I0660461

HYENAS IN A DOMED SAVANNA

Copyright, 2022

by

John Rigol, Jr

ISBN: 978-0-578-35373-9

Front cover artwork by Katy Rigol.

dominates the New Orleans cityscape,
a trenchant reminder of the State's corrupt politics.

DISCLAIMER

This is a work of fiction. Names, characters, events and incidents are the products of the author's imagination. Any resemblance to actual persons, living or dead, or actual events is purely coincidental.

This novel's story and characters are fictitious. Certain long-standing institutions, agencies, and public offices are mentioned, but the characters involved are wholly imaginary.

John Rigol, Jr.

DEDICATION

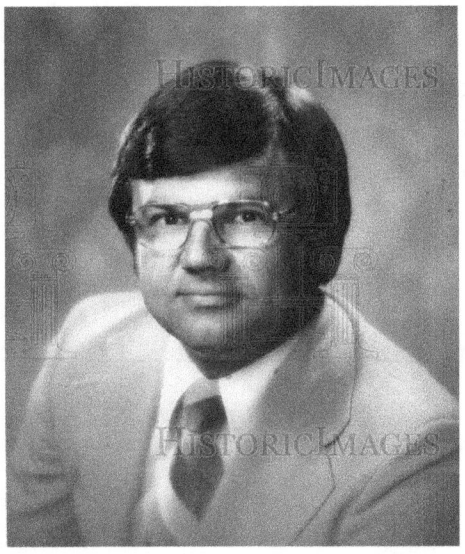

1

The White/ Knight of the Louisiana State Police.

Don Thibodaux wasn't simply charismatic; rather, magnetism effused from him as if it were lava from a volcano at maximum ejection. It was fiery, spectacular, and overwhelming.

Bordering on being corrupt and rife with politics before Colonel Thibodeaux became superintendent, the Louisiana State Police was, at best, a mismanaged

---

[1] August, 25, 1937—September 23, 1993.

organization. Given loose rein in his appointment by then-Governor Edwin Edwards, he set about a campaign to undo the damage and revitalize the flagging outfit.

And rejuvenate the State Police, he did!

After Thibodeaux died, his wife, Alice, told me Donald repeatedly said to her, "John is the smartest man on State Police." (I trusted what she told me was true, but in my heart, I believed he had been misled.) She also informed me he had said I was the only trooper who would disagree with him on matters of State Police policy. And I knew that to be true. It seems Thibodeaux could sense my uninhibited zeal, because I ate, drank, breathed, and almost lived for the State Police.

Colonel Thibodeaux embraced, nay, celebrated my Don Quixote-ish comportment. And it was he who assigned me to the Louisiana Superdome to give order to the criticized security effort there.

It was the pinnacle of my police career, and that posting copiously enriched my life.

Thank you, Chief.[2] I miss you.

---

[2] His wife, Alice, and others have told me he would allow no one else except me to call him "Chief."

[New Orleans] is famous for its gamblers, prostitutes, exhibitionists, Antichrists, alcoholics, drug addicts, fetishists, onanists, pornographers, frauds, jades, litterbugs, and lesbians, all of whom are only too well protected by graft.

Ignatius J. Reilly
in *A Confederacy of Dunces*

Times are not good [in New Orleans]. The city is crumbling into ashes. It has been buried under taxes and frauds and maladministrations so that it has become a study for archaeologists....

Lafcadio Hearn
Inventing New Orleans: Writings of Lafcadio Hearn

TABLE OF CONTENTS

PART ONE

PART TWO

ACKNOWLEDGMENTS

I can no other answer make, but, thanks, and thanks.
--William Shakespeare: *Twelfth Night*; Act III, Scene III

Where would I be without family and friends? I don't know. But I do know I couldn't have written this novel without them.

Aware that most of the following who are lauded here would eschew these panegyrics, I nonetheless deem myself obligated to cite them. And even though I didn't always follow their advice, all made significant contributions to the book. If I should have followed all their recommendations but didn't, then any shortcomings are mine to bear.

Over fifteen years ago, Cherie, my eldest daughter and the family matriarch, began to badger me to write my autobiography. But when I finally did so, she said it was too raw. (I'm sorry, Cheesh, but the truth is I've lived a lewd and salacious existence.)

Yet undaunted, and with her iron fist in a velvet glove, she simply switched gears and needled me to write a "faction"; i.e., a fiction loosely based on my life experiences. Thus, it was she who planted the seed for *Hyenas*.

You had more confidence in me than I did, my amazing daughter and *fidus Achates*. If it weren't for your ex vivo insemination, this book would have been an infertile ovum to be expelled in conjunction with the lunar cycle. Thank you, *mon très cher*.

My enchanting and devoted spouse, Gena, has iteratively parroted Cherie's sentiments. And besides that, she has been my literal in-house editor. Sans her contributions, the writing would have been pedestrian and wanting.

And her ideas! Her conceptions were florid; she gave me singular concepts that I employed but would never have imagined on my own.

Moreover, she has spent days upon days helping me edit, and re-edit, and re-edit, and re-edit the manuscript. Her untiring dedication thwarted errors in syntax, structure, and grammar. I love you, my wife, life partner, and confidant.

But like the tentative protagonist in the book, Johnny Régis, in this writing—

even with the encouragement of Cherie and Gena—I was still sheepish about my virtuosity to write a novel. And who but Doug Dodd, who coincidentally worked at the Superdome with me, would be the catalyst in the reaction. Doug is an outstanding human being; he is erudite, clever, compassionate, and along with my son, John III, the most noble and loyal man I know.

Like Cherie and Gena, Doug, too, encouraged me to write fiction, saying, "Write about something you've lived. With all your adventures and life experiences, certainly, you can write a novel." Thus, it was he who rendered the watershed moment.

Besides that, Doug has been my shadow editor. Behind the scene, he has instructed and prodded me to create a better outcome.

Doug, please accept my endless gratitude for your inspiration, your advice, and your endearing and enduring friendship.

Midway through the inscription process, I was bonused with the assistance of my beautiful granddaughter, Katy Rigol. Alas, we had theretofore been somewhat disunited, but this book has brought us together—an ecstasy for an old man in his dotage.

Katy is intelligent, perspicacious, and tender. As a developmental editor, she brought a youthful, fresh perspective to the writing, and she has been the principal motivity of the romantic aspects of the writing. I am indebted to her for attentiveness, her efforts, her candor, and her perseverance. If this novel is ever published, Katy can claim a large share of its actualization.

An angel from heaven, Lisa Worobetz, took the time from her burdened schedule to beta test the manuscript, and as expected, her comments were thought-provoking. Because of her insights, I was impelled to take a fresh look at sensitive aspects of the work. I am honored to call Lisa a dear friend and astute advisor.

Moreover, Katy, Gena, and Lisa rendered indispensable advice for the humancentric feminine spheres of life. Without their enlightened counsel, the plotline would not have had those delicate touches, and the novel would have otherwise been lackluster.

My noble erstwhile British neighbors, John and Lynda Harper, both of whom are brilliant, took upon themselves the onerous task of editing—a Herculean endeavor considering my innumerable grammatical errors. I am deeply

indebted to them for their munificence. And since they repatriated to England, I miss them terribly.

After a hiatus of forty-plus years, via Facebook, Larry Gould reappeared in my life. What a windfall that was for me! We not only re-established communication and friendship, but he has been a capital asset as a contributing editor.

During my repetitive edits, I was reminded of how much he contributed to the writing. With his ideas, six blue-pencil exertions, his line-by-line corrections, his scholarship, and his analytical mindset, he has shepherded me not just around potholes, but chasms too. I am not only fortunate for his help; I am also blessed with his society.

Nearing the end of the book's inscription, via a quirk of fate, I had the profound delight of meeting and becoming friends with Tom Aswell, a celebrated author, a trenchant investigative journalist, and a noble and most interesting man. His writings of news, fiction, and editorials are phenomenal!

Antipodal to a retired police author I had previously tried to contact and who had ignored me, Tom embraced my writing and with a cornucopia of enthusiasm, and gave me scads of encouragement and learned advice.

With a professional eye, he laboriously edited the entire work. And with his literary acumen and his good offices, he afforded readability and polish to my theretofore rough-hewn effort. It has been indeed felicitous for me to have his amity and aegis.

Thanks to my parents, John and Lily Rigol, who encouraged me at a tender age to read, and read, and read some more.

My son, John III, gave me encouragement along the way. And with his computer talent, he diligently helped me with quirky formatting.

A special thanks to my patron saint, Jim Champagne who restimulated and impressed me into developing my writing skills when he was my commander at State Police.

Although my former neighbor in Hammond, Louisiana, Larry Gray, did not directly contribute to this work, his creative writing tuition in that endeavor was an immense help in the preparation of my autobiography. And from his tutelage, I learned a lot.

Larry is a professor of English, a dramatist, a published author, and an

awarded playwright. With his wealth of knowledge and erudition, he vicariously obliquely provided me invaluable insights and revelations in scribing this novel. Whatever coherency this book might have is mostly because of his previous conscientious and scholarly help and I am keenly beholden to him.

Having never self-published, I owe a debt of gratitude to Anthony Cassard of Claitor's Law Books and Publishing Division. With remarkable patience, "Mr. Anthony" took the time to tutor and guide me in the publication process...and that wasn't an easy chore!

And thanks to those who gave their time to do partial reviews: My brother, Jimmy Rigol; my soul brother, Ben Burks; my sister-in-law, Phyllis (Peedy) Smith; my longtime friend, Al Plaeger; two of my lovely current neighbors, Laura Eyth, Linda Rosenblatt; and Pam Cox.

FOREWORD

I suppose I never really met my grandfather until I met Johnny Régis, the protagonist of this novel. Growing up, I heard inklings of the wild stories and the darkly-humorous escapades of John Rigol Jr., always recounted to me with the loving disclaimer: "He's your Grandpa."

My dad, John Rigol III, and I share a long-running joke; if my lovable brother happens to say something goofy (he is an endearing goof-ball, for sure), Dad teases to me, "He's your brother!" To which I reply, "He's your son!" The same skit arguably works better with Grandpa. We toss around our relation like a hot potato— "He's your Grandpa!" countered with "He's your Dad!"

Some of the crazy Johnny Rigol stories, I must admit, are genuinely disconcerting. I was afraid this quasi-autobiographical fiction would somewhere retell a depressing domestic drama, but for better or worse, that fear was not realized.

Undoubtedly, John Rigol Jr. lived the life of Johnny Régis, whom you'll soon discover was a competent Chief of Staff Security at the Superdome (an early edition plagued by old New Orleans politics and scandal). Back then, Louisianians would refer to our losing Saints football team as the "Ain'ts. The name fits Johnny Régis and his living counterpart well—they ain't Saints.

I believe I'm perceived as quite the opposite: I am passive, modest, patient, and soft. Without any conflict caused by the author's and my clear personality differences, I've been generously credited as "Developmental Editor" for a novel which I love and am proud to have my name printed on. As I craft this foreword in my college dorm room, I hope to enter a career in writing myself.

However, despite my potential for tunnel-vision inducing dreams of a journalistic, and literary career as well as my undeniable fondness for this story and its author, editing the various elements of this book has been a knotty task. Grandpa and my mother, according to the stories, had their differences—and I am very much my mother's daughter, having inherited her appearance and disposition, the two of us having supported each other through many difficult circumstances.

I am unable to definitively decide which narratives—the real or the fictional ones—bear more weight in my mind and heart, and I cannot verily say whether I forgive all on behalf of various loved ones.

Forgiveness withheld or spared, no one could forget my Grandpa, just as you reading this novel could not—will not—forget New Orleans and its political bogs of depravity. Fortunately for you, this murder-mystery is somewhat light-hearted, as also seems my grandfather. However, if you want to discover the truth, to resolve both the mystery and the enigma of Johnny Régis, you must explore every fleeting shadow.

This exploration projects an existential question. Perhaps our lack of certainty is a matter of denial, in that the answers we seek are not always the answers we prefer.

You will come to love and hate certain characters and probably formulate theories of your own; the culprit may or may not be who you suspect.

Or worse, the culprit may not be who you wish.

Katy Rigol
Natchitoches, Louisiana
November 2020

PART ONE
PROLOGUE

He looked like uncooked dough that had fled the pizzaiolo's hands and landed atop a stove with cooking utensils on it.

Ghost, as twisted as the trunk of a venerable, gnarled olive tree, was draped over seats 15, 16, and 17 in Section 281 on the Plaza level of the Louisiana Superdome. With blood in the first stages of gelation having run out of his nose, mouth, and ears, he was quite recently dead.

It was apparent my subordinate, Agent I Langdon "Ghost" Dickerson, had fallen from the Loge level above somewhere in front of Section 347. But how and, the more significant question, why?

I didn't know it then, but his death would transform my pedestrian life into a gruesome fairy tale.

CHAPTER I
An Ugly Dismissal

From the playing field, the investigators evoked an image of gnats in an empty, eighty-quart crawfish pot, almost lost in the immensity of a Pharaonic stadium that can welcome a seating capacity of 76,468 spectators.

As Chief of Staff Security, I was to be notified of any major security breaches in the Dome. After being rousted from sleep at home by Superdome security, when I arrived there at 2:30 a.m. on Wednesday, the New Orleans police—uniformed officers and plainclothes detectives—were chuckling and palavering among themselves. And so was an on-duty Dome security guard.

In truant nonattendance were the contracted security administrators, Shallier Corbin and his partner Donatien Huberty as well as their Chief of Line Security, Jim Rieglé. Why weren't they present?

Other than the police photographer taking pictures and the police technician dusting for fingerprints, no one except the coroner's investigator, who was conducting a hands-off inspection of the body, no one else was doing much of anything.

I began to ask a few questions, but the two detectives, led by Rosh Macklin, one of four sergeants in the New Orleans Police Department (NOPD) homicide unit, gave me the brush-off. Macklin and I had obliquely crossed paths before, but the encounters were so brief we couldn't be classed as colleagues.

The NOPD didn't cotton to my presence there, and they didn't hesitate to show it. But I persisted until Macklin, girdled by a wet bovine effluence and registering a scowl, told me, "Back off! This is a crime scene, and we're in charge. You can get your answers when we file our report." Although distraught at Dickerson's death and outraged by Macklin's consequent dismissal, I stepped away despite being averse to doing so.

CHAPTER II
Politics Amuck in the Queen City

The Louisiana Superdome (aka, the "Dome") had been a case study of monumentalism—a campaign of then-Governor John McKeithen, who, when touring the Astrodome in Houston, Texas, in 1966, was quoted as saying, "I want one of these, only bigger." And he proceeded to push his pet project through the Louisiana Legislature.

The stadium is a domed sports and exhibition arena located in the Central Business District of New Orleans. Its steel frame covers a 13-acre expanse and the 273-foot dome is made of a lamellar multi-ringed frame and has a diameter of 680 feet, making it the largest fixed domed structure in the world. The structure boasts a massive Hypalon plastic roof.

One most often becomes wealthy in Louisiana only if he sells his soul to Azazel from the South. In their gluttonous rapacity, all seasoned politicos—and some neophytes too—who could involve themselves in the project wanted a rake-off of the pickings. And in their zeal to build the stadium, they erected the behemoth over a disestablished graveyard, Girod Cemetery.

The Saints were later to become the losing "Aints." Fans sought reasons for the team's continuing bad luck, and many were blamed—owners, managers, coaches, and players.

But in the most haunted city and voodoo capitol of North America, many came to believe that the aggrieved spirits of the old cemetery, disgruntled that their resting places had not been final, put a gris-gris on the Dome and the team. And even I trifled with the notion, *Could that have been why Ghost had lost his life?*

It was anticipated the stadium would be ready in time for the 1972 NFL season, and the final cost of the facility would come in at $46 million. But neither of these goals was realized. The final price tag of the stadium skyrocketed to $165 million. And due to political delays, construction did not start until August 11, 1971. It was not finished and opened until August 1975.

The State Legislature forged a newly-minted Superdome Advisory Board to oversee operation of the facility. The Board was composed of various politicos from throughout the State but more to the point, from New Orleans. I thought

6

most of them were little more than political hacks.

In turn, the Board let a contract to the Superdome Management Corporation to oversee operations of the arena. And they, in turn, let cost-plus sub-contracts to other entities to perform day-to-day operations.

Macklin was a twenty-nine-year police officer who, of late, had enjoyed a capital career. Now because of his longstanding position as a detective sergeant in the Homicide Unit, he now seemed to believe seniority—rather than performance—was the Holy Grail of policing. I presumed he was unfamiliar with the term "twenty-year rookie," meaning seniority was as useless as a screwdriver on a bolt for gauging a police officer's competence.

Macklin chain smoked and had a penchant for polyester, wide-lapel suits. He was scruffy, portly, balding, and olive complexioned. Long, black bristles extruded from his nose and ears.

He could be crude and crass, and recently, more than when I had known him beforehand, he presented those traits as badges of honor. Indeed, he exhibited the earmarks of a man with a splintered 2x2 stuck up his corpulent derriere. What a "chookee" (a New Orleans toned-down version of "asshole") he had become!

Noting the police technician was dusting around the body, I thought it to be an exercise in mental masturbation because three nights before, the Saints had played—and again lost—to a sellout crowd. As if they were seeds thrown from a basket by a Tharu farmer, fingerprints would have been strewn and smudged over the entire area. Afterward, the technician did the same above the body on the Loge level.

Dickerson, in coat and tie, was wearing his holstered sidearm. This would be a potential clue as to what had happened, although it was only a diminutive piece of what was to become a very large puzzle.

Macklin knew me and what my role was at the Superdome. But the jerk was right of course—it was his investigation. Other than Dickerson being one of my team members and the incident having occurred in the Dome, I had no dog in that fight. So I stayed out of his way. Macklin would later want to interview me, but he seemed to be in no rush to do so.

His behavior provoked me to flash back to not that many years ago when I had been a homicide detective in the micro, three-man homicide squad in adjoining Jefferson Parish.

Homicide detectives are almost always pretentious, and I, too, had suffered the same illusion of grandeur—I had been a chookee too! And it wasn't until later in hindsight that I came to the humbling and haunting realization I couldn't detect the odor of shit in a shithouse.

Having been christened, Jean Regis, I was given the nickname, "Johnny," and it stuck. I lived my youth and adolescence in the Fabulous Fifties, and I still felt that aura of innocence and immutability.

I had been raised in Old Metairie (called "Metry" by the locals), an unincorporated area of Jefferson Parish that shared a common border on the west side of New Orleans. When asked by outsiders, most Metairie residents would say that they were from New Orleans.

My juvenile years embodied the words of Socrates, "Not life, but [a well-spent] life, is to be chiefly valued." And I did have a rare, well-spent life. And I never once smoked the Devil's lettuce.

When I was ten years old, I was "commissioned" a Junior Deputy in then semi-rural Jefferson Parish by a family friend, Chief Deputy Jorge Gutiérrez of the Jefferson Parish Sheriff's Office. That cinched it—I was going to be a cop when I grew up!

And eleven years thereafter, when I was twenty-one, on the back steps of the Gretna Courthouse, Chief Gutiérrez did, indeed, swear me in as a full-time Jefferson Parish Deputy Sheriff. I had arrived!

But soon realizing how much politics played a role in the Sheriff's Office, I sought someplace better. I learned that the Office of the State Attorney General was also a law enforcement agency and maintained a police component to enforce laws and conduct investigations throughout the State. I applied for and was hired as an Attorney General Special Agent I; I had arrived again! And I had been twice promoted since then.

The AG, Guillaume Gustave, had many years earlier been a tailback on a better-than-average Louisiana State University football team. He was of medium height, with a strong bearing, and he had keen eyes that could lead some to believe that he could read their thoughts.

Graduating college, he gained employment with the Louisiana State Police, but the challenge was not there for him. So he matriculated into law school, after which he worked for the U.S. Attorney General's office for the Western District of Louisiana.

He was known for his honesty—a rare trait in Louisiana politics—his political acuity, and his ability to build a team of experts around him. His preamble onto the Louisiana political scene was his first run for State Attorney General, and he won in a landslide. Unless he chose to run for Governor, he could be AG for life. He was much too savvy about the politics and the politicos of Louisiana.

The Superdome had only been open for about eleven months, and from the beginning, political self-interests perforated and then began shredding everyday operations. Moreover, the Dome was increasingly plagued with almost daily adverse press reports about inferior security.

Ghost was assigned to me when the Governor, Edwina Entremont, disturbed by the continual avalanches of negative press reports about security at the Superdome, requested a task force of investigators to be assembled from the Louisiana Office of State Attorney General.

The five of us dispatched to the Dome were all special agents with the AG's office. Assigned the mission title of Chief of Staff Security, I was the team's commanding officer. We were temporarily deployed there to oversee and evaluate the politically riddled and hotly criticized Dome security force—the Superdome was a State of Louisiana holding.

I knew the Dome was a flash point, but I had not even an inkling of the caliginous passages of horrors and survival struggles I would experience while there.

The press had lots of red meat awaiting them; thus, they delighted in an abundant feast at the scandal trough. The minority-held group, C&H Services, headed by Shallier Corbin and Donatien Huberty, was the *high* bidder and had snagged 71% of the total cost-plus sub-contracts let.

And to further fuel the fires of the media, Corbin and Huberty did not meet a fundamental criterion to qualify for the security contract; that is, the sub-contractor had to have had security experience, and the Corbin and Huberty, (C&H Services) group had none.

Therefore, to comply with the security experience requirement, C&H let a sub-sub-contract to a security company, NOLA Security Services. Of course, that was cost-plus too, and C&H was still responsible for the actions or inactions of the sub-sub-contractors—the security buck stopped with them.

Corbin was an enigma who seemed to almost appear out of nowhere; he said

very little and revealed even less. He was a transplant from North Louisiana and seemed to be involved on the periphery of many political deals. But until his landing of the Dome sub-contracts, he was never at the top of the food chain.

It was rumored that, among other things, Corbin had recruited prostitutes in New Orleans for work in brothels in Central and North Louisiana. But the claims never materialized; perhaps they were generated by those who were envious of his ascension in the New Orleans political milieu.

Huberty, on the other hand, was a high-profile example of home-grown, New Orleans-style corruption. Huberty had come to be the co-owner of the C&H outfit not because he had experience in security or any other of the Dome's functions, but because of an incident in the Desire Street project and because his father had money and, at one time, had been well-placed in the New Orleans political structure.

What Huberty lacked in intelligence, he made up for in his sleazy approach to women. No one would ever mistake him for a gentleman or a subdued small-town librarian.

If one wanted to find Huberty, the office would generally be the last place they would look. More likely, Huberty could be found at Kolb's just off Canal Street. By noon he would be ensconced at a back table drinking German beer and dining from their German menu.

By mid-afternoon, with unconstrained eructations, he was usually drunk and acting the role of an insufferable asswipe. One could almost always tell what he had been eating, since it was usually dribbled all over his garish polyester suits along with a nimbus of repellent exhalations that enveloped him.

Besides Corbin having been an unindicted co-conspirator in a Children's Health and Safety Foundation fraud, another censure emerged when he was accused of receiving payoffs from companies seeking to obtain contracts from City Hall. The entire Dome setup was a suicidal *coup d'état* that had Louisiana government begging, "Please steal from me!" and the press saying, "*Bon appétit.*" New Orleanians, with their congenital predilection for scandal, were elated.

We were the AG's go-team. While we were primarily assigned to the New Orleans and Baton Rouge areas, we could—and did—work in any part of the State where the AG felt the locals needed help with an investigation or where the locals, themselves, needed to be investigated.

We were provided a well-lit, commodious, non-partitioned office with six brand-new desks, telephones, and two electric typewriters. (The latter were almost pointless, since only one of my subordinates, Zitzy, could type.) The space was arrayed with a bank of windows overlooking Mid-City and the upper tier of one of the Dome's parking lots.

North of the noise and saturated color of the French Quarter one finds a New Orleans neighborhood that's perfected the art of living. "Welcome to Mid-City," read the signs on the neutral ground (median). It's the kind of place where your auto mechanic invites you to a crawfish boil and a total stranger may buy you a drink at an Irish pub or cannoli at an Italian bakery.

One can take the red streetcar line up Canal to the Cemeteries (Mid-City's dead neighbors, housed in above-ground tombs, are as interesting as the live ones) or bike the 2.6-mile-long Lafitte Greenway that stretches from Basin Street to Carrollton Avenue and conveniently stop at a po-boy shop, a sno-ball stand, and a micro-brewery thrown in for good measure. True southern-style buttermilk biscuits, New Orleans po-boys and red beans and rice are everywhere. Live music abounds. And a bowl of Vietnamese pho is just around the corner.

I liked the layout of the office. We were an intimate crew, and it encouraged group participation. And with few exceptions, Superdome management left us to our own devices, so we had carte blanche to function as we wished.

Our squad had been in operation for eight weeks. And among other activities, we had been reviewing the Superdome Security Procedural Manual; incident reports generated by the security force; contracts among Olson, the food service provider; the security and other sub-contractors; and the Superdome organizational structure.

Two of my thorny assignments were sometimes dealing with a frenzied press and occasionally publicly addressing the Superdome Advisory Board to report on our progress. Amid the political squabbling, one ill-considered indiscretion would doom my career.

Dickerson had been a prized contributor to our team, the only Black in the group. I had nicknamed him "Ghost" for several reasons. He was the most reclusive, reticent, and taciturn man I knew. He required minimal supervision, and his assignments were always completed with celerity, with adeptness, and without flourish. Composed, tall, and slender, he seemed to specter-materialize

11

in and out of our Superdome office. I often wondered what kind of private life he led.

But Ghost was not only phantasmal during normal working hours. Unbeknownst to me, unannounced, and on his own time, he would appear at the stadium under the cloak of darkness.

For a while, I was unaware of his nocturnal forays because he had not claimed overtime for them. But when I learned of his activity I asked him, "Why are you doing that, Ghost?"

He responded saying, "I just wanted to make sure the guards were doing their jobs."

"And what?"

He told me he had found no discrepancies. Lauding him for his dedication, I said, "Well, I suppose you're finished?" He agreed, and I assumed he would shelve it. Our conversation over, he dematerialized from the office. *But why did he again show up last night after he told me he was finished with it?*

Of course, after I left Macklin to his industry, it was pointless for me to return home.

Sitting at my desk, I thought Dickerson's death "could" have been an accident, but that was improbable. Suicide was even more far-fetched; having been a cop, it was most plausible Dickerson would have eaten his gun as most suicidal policemen are prone to do. It had to have been a homicide, and even though not on top of his game, Macklin surely would have surmised or known it was.

I called Natalie, my bonny wife, briefed her on the situation, and told her not to expect me home until later that evening. After the call, I again puzzled over the circumstances, lit a cigar, braced myself with a stiff slug of Jim Beam I kept stashed in my desk drawer, and prepared for my call to the AG. One of the first things I would have to do during working hours was to advise him of the situation.

I also planned for the scrum of reporters who had been kept from the crime scene by the Dome's security guards. And being rattled, I was relieved I didn't have to convey the death notice to Dickerson's next of kin; the Coroner's Office or the NOPD would do that.

But what was *I* going to do?

CHAPTER III
"Find the Motherfucker"

My crew—less Dickerson—arrived at the Dome at 8:00.

Except for Agent II Elvin Leman, nicknamed Zitzy, and Agent I Dan Brisolaro (Cool Breeze, shortened to Breeze), we wore khaki pants and nondescript AG royal-blue blazers fitted with breast-pocket badges.

Nicknames tend to be more prevalent in the South than they are in other parts of the country. And southern nicknames, especially police nicknames, most often have a semblance of teasing disparagement attached to them. The sobriquets fit in perfectly with the police penchant for "playing the dozens"—the activity of making deprecating remarks in jest among friends, a popular police and New Orleanians' pastime.

I didn't have a nickname, per se, but on a few occasions, I had overheard some team members referring to me as "JR," which I supposed was a reference to the both famous and infamous character on the TV series, *Dallas*.

Breeze was the antithesis of prosaic. Although married, he was a bon vivant, who enjoyed life and the ladies and, contrary to biblical dictates, was always dapper in a linen and light wool three-piece suit, even in the sultry Louisiana summers. No cheap polyester for him!

It perplexed me he didn't succumb to heat exhaustion, but I never once saw him perspire. He adored fine wine and a good joke, and he was never lacking a potpourri of paramours—Breeze loved them all.

Antipodal to Breeze, Zitzy was balding (he wore a rug), and dressed in tieless, double-knit leisure suits with synthetic Hawaiian shirts opened to the third— sometimes to the fourth—button to expose a gold necklace and cross and his muscled, hairy chest. Sometimes during the winter, he would don an Irish tweed Celtic cap and wear it inside or out all day long. I supposed he didn't wear his hairpiece on those days.

He appeared to be dispassionate, but to assume so would be a huge mistake. He had a disarming manner, and he was every whit a professional.

Briefing them, they barraged me with questions. All the agents had police experience, and their curiosity impelled them to press me for details. I told them

I had only a few answers—Dickerson had been murdered and Macklin had dismissed me.

The call with the AG didn't go well. After outlining the circumstances, he said, "Find the motherfucker, and find him fast!" *Tell that to NOPD; they're already being impossible pricks.*

It would have been to no avail to outline the nightmarish logistics I would have to wend my way through to "...find the motherfucker and find him fast!" Besides that, I didn't want to appear to be a whiny, crybaby bitch, so I didn't complain. I wanted more than anything to "find the motherfucker." But no investigation can move faster than the collection of facts allows, and I had only a paucity of those.

I was angry about Dickerson's death and resentful toward the AG for thunderstriking me with this. I felt as if I were playing a character on *Mission Impossible*, that is, "Your mission, should you choose to accept it, is to face your fate. Pursue us, you'll be caught. Resist us, you'll be killed. And your precious Attorney General will disavow any knowledge of your actions. Good luck, Mr. Régis." Except I wasn't offered the option, "should you choose to accept it"

Of course, I had already planned to get the scumbag who killed a cop, my colleague, my friend, and such a principled human being. But I knew from the onset it would be a punishing venture. And the short time onus imposed by the AG was particularly disconcerting. With that, I began an odyssey onto a stage not of my making with a script that had yet to be written.

After the call, I again gathered together my staff and announced, "We have a problem, Houston." With very few words of encouragement, I advised them of the AG's order and then outlined the daunting obstacles we were facing.

The megalomaniacal Mayor of New Orleans, Luna Langlois (pronounced **lahng**-lwah) was pudgy, squishy, and almost neckless. Her distinct characteristics were her hazel eyes. Squinty due to the fat of her face compressing them, they were adorned with fake, dust broom-like eyelashes. Her artificially colored blonde hair had been straightened and dyed so much it was as arid as the Atacama and as brittle as dried straw. It appeared to be a cheap wig...maybe it was a postiche and a leftover from a chintzy Halloween costume.

Langlois was a light-skin quadroon, the child of a mulatto mother and a white father (a mulatto is the child of a white parent and a Black parent). For most of her life, she "passed" as white, and when she was confronted about her racial

heritage, she disingenuously said she was "Creole." But a Creole is one who has mixed French and Spanish Caucasian blood. However, when the populace of New Orleans became mostly Black, she shed the artifice.

Langlois showed the wear of many hands. From the time Luna was a more svelte and appealing *fille* of fifteen until she graduated Louisiana State University New Orleans with a degree in Government at the age of twenty-nine, she had been a *placée*—literally: "Care to have a better place or to have a better seat."

But in the diverse City of New Orleans, *placée* is used to define a concubine or kept woman. And because of Langlois' ambitious drive to realize a "better place," she passed herself around like a bottle of Thunderbird wine on Saturday night in Congo Square or in front of the Little Rumboogie, a Black bar in the Upper Ninth Ward. Those who couldn't afford drinks inside the bar drank cheap wine outside of it.

Moreover, the "Honorable" Luna Langlois was a narcissistic harridan. Her apparel of choice was rusty chic—tawdry, big-legged, double-knit pants suits and short platform clogs. Sometimes, she wore a tignon, a headdress once used to conceal hair adorned by free and slave women of African ancestry in Louisiana in the eighteenth century. Minus the hairy chest and the tignon, she could have been a sartorial clone of Zitzy.

She had the penchant of poking her short, stubby right index finger at those who crossed her. Her affectation, which probably got her elected—after all, this was the prodigal New Orleans—was that she smoked cigars.

Although perceived as outré by non-natives, Langlois' mannerisms were apposite in a city of artists, eccentrics, devotees of the Erotes, masters of bizarre expressions, and despoilers of the English language. The New Orleans lingua franca includes a primo exemplar in the greeting, "Where ya at?" in place of the customary, "How are you?" "Good morning" and other accepted salutations.

And Langlois was shrewd. She held advanced figurative degrees in manipulation and control. She had the tempo of the Big Easy in her veins. She knew of—and capitalized on—the *joie de vivre* and *mañana* attitudes of the New Orleans' denizens who only needed red beans and rice, crawfish, beer, sports, and their innumerable parades to make them happy. Moreover, New Orleanians were habituated to electing scoundrels and demagogues.

Unmarried, overbearing, and dictatorial, she ruled New Orleans with

despotism. Mirroring so many other natives of the Crescent City, she deemed that life and culture stopped at the city limits. The rest of Louisiana was an afterthought and an annoyance to be to tolerated.

She didn't look with favor on police—even the NOPD. However, that did not mean that she did not use them to satisfy her own agenda. And the parochial termagant harbored a consuming animus toward any other law enforcement in "her" city, including the FBI. Shit rolls downhill, so it wasn't surprising the NOPD was infected with her acrimony.

Langlois was also the chairperson of the Superdome Board of Advisors. And very much so she resented our presence in the Superdome, even though the Board and her position on it had been created by the State Legislature.

She had been quoted in the media with the canard, "The Superdome is in New Orleans. We don't need makeshift secret agents from the State to infiltrate our stadium." In private, she had reportedly referred to the AG detachment as the "doodlebug squad."

It didn't matter to her we weren't makeshift, we weren't secret, we weren't infiltrators, and the Superdome stadium was a State of Louisiana property. It was an understatement to say we weren't going to get any assistance from the mayor's office. Nor did I expect to receive help from the NOPD.

New Orleans has rarely had a municipal administration that hasn't shamed it. Bad government had always been the accepted—and expected—paradigm. Corrupt politics had been treated as enlightened conduct, a perverse game.

Millenia ago, a chunk of the South American continent must have broken off, was caught in the Gulf Stream, and swept north and west by the Gulf Stream. It collided with, and then semi-attached itself to, Louisiana, where it formed the Isle of Orleans (the city is virtually surrounded by water).

In any event, it's an undeniable fact New Orleans, with a consolidated city-parish government, is the most northern Banana Republic. And if it weren't for its laid-back, acquiescent citizenry, New Orleans would have had a long history of *coups d'état*.

The streets of the Vieux Carré after Mardi Gras day and past governments of the city have had the stench of bodily excretions, but the mephitis from this New Orleans regime was even more noxious than usual.

The city was in shambles, and its infrastructure was collapsing. A significant

one-quarter of its denizens were living below the poverty level and on all types of subsistence programs.

Crime statistics told the sad tale, and they were off the Richter Chart. The murder rate had eclipsed all previous records. Along with Memphis, Tennessee, the city was leading the nation in per-capita homicides.

At one time, the New Orleans housing projects had been among the best in the nation, with vegetable gardens and flower beds in abundance. But they had morphed into wastelands of proving grounds for criminals.

Armed robberies, burglaries, and missing persons, including children, mostly from the impoverished housing projects and the lower garden district—the Latino sector—were systemic and at all-time highs. And the Faustian dystopia was so commonplace it was blasély accepted as a *fait accompli*.

Tourism, one of the mainstays of revenue in New Orleans, had plummeted. One may consider that, next to the French Quarter, the Superdome was the biggest touristic draw for the city. But the Dome's security distemper was as infectious as malaria, and Dome attendance was dwindling. The miasma was being exacerbated by national media coverage.

From a jaundiced point of view, perhaps the drop in tourism was a perk—afflictions are sometimes good blessings. Changing demographics have led to concerns that *La Nouvelle-Orléans* is beginning to lose the very thing that attracts new residents and tens of thousands of visitors here each year—its culture.

Enchanted by its charm and zaniness, many non-natives who visit the moated city stay or come back to take up residence. And with that, they bastardize the cultural allure that so mesmerized them in the first place.

A remarkable indicator of the City's fetor was the incongruity of Langlois' undisguised animosity toward the AG's Superdome detachment. Yet it was clear the city and the Dome needed help...any help. It seemed Langlois would have welcomed us as adjuvant allies; rather, she was disparaging those who could be of assistance. And it was another "why" to add to a growing list of anomalies.

How did she get away with her totalitarianism? After all, she represented only one of the three arms of city government, the executive branch. There were still the legislative branch (the City Council) and the judicial branch (the Courts). Nevertheless, she ruled with an iron heel. If raw success is the measure of an individual, Langlois was twelve feet tall.

The key to success in Louisiana and New Orleans politics was simple—have the sleaze on others, and one could control the patronage. *What sleaze did the mayor have on the others?*

Our task was daunting. But at least we had a staunch ally on the Dome management group, Wilhelm Conrardy. Known as Willy, he was the operations manager. Besides having a prestigious job with the Dome, Willy was also connected with a segment of the New Orleans political machine. And he wanted to help us!

In our pursuit of Langdon's killer, Willy promised his full cooperation and assistance—he knew the political landscape. He told me he was aware of the challenges we faced, and he was poised to lend his full support. And from time to time thereafter, he could be my sub-rosa contact with the Dome executive group. I needed an in-house ally, and our desiderata would require all the help we could get.

That is what I laid out when I collaborated with what was to become my war cabinet, notifying them all hands were to be on deck; all days off were canceled, and we were going to kick ass and take names. I had no idea how much *our* asses were going to be kicked along the way.

CHAPTER IV
Where to Begin?

We needed a starting point. But what could it be? The police report would be a good launchpad for our probe, but it was unavailable to us. The crime scene was still taped off; and we couldn't interfere with the NOPD investigation. We did, however, have authority to review the Dome's security records.

Zitzy, a protean agent with a bulldog jaw, was my assistant supervisor. He had been a Navy seal, had worked in naval intelligence, and he was a bodybuilder—no steroids there.

His bushy eyebrows appeared to be two ravens perched above piercing and quite active oculi. What I supposed was a tic, his steel-gray eyes continually darted from side to side, whence came his nickname, Zitzy. But only his dear friends dare call him that without being the victim of a trouncing.

Zitzy commuted from Algiers, the part of New Orleans frequently described as Siberia because it was only a small portion of the city located across from New Orleans proper on the West Bank of the Mississippi River. As all native New Orleanians, his accent was thick and sultry, and he mispronounced many words, such as "buttah" (butter), "dahlin" (darling), "dere" (there), and "Kennah" (Kenner), as well as the frequent use of "Babe." But then, all indigenous New Orleanians call everyone "Babe."

Zitzy had a near-obsession with details. Therefore, I assigned him to obtain copies of the security records for the previous two months and pore over them. I also told him to focus on nighttime ingresses and egresses at the Dome, the first priority being last night and this morning. And in particular, to look for any peculiarities.

Another of my group was Agent I David Dosstein, who was a follower of Reform Judaism. Dosstein was pasty and fleshy, so much so we called him the Pillsbury Doughboy or just Doughboy for short. Hyper-intelligent, perspicacious, and jovial, he was the *ne plus ultra* of common sense and the wittiest person I've ever known.

One or more of the Dome's security guards could give us a lead. But it would be difficult to get that inroad because we had to infiltrate the almost all-Black

security force and ferret out an informer or informers, and we had lost our only Black agent. The only whites on the Dome's security staff were Gerald Bowditch, a shift supervisor, and Jim Riegelé, the line-active Chief of Security.

Doughboy was my first choice. I anticipated his being Jewish and having been discriminated against, he could more easily interact with the Black security guards. Combining that with his affable and gregarious personality, if he couldn't pull it off, no one could.

I decided my two other subordinates should continue working on the Dome projects to which they were previously assigned. And I would utilize them in the murder investigation as they might be needed.

And I notified them that every morning we would have a staff meeting to discuss our progress, but that did not preclude them from immediately reporting to me any new developments on the case. I also admonished them we were in crisis mode, and our investigation was top secret. "Under no circumstances, should you discuss this with anyone, even those with *Smilin' Faces* [the title of a popular song at that time]."

As for me, besides coordinating the investigation and still overseeing our quotidian activities, I would have to deal with the AG, Macklin, and quite possibly, Langlois. I wasn't looking forward to tackling any of those.

Later in the day when I was interviewed by the press, my comments were brief, and the interview was not as difficult as I had earlier anticipated. I was asked by reporters if I could have prevented the incident—the death was not yet classified—had I had more personnel. I reminded them we were only there in a staff, not line, status to oversee and evaluate the security function, and as such, we did not execute or supplement every day security obligations.

And my license to slide was that the matter was in the hands of the NOPD; however, I emphasized that, without question, we were looking into it from the perspective of Dome security. I also took the opportunity to commend Dickerson's work, and I painted him as the proficient agent and noble individual I knew he was.

Frazzled after a long day, I went home to Natalie, colleen nonpareil. Luxuriant black tresses cascading to her shoulders embraced her slender neck, Vendela rose-complexioned visage, and her translucent cheeks tinged with the softest pink coralline. Coupled with her hourglass figure and patrician bearing, she is the

apotheosis of femininity.

And her loveliness isn't miserly to her extrinsic carriage. Her brilliance of mind, depth of compassion, and her deep well of empathy presented as brightly as did her countenance.

Natalie is way overqualified for her role as a homemaker. Housewifery had declined in status over the preceding twenty-five or so years, but Natalie calligraphed it into an art form. Her chefery included New Orleans cuisine prepared as exquisitely as Michelin-level menus. Our home was welcoming— cozy, tidy, and eclectically decorated. Because of her, we enjoyed an atmosphere of serenity and joy living there.

Over a dinner of a salad laced with caponata accompanied by butterflied pork chops stuffed with dirty rice, we chitchatted about trivialities. But with a worried look, and always sensitive to my peace of mind, she said, "Let me know when you are ready to talk about what's going on; I'll be an active listener."

"Just for now, I'll tell you that something bad has happened at the Dome, and my team and I are in the big middle of it. Let' sleep just a bit, and tomorrow I'll share with you an interesting story, at least as much as I know to this point."

In an attempt to wash away the feculence of the day, I showered and vigorously scrubbed myself, collapsed into bed, and almost immediately drifted into the waiting arms of Morpheus. Natalie remained awake, and before I sloped off the cusp of reality, I could hear the tinkling of her rosary beads. Natalie was not at all lazy in love.

CHAPTER V
"Handling" Me

After our previous day's meeting, Zitzy and the Pillsbury Doughboy had jumped into deep waters. I didn't see them for the rest of the day, in part because I had spent so little time in the office and in part because they were motived to get things rolling.

I chanced upon Corbin and Huberty in the Superdome canteen. Except for the political ramifications of bad press, the pair expressed little interest in the possible murder. Although Corbin evinced at least some curiosity, Huberty was altogether dismissive. I wasn't going to have any help from them either.

I went to NOPD Headquarters to see Macklin and get a copy of his preliminary report. There, I was notified he was unavailable, but I could see him in an hour.

Slipping out and going across the street to the Crescent Bar, a hangout for NOPD officers, I ate a roast beef po-boy.

A po-boy is a sandwich made on "New Orleans" French bread; that is, a type of bread usually made by one of the Gendusa, Reising, Gambino's, or Leidenheimer bakeries. Po-boys—New Orleans "fast food"—are most often served wrapped in white butcher paper.

When I returned, I was notified Macklin has been called away and would return in about a half-hour. I sat on a hard, wooden bench outside the Detective Bureau and waited...and waited.

After about an hour, I again spoke with the receptionist who told me Macklin hadn't returned. I wasn't positive, but behind the closed doors of the detective offices, I thought I could hear Macklin's gravelly voice with his heavy New Orleans brogue. As I suspected, he was "handling" me (a police term for "fucking with").

There are seven distinct accents in New Orleans. The type, strength, and lexicon of the accents vary from section to section of the city's metropolitan area. Longtime residents can often tell from which neighborhood the other residents are by their accent. Speakers of this dialect originated in the Ninth Ward, as well as the Irish Channel and Mid-City, but as the city grew, the articulations altered.

Frustrated, I left and went downstairs to the morgue in the basement of the police headquarters building. On the jaded—but not unclean—side, the morgue

was somewhat a reflection of the NOPD and New Orleans in general.

Unlike state troopers, who took pride in their appearances, many NOPD officers reveled in looking shabby. It was as if they were trying to convey an image of a rough and tumbled, dust-covered, gun-slinging cowboy after a roundup.

The morgue and the rest of the city—except for the Garden District, parts of the Faubourg Bywater, and the subdivisions at the lakefront—embraced that sullied, bedraggled, and apathetic look too. The Great Lady of the South was gasping in the throes of her demise.

At the morgue, I inquired about the time and date of Dickerson's autopsy; it was scheduled for two days later (Friday) at 1:00. The sultry and trash-littered streets outside NOPD Headquarters were a welcome treat after the dank, fetid air of the New Orleans Morgue.

Having had ingested enough squalor and antipathy for the day, I went back to the office. Arriving there after 4:00, and while packing my briefcase, I noted a stack of documents on Zitzy's desk. I was curious, but I didn't disturb them.

I then returned to the oasis of my home. My haven was serene yet electrically charged. Natalie was dressed in a short woman's tie front shirt with an overhand knot just above her navel and with short shorts that barely covered her pubis and the gluteal folds of her buttocks. As always, I was spellbound by the sexual prowess of her thighs.

She had prepared a repast of shrimp sautéed in olive oil, butter, lemon, and garlic served over rice. In the interest of healthy eating, she included buttered cornbread and a side of mustard greens cooked in onions and, yes, thick cut (healthful?) bacon.

Conversing with her about the case took some of the edge off of my harried day—Natalie was an attentive and non-judgmental listener.

CHAPTER VI
Zitzy Zitzing

After a night of fidgeting and half-sleep, I awakened unrefreshed at 4:30 the next morning. I gingerly stepped out of bed so as not to awaken Natalie and went to the kitchen. After brewing a pot of stout Union Coffee and Chicory I prepared a *café au lait* and noshed on some left-over cornbread with butter.

I mulled over the events of the previous day and, in abstract, laid out an implementation plan. Not long thereafter, leaving Natalie asleep, I, went to the office, arriving there a little before 6:30.

My team rolled in at about 8:00. We had a general debriefing, and I then asked Zitzy and Doughboy to step aside and update me on what they had so far found.

Zitzy had at first encountered resistance obtaining the necessary security documents. The security office supervisor, Elvis Leasean, was not amenable to providing them without his supervisor's approval. But Leman, with his zitzy eyes, was formidable—a sane person would not be inclined to provoke him.

Ultimately, however, the Chief Security Officer Jim Rieglé, an ex-FBI agent, authorized the documents to be released. But he told Zitzy it would take a few days to get them to him. Zitzy made it clear that was unacceptable.

And Zitzy's eyes started zitzing. "Under the noses of your security personnel, a likely murder has been committed. And you want to impede an investigation into it? If I don't have them within an hour, our group is going public and expose your unwillingness to work with us. Is that what you want?"

Rieglé was no stranger to the sub-contractor's tenuous standing in the community and even more cognizant of Zitzy's zitzing steel-greys. I later learned that, discretion being the better part of valor, Rieglé capitulated and produced copies of the records within an hour. But with the delay, Zitzy had little time to adequately review them that day. Nevertheless, he called me that evening and promised to peruse the paperwork and report back to me ASAP.

Against the odds, Doughboy informed me he had made some progress. With his well-oiled discernment and savoir-faire, he might have unveiled an inroad.

It is quite often said, "Home is where the heart is." And another well-used expression is, "The way to a man's heart is through his belly." Home for supper,

Natalie had prepared nostalgic comfort food for me—shrimp-stuffed mirlitons. Although long ago, she had commandeered my essence, the mirlitons were finishing touches to the rapture she ignited in me.

CHAPTER VII
Doughboy Meets "Tips"

The following day, Doughboy gave me his full report.

Security Officer Jacquelyn Tippers had been working the day shift. She was one of three females of the forty-eight personnel on the Superdome security staff. And she wasn't happy.

I had heard Tippers was a fox. The men called her "Tips" because of her name and because her large nipples sometimes jutted through her unlined bra and uniform shirt. She was tall and lithe, yet curvy with an isthmus-like figure. In her late twenties, she was said to be alert and vivacious.

Tips was fawn complexioned with imposing high cheekbones, mocha-colored lambswool-rippled tresses, and inquisitive tawny eyes. She was wreathed by a zephyr of equanimity and grace that sallied forth and enveloped her. Even in a police-type uniform, she still had the presence of a glamour model.

The indicated reason for her distress was that she was propositioned over and over by drooling males with whom she worked. But it wasn't only the men—one of Jaquelyn's rough-hewn and very butch diesel female associates was after those orbicular buns too.

Unable to seduce her, her male co-workers began to badger her. The rank-and-file hassles didn't bother her too much. But long before sexual harassment was a hot issue and she could complain about it, the advances by Donatien Huberty, the co-owner of the sub-contracting security outfit, distressed her.

Walking around the Dome with her, Doughboy had the impression that, because of her extraordinary allurement, Jaquelyn had most often been treated as a sex object and not recognized as the professional she was.

Along with that, with his finely tuned perspicacity, Doughboy perceived latent acuteness and constituent humanity within her. He also discerned in her a certain *je ne sais quoi.*

Gallant, and as if he had kissed the Blarney Stone, Doughboy, an old-school gentleman, could seduce an Amazon crocodile if he chose to. But oddly enough, he didn't know it, and his love life was almost nonexistent.

Chatting Jacqulyn up with quips and witticisms, and keeping the conversation

26

focused on her, he eased her into relaxation. He learned about her morale problem at work. And when he treated her to lunch at the Superdome canteen, she revealed additional facets of her workplace conflicts, but she swore him to secrecy.

Doughboy, interlocutor extraordinaire, commiserated with her, and he learned she was from Saint Martinville, a small town in South Central Louisiana near Lafayette. She had taken leave of Saint Martinville to get a job at the Superdome.

Doughboy asked her what name she would prefer being be called, and she said, "Jackie." With a conspiratorial grin, Doughboy confided, "Okay, I'll call you Jackie, and you can call me Dave."

Apparently, mesmerized by his twinkling cornflower-blue eyes, his inherent charm, his concern, and his lack of chauvinistic dominance, Jaquelyn was captivated by Doughboy...or so it seemed. It couldn't have been mere coincidence she inquired about his marital status (a three-year divorcée). And as she was leaving to return to duty and thanking him for lunch, she squeezed his shoulder— an inveiglement perhaps?

So much titillation; so much romance! All ears to his narration, I felt I was listening to an excerpt from *Sense and Sensibility*.

"But," said Doughboy, "my instinct tells me whatever it is unsettling her, it's deeper than she's disclosed." He told me he would follow through and pursue what he saw as an opportunity to learn more from Jackie.

Although in drawing out the information—if there were any to be had—he said he would have to be patient. He didn't want it to appear that she was just a tool in our investigation. This was to later pay off handsomely.

Yet, did I not see more than just a twinkle in his eyes? Hmm. Was Doughboy, too, not a little enchanted by Jackie's air of mystery? I chose to say nothing and let it play out on its own. He was a good investigator, and he knew not to cross the line of professionalism...at least not too quickly.

I asked Doughboy what MO he had employed to place him in such a propitious position. He told me he began by going to the security office and asking for someone to show him around the Dome. Of course, the security contingent knew him, and there was no perceptible antipathy between our group and the proletariat security officers, themselves.

He continued about his conversation with Leasean, "This place is a maze; even though I've been here for over a month, I still can't find my way around. Could you get someone to help me?" he had asked him. The request was not unreasonable; the Superdome was a labyrinth with hidden corners, nooks, and crannies.

Leasean agreed to help him, and he made a call on the radio. Moments later, Doughboy, with some levity, was introduced to "Tips." The supervisor was blasé and seemed to be unconcerned his subordinates would be jealous of Dosstein— not to worry, Tips could never be attracted to the chubby and baking-soda-white Pillsbury Doughboy.

But as Jerome Lawrence has said, "The man who has everything figured out is probably a fool."

CHAPTER VIII
Pontius Pilate II

I spent most of the day on the telephone. I wasn't the only one seeking information about the incident; more so than other similar investigations, the press was also. But they were put off by the police. Reporters clamored for a press release, but they only received a statement saying, "The matter is still under investigation." Likewise, their calls for a news conference with the NOPD Chief of Police were brushed aside.

A queer cone of silence had fallen over the investigation. Another piece of the puzzle, and I couldn't figure out why.

I left three messages for Macklin—all went unanswered. I found this too to be a bit odd; even police agencies that did not function well with each other shared at least some information.

Telephoning Corbin, I asked him if we could meet in my office. Ever pretentious, he said he was busy, but I could come to his office and he'd receive me for a short conference. I left my sunny suite and descended into the bowels of the Superdome.

Corbin's office suite had no natural light. It was populated with female cost-plus employees working with dimmed illumination. Only a few were busy; most of them were eating cookies and bags of chips and prattling among themselves. And all of their desks, sagging under the weight of papers, junk food, and trivial personal items, were in disarray.

I was dispatched to Corbin's private office, which was as dismal as the ante-office. "Handling me," he didn't arise from his chair behind his large desk nor offer to shake my hand. Huberty was seated to Corbin's right, and he, too, did not rise or extend his hand.

In the Southern culture, in which even the most contemptible of political enemies shake hands, that was an obvious sign of disrespect. Furthermore, it was clear from the seating arrangement that Corbin was in charge.

The two were dichotomies. Like Richard Cory, Corbin was "clean favored and imperially slim." He was caramel complexioned, and although somewhat hidden, he still betrayed a sense of affability, humor, and maybe even compassion.

29

Without doubt, I recognized he was the more politically astute of the two.

Conversely, Huberty was a large man and darker than a hundred midnights down in a cypress swamp. In the dimly lit office, he was almost invisible.

As if someone had thwacked his face with a two-by-six and flattened his nose; it was smeared across his face, his wide nostrils conveying the impression of an extra set of dark, ominous eyes. He personified the Oscar Wilde quote: "Some cause happiness wherever they go; others whenever they go."

He carried the aura of stale beer and grunge about him. And he seemed to be devoid of personality; indeed, his body language said, "I don't like you; don't come near me." It was of no little wonder that Jacquelyn was so repulsed by him.

I was met by both of them within a noxious climate of disdain. Corbin, who emoted the role of a high-octane executive, directed me to a chair so low my butt could just as well have been on the floor. The entire scenario screamed intimidation ploy.

I asked Corbin if his security guards had come up with anything on Dickerson's death. And insouciant, he said, "No, and we don't intend to; it's an NOPD matter."

I knew that, having snagged the prized contracts, Corbin was hooked to the New Orleans political machine, so with little expectancy, I also asked him if he could get a copy of the preliminary police report for me. Without any hesitation, whatsoever, he curtly said, "No."

So much for that! With some difficulty, I arose from the low chair and began to leave his office. Stopping at the door and turning to face them, I said to Corbin, "You sir, are going to regret your Pontius Pilate non-involvement in this tragedy."

Both of them smirked at me. And I wondered for a moment if they even knew the story of Pontius Pilate's washing of hands. They probably thought it was an exotic cocktail served at Pat O'Brien's or another one of New Orleans' famous bars.

I was desperate for a copy of Macklin's complete report—the narrative, photographs, and forensics, although I would have settled for just his preliminary report. Frustrated, I decided to call the NOPD Chief of Police, Claudio Giovanni. But at the last minute, I changed my mind.

Over the years, the NOPD had suffered and regressed because of nearly fourteen years of flawed administration by the Giovanni brothers, Giuseppe and Claudio, both of whom served as superintendents. The brothers, more firmly than

ever, inculcated the Department's parochial attitude. As the largest police department in the State, they adhered to the deluded platitudes, "Bigger is better" and "We handle Mardi Gras."

Giuseppe was intelligent, but he was influenced by autocratic tendencies. Claudio shared the same debility. However, compounding that, Claudio lacked Giuseppe's intellect—he had an attention span of thirty seconds. Not long thereafter, Claudio survived a blood clot on the brain. I often wondered if he hadn't had a series of mini-strokes before I had met him. The brothers consecutively served about sixteen years as NOPD superintendents.

The NOPD did have competent officers, and Lieutenant Jack Huggins, the administrative assistant to the chief, was one of them. Aware of the Chief's limitations, I instead placed a call to Huggins.

In the past, Huggins and I had collaborated on a complex joint police project. I knew him to be articulate, dedicated, and open-minded. Although we had represented different positions, we had arrived at a compromise, and we parted as amicable acquaintances.

Unlike Macklin, Huggins did take my call. I explained my situation to him, and I wasn't surprised he understood. He told me he would look into it and get back to me as soon as he could.

Within an hour and a half, Huggins contacted me. I was pleased with the quick turnaround, but he bore bad tidings. Sotto voce, he said he couldn't help, and even the Superintendent, himself, couldn't help if he wanted to. "The mayor's office has placed a hold on the report and press conferences are on lockdown. The report can't be released until we receive word from her." I could tell he was puzzled, so I thanked him, said I owed him a favor, and we signed off.

Besides the other "whys" of Dickerson's murder, we now had another one—why were the clamps put on what should be a straightforward homicide investigation? The situation reeked of a coverup. But a coverup of what, why, and for whose benefit?

Putting my feet to the fire, I decided to call the mayor. Although I expected to be given the runaround, to my amazement, after I spoke with the gum-smacking receptionist and waiting only about two minutes, Luis Irvando answered the phone. Although we had never personally met, I knew who he was, and he knew who I was.

Too delicate for matrimony, Irvando, also a member of the Superdome Advisory Board, was an obvious dash of lavender. He was a fat, obsequious toady, who prig-strutted and functioned as Langlois' simpering administrative assistant.

Always dressed in nouveau chic and with a flawless, sprayed coiffure, he still smacked of a slob (or a "slab," as my French father used to say)—so much so his foppish bleached blonde hairstyle appeared to be fertile ground for pediculosis. I shuddered when I imagined lice cavorting in there.

As I had with the others, I solicited Irvando's help in procuring the police report. He was pleasant enough, but beneath the façade, I could detect a sharp edge. He told me as far as he knew, it was still an open investigation, and because it was, the police had not yet issued a report.

As proof, he cited the absence of the autopsy results as one of the reasons for the delay. It was a good point as far as it went. But it did not explain the lack of the usual police updates to the press nor the non-production of a preliminary report to a sister agency.

Without revealing my source, I told him I had heard the police were sitting on the report because they were ordered by the mayor to do so. A coiled snake lashed out, and his counterfeit amicability evaporated. In his high-pitched, lisping voice, he shrieked, "You're a fucking liar! If I were you, I would watch my mouth and what comes out of it! The mayor would *never* do anything like that." *It didn't take a lot of imagination to know. where he put his mouth and what went in and out of it*

"Okay, okay; I suppose my information was wrong."

Not satisfied, he continued, "Don't forget; you're here at the pleasure of the mayor." That was an *ipsi dixit*, but I agreed with him anyway—why argue the point with a two-bit political hack?

So, we ended our little chat. I did, however, find it a bit humorous that a popinjay like Irvando tried to carry off a veiled threat. It reminded me of the cartoon of the mouse flipping off the eagle, just as the eagle is about to pounce and claw the life out of it.

Sitting alone, I at first felt as if I had had an unproductive day. Yet upon reflection, I considered otherwise. I hadn't made any progress with the case, itself, but I did have some facts I hadn't had before.

Although initially I *thought* it was a coverup, I now *knew* it was. And that was

32

a big "why." Of course, all the other "why" questions were there too, and I couldn't begin to fathom answers for them. And besides having no answers, I felt I didn't even have rudimentary clues to the overriding "why" queries.

Yet I did answer—at least in my mind—one question. I reaffirmed this was New Orleans, the epicenter of corrupt politics. And Langlois must have a lot of dirt on a lot of people; therefore, she could brandish her double-balled antipathy-mace with impunity.

I had no opinion about her relationship with the courts, but I recognized the City Council was her *Punch and Judy* puppet show, and she was the puppeteer. However, at this point, I had no reasonable expectation of learning the specifics of how she accomplished what she did. Nor did I think that an integral cog in my investigation.

Oh Johnny, why categorize that as a backwater? You are familiar with Hamlet's quote, "There's a special providence in the fall of a sparrow...," aren't you? Don't you know a competent investigator considers every piece of the puzzle, even if he later learns that it is not a piece to the puzzle after all? Apparently, I didn't.

During my musing, Conrardy stepped into the office and asked me if I could use help, and I told him, yes, I could use more manpower. He said he couldn't provide that because he had no access to anyone with police-type training, but he condoled with me and again offered any assistance he could render. It was comforting to know he had my back if I needed him.

When I arrived at Chez Régis, I found Natalie had prepared one of my favorites—pan-fried speckled trout, with lemon and butter sauce on the side and accompanied by Brussels sprouts with cheddar cheese and bacon. Of course, it was not Monday, so I had no red beans and rice.

Over dinner, she peppered me with questions about the case. I gave her as much as I knew—which wasn't a lot—and she offered a few suggestions. She had always been a good sounding board. But in this matter, her ideas were all things I had already considered, yet I loved her so much involving herself.

Throughout my life, my father told me I had been born with a Silver Star up my ass, and it seemed to be true. In marrying Natalie, however, it had to be on overtime. Besides being loving, compassionate, and devoted to me, she was

brilliant. Indeed, she could have done so much better, so why did she make such a pedestrian selection in choosing me?

CHAPTER IX
Sleuthing

We had our staff meeting the following morning. One of my other investigators, Agent I Brent "Dupes" Dupuy, a superb undercover agent who consistently "duped" criminal adversaries notified me he had to return home because his wife, Nancy, was in labor and about to deliver their third child; thus, his wife would need him. (No kidding!) I told him to take the following two weeks off, and he could take more time off if necessary.

That handled, I told Breeze, to forget about the days-off cancellation and to enjoy his weekend. He tried to demur, but I insisted, telling him to rest up; it would be asshole and elbows next week.

Then Zitzy and Doughboy gave me their reports. Zitzy advised me he could find no untoward activity or no unusual Dome entry in the security logs for the evening/night of Langdon's death.

The logs were pre-stamped with continuous page numbering using a Bates page number stamp. A new log sheet was started with each shift change, and they recorded security officers on duty, work station assignments, comings and goings of persons at the Dome, and unusual events—a fire, a burned-out light, the need for an emergency vehicle, a death or injury inside the Dome or on its peripheral premises, a sick security officer, a pile of trash where there shouldn't be any, or any other anomalous situation.

He also said, "The shift supervisor typically sits behind a teller station in the security office at the main entrance, assigns officers to security patrols, handles telephone calls directed to the security desk, monitors traffic over the Dome radio network, and directs ongoing security activities. It is generally he who fills out and signs the log for his shift."

"What, if anything, did you find there?"

"It seems that besides recording Dickerson's death—not murder, not an accident, simply a 'death'—the changes of the twelve-hour security shifts, unusual incidences, and non-event ingresses with intended destinations and egresses, the logs were unremarkable. The logs even listed visitors coming to our office."

"What time did Dickerson enter the Dome?"

"They don't record the entry of Dome personnel with Superdome badges, the FBI, emergency personnel, the NOPD, nor us."

"Did you find out if anyone knew what time Dickerson entered?"

"I asked, but I was told there was another shift on the night watch that evening. I'm coming in tonight and ask around."

"Okay, Zitzy. But you know how you can't suffer fools. Schmooze them a bit, and if you can't get what you want, let it drop. Those guys might have some valuable information, and if not now, one or more of them might let something slip later on."

Zitzy suppressed a chuckle. And with a smile, he assured me he understood, and it would be no problem.

I segued, "What do you have, Doughboy?"

"Well, I 'toured' with Jackie as she made her key punches again yesterday. She received permission to have an extended off-campus lunch, and I took her to Mother's Restaurant, where we each ate a small Ferdi Special. Not wanting to appear too zealous, I didn't press her about the work environment.

For some unexplained reason, I sense she has good information, yet she's withholding it. Then again, maybe she doesn't, but I have this feeling…. So at this point, I'm only trying to gain her trust.

"After our tour, I took the liberty of a *passe-partout*, and I explored on my own. Lo, this place is a cavernous warren…and complicated! I observed innumerable closed doors to rooms with no nameplates on them. And those with nameplate-type signs were usually, 'Caution Keep Out', 'Do Not Enter,' 'Danger Live Wires,' or something to that effect. I assumed they were engineering and maintenance portals. The Olson Foods warehouse and cold storage is completely fenced off."

"What about entrances other than the main ones?"

"There's a slew of them. I'm not sure if they're alarmed or not, and I don't know how they are keyed, but perhaps I can find this out from Jackie."

Mentally kicking myself, I realized I should have obtained that information when we first arrived. *Oh, Johnny, what a piss-poor security administrator you are.* "See if you can get a schematic with those portals and check them out."

"Okay."

"Let's get to it. And as soon as possible, question the Dome reporting officer for not only facts but for his opinions too." I was hoping we'd get to him for a detailed interview before Macklin did, even though I knew Macklin would have questioned him—or her—at the scene on the night of the homicide.

CHAPTER X
At Death's Doors

The next day, I arrived at the morgue at 12:35. And after checking with the dowdy and bedraggled receptionist, I was curtly directed to sit and wait on (another) hard wooden bench. My skinny tush doesn't take kindly to hard seating, but I suppose citizens' comfort is not a priority in New Orleans public buildings.

The waiting room, most often a place of grief and despair, was not conducive to even an iota of cheer. The ceiling, originally white, was, because of cigarette smoke, a smudgy beige. The walls were government green, and they too were coated with a film of cigarette tar. The once-white tile floors were stained with grime and the tears of the bereaved. With an invisible fog, fetor hung in the air, and with only a little imagination, one could envision it as the effluvium of the Grim Reaper's crotch.

As if that weren't enough, more mephitis invaded the space—Macklin. He knew the drill, so he didn't need to speak with the receptionist, and he chose to sit down on the bench beside me. Without acknowledging me, he began to speak, "You know the expression, 'Don't put your shovel where there ain't no shit?'" Not waiting for an answer, he continued, "Régis you're smart enough to realize what the deal is. It's our investigation—back off, let us handle this."

Our AG badges were boot-shaped in the outline of the State of Louisiana; thus, the City of New Orleans, and the rest of the State, was within the purview of our police authority. So I said, "There are no holes in my badge, Macklin. An AG agent was murdered, and you expect me to let it go?"

"Wait a minute, Pal. Who said Dickerson was murdered? It was an accident."

"That must be your ass talking because your mouth knows better."

With a sneer, Macklin said, "Well, we'll see, smart guy." *Uh-oh, this coverup was even more enrooted than I had believed it to be. And the coroner must be in on it too.*

We hunkered down into a loud silence.

Anon, Dr. Charles Odom, the coroner and pathologist, attired in green scrubs, a plastic apron, a face shield, and surgical gloves opened the exam room doors and motioned us to enter. In his mid-fifties, Dr. Odom, lank but physically fit, wore

his long gray hair in a ponytail.

He had seen over a quarter of a century of death and tragedy, yet his cerulean eyes frolicked, and an almost indiscernible, impish smile creased his lips bringing life and freshness to that domicile of dissolution. It was apparent that being the coroner was for him not a necessity but a labor of love.

Barely inside, Macklin said to Dr. Odom, "He doesn't belong in here. This is an NOPD matter."

Turning around, Dr. Odom said, "Sergeant Macklin, you run your investigation, and I'll run the Coroner's Office. Mr. Régis is welcome to attend."

Squinting his saddle-brown eyes, Macklin sputtered, "But…," and stopped. He glowered at me, but I just smiled, shrugged my shoulders, and followed Dr. Odom.

It gut-wrenched me to look at what was once my friend on a table lying naked on his back in a shallow stainless-steel pan. There was no partial sheet over his private parts as seen in the movies. I had to get the bastard or bastards who had done this.

His brown eyes were wide open, staring straight ahead. Were they looking at his killer? I tried to divine if they were, but I met with no success.

Macklin, with palpable impatience, and I, with avid interest, watched, Dr. Odom undertake the autopsy.

Dr. Odom began by making a meticulous examination of the front of Langdon's body, including the inside of his mouth and other orifices, the groin area, the armpits, and between the fingers and toes; he often used a magnifying glass and flashlight to do so. In the process, he photographed the body noting bruises and other anomalies. And as he did throughout the entire procedure, he spoke into a mic suspended from the ceiling.

After that, with the help of an orderly, he rolled Dickerson's cadaver over and began another minute inspection of the back side of the body. While doing so, he noted a pinprick with a small bruise on the left rear quarter of Dickerson's neck. He excised a small plug of the tissue around it and placed the sample in a small collection tube. Inexplicably, with keen interest, that procedure seemed to rouse Macklin.

Dr. Odom and the orderly then rolled Langdon's cadaver back to the face-up position on the gurney. Under Dr. Odom's watchful eye, the orderly, with a bone saw and hooked hammer, removed the skullcap, exposing Langdon's once active

and insightful brain.

Following that, the orderly cut a large, deep, and angular Y-shaped incision from shoulder-to-shoulder meeting at the breast bone and extending down to the pubic bone. Providing access to his internal organs, Langdon's ribs were broken with rib shears and the chest and the abdomen cavities were splayed open.

Dr. Odom extracted, weighed, and dissected Dickerson's organs. Rifling through them like a deck of cards, he examined each one. He placed small pieces of each in a communal jar, and he collected blood samples directly from the heart and labeled them in three separate hypodermic vials.

Finished, he, replaced the unsaved organs in the body cavity and directed the orderly to sew the corpse back up with white cotton string.

Breaking the silence, Macklin said, "Well. What's the verdict, Doc?"

"I can't give a definitive opinion now, but I think it's a homicide."

"Ya' gotta' be shittin' me. Didn't you review my preliminary report?" exhorted Macklin.

"Yes, Mr. Macklin, I did read your report. And at this point—my opinion might change—I believe you made a mistake. This was no accident." *Voila! One for the good guys.*

"Have you spoken with the mayor about this? You know that's going to be bad publicity for the city."

"Well yes, the mayor called me, Mr. Macklin. And I'm fully aware of the negative press it will generate. But she has her responsibilities and I have mine."

So, the "accident" spin was why Macklin, Irvando, the NOPD, and Corbin stonewalled my requests for the preliminary report. And Dr. Odom was a stand-up guy!

Again, Macklin almost drooling, sputtered, "But...."

However, it didn't matter whether or not Macklin could have finished his sentence, because Dr. Odom said, "If you'll excuse me, gentlemen, I have two more autopsies today," and he ushered us to the door.

On our way out, I asked Dr. Odom when I could have a copy of his report, and he told me he had to wait for the lab results, but it would probably be less than a week.

Once outside, I smirked at Macklin and in my best sardonic tone said, "An

accident?"

Macklin's response was, "Fuck you, Asshole," and he stormed off. Besides being vulgar, it seemed Macklin was vocabularily handicapped too.

This wasn't a bad day after all, I said to myself as I walked to my car. I had the box of Tinkertoys, but I didn't yet know how to assemble the pieces, or what I was going to build with them when I learned how they could be put together.

CHAPTER XI
Schmoozing the Security Staff

When I returned to my office, it was clear that Doughboy and Zitzy had some good news. Talking over one another with unrestrained enthusiasm, they began to both give their reports. Most likely, they each had a good day too. Calming them down, I said, "Wait a minute, guys; I can't understand what you're saying if you both speak at the same time."

Doughboy deferred to Zitzy's senior status, saying, "Go ahead Zitzy, I'll wait."

"You remember I spoke about Leasean, one of the security supervisors? Well, I think he might be able to help us. Leasean is upright, so upright he doesn't flirt with Tips. He's taking classes at the Baptist Theological Seminary to soon become a minister. He might be a weak link in the coverup; he needs the job, but his ethics and morals come first. I believe I can work him."

"Fantastic! Follow up on it. What about your re-review of the logs and your take on the incident report?"

"That was the big break! Although the incident report, itself, is generic and limited—brief and a few facts we already know—there's a peculiarity between the log and the incident report.

I had seen that, and I assumed it was SOP. But according to Leasean, it wasn't. At about the time of the murder, the handwriting in the log changed. And the original handwriting is the same as the incident report, but the later log entries and the incident report don't match."

"Do you know who the two authors were?"

"I have the name on the incident report and the initial log inscriber, Gerald Bowditch—it's on the log itself. But right now, I don't know who the intervenor at the desk was because I can't decipher the signature. I'm planning to see Leasean again and get that info from him."

"Good job. Follow up and let me know. And after Sunday, call the Coroner's Office every day for a copy of the autopsy report until you get it.

"What do you have Doughboy?"

"My report isn't as pithy as Zitzy's, but I've made a little headway.

"Jackie's off this weekend. And she's a no-bullshit chick. She asked me to go

on a picnic with her Sunday afternoon!"

"I hope you accepted."

"Of course, I did! Normally, I'd be apprehensive about a setup, but after what she told me today, I think she favors white guys, and she likes *me*."

"Well, she can't find any whiter than you. What did she say?"

"Something must have happened in her past, because she bitterly complained about Black men. She told me they're all excessively macho, and all they talk about are their big dicks."

"I knew I selected well. You're the quintessential man for the job—you're sensitive to women, and you won't be bragging about your parlor peter." (Think about it...historically, the parlor was a prim and proper place to formally entertain genteel guests, such as those having high tea. Men tend to think of their personal appliances as menacing weapons of destruction rather than delicate utensils as fragile as China teacups.)

"Yeah, yeah; I got it. But what do you think about me going on the date?"

"Go for it. But don't boff her. We don't want this thing to explode in our crotches. And I'll tell you both why."

I informed them what happened at the autopsy and then said, "All indications are we're up against a powerful political machine. And our Higgs boson, the theorized 'God particle,' will ignite a major revision in New Orleans politics, much as the Higgs boson is believed to have ignited the Big Bang,"

"The Higgs 'whatever' is over my head, but I get the point, said Zitzy. There'll be a Vesuvian detonation if we're successful."

"Exactly. And for that reason, I want you to dot the I's and cross the T's. They may already be on to us, so we can't afford any mistakes."

Narrating my tiffs with the security contractors, the NOPD, the Mayor's office, and Macklin, and iterating what had transpired at the autopsy, I summed up, "I don't want to come across as a conspiracy nut, but I believe this is more than a murder case. Whatever it is, it's big. We're controverting an entrenched consortium, and we might end up being sacrificial lambs.

"In this case, sorting out the information is the same as dealing with quantum entanglement—each piece cannot be described independently of the state of the others, and we don't even have a handle on the state of the others. But keep going at it. Facts give rise to observer participation; observer participation gives

rise to information; information gives rise to more facts."

I still had to call the AG and give him my report. And report I did. He didn't take the delay of the apprehension well. But to my surprise, he gave me the option to bail if I wanted to and leave the investigation to the NOPD. Had I had a crystal ball and could have foreseen the future, I *might* have earlier chosen that opportunity.

But I wasn't given a choice. I didn't have a crystal ball, and my friend and colleague was murdered on my watch. Nevertheless, at this point, I was committed— "In for a penny, in for a pound." Thus, I declined his offer.

However, the AG made it clear: The situation was political dynamite, and I could expect little support from his office. Johnny Régis was standing naked in front of his enemies.

It had been a brutal and harrowing few days. And in the process, I had neglected to oversee the projects assigned to my other two subordinates. So I spoke with Breeze and requested he give me his and Brent's progress reports, which he delivered with dispatch.

They were two good men. And...they had been doing quite well without my direct involvement. *The lesson: There is no need to micromanage competent personnel.* I told Breeze to enjoy his weekend but to remain on standby in case I needed him

It was after six when I opened the back door to our bungalow. And I was—at least for the time being—in Nirvana. I had it all...a snug roost, a loving wife, *and* epicurean seafood gumbo with South Louisiana rice! Following that succulent repast, I showered, climbed into bed, and Hypnos ferried me onto and across the River Lethe.

CHAPTER XII
Occam's Razor with a Dull Blade

At six-thirty I awakened, the Saturday morning sun cascading through the unshaded fanlight above my bed. And I could hear the muted sounds of Natalie puttering about in the kitchen.

How fortunate I was to have Natalie. We married young and immature. But we made it work, even though we are a most unusual couple—a fairy princess and a troll. Marrying her, I was inseminated with an immutable enthrallment.

It has always amazed me that men are so intolerant of women; e.g., too fat, too skinny, too old, and other tasteless criticisms. Yet women are so uncannily tolerant of men. From my perspective, Natalie could have been a non-emaciated runway model. I, on the other hand, was short, prematurely balding, and unattractive. But it didn't matter to Natalie; she took me as I was—warts, feathers, and all.

Lying in bed half-awake and half-tumescent, it hit me in a flash! With all the helter-skelter of the preceding days, I had somewhat neglected my husbandly duties. And as I lay there thinking of Natalie, I heard the bedroom door ease open. I rolled over to see what was happening—Natalie entered and silently glided in.

And presto! She was at her side of the bed, her nightgown glissading to the floor. Natalie was not going to allow me to be derelict!

At breakfast, I gave her an update on the situation I was facing—I was quite apprehensive, but I wasn't about to let her know that. "Well," she declared, "you have two days of rest ahead of you. It's a beautiful October day, and you and I can enjoy it together—maybe sit at the Lakefront, drink beer, and eat boiled crabs. I'll prepare an ice chest."

"No, Babe, I'm sorry," I said with a pained locution. "As I told you, this thing is huge, and I'm in the sights of the AG *and* the bad guys. I have to wrap it up as soon as I can But after that's settled, with my accrued k-time, we'll take a vacation."

Displaying a moue, she upbraided me, saying, "You're becoming obsessed with this case." Yet capitulating, she granted me license to believe she understood.

When I showed up at the office at about nine-thirty, Zitzy and Doughboy were already there. Those guys are stellar. They had come in early, and they had been poring over the obtained security documents and making notes of, and discussing, their individual efforts.

"Glad you could make it," simpered Zitzy.

Animated, they again both began to speak at the same time. And as before, Doughboy demurred to Zitzy. "I got lucky. Leasean was supposed to be off this weekend—Friday, Saturday, and Sunday. But he tries to work on the weekends, so he has time off during the week to attend seminary classes. It's Jack Spratt and his wife—he sometimes trades days with other officers, most of whom would prefer a free weekend.

"Therefore, I had the opportunity to wriggle some more information from him, stuff I hadn't heard before.

"The evening/morning, 6:00 p.m. to 6:00 a.m., shift supervisor on duty during the apparent time of the murder was Bowditch. He initiated the log and sat at the security desk until quarter-past midnight when he called the security guards in for training. During the training, Bowditch told the crew he was stepping out for fresh air, and he left Bill May in charge of the command desk and the rest of the training session.

"And as you can see by the change in the handwriting, he signed off, and May signed onto the log; however, Bowditch never resumed desk duty that morning. And at 1:15, he radioed May and told him he had discovered Ghost's body, to call the NOPD, and to send the guards back to their posts. He was probably at the scene when you got there.

"But here's where it gets strange. Leasean said it was highly unusual for a supervisor to be patrolling the Dome, especially at night. And as you know, although the arena stays illuminated, the lighting is dimmed to about one-third of what it is for an event. It's enough to find one's way around, but that's it." Of course, by the time I arrived at the scene on the morning of the murder, the Dome's lights had been fully illuminated.

"Did you interview May and Bowditch?"

"No, I couldn't. With those twelve-hour shifts they have, this is their long weekend off."

"Well, contact Rieglé, get their home addresses, and interview them there.

46

And let me know how it goes."

"I don't believe we should," said Zitzy. "If we approach them at home, they'll probably be resentful and clam up more than they would do if they were here."

"You're right, Zitzy. Cancel that, but follow up."

Doughboy said, "Once again, my report is not as compelling as Zitzy's. Jackie and I exchanged telephone numbers, and…"

Ring, ring! The telephone interrupted us.

"Régis," I answered.

"Johnny, Dickerson's wake is tonight starting at 6:00; his funeral is tomorrow at 1:00 p.m." The voice was that of my immediate supervisor, Agent IV Jim Chatelain. "If you can't attend the wake, you have to attend the funeral. Most of us from the office will be going to the wake but not the funeral. The religious service will be held at the funeral home chapel at 1:00."

Of course, I had already decided to attend, but I was surprised at the order, itself and that the funeral would be celebrated on a Sunday.

"Where?"

"Jacque's Funeral Home, on Saint Claude Avenue. Burial will be in Saint Vitus Cemetery #2 on Louisa Street."

I jotted it down and said, "Okay, got it. Don't worry about representation at the funeral; Zitzy, Doughboy, and I will be there." And I disconnected the call.

I notified Zitzy and Doughboy about the directive I received. Both were disposed to attend, although Doughboy said, "But that's when I have the picnic date with Jackie."

And with an inspirational glint, I said, "Doughboy, could you convince Jackie to go to the funeral with you. The attendees are going to be mostly Black, and the family and others will take note of an AG with a Black woman there to pay his respects. We might gain a lot of mileage, and perhaps we'll be able to use it to our advantage."

"I don't know, I'll try, but I won't press her. This is a delicate situation, and I don't want to mess it up.

"Anyway, I was about to tell you that I sense Jackie wants to work with us. Given that, it's likely she'll also want to participate."

"It sounds good. But I'll defer to your judgment.

"Okay guys, go back to what you were doing." They did, and I had the rest of

the day to outline, contemplate, and analyze the skimpy facts I had.

Everything that I had seen so far foreshadowed that the fix was in, but why? Maybe if I knew the reason there was a coverup, I could find Dickerson's killer or killers. What could be so important to obfuscate the murder of an AG agent? Whatever it was, it had to be big.

In an effort to be objective, I questioned my massive conspiracy theory about the murder. Could it not just be a political effort to avoid negative press? Could it not be I was overreacting?

But when I applied a rusty version of Occam's razor—entities should not be multiplied beyond necessity—I found very little to shave off. It seemed the most likely option was that something more than protecting the image of the Superdome was the motivating factor for the coverup. I still wasn't sure, and I still didn't know the "who," the "why."

At about 1:00, I decided to pack it in. But instead of going home, I drove to my meditative stupa and parked in one of the bays on Lakeshore Drive not far from the Coast Guard station. (I couldn't tell Natalie I did, but I needed a place where I could contemplate without distractions.) And I sat on the seawall hoping to have insight.

A light breeze ribboned the water. And the usual muddy-looking lake beneath the celestial blue sky broken only once in a while by popcorn clouds appeared to be blue too. The sound of the ripples tickling the lower steps of the concrete bulwark, fusing with the squawking of seagulls, made a sweet melody. And at this time of the day there were only a few sailboats out on the lake, not nearly as many as there would be for the later-afternoon regatta.

Embracing the lacustrine ambience, I melded into the environment. I sailed those waters when I had time off, and this spot allowed me to empty my mind of extraneous thoughts and put a laser focus on the prevailing situation, just as I focused on the wind while sailing.

But it was futile; Minerva didn't appear out of the wavelets to guide me, and I was rewarded with no effulgent glimmer of intuition. I was distressed I couldn't get a handle on the status quo. And I was becoming more frustrated and unsure of myself. *Johnny Boy, perhaps you've exceeded your limitations.* And with nary a trinket of discernment I went home to Natalie.

She sensed I was burdened, so she put a Mario Lanza $33^1/_3$ on the stereo. It

helped; I could feel the tension evaporating from my body. For dinner, she had prepared one of my favorites—spaghetti bordelaise with Italian sausage and fresh French bread on the side. We made small talk and shared a bottle of white Graves.

As Natalie was cleaning up, I hit the shower. Later, we had a replay of the morning's bacchanal. The last conscious thing I remember before I drowsed off was being nestled in the fragrance and sweet caress of her bosom.

But my contentment was short-lived, for it did not follow me into slumber. I dreamt I was alone on my sailboat, and the wind sat down to an eerie calm. I was deadlocked in irons, and I wasn't going anywhere until I had an airstream to propel me forward.

An angry nor'wester was on the horizon and headed my way. As it stood, I'd never make it to port before the gale was upon me, and I was unsure if I could single-hand through it.

There was no chance to reef the main. Along with a bolt of lightning and a leading edge of pelting rain, the wind came up in an unrelenting ferocity. The mast broke, and I began to take the wind and waves on the beam; and a rogue wave caused the boat to capsize and turn turtle.

Trapped beneath it, I was drowning, and I awakened shivering in a cold sweat.

CHAPTER XIII
A Modified New Orleans Jazz Funeral

Funerals. Even though I know they supposedly serve a purpose, I hate them; I think they're barbaric. The platitudes are usually boring, hackneyed, and more often than not, the preacher barely knows, or doesn't' know, the deceased. The loved one is gone, and all the looking at his or her corpse won't bring them back. I tried to avoid funerals, but I would never consider dishonoring my friend that way. So I had to go to one today.

Awakening at 7:30, I had coffee and cheese grits with Natalie and waited until 8:00 to call Doughboy. He answered on the first ring and said he was waiting until eight to call me.

He said, "I have good news. Not only was Jackie okay cancelling the picnic, she was thinking of asking me to take her to the funeral. It seems that, during Ghost's nocturnal peregrinations around the Dome, she and Langdon had become friends. And she is distressed about his death."

"Great! Did she provide you any other information?"

"She didn't volunteer, and I didn't ask. You do remember we agreed to take it slow, don't you?"

"Yeah, you're right. I suppose I'm overly anxious to get some facts and speed up the investigation." *Notes to self: 1) You're luckier than a dog with two dicks to have such a prudent subordinate, 2) don't hotfoot it—you should know better, and 3) don't truckle to your perturbations.*

"I think we should arrive early. I have no idea what the turnout will be, but inasmuch as it's on a Sunday, I'm assuming it will be low. How about if we meet there at about 12:15?"

"That's fine. I'll call Zitzy and let him know."

"Thanks."

Boy, was I wrong about the turnout! I arrived at the funeral home shortly after twelve, and already the parking lot was filling up. I went inside—Zitzy and Doughboy would find me; hell, I was the only white face in the bunch. And I queued up in a receiving line to meet Mrs. Dickerson.

While waiting, I noted four quiet, well-behaved, well-groomed children seated

in the right front pew. I estimated their ages ranged from about five to twelve. They were accompanied by a lady who appeared to be in her mid-fifties, whom I presumed was their grandmother. In the left front row were seated those who I assumed to be relatives.

Langdon's casket had a golden-copper hue, and it was adorned with a large white rose spray on the lid covering the lower half of his body. And spray upon spray lined the walls of the chapel.

It was a short wait. Mrs. Dickerson appeared to be intimate with the other mourners, and they had probably attended the wake. When it was my turn, I took her right hand in both of mine, and when introducing myself, she said, "I know who you are."

She had run out of tears. I could see through the veil lightly fallen over her face that her goldenrod eyes were puffy and dry. But *mine* weren't. I thought of Langdon, his widow, and those whom I supposed were his now-fatherless children. Teardrops trickled down my cheeks, as I told her what a beautiful human being Langdon had been.

Assuming a slight smile and trying to give *me* solace, she said, "I know how you felt about him, because he felt the same about you. I also saw and heard what you said about him on TV."

I hugged her lightly and turned around to find a seat midway between the front and the back of the chapel—I didn't want to closeup-view his body; I wanted to remember him alive. And I didn't let myself recall seeing him naked, dissected, and very dead on an autopsy table a couple of days ago.

Zitzy, Doughboy, and whom I assumed to be Jackie were only four or five persons behind me. After they offered Mrs. Dickerson condolences, they viewed the body and then sat in the pew alongside me. I noted Jackie, too, had wept.

The chapel filled, the receiving line lengthened, and finally, there was standing room only in the vestibule. When I turned around to see if there were any Dome security representatives of other AG agents present, I noticed three somewhat elderly, white-haired, gaily bonneted, and well-attired ladies standing there. I bade them come over, and albeit hesitatingly, they did so.

I nudged Zitzy and head-motioned Doughboy, and we gave them our seats. Very alert, the gesture wasn't lost on Langdon's wife, for I saw her looking at us. Nor did it escape Jackie. We took the ladies' places standing in the vestibule.

Earlier, a bass player and a saxophonist had set up to the left of the casket in front of the sprays. The musician who played the bass was a handsome, shaved-head, tall and muscled Black man who donned a large gold bangle hanging from his right ear. And the sax player was of medium height sporting an afro. Both wore tuxedos. I judged the musicians to be a nice—but expensive—touch.

At 1:00 sharp, the pair began to play. They opened with the instrumental, *Slow Blues,* and followed up with *Precious Lord, Take My Hand; Swing Low Sweet Chariot; When I Lay My Burden Down; Take Me to the King,* and ending with *Amazing Grace*, all sung in a mellifluous rich baritone by the bass player.

It is said music seems to say what the heart has trouble finding the words for. And it certainly had that effect on me. Maybe funerals—more so Black funerals—aren't so barbaric after all.

Due to the long receiving line, the service was somewhat delayed. But eventually, Mrs. Dickerson took her seat next to her children, and the preacher emerged from the vestry assuming a position at the lectern. He was not tuxedoed; rather, he was wearing a purple robe and a gold sash. And he could have been a younger brother of the bass player. I later learned he was.

Besides delivering appropriate, but non-hackneyed, biblical quotes about death and spiritual resurrection in the House of the Lord, the Reverend, with a personal touch of heart and soul, eulogized Langdon.

He informed the congregation he was the pastor at the New Testament Baptist Church, and Langdon was an assistant deacon there. He lauded Langdon profusely, and quoting 1 Peter 2:13, Titus 3:1, and Romans 3:31, he said Langdon died doing the work of the Lord. Following that, a robust "Amen" was issued by the communicants.

Following his dialogue, he solicited eulogies from those gathered. And after a brief pause, a wizened figure, who I later learned to be Langdon's maternal uncle, gave paeans to his nephew, affirming Langdon as a good family man and a credit to the community.

When he finished, the preacher again asked if anyone else would like to say a few words. As if a shadow had nudged me, I stepped forward from the vestibule, and I thought I heard gasps from the other mourners—I could certainly hear them murmuring. I took the lectern, introduced myself, and spoke about our working relationship, praising Langdon as a dedicated officer, a noble man, and my friend.

In confirmation, I contended this overwhelming crowd was testimony to that which I had said.

Summing up with rheumy eyes, I looked at Mrs. Dickerson and told her we would never forget Langdon and we would be there for her and her children whenever she needed us. The last words I said were, "God bless you and your children, Mrs. Dickerson."

I then returned to the vestibule wading through a long round of applause. And that's when I noticed Macklin was standing off to one side in the rear of the crowd.

The service over, the undertaker, with Mrs. Dickerson and her children present, closed and locked the casket lid. Mrs. Dickerson wailed, and aided by her eldest son, stumbled to her pew. Listening to her muffled sobs, there were a few moments of silence, and no one moved. And modeling a jazz funeral on the way back from the cemetery, the duo picked up the beat with *I'll Fly Away*, *Down by the Riverside*, and ending, of course, with *When the Saints Go Marching In*.

It wasn't a far distance to Saint Vitus Cemetery, but even with a police escort (the NOPD had graciously provided a three-motorcycle team, as I later learned, arranged by Zitzy's brother), the trip took about forty minutes.

Giving the last rites, the preacher assigned Langdon to the earth, and his wife and each child threw a single rose and a handful of dirt onto the casket. The funeral ended, and the mourners, as we did, began to disperse. I again saw Macklin, this time walking toward his unmarked police unit.

When we were halfway between the burial site and our cars, a youngster, Langdon's eldest son came running up to me and said, "Mister, Mister Johnny, my Mama told me to ask if you could wait a minute."

"Tell her," I said, "of course I can. And tell her not to rush; we'll wait as long as necessary."

About fifteen minutes thereafter, her veil pulled up over her hat, Mrs. Dickerson approached us saying, "Please pardon me for making you wait."

"There's no need of a pardon, Mrs. Dickerson, we were glad to do so."

"Please call me Gayle."

"Only if you'll call me Johnny; I believe you met Jackie, Elvin, and David." Nodding, a slight smile skipped across her lips when she looked at Doughboy and Jackie standing close to one another.

"I'm pleased to meet you," she said. "First, I want to thank you for the beautiful eulogy you gave. And secondly, will you do me the honor of coming to our home and join us in an after-funeral party?"

Chris Rose has said, "[New Orleanians] dance even if there's no radio. We drink at funerals. We talk too much and laugh too loud and live too large and, frankly, we're suspicious of others who don't." Perhaps in other areas of the country, Gayle's social gathering is referred to as a post-funeral reception, but this was New Orleans, and we call it what it is—a party!

"*Au contrarie*, it would be *our* honor to be there."

"Good. I have to go back to the funeral home first, so please give me about a half-hour. My address is 581 Piety Street in Bywater or the Upper Ninth Ward."

"We'll find it. And thank you."

After she left for the limousine, I said, "Perfect timing, I need a cup of coffee. What about y'all?"

They agreed, and Doughboy said, "I know a coffee shop near here; you want to follow me?"

Freddy's One Stop Food Store, a typical New Orleans corner grocery, was a block and a half from Langdon's house. It was sheathed in timeworn cypress weatherboards coated in light blue paint that had long ago oxidized. Inside, we sat at one of the four wooden tables surrounded by cans of foodstuffs, bags of rice, flour, and beans. A nearby upright cooler was crammed with soft drinks— Coca-Colas, RCs, and 7 Ups, as well as Jax, Regal, Falstaff, and Dixie beers.

Hubig's pies and MoonPies were piled on the cashier's wooden counter, which was scalloped and polished by years of wear. Next to the counter, a deli and meat case displayed an assortment of processed meats alongside fresh pork, beef, and sausages.

The specialty of the house was a Fred's po-boy with liver cheese, fried bologna, fried luncheon meat, hogshead cheese, and mayonnaise. And, of course, "dressed" with lettuce, tomatoes, and mayonnaise.

In the mid-1910s, Bennie and Clovis Martin moved to New Orleans from their home in Raceland, Louisiana, to work as streetcar conductors. In 1922, the brothers decided to open their restaurant, Martin Brothers' Coffee Stand and Restaurant, specializing in French loaf sandwiches with anything you wanted on them.

Those sandwiches wouldn't be called po-boys until 1929, when members of the Amalgamated Association of Street and Electric Railway Employees of America, Division No. 194, went on a four-month-long strike, thereby leaving over a thousand union streetcar workers lacking a source of income. The Martin brothers, to show their support for the workers affected by this strike, wrote a letter to the *New Orleans States* stating that they would give a free meal to any members of Division 194.

Legend has it that when the brothers saw one of the union workers walk into their restaurant, one of them would yell, "Here comes another poor boy!" Since the free meal given to these workers often included the customary sandwich, the name "poor boy" gradually became associated as the sandwich itself, and they were eventually called po-boys.

Po-boy restaurants and even kiosks can be found throughout the city. Po-boys are simply a superior form of fast food—New Orleans style.

While we were drinking our steaming cups of chicory coffee, I finally had the opportunity to fully appraise Jackie. Everything I was told about her appearance was understatement.

She had a haunting beauty. Small boned and lithe with an hourglass figure, she exuded poise and elegance. And beneath it all on her character menu, I presaged an apéritif of wit, canapés of humor, an entrée of compassion, and confections of inscrutability. In short, she was delectable. And I couldn't help but notice the furtive glances between her and Doughboy.

Feeling comfortable with her—I assumed Doughboy had told her we were investigating the murder—I opened the conversation, "That son-of-a-bitch Macklin was at both the funeral and the burial. I don't know if he's tailing us, looking for a suspect, or curious. But I'd give long odds he wasn't there to pay his respects. Did you guys pick up on any suspicious activity?"

Zitzy said he hadn't, and Doughboy shook his head from side to side. And I asked the three of them, "Did you see any of the Dome's security personnel there?" To which they all responded in the negative.

We were silent a few minutes, each of us adrift in our own thoughts, when Jackie interrupted our reflections. "And she has four children to raise."

Registering what she had said, suppressed anger roiled within me. I had to tell myself, *Don't let rage obscure your goal; adhere to the adage, "Vengeance is a*

dish best served cold." And doing so somewhat calmed me down.

When we finished our coffees, Zitzy said, "Johnny, I have to spend some time with my wife and kids. If you don't need me, I think I should go home."

"Of course. Go for it." He told Jackie it had been a pleasure to have met her, and he left. I picked up the check, and we, too, left shortly thereafter.

CHAPTER XIV
Langdon Had Been Acting Oddly

The Dickerson abode was five blocks from the Mississippi River. Throughout the neighborhood, as it had been at Freddy's, one could whiff the pervading tang of Old Man River, the second-largest—but greatest discharge—watercourse in the United States.

Bywater has an interesting history. It has always been a neighborhood in transition. First known as "Faubourg Washington," it was part of the predominantly Francophone "downtown" section of New Orleans. It had been a planation at one point, but over time, it became the homes of White Creoles of Spanish and French descent followed by continuing waves of new arrivals such as African-Americans, Germans, Italians, and. some Irish.

Much of New Orleans sits in a pronounced, half-circle crook of the Mississippi River on the south and Lake Pontchartrain on the north. And most of her streets either parallel the river or run perpendicular to it creating a spider web effect. Therefore, it is impractical to say, "Go north, south, east, or west on such-a-such street." Therefore, New Orleanians give directions as lake-bound, river-bound, uptown, and downtown.

Lake-bound (north) and river-bound (more or less south) are self-explanatory, but some clarification might be in order for uptown and downtown. New Orleans' main drag, Canal Street, essentially runs northwest-southeast and bisects the city. Once touted as the widest street in America, Canal Street has an ultra-wide neutral ground (called a median in the rest of the country).

That part of the city downriver from Canal Street is called downtown and, historically, was the French sector. Anything on the upriver side of Canal Street is considered uptown and, in days gone by, was the American sector. Thus, New Orleans' four "compass points" are Lake-bound, River-bound, Uptown, and Downtown.

New Orleans is a town fraught with dichotomies. And one of them is that there has never been a canal on, or anywhere near, Canal Street.

As were most homes in downtown Bywater, the Dickerson's was a raised and tidy shotgun double, which had been converted to a single. Bright, but not garish,

it was painted with a multitude of colors; the most prevalent one was lilac.

In true Crescent City style, the ceiling of the spacious front porch was sky blue and sported white gingerbread with navy blue finials. Its two front doors were fire-engine red. Similar to most shotgun doubles of New Orleans, the porch windows were floor to (fourteen-foot) ceilings.

Mostly built in the early 1800s, shotgun doubles were constructed with large windows which were dual purposed: First, they provided much-needed ventilation during the oppressively hot and humid New Orleans summers, and secondly, they occasioned a property tax break.

In that era, a crazy property tax law determined the amount of taxation by the number of doors a house had, and the tall windows provided ventilation and ingress and egress almost as well as doors did.

The *grande dame* I deemed her to be, Gayle exuded warmth and charm when she met us at the front door and introduced us into her home. Taking me by the hand, she said, "Please come in."

New Orleans, pure New Orleans! Her home was appointed with comfortability. In the parlor, which was refreshingly devoid of a television set, I espied a dark brown recliner with a stack of books alongside. I assumed the chair to have been Langdon's refuge after a long day.

Separate from that was a well-used brown leather, three-seater Chesterfield sofa, and a floral-upholstered Lincoln rocker with a small footstool. I envisioned Gayle rocking there and chatting with Langdon in the evening.

The walls of the parlor were not splashed in artwork or geegaws, but they weren't bare either. Rather, they were replete with old photographs of what I assumed to be forebears. And there was also a framed 10×20 sepia photograph of the handsome couple on their wedding day. It was apparent that family was an important factor in their lives.

The dining room sported a large, well-worn oak table. Entering there, I was met by a medley of rich aromas. And I was dazzled by the dining room table laded with soul and Southern food—fried chicken; seafood gumbo; potato salad; black-eyed peas; mustard, collard, and turnip greens; macaroni and cheese; rice—lots of rice—and a host of other savories.

And for the brave, there was poke sallet and chitterlings, as well as a pot of dark chicory coffee, and a dessert of *pain perdu* (lit., "lost bread') blanketed in

fresh strawberries. The table looked as if it might collapse under the weight of the cornucopia of good groceries (New Orleans jargon for succulent foods).

The walls there displayed some Clementine Hunter prints and other rustic-type works interspersed with more of what I presumed to be family portraits.

She began introducing us to other guests, almost all family members. Then, she escorted us to the kitchen/den sprawled across the back of the house to meet her mother—the lady I had seen in the front pew—and their handsome children. I later learned Langdon's and Gayle's fathers were dead, and Langdon's mother was in a nursing home suffering from advanced Alzheimer's.

While in the kitchen/den, I happened to note a small TV and several ice chests of short-bottled red and white wines, Regal and Dixie beers, Cokes, and Barq's root beer.

My view was that children's manners had mostly gone out with high-button shoes. But not so the Dickerson's offspring. Sad, but still full of life, they were among the most respectful and polite kids I had ever known.

Gayle redirected us to the dining room table. "Eat well," she said; "mingle, and I'll get back to you later."

As we savored the offerings, we socialized. All the other mourners lauded Ghost, as did we.

Although Doughboy and I were the only two whites in attendance, the Black condolers affably accepted us and besieged us with questions about Dickerson's death. We had no concrete answers to give them, and we were careful to avoid divulging the few details we did have about our investigation.

Later, the ladies helped Gayle clean up. And shortly afterward, amidst sobbing, weeping, and lots of hugs, the crowd began to disperse. About that time, Gayle approached us and under her breath said, "Please don't leave until I can speak with you."

Not long thereafter, she gently nudged the other remaining guests out saying, "If you'll excuse me, I have to speak with Mr. Régis and Mr. Dosstein." The remaining family and friends understood, and after more commiserations and crying, they too departed.

That done, Gayle told the children to watch television with their grandmother in the den and directed us to the parlor. "I must confess that besides liking you and wanting you to be here, I had an ulterior motive—I wanted to speak with you

about Langdon."

I simply nodded my head. Starting with questions from us would be distracting and superfluous. If I let her do it in her own time and in her own way, we'd probably glean more information.

She began by telling us about being interviewed by Macklin. She didn't like him, because she found him to be crude. Thus, knowing we would also investigate, she didn't give Macklin a lot of information.

"It appeared he was trying to assert that Langdon's death was an accident or a suicide. He kept pressing me about Langdon's mental and physical conditions and whether Langdon was clumsy." And with an impish smile, she said, "My husband was one of the most stable, healthiest, and most agile men I know; after all, I am his wife.

"He also asked me if Langdon had been behaving strangely. I lied and said to him, 'Other than putting in a lot of hours at work, no.' But Langdon *had* been acting oddly. He was still attentive to the children and me, yet at the same time he was distant—perhaps I should say distracted. Could you tell me why that was so?"

"Not now. We're still trying to give form to the mystery. Did Langdon keep a diary or a journal?"

"None I know of."

"Well, when you begin to go through his things, if you find one, will you notify us immediately?"

"Of course."

"Are you aware he was off-duty when he was killed?"

"No, I assumed he was working."

"Gayle, I'm sorry to tell you that, although he was probably working, he wasn't doing so at the direction of the AG's office. I don't even know what he was doing there. And it might negate any benefits due you."

She gasped. "Oh, no! I have four children to raise without a father, and I don't want them to be latchkey kids." She again began to cry.

As her sobbing reduced to sniffles, I said, "Gayle, I promise to do everything I can to help you. I don't want to give you false hopes—the odds are stacked against us, but I'm going to fight to get it done." And she began to sob again.

When she recovered, I asked, "I don't want to be personal, but how did you

afford such a beautiful funeral?"

She cocked her head up and said, "You probably noted we have a large family. Besides that, Langdon had a substantial following, and he was highly respected in our community. In fact, to many he was known as the Sheriff of Bywater."

"I *was* surprised at the unusually large turnout for his funeral, especially on a Sunday."

"The only money I contributed were the proceeds of a small insurance policy he took out right after we were married. The rest was provided by our families, the community, and the New Testament Baptist Church, where he was an assistant deacon. The preacher, who is a brother of the bass player, and the two musicians, who are members of the church, donated their time."

Well, that clears that up, Johnny.

"Why was he called the Sheriff of Bywater?"

"Langdon was the only law enforcement officer in our neighborhood. So our neighbors came to him about criminal-type problems such as home burglaries, car thefts, missing children, etcetera."

"And what kind of help did he provide them?"

"More than anything, it was advice and counsel. In some cases, he followed up with a Black detective, Henry Jackson, with the NOPD, and Langdon would report back to the victims what he had learned. He and Jackson had grown up together. I suppose, more than anything, Langdon was a conduit of information when the residents could receive little or no information from the police."

"Was he working on any particular case before he died?"

"None that I know of during the last three or four weeks. Considering how much work he was putting in with your office, he didn't have enough time for anything else."

I avoided reminding her some of Langdon's "work" time was off-duty.

"Did he receive any strange or upsetting phone calls?"

"Macklin asked me that, and I thought better about it and told him I didn't know of any. But it seemed like he did receive two or three."

"What do you mean 'seemed like'?"

"After the calls, he became withdrawn and pensive."

"Tell me about them."

"They were short. Of course, I don't know what was said on the other ends of

the lines. And his responses were usually clipped; I forgot what the actual conversations were about. When I asked, Langdon about them, he would be dismissive saying something vague about work. But again, they were always brief."

"Can you tell us anymore?"

"Not now; I'm upset and confused."

Interjecting herself into the conversation, Jackie said, "Did he tell you anything about missing children here in Bywater?" I was surprised by her forwardness, but I didn't take umbrage

None of us has all the answers or, in this case, all the questions. Did Jackie have information we didn't? I'd have to ask Jackie about that. I didn't know then, but in a short time, I would learn from Doughboy what she knew and why she knew it.

"I think he got updates from Detective Jackson and passed the information along to the parents of the children."

Gayle *was* becoming tired. She had had long day—a very long day. And she had had four difficult days before that, so it was our cue to leave. "Thanks for your hospitality and time Gayle. We'll keep in touch. Here's my card—I'll write my home phone on the back. Call anytime. We can't falsify official time records, but again, I promise to work tirelessly on getting you full benefits."

Before leaving, I cautioned her to keep what she had given us to herself, "Discuss it with no one, especially Macklin—I don't trust him." And she nodded her agreement.

She walked us to the front porch. With tears in her eyes, she hugged Doughboy and me. But when she hugged Jackie, both she and Jackie broke down and bawled.

Outside, darkness had fallen as soft and gentle as a brown leaf descending from a Southern Sugar Maple tree. In the quiet tranquility of the neighborhood, it was difficult to acknowledge the horror of the preceding days.

I told Jackie it had been an immense pleasure to have met her. She kissed me on the cheek and again hugged me tightly as I did her. I told Doughboy I'd see him in the morning, and we departed—I to my home sanctuary, Doughboy and Jackie to points unknown. In true Creole fashion, Gayle was still on the porch waving as we drove away.

Natalie had again worked her magic in the kitchen—stuffed eggplants served with angel hair pasta, succulent mustard greens with bacon and onions., and a slightly chilled bottle of Frascati.

Quite satisfied and relaxed, I went to bed and sailed off in a wooden shoe with Wynken, Blynken, and Nod.

CHAPTER XV
Doughboy's Admission

The next morning, my crew, sans Doughboy, was waiting for me when I walked in. They appeared to be refreshed and eager to get started. And I was glad they were; we had some grueling days ahead of us. We were still far off target, and I was evidently not the homicide investigator I would have liked to have been.

I first attended to daily business with Breeze, who was not yet working on the Dickerson case. He wanted to know how the investigation was going, and I told him I'd fill him in later.

I turned to Zitzy, "Have you heard from Doughboy?"

"Nary a word."

So I briefed him about our interview with Gayle. And about the time I was finished, Doughboy, looking drawn and peaked, came in.

"Glad you could make it," I said. "It looks like you had a rough night."

"Three and a half hours sleep doesn't get it. But I do have some interesting and perhaps some helpful news."

"Let's hear it."

"Okay, but first I need a strong cup of coffee."

Zitzy, realizing his partner was fatigued, offered to make him one. "Cream and sugar?"

"Yeah, thanks. Three sugars if you don't mind."

Taking his first sip, Doughboy began to narrate his report. "After Jackie and I left you, we drove to her apartment in Metairie's Brunche Village, and she invited me in for a nightcap. I think we were both mentally drained from the stress, and I decided I could use a little drink." (Brunche Village is a vaguely defined area in Metairie, the populace of which was almost all Black.)

"Hmm," said Zitzy with a leering smile, "the plot thickens."

"Continue," said I.

"Entering her somewhat bare, but tidy, apartment, she offered me wine, beer, Irish whisky, or chilled vodka. I opted for the Irish whisky—neat. She drank iced vodka with a splash of cold water.

"We sat on the sofa and discussed the funeral and Gayle's plight. It saddened

64

both of us, so I steered the conversation around to her.

"She had obtained a degree in criminology from the University of Southwest Louisiana in Lafayette and applied to be a deputy with the Saint Martin Parish Sheriff's Office, but it's a small agency, and there were no openings.

"Wanting to be near her mother ailing with rheumatoid arthritis, she landed a position at the post office and became a Saint Martinville mail carrier. It wasn't her dream job, but she enjoyed it, and she could attend to her Mama. But after working a few months, she decided she would make a career there and eventually apply for the United States Postal Inspection Service."

"Well, why did she leave her mother *and* the post office?"

"Patience, I'm getting to that."

"Okay, continue."

"She has a large extended family and a sister named Céline Tournoi. And one of Céline's children, eleven-year-old, Adeline, had gone missing on the same day she went on a church tour and went to the Dome. And as you know, the Saint Martinville Police Department is somewhat of a hayseed department; therefore, she wasn't getting any satisfaction from them. So she turned to Jackie for help.

"Jackie also said, 'With a population of only 6,114, Saint Martinville is a small community, and gossip swarms as do bats at eventide from the Bracken Bat Cave near San Antonio, Texas.' Somehow, Céline had picked up on a rumor that abducted children were taken to New Orleans and impressed into the sex slave trade. Another weird rumor had it that the focal point—where the big money was—were major events at the Superdome."

"You've got to be kidding me!"

"No. So Céline agreed to care part-time for their mother, and Jackie applied for a security job at the Dome where she was immediately hired. A degreed Black female on the security roster was a blue ribbon for the security contractors. It wasn't front-page news, but the *Times-Picayune* noted it in an article on page two, and it received a few blurbs on the evening news shows. It made good press for Corbin and Huberty's security effort.

"When Jackie worked night shifts, she occasionally bumped into Ghost. And as did all the other security guards, Jackie suspected Langdon was making his evening visits to check on them. She had nothing to hide—she was doing her job—so she chatted with him. And after several encounters, they became

65

friendly.

"One evening, in an attempt to obtain information from him, she asked, 'Have you heard anything about abducted children being farmed out here during events?' As perspicacious as she is, she could see he was taken aback, even though he tried to hide it.

"But he deadpanned her and said, 'What are you talking about?'

"Nevertheless, she had a good feeling about him so she propelled forward saying, 'It's a rumor I heard, and I wanted to know if there was anything to it.'

"Langdon replied he hadn't heard anything as crazy as that, and they changed the subject. They continued strolling and chatting, and she made her required security keypunches.

"The next time they saw one another, Langdon pumped her for information. Feeling she could trust him, she acquiesced to his probing. At that point, he confessed what she already suspected. He had heard the same rumor.

"And inasmuch as he coincidently had been assigned to the Superdome, he decided to follow up on it. But each of them revealed to the other their labors were unrewarded because they had developed no clues, whatsoever."

So that's why Jackie had asked Gayle about Langdon's missing persons activity.

"Wow—what a treasure trove you've uncovered! Do you have any more for us?"

"Well, not exactly."

"What in the hell does 'not exactly' mean?"

Flushing, Doughboy said, "I violated our agreement."

"Oh?"

"In the course of the evening, she divulged personal information. And she teared up quite a bit. Perhaps because of the funeral and her missing niece—remember, she and Langdon had become friends—I believe her emotions were running full throttle."

"What personal information did she reveal to you?"

"Other than she had a hard life with men as a kid and as later as an adult, I'd rather not say."

"Doughboy, it doesn't take a mental giant to deduce she had been abused as a child, or raped, or both."

"Well...yeah."

"But what does that have to do with 'not exactly'?"

"She told me she never married and had had few boyfriends—all Blacks—who had mistreated her, and she hadn't had sex in over three years."

A big grin creasing his face, Zitzy said, "I know where this is going."

"Of course, you know I don't have Breeze's allure, and my love life has been in the pits for a long time now."

"Yes...and...?" said I.

"After a few highballs between us, she went to the bathroom; I assumed she had to pee, which she might have done. But when she returned, she had on a light flowing robe. And it was untied and *open*!

"She looked me straight in the eye and uttered a sensual, 'Come.'

"Recalling our agreement, I paused for a second—but only a second—and I followed her into the bedroom. I'm not going to give you any details, but guys, it was absolute bliss."

"Well, you deserved to let yourself go," I said with a smile, "especially with the information you developed. Take the rest of the day off; go home, rest, and prepare yourself for a very active week ahead. I'll need you on your toes."

He said "Thanks." And as he headed toward the door, it must have been my imagination, but I could have sworn he was walking on air.

CHAPTER XVI
Challenged by Zozobra

Zitzy reminded me he had been unable to contact May or Bowditch.

"I don't want to be overly confident, Zitzy, but I think we have something. The puzzle isn't solved, but at least we have a few pieces. And we can't sit on our asses and wait for a solution to come to us.

"You need to follow up with Leasean, May, and Bowditch. And see what you can find out from Jackson. If possible, develop a rapport with him. He might have some information that will help us. Also see if you can profile Macklin."

"Got it. You know my brother works in the Fifth District. I'll see if he knows Jackson and Macklin and if he can help us with any of this."

"Good. But don't give away any of our sensitive information, even to your brother."

I try not to fool myself and I recognize I am the most able person to do so. Each of my agents was a better investigator than I. Lamentably my M.Crim. (Master of Criminology) didn't knight me as an ace detective. I had to keep reminding myself of the unwritten management rule, "Surround yourself with subordinates who are brighter and/or more competent than you are. And make sure you give them plaudits and credit when they deserve it." I hope I lived up to that with my team.

So much for ruminations; I had to get to work.

More analytical with pen and paper, I sat at my desk and began to outline in no particular order the information we had accrued—I check-list recorded them by hand as they came into my mind. I no longer have my notes, but they went something like this:

- *Who killed Langdon, and why was he killed?*
- *How was Langdon killed? (The autopsy report should reveal that.)*
- *A coverup—why?*
- *Was the murder a conspiracy?*
- *If so, who were the conspirators?*
- *Who were the originators of the rumors about the abductions at the Dome?*
- *How and why was Langdon involved?*

- *Why did Langdon persist after he told me he was shutting his "inspections" down?*
- *What did Langdon know?*
- *With whom did Langdon share his intelligence?*
  Gayle,
    Jackie,
  Jackson?
- *Why didn't Langdon share his information with me?*
- *Macklin—background, Zitzy.*
- *Jackson—possible source, Zitzy.*
- *Leasean—possible source, Zitzy.*
- *Rieglé—background, Zitzy; interview, me.*
- *May and Bowditch—Zitzy.*
- *Bowditch—background, Zitzy.*
- *Jackie—press for more info, Doughboy.*
- *Autopsy report, Doughboy.*
- *Follow-up—Gayle, me.*
- *Langdon's benefits, Gayle—me.*

I felt as if I were in a henhouse trying to catch all the chickens all at once. Able to snag one or two, I'd reach for another one, and the chicken I had in my hand would fly away. Questions, questions, questions, and no answers. I sat back and pondered them and my situation.

I sucked 'em up and called the AG. He was unavailable, so I left a message for him to call me. Disappointed with myself—I'm my own harshest critic—I was quite negative, and I wondered if he were avoiding my call. He seemed to be trying to distance himself from this snake pit in which I found myself. Would I end up being the scapegoat to preserve his political career?

The word "zozobra" is an ordinary Spanish term describing "anxiety" but with connotations that call to mind the wobbling of a ship about to capsize. And I didn't know if my abilities were enough to prevent my career's boat from foundering.

Zozobra had sheathed me in its clutch.

CHAPTER XVII
Honeymoonetting

At about 3:00, Doughboy came back in looking much spryer than he earlier had. I attempted to hand him my list, but he waved it away almost breathlessly saying, "We have another quasi-team member—Jackie!"

"What do you mean?"

"With her accumulated k-time, she's taking three days off—actually, with the twelve-hour shifts, it'll work out to seven days. And she's going back to Saint Martinville to trace the rumors, and see if she can uncover any clues about the abductions, if of course, there are any to be had."

"Have you briefed her about where we are in our investigation?"

"A little; I told her we don't have much, but I would fill her in as we move along."

"Good. I think she could be a font of information for us. How would you like to visit Saint Martinville?"

Doughboy smiled so widely it seemed his face would shatter. "Wow—I'd love to! Incidentally, Jackie asked me if I would accompany her, and I was going to ask you for k-time to do so."

"Well, you won't be on k-time; you'll be on company time. And I don't mind if you have a honeymoonette there, but I do expect you to develop some leads. More particularly, find out who started the sex-slave children rumor and more importantly why."

"This is birthday and Christmas all rolled into one!"

"I'm assuming she'll stay with her Mama. Rent a mom-and-pop motel for four nights; that should give you enough time. And claim the rental and per diem on your expense account.

"I'll need her mother's phone number and also the telephone and room number of the motel at which you'll be staying. I'm not going to micromanage you, but try to report in every evening—more if you develop something big. Don't hesitate—you have my home phone too.

"Call our detachment in Lafayette if you run into trouble, and have them call me right away. They have my home phone. Travel there in separate cars, and

keep your radios on. Above all, be discreet, and tell Jackie to be prudent too. If you aren't careful, this whole thing could be met with disaster."

It was a gamble. I had confidence in him, but I was still anxious. It was as if I were sending a pre-adolescent son out on his first solo hunting trip.

"When do you plan to leave?" I asked.

"I suppose after her shift ends at six in the morning."

"Take two of the portable radios. Give her one, and tell her to use it only to keep in touch with you She will have been up all night, so encourage her to stop often for coffee. Now go home, pack, and rest up for your trip tomorrow; from what you've told me about your extracurricular activities, you'll need it."

"Got it. Thanks!"

After he read my handwritten notes and said he had committed them to memory (which for him was a cakewalk), he picked up two radios. As he left, he wasn't walking on air as he did before; this time he was *wafting* on air.

CHAPTER XVIII
Quid Pro Quo?

About a half hour later, unannounced and baggy-looking, Macklin, with his rumpled, croaker-sack-brown suit and loosened soiled tie, rumbled into our office as if he owned it—using borrowed space, we had no personal secretaries nor a receptionist. His face was flushed with hostility and with no salutation, he growled, "Régis, we have to talk," as his fat ass plummeted toward an unoffered chair facing my desk.

Covering my notes with a legal pad as if I were preparing to take notes, I considered having him ejected. But I had to be interviewed sometime and decided perhaps it was best to get it over with. So dripping with sarcasm, I said, "Well thank you for making an appointment."

He ignored the reproach and brusquely said, "I know you're working on the Dickerson case, and I need to know what you've developed so far."

"Is this the same man who refused to return my calls and dodged me when I went to his office? No pal, it doesn't work that way. I've not even had the opportunity to see your preliminary report, and you have the balls to *need* the results of my investigation? Fuck you and the horse you rode in on!"

"You're making a mistake Régis; I can make things difficult for you. You're impeding a police investigation by refusing to answer questions concerning a homicide."

"Oh, *now* it's a homicide. That isn't what you suggested to the coroner."

He brushed aside the gibe and continued, "Just tell me what you have."

"Are you fucking kidding me? Other than your pig-ignorant demand for my investigative results, you haven't even asked me one question. Ask away, simpleton." And with that, I extracted my tape recorder from my drawer, turned it on, and placed it on my desk between us.

Taken aback, he hesitated. But undeterred, he retorted, "Have you been investigating the murder of Langdon Dickerson?"

"I have."

"I demand to have access to your work product."

"Mr. Macklin, I've not generated a work product," I said flaunting a Cheshire

Cat grin. It was only partly true—I did not have a report, per se, but the notes I had completed could have been considered as work product. Of course, no one else except Doughboy and I knew of their existence, and I wasn't under oath.

"Did Dickerson work for you?"

"He worked for the AG's Office, but, yes, I was his supervisor."

"What was he working on the night of the murder?"

"I don't know."

"Your lying isn't going to sit well with the judge when you're issued a subpoena duces tecum. I figured you might do this, so I checked with our counsel, and he's already prepared the request for the court."

"Macklin, go ahead and waste your time and make an ass of yourself. Dickerson wasn't on the clock; our records will bear that out. And as I told you—and I'll tell the judge—I don't know what Dickerson was doing at the Dome on the night he was murdered." Of course, I had a hunch, but I didn't *know*, and he didn't merit my opinions.

Macklin switched gears. He must have considered me to be an illiterate, non-streetwise suspect because he donned the "good-cop" hat. "Look Régis, we both want to catch the slimeball who killed your agent. Give me what you have, and if we work together, we can do it."

"No Macklin, it doesn't work that way. You can shake that tree all you want, but all you're going to get is a shriveled peach. We aren't going to be manipulated or coerced by you. You conduct your investigation, and we'll conduct ours. And when you're ready to *truly* share information, we'll consider working with you."

He sprung from his chair, pointed his finger at me, and snarled, "You're fuckin, up, Régis. This isn't a hayseed hick town like you're used to, and you're messing with the wrong people. You're fixin' to be shredded." That splintered 2x2 up his ass must have been working overtime.

Raising an eyebrow, I was so bold as to presume Macklin was not a graduate of the Dale Carnegie course, *How to Win Friends and Influence People*.

"They won't be getting a cherry. Goodbye, Macklin." And I guffawed a belly laugh as he left appearing as though his scrotum was contorted in granny knots.

CHAPTER XIX
Macklin at Wal-Mart?

I called and left a message for the AG.

It wasn't long thereafter when Zitzy came in, and he gave me his report. "I had lunch with my brother at Jack Dempsey's, and I asked him if he had heard any chatter on Macklin. He told me that, up until recently, while Macklin was old school and a bit on the rough side, he had a sterling record. He was a highly successful homicide detective, and although sometimes crass, he was one of the most affable and jovial men on the department.

"The only thing 'odd' about him was he never cheated on his wife, as many policemen do. But now, for reasons nobody is sure of, he is on shaky ground with the NOPD."

Macklin was oftentimes an intransigent jerk, but I had sensed in him an anger I had not seen in our previous brief encounters. "Is his work performance off?"

"Yeah, but that isn't all of it. His wife of thirty or so years has lingering terminal cancer. And he seems to always be testy with his subordinates, his peers, and although not as overt, even with his supervisor.

"Coupled with the fact he's perceived as a dinosaur, he's a step away from being forced to retire. Of course, he'll receive his pension and benefits, but it's not enough to take care of his wife's nursing and medical bills. At his age, with his lack of experience in other areas, and his roughhewn mannerisms, he'd have trouble getting a job as a Wal-Mart greeter."

Laughing out loud I said, "Can you imagine that? Picture this: An obese woman in her mid-thirties, with greasy, stringy hair, wearing soiled pink stretch pants and a dirty 'Fuck the Pigs' T-shirt, and who appears to be otherwise healthy, comes into the store and starts bitching him out because there are no available electric carts.

"Macklin, definitely not the most genteel of men, snarls at her saying, 'Get off your fat, cellulite-cratered, hemorrhoidal ass, walk around the store, get some exercise, and you won't *need* a fucking cart, Bitch!' "

Zitzy laughed and said, "Wonderful PR for the already beleaguered Wal-Mart. And it so fits Macklin."

"Does anyone have a clue as to what's provoked the change in him?"

"Some say it's because his wife is dying, but no one really knows." I'd have to add that to my "why" list.

"Good job, Zitzy. What about Jackson?"

"My brother says Jackson's almost as spectral as Ghost was. He keeps to himself, and he doesn't socialize with other cops.

"He has an impressive work history for solving cases, and he'll probably soon be promoted to detective sergeant. But he plays his cards close. Although many have tried to find out, no one knows what the key to his success is."

"He sounds like a clone of Langdon," I responded. "Did you have the opportunity to interview him?"

"No. I tried, but he's off today, and I didn't want to bother him at home. Moreover, I think he'll balk if we don't handle him with kid gloves."

"Okay, but get to him as soon as you can."

CHAPTER XX

On the Wings of a Dove (or a Hog), Pumpkin Glides In

The telephone interrupted our conversation—it was the AG.

"What do you want Régis?"

"I simply wanted to bring you up to speed, General."

"Okay, shoot."

I gave him a condensed version of what I have narrated—it was still about ten to fifteen minutes of non-stop talking. He listened with patience—he did have a knack for paying attention. At the end of my monologue, he said, "Put it in a report and send it to me."

"If that's what you want, I'll do it, Sir. But do you remember what I told you about Macklin and the production of documents?"

"Oh, that's right. Then provide me with verbal reports. And by the way, I know you lost a staff member due to maternity leave. But even though we're shorthanded, I'm going to send you a replacement, Benicia Burchett."

"Tremendous! Thanks." Maybe the hard-nosed son-of-a-bitch had a soft spot after all.

Benicia Burchett? Mamma mia! It might be hard to believe, but she was finer than Jackie. She had a peaches and cream complexion and an androgenous countenance. But androgyny in a woman is widely accepted as a physiognomy that enhances a woman's beauty—it certainly worked for her.

Flaunting sinuous and proportioned curves and a fantastic tush, Agent I Benicia Burchett was a stunner. I flushed when my memory board alit reminding me of the backwash of an AG Christmas party several years ago when we were both single and tipsy with cocktails. *Careful, she could easily be your downfall.*

Once, caught in an unexpected thunderstorm without a bra and umbrella, she was wearing a bright orange T-shirt. Wet, it profiled her pert breasts and diamond-hard nipples, so that, even without the orange of the T-shirt, her tits favored young gourds. As such, she acquired the nickname, "Pumpkin." It was rumored the sexually frustrated Doughboy, seeing Pumpkin in that consequence, had an in-pants, unassisted orgasm.

Pumpkin was beyond interesting. Besides her sensual curves, wide emerald eyes, remarkable soft-chiseled visage, and flowing blonde hair, standing 5' 10", she was as strong as most men. Off-duty, she wore Levi blue jeans and cowboy shirts and, in the winter, a black leather motorcycle jacket. On duty, she dressed in pink, white, or blue button-down blouses, khaki pants, brown penny loafers, and white ribbed socks, all with an AG blue blazer.

And she had pizzazz. Full of life, she was witty, articulate, charming, and alluring. Saying it suggested friendship, she boldly sported a large tattoo of an angry dragon on her left forearm.

She had an intriguing and lilting mezzo-soprano voice. But on the downside, she could never get the New Orleans-treasured guttural "mothafucka" right.

And although she didn't hang with bikers, in her free time, she tooled around town on a pearl white BMW K 1600 GTL—a German "hog." Yet beneath the rugged exterior, she was gentile, refined, and charming.

I had often fantasized about riding behind her on her BMW, both of us naked, with my crotch firmly nestled against the cleft of her callipygous tush, her blond hair tickling my nose, and with my hands cupping her firm—and natural—mammaries. And they talk about the thrill of driving in a NASCAR race—pshaw!

What a swine you are! You have a beautiful wife at home who loves you, cares for you, and prays for you. And you would risk devastating her for a tryst with another woman. You have no honor, you creep.

The *pièce de résistance* was that Pumpkin played the cello and played it well. Yet Pumpkin had a set of stainless-steel balls. If I were ever in a firefight, I would want her at my side.

Pumpkin was born, raised, and still lived in Bucktown, located in the far northeastern corner of Metairie in Jefferson Parish. With its own distinct culture, Bucktown could have been a remote island in a faraway land.

It was developed during the late 19th century. By the early 20th century, wooden camps were built on stilts with wide galleries covered by shingle or tin roofs, and they lined the canal that serves as its eastern border. There were also mom and pop retail stores, a schoolhouse, and a jail, as well as saloons, gambling houses, dance halls, and clubhouses for sportsmen.

At the very edge of Lake Pontchartrain, Bucktown had weathered a plethora of destructive hurricanes, and its hardy denizens had always rebounded. That

resilience, coupled with the fact that the industry of the hamlet has historically been trapping, hunting, and fishing, Bucktown has brought forth generations of burghers cut from stout cloth. Bucktown's bars were in a higher percentage to its population than those of the Vieux Carré.

I had the pleasure of meeting Pumpkin's Mama, Samantha—or "Sam"—wearing a red blouse and red split-legs pants that revealed a pair of svelte, well-toned appendages. With both feet on the ground, she was a diamond in the rough. Although no spring chicken, Sam was an inveterate flirt. And she had the vigor and the adorability of an effervescent teenager.

Pert, robust, charismatic, and endowed with camouflaged culture, Sam was the living personification of that intrepid settlement, Bucktown. And more than a daughter, Pumpkin could have been a younger replicate of her mother. Thus, it was no small wonder that Pumpkin was such a luminary.

Like Zitzy, Pumpkin—and, I believe, her Mama, too—didn't suffer fools. Passionate, when it came to police business, she had a glacial, rational mind of the first water along with an arrogant integrity. But her lack of diplomacy did not have an untoward effect on her work. She was a distinguished agent, dispelling the prejudiced myth women were not analytical or logical; the logician in her solved many of our most difficult cases.

In so many ways, it was going to be a gratification to have her on our team. And in the midst of this crisis, we could all use her cheerfulness and sagacity.

Hanging up with the AG, I told Zitzy about Pumpkin's assignment to our team. "She's sizzling!" he exclaimed.

"Yes, she is Zitzy, but we can't let that tower above our investigation."

"She can tower on top of me any time she wants—preferably naked."

I could well-understand his enthusiasm, but I said, "Okay Zitzy; calm down, Boy." *In admonishing Zitzy to "calm down," was I not trying to convince myself to do so too?*

Returning to my briefing of Zitzy, I said, "I had initially wanted Doughboy to sit on the Coroner's Office for the autopsy report. Do you think you might have the time to do it?"

"Yeah, it ain't no hill for a stepper."

"Well, there isn't much more we can do today. How about we take it to the house?"

"Okay by me."

Driving home, I replayed the events of the day. I again questioned my wisdom in sending Doughboy to Saint Martinville. I reflected on the run-in with Macklin, and I recognized the tiff wasn't over, and I'd most probably fade some heat from it. And as I struggled to focus, I tried forcing myself to thwart my salacious fantasies about Pumpkin.

One of those problems, however, was resolved when I entered my home and saw Natalie—all prurient thoughts about Pumpkin were banished.

Pregnant about three years before, Natalie had miscarried. Her obstetrician told her that it was near impossible she could ever carry until term, and it would be unsafe for her to try again. Disappointed but practical, we decided to remain childless.

It was Monday, and Natalie had prepared her creamy, long-cooked red beans and rice with ham hocks and andouille sausage, Natalie always bought the best andouille, which came from Jacob's in Laplace, just upriver from New Orleans and touted as "The Andouille Capital of the World." And she served the beans with French bread too! As Mark Twain said, "New Orleans food is as delicious as the less criminal forms of sin." And it doesn't get more New Orleans than red beans and rice.

I assumed Natalie granted me the allowance of pretending such an intelligent, insightful, and articulate woman could not see my many flaws. And especially while in the midst of this tornadic investigation, I risked falling into that dreaded ego trap. I had already caught myself about two steps away from the snare recently when I was "the man" just because I had perhaps beaten Macklin in one minuscule round of his diabolical game.

The steam from the plate of red beans and rice taunted me, enticing me to eat, but prohibiting me at the same time lest I singe my tongue. Natalie knew the true secrets of not only of how to cook hedonistic red beans and other culinary delights, but of life as well. She took this indecisive moment to ask how the investigation was going. Her advice and counsel have always been restorative elixirs for me.

As I was recounting my day, I was sure she possessed and utilized the telepathy a wife naturally wields when her husband tries to skim past the mention of a woman like Jackie or Pumpkin. Natalie, in her infinite patience and quiet yet

certain knowledge of my weaknesses, did not flaunt her amazing powers.

Once, drinking wine together—*in vino veritas*—I asked her whence came her equanimity. She was surprised by my question, but with a patient smile, she said, "You know! I was raised Catholic; thus, at an early age, I acquired a healthy belief in Christ. He preached love and tolerance, and I try to practice what he evangelized." Indeed, she did, and she did it so well. How fortunate I was to have her.

CHAPTER XXI
An Unforeseen Clobbering

I had prepared myself for a tough day, but I had no idea how challenging it was going to be.

When I strolled in, my crew—Zitzy, Breeze, and now, luscious as ever, Pumpkin—were at the office which was permeated with the spoor of testosterone.

Zitzy greeted me with, "Have you read the morning paper?"

"No, I subscribe to the evening paper, the *States-Item*. Should I have?"

Without responding, Zitzy handed me a copy of the morning paper, the *Times-Picayune*. An article in the lower right-hand corner of the first page was entitled *Attorney General's Office Refuses to Cooperate with NOPD*.

The article went on to say an unnamed source stated that the AG's security detachment had rejected attempts by the NOPD to work together to solve a mysterious death—possibly a homicide—at the Superdome.

The article, with the byline of Edmund Sanderson, questioned the need for the AG's security detachment's secrecy as well as the need for the detachment, itself. Macklin was right—I was playing sandlot ball in the major leagues. It was a blow to the AG's public relations image, but I was not about to allow it to be a fatal one.

Stifling my insecurities, I declared to the crew, "The sword of Damocles is hanging over our heads, but I have a trump card."

I then took the time to warmly greet Pumpkin. As usual, she was sensational. She was buoyant, and she infected the rest of us with her sunny disposition. And at this point, we certainly needed some sunshine.

With nary a hint of emotion, Breeze gave a succinct report regarding his previously assigned Dome duties, and he was on track. How fortunate I was to have subordinates who needed so little supervision. I directed him to apprise Pumpkin of his and Brent's projects and that they should begin working together. I'd bring Pumpkin up to speed on our Dickerson investigation later.

Zitzy asked what my trump card was, and I played the Macklin tape I had recorded. "Macklin knew he was stonewalled via legal channels, so he resorted

to sleazy and underhanded tactics. But we have this." Listening to it, the group lit up. Zitzy managed our audio equipment, and I directed him to make eight copies, distribute them to the team members, and secure the others in safe places.

I told the crew I found Macklin's action curious. He was aware I had taped our conversation that would disclose the reasons the AG's office was uncooperative. Why would he push the issue when he knew he would be exposed? The crew didn't have an answer, and as hard as I tried, I couldn't envision one either.

Having his work cut out for him, Zitzy hopped to it. And certain he, Breeze, and Pumpkin would do their tasks well, I went on to other things.

At about 9:00, I received a collect call from Doughboy. Traveling I-10 west, he and Jackie had stopped at the Racetrack service station in Port Allen on the west side of the river from Baton Rouge. Armed with stout cups of Community dark roast coffee, they were ready to proceed on to Saint Martinville.

Doughboy said, "We got off to a late start because Jackie had to go home, freshen up, and gather a few things for the week. I'll be staying at the only decent hotel I could find near Saint Martinville, the Maison Des Amis in Breaux Bridge, about eleven miles away from Jackie's home."

He also told me the hotel was located on the highway before Saint Martinville, and once there, he and Jackie would part ways, he to the hotel and she on to her mother's house. She would sleep and call him when she awakened.

"Okay, call me after you finish for the day."

CHAPTER XXII
Meet the Press

I wasn't surprised when I received a call from the quite perturbed AG. "What the hell's going on down there, Régis; we can't afford this bad press!"

"I'm on top of it General. Do you remember I have an incriminating tape of Macklin's and my meeting?"

"Yeah, you told me about it, but I haven't heard it."

I played it for him, and afterward, he seemed to calm down. I told him I was going to call a press conference to clear the air. "This is not going to be a he-said/he-said affair."

"Okay, but do it fast; we don't want this thing to snowball."

The press conference was scheduled and went well, very well. I might have been playing in the majors, but even a sandlot player can occasionally hit a home run.

After conferring with my crew, I had spoken with the Dome's PR representative and had asked him to arrange one for me in the afternoon. Shortly afterward, he notified me it was scheduled for 3:00 in the Board of Advisors meeting room.

I was sure it would be well-attended, and it was. With a score to settle, I hoped the journalist, Sanderson, was there. My team members were pursuing other assignments, and I was alone—I usually attended those meetings with my team there to back me up. Moreover, I was cautious; I did not want to reveal our new member, Pumpkin, and I didn't want to answer unexpected questions about Doughboy's absence.

When I began, I had a knot in my gut, and I started with a prepared statement saying how much we lamented the loss of our colleague, Dickerson, and we, along with Dome security (which wasn't true), were conducting an internal investigation into his death. I transitioned, restating our mission at the Dome; i.e., to review security procedures with the aim of making the Dome a safe place to visit and emphasizing we performed no physical security functions.

Next, I addressed the news article in the morning's *Times-Picayune* ruing the fact the reporter had not contacted me before publishing it. I gave a brief synopsis

of the meeting between Macklin and me, omitting my opinion of Macklin's injudiciousness. And I played the tape for them.

Except for the subdued woosh of the tape and its narrative, silence—not even the rustling of movement. After playing it, I asked, "Do you have any questions, ladies and gentlemen?" And there was a flurry of them. I told them I would answer each and every one and suggested we continue with the raising of hands to ask theirs.

What follows is a summary of the challenges I received and answered:

"Was Sergeant Macklin aware the conversation was being taped?"

"Yes, I told him so, and I placed the recorder on my desk between us."

"How can we know that?"

"Because I'm telling you, and it's a fact. I don't record conversations without advising the other party. But even if that weren't the case, Federal law 18 U.S.C. § 2511 only requires one-party consent, which means one can record a phone call or conversation so long as he or she is a party to the conversation. Louisiana has adopted the same measure."

"Why are you laughing at the end of the tape; you didn't consider the situation serious?"

"The situation, itself, is serious, but I thought—and still think—Sergeant Macklin's threat was foolhardy, impetuous, and ludicrous."

"As of now, what have you uncovered?"

"I'm sorry, but I can't disclose that. Like the NOPD has told you, this is an ongoing investigation."

"What was your agent working on when he met his demise?"

"That, too, I can't say because I don't know—and it's part of an ongoing investigation."

"You told Sergeant Macklin Agent Dickerson was off-duty at the time, didn't you?"

"Yes, I did."

"Then what was he doing in the Dome sometime around 1:30 a.m.?"

"I don't know—that's also part of our ongoing investigation."

"Don't you find his off-duty activities odd?"

"Yes, I do. But it is not altogether unheard of. Our agents are dedicated, and because of that, they occasionally work on their own time without asking for

remuneration."

"Did you know he was doing so?"

"A couple of weeks ago I learned he was, and I asked him about it. He told me was sporadically checking security activity during non-event hours. I asked him if he found anything out of order. He said no, and I suggested he discontinue. He agreed, and until the night of his death, I assumed he had stopped."

"Why won't you cooperate with the NOPD?"

"I initially tried to, but I was banned from the crime scene. And the NOPD won't even provide me with a copy of their preliminary report much less photographs and forensic evidence they have collected. I have been stalled as much as you have, and at this point, I can't imagine it would be a mutually shared or harmonious relationship.

"Besides that, we're two law enforcement agencies, and we have somewhat different responsibilities. Theirs is to the public at large. And although we, too, have a responsibility to the public, our focus is now primarily on the Dome security function. Moreover, it is de facto that any crime that occurs in the Dome now falls under our purview too.

"And as two separate organizations, we have different operating procedures which might at times conflict. It's the same as the oftentimes divergent relationship local police agencies have with the FBI."

"Can we have a copy of the tape you played?"

"Of course, you can; it's not germane to the investigation. Leave your cards on the table, and we'll make copies of it for you. You can pick them up tomorrow from Mr. Boudreaux, the Dome's PR representative."

"When will you wrap up your investigation?"

"I don't know. All I can tell you is we'll be finished when we finish."

"Will you eventually share your findings with the NOPD.?"

"I'm not sure. After my meeting with Sergeant Macklin yesterday, I'm reluctant to do so. And besides that, as of now, we have no findings to share."

"Why didn't you tell Sergeant Macklin that?

"Before I started taping our conversation, I did. When he demanded to see our work product, I told him we had none."

And so went the press conference; I felt I had done well.

The reporters packed their gear and filed out. All except one—Edmund

Sanderson.

"Agent Régis, it seems I owe you an apology. I'm Ed Sanderson, and I wrote the *Picayune* article."

"That's okay. It's a pleasure meeting you."

"We received a tip from the mayor's office, and I ran with it. I should have fact-checked the information and called you before I published it. It's a hard lesson for me, but I've learned from it."

It was a stretch, but I again said, "That's okay." And I segued, "But I have a question Mr. Sanderson. I know you can't reveal your sources, but you said in the article you received your information from the mayor's office, right?"

"That's correct."

"May I then assume it wasn't from the police department?"

"Yes, you may."

"Well, when you have any questions in the future, please feel free to call me. I'll gladly answer them if I can."

"Thank you."

I let myself believe I now had a contact in the media—I hoped I wasn't fooling me.

More "whys" and, this time, a "who." Why did Macklin mislead someone in the mayor's office? Why did someone run with it without fact-checking? He or she could have easily contacted me to verify and/or expand on it. Who divulged the distorted information? And why was the release issued at all? Although unsure, I surmised I had the answer to the latter one—there was a conspiracy to oust us from the Superdome.

Nevertheless, the Mayor's Office was discredited. And for the AG's office, the ugly duckling press release became a lovely swan.

CHAPTER XXIII
Zitzy Susses Out

Zitzy was waiting for me in the office. "How'd you do?"

"I believe it went well." And the phone rang.

"You did a good job, Régis!" bellowed the AG through the telephone receiver. "We gained a lot of mileage with the media." *More than you know, General.*

Continuing, he was gleeful, "Heads are going to roll in the NOPD and the Mayor's office. And maybe in the future, they'll accept our presence and respect our work at the Dome." *Yeah, General, when New Orleanians stop going to parades, drinking, eating po-boys, crawfish, and red beans and rice!*

"Thank you, General," and we clicked off.

I was quite proud, but with a self-delivered thump on the head, I reminded myself, *"Pride comes before the fall." Don't fall into that trap.*

"The AG liked it," I said to Zitzy. "Now, what do you have?"

"After I copied the tapes, I went to the NOPD and found Jackson in shirtsleeves at his desk in the overcrowded, smoke-filled Detective Bureau, where many of the detectives were sitting on desks and chairs prattling with their colleagues." *Hmm. That sounded like a replay at the scene of Ghost's death.*

"I told him who I was and what I was doing. As I was doing so, he continued to interrupt me with irrelevant questions and made notes. Finally, he loudly said, 'Get the hell out of here, I don't want anything to do with you!' But he discreetly passed me a post-it note, which I eased into my pocket. It all seemed clandestine to me.

"Of course, I didn't look at the note until after I left. He had written, 'NOMA, 1:00 p.m.' I knew NOMA was the New Orleans Museum of Art, and I knew where I could find it in City Park. I had time to spend, so I stopped at the Parkway Bakery near the park and had a shrimp loaf and a Dixie beer."

Now called po-boys, fried oyster and fried shrimp sandwiches on New Orleans French bread were originally called loaves.

"At about 12:30, I went into the park, positioned myself in front of the Neo-classical Beaux-Arts Museum beneath the blossoming and perfumed magnolia trees lining Leland Avenue and waited."

Feeling the need to give me all the details, Zitzy said, "Jackson, well-groomed and wearing a subtle, plaid Corneliani sport coat, arrived when he said he would and sat in my car. Like Ghost, he's tall and wiry. And man, he has laser penny-copper eyes that could bore a rivet hole in a steel girder! But even though he's reserved, I was able to extract a few pearls from him.

"Our group is definitely *personae non gratae* with the NOPD; that's why he gave me the bum's rush in front of his associates.

"He told me he sized us up at the funeral and realized we weren't the bad guys we're purported to be. He was definitely fond of Dickerson, and Dickerson must have loved you, because he often sang your praises to Jackson. Jackson said Dickerson planned to tell you all about his findings when he had developed something substantial.

"He and Dickerson grew up together. Although they were both mostly working as independents, they were still comparing notes in unison about missing children—about nine-to twelve-year-olds, both male and female, but mostly female."

"Is he assigned to Missing Persons?"

"No, General Assignment. And that's an interesting part. There seems to be a rub there. He didn't go into detail, but he indicated the Missing Persons Unit gives priority to white kids and short shrift to Blacks and Latinos. When he's inquired about the Blacks and Latinos, he was cold-shouldered.

"Besides the Blacks and Latinos, the Missing Persons Unit gives little attention to almost all missing Asian children—most of whom are girls. They automatically assume the Asians are sold by the parents on the black market, and the parents report them as missing to cover up the sales. It's weird, but that's what he told me."

"What brought the case or cases to their attention?"

"Jackson lives in the Lower Garden District, which is mostly Latino. And many neighborhood Latino parents of the missing children, although quite a few Blacks too, have come to him for help."

"Why haven't the parents gone straight to the Missing Persons Unit?"

"Again, the detectives there—almost all white—are dismissive, giving them the spiels, 'We're working on it,' 'We have a backlog of cases,' or the favorite, 'Your kid is probably a runaway.' So they've gone to Jackson and Dickerson for

assistance."

The Crescent City has had a bewildering olio of racial attitudes. Well before the Civil Rights Act of 1964, due to the shortage of dry land, there were many mixed neighborhoods. Neighbors affably greeted neighbors, but whites tended to socialize with only whites and Blacks with only Blacks. There were white-only barrooms and restaurants, and except for Dooky Chase's and Buster Holmes', there were Black-only establishments.

And in a curious twist, except for a few exceptions, there was little racial tension. Moreover, the New Orleans lexicon was, and has been, heavily infused with Black humor, epithets, expressions, and stylistics.

But entrenched customs of yesteryear tend to persist. Racism was an institutionalized sacred cow of the NOPD. Upon being arrested, Blacks could almost always anticipate being man-handled and treated with disdain. Thus, it was not surprising that missing persons detectives marginalized their efforts to find missing Black children, and their parents knew the police did so.

"How did Jackson and Dickerson tie up on this?"

"When Dickerson received no satisfaction from Missing Persons, he contacted his old friend. Jackson essentially provides the same type of help in his neighborhood in the Lower Garden District as Dickerson did in Bywater. They compared notes and began conferring.

"Dickerson had learned that, while on a field trip to the Superdome with her Saint Demetria Church's children's group, an eight-year-old named Lashanna Brown went missing. He contacted the church and found out the children on the field trip were in the care of the associate pastor, Father Baugh Duncan, who organized and led the trip. He contacted Father Duncan, and they teamed up in the hopes of finding Lashanna."

"Why did the kids tour the Superdome?" I queried. "There's no religion there."

"Dickerson asked the same question, and Father Duncan told him that mostly the trip was of a religious nature—Saint Louis Cathedral, the Ursuline Convent, and St Augustine Catholic Church. But he didn't want to weigh down the kids with pietism, and he thought it would be a bit of a diversion to let them tour the Dome."

"That makes sense. Did Dickerson and the priest have any luck, any leads?"

"No. And in the end, Father Duncan finally threw up his hands and said

89

Lashanna was probably a runaway. But here's the twist—Ghost knew the parents, and he knew the little girl. Dickerson had told Jackson Lashanna is timid, a good student, respectful to her parents, and seemed content with a loving family."

"What's Jackson's take on it?"

"Jackson doesn't have a take. Ghost said the priest was obviously upset, because he wept several times during his and Langdon's conference. And Langdon believed Father Duncan's 'runaway' conclusion was an emotional response to rationalize his failing for letting it happen."

"What were the facts of the disappearance?"

"That's an interesting point. Do you remember Ghost had told Jackson that Lashanna was timid?"

"Yeah. Well, there were forty raucous kids on the tour, and they were conveyed on a standard school bus. Jackson suggests because of her shyness, perhaps Lashanna's social skills were lacking, and she kept to herself because she didn't have close friends. So she might have isolated herself from the group. The last tour was the Superdome.

"By that time, fifty-nine-year-old Father Duncan was tired, harried, and inattentive—he admits he didn't make headcounts as he should have. The Dome was the last tour, and it wasn't until they returned to the church and Lashanna's mother didn't see her daughter that anyone realized she was missing.

"In a panic, they called the Dome's security force as well as the Saint Augustine church and notified them of the situation. In Father Duncan's car, he and Lashanna's distraught and wailing mother rushed to the Dome. And when they arrived there, the security supervisor told them Lashanna was not to be found.

"They again called Saint Augustine's church, and the rector told them he and another pastor twice swept the church with microscopic attention, but it was all to no avail. It was the same with the Ursuline Convent and Saint Louis Cathedral." Of course, they filed a Missing Persons report with the Dome and the NOPD."

"Get copies of the Dome's incident report and the NOPD Missing Persons report."

"I already have the NOPD Missing Persons report on Lashanna's disappearance as well as several others Jackson's working on. Jackson figured I'd want them, and he made copies of his for me before he left his office."

"Then sort out all the Dome's Missing Persons incident reports, and pore over

those and any synchronized police Missing Person's reports. Let's see if we have a pattern here." *Why hadn't I realized this beforehand?* "You have a hard two or three days ahead of you, Zitzy."

CHAPTER XXIV
The Tittle-Tattle Telegraph

That evening, Doughboy called me at home. From an investigative standpoint, he hadn't accomplished much. He had waited in the motel room reading (he's a voracious reader) until Jackie awoke and called him at about 3:00.

They met at Boudin on the Bayou Shop near the motel, a small, four-table charcuterie specializing in boudin and other Cajun savories such as alligator, crawfish, goujons, and frog legs, where they talked over a late lunch.

"I couldn't believe Jackie looked so good after only a few hours of sleep," Doughboy said. And by then, I was hungry as hell. I ate three links of boudin; we shared a basket of alligator nuggets; and we each had a Delaware Punch. The cuisine there is so divergent from the fast food of the national chains as to compare a po-boy to a white bread sandwich."

Cajun boudin, also known as boudin blanc, is a traditional mixture of pork meat, pork liver, and rice, along with onions and seasonings. The stuffing mixture is similar to Cajun dirty rice. It is popular in Southwest Louisiana and Southeast Texas.

"It seemed Jackie had a schedule in mind for us. She said she had briefed her mother on our mission, but if we were going to work together in her small hometown, I'd first have to have her mother's blessing. Jackie also said, because she had been so abused by men in the past, it wasn't going to be easy. 'She's just wary of me being taken advantage of again.'

"And due to the fact I'm white *and* Jewish—they're Catholic—it might be even more difficult. I promised to rely on my instincts and give it a try.

"Their home is a humble, whitewashed, L-shaped, cypress-weatherboard, Cajun cottage, somewhat in need of a little TLC. A wide porch wraps around the front and the front L-side of the house. And besides the front door, there was a door leading into the house from the porch on the short side of the "L"; both had attendant screen doors.

"After parking in the oyster-shelled driveway and approaching the house, I told Jackie I was apprehensive. She told me not to worry, and if anyone could pull it off, I would.

"The interior of the house was pristine. With tiny bedrooms and a small hall off to one side, we entered the narrow living room, where there was a yellowing picture of Christ with children as well as a well-worn sofa, eclectic end and occasional tables covered with starched doilies, and what I presumed to be family photographs.

"As we passed through the small dining room, which was narrow like the living room, I found it to be cramped because the dinner table was quite large. The unfinished wood floors in both rooms were a dull whitish-gray from years of toiled scrubbing.

"We entered the kitchen. *Huzzah*, what a kitchen it was! Sprawled across the rear of the house, it was huge. Besides the impressive Chamber's Range—food must be a major part of their lives—the round-topped vintage refrigerator, and yards of countertops and cabinets, there were two rocking chairs and a six-seater round table. And there was still open space to comfortably walk around. Miss Marie, like most Cajuns, keeps a more modern refrigerator and a chest freezer on her back porch."

"Doughboy, the tour was nice, but cut to the chase."

"I just wanted to give you the background where I'll be working." *That was dumb. He's a good investigator; let him narrate at his own pace.*

"Please continue."

"Entering the kitchen, I was assaulted with the delightful odors of fresh-brewed coffee, cornbread, and mustard greens with ham hocks.

"Jackie's mother was alone—Céline had taken time off while Jackie was there—and she was seated at the table alongside a well-used, black, rotary telephone sipping a hot cup of coffee. As lithe as Jackie is, her mother is that plump. Attired in a gaily printed housedress, she radiated poise and grace. When she spoke, her antique-parchment eyes shimmered with innate brilliance. I was impressed but not surprised; after all, she's Jackie's mother.

"Jackie introduced me as David Dosstein and her mother as Marie, and I said, 'It's a pleasure to meet you, Miss Marie.' She invited me to sit at the table next to her and directed Jackie to serve me a cup of coffee, which she poured from a tall, narrow, white-enameled coffee drip-pot.

"Miss Marie cautioned me it was strong, and she told me to make myself at home. And I could see an immanent skepticism and burning curiosity in her large

eyes. I was heedful this was going to be an interrogation.

"Miss Marie seemed to have the uncanny knack to make her questions granular—to focus on the kernels of the matter she was pursuing. And she launched her examination that went something like this:

"With her head somewhat cocked to the side, and with a slight squint of misgiving eyes, she said, 'So, where are you from, David?'

"'I've lived my entire life in New Orleans.'

"'Where in New Orleans?' She seemed to have a working knowledge of the city.

"'I was born, raised, and grew up on Palmer Avenue in the Audubon neighborhood.'

"'And where did you go to school?'

"'Jewish Community Day School, Newman Isidore, Tulane, and Loyola.'

"'You must be Jewish?'

"'Yes, Ma'am; I am.'

"She then asked me, 'And what degree did you receive?'

"'I graduated with a B.A. from Tulane and I earned my Master of Criminal Justice from Loyola.'

"For being a small-town resident, Miss Marie was quite savvy. I'm convinced she is a notable in the almost all-Black community.

"And for about a half-hour more, it continued on from there.

"Then, an unexpected thunderclap! Out of nowhere, she asked, 'Why *my* daughter?' She had the insight to see the chemistry between us.

"Caught off guard, I was unprepared for it. But you know what? It went easy.

"Having been seated at the table with us, Jackie had been silent the entire time. I think she was absorbed by the interview—her mother asked the same questions she might have if she had had time beforehand to do so. Nevertheless, she cried, 'Mama!'

"I didn't let her flurry deter me, and I plunged forward. 'It really shouldn't bewilder you, Miss Marie. Surely, you're aware of your daughter's charm and integrity. I'm not a virtuoso, and I'm abundantly endowed with failings and shortcomings, but I *am* discriminate—I know character when I see it.'

"Almost in a twinkling, her skepticism seemed to disappear, and she said, 'I believe I like you Mr. Dosstein.' And with an almost imperceptible nod of her

head, she delivered what I believed to be her stamp of approval to Jackie.

"'Please, just Dave,' I said. She gestured agreement and asked us to have supper with her. I thanked her, explained we had just eaten, and told her we had work to do. So we exchanged goodbye pleasantries. I kissed Miss Marie's hand; Jackie bussed her mother; and we left."

"Okay, lover boy. Are you moving in?"

"Absolutely not. However, after we left her Mama's house together in my car, we went to the motel to discuss our investigative plans. On the brief ride over, she said, 'I hope you understand, while here, we can't spend nights together, because I have to spend them at home.'

"A bit disappointed, I told her I understood. 'But,' she said, 'that doesn't prevent us from having matinees!'

"Apparently it didn't! I had barely closed the door when she locked me in a one-armed bearhug. With her lips clamped onto mine, her free hand began to unbuckle my belt. And without warning, my pants and drawers were around my ankles. Hobbling like I was in leg irons, she dragged me to the bed. And in short order, with our clothes strewn all over the floor, I was in the Promised Land.

"Afterward, lying depleted next to one another with her head on my chest, neither of us said a word. I don't know what she was thinking, but I was over and over replaying the events that had just happened. Then she snapped me out of my dreamworld saying, 'That was wonderful!'

"I was surprised, and I asked, 'Wonderful? Really? Jackie I'm an inexperienced lover; it couldn't have been *wonderful*.'

"She rejoined with 'No, not the sex, Silly. You were more than adequate sexually, but emotionally, you're a megastar. We'll work on the raw sex as we go, but never lose your passion for empathy and tenderness.' And she kissed me with affection and, what I let myself believe, love.

"Perhaps the 'not that' should have chinked my ego, but what she said and how she said it made my heart flutter. *And* she said, 'as we go'! This doesn't look like it's going to be another short-term, disappointing romance—at least I hope not.

"She then said, 'The wonderful I was talking about was how you so impressed my Mama. I knew you could do it, but I never imagined you would do it so well. I know my Mama, and I could read the approval in her eyes. And there's even more

than approval; I believe she's beguiled by you.' "

"That's what I've been telling you. Even the older ones are fascinated by you."

"I think I've uncovered Jackie's *je ne sais quoi*—she might have been an Indigo child."

"What is an Indigo child?"

"They're also referred to as a crystal or star child, or a child with a third eye. An indigo child is one who has come into this world destined to create change and spiritually awaken humanity. Indigo children are considered to be freethinkers with profound discernment of the human condition and an ability to see the truth clearly."

"Uh-huh. What happened next?"

"She said, 'Let's not discuss work; I want to go to sleep and have uncluttered dreams about today. And I don't want to press it with Mama, so now, I should go home.'

"I said 'Okay, how about starting on the case at 8:00 tomorrow morning?'

"She answered, 'That's fine with me.' And in near silence, we drove the fifteen-minute trip past farmland of soybeans and then crawfish ponds to her home. When we arrived, she kissed me on the cheek, hopped out of the car, and ran inside."

Doughboy concluded with, "Well, that's all; we'll be up and at 'em tomorrow."

"Good. Your report sounds like an X-rated Harlequin romance. Now let me brief you about what's going on here." And I narrated what we had learned to that point. "Hopefully, we'll be able to tie it all together.

"And I'm happy you had such a spectacular day. I realize it wasn't all fun and games. And with a little luck, Miss Marie is on the Saint Martinville tittle-tattle telegraph opening doors in the Black community, and you'll have a Saint Martinville Type A Diplomatic Visa to freely investigate. Get a good night's rest and have boots on the ground in the morning."

CHAPTER XXV
Shifting Priorities

At our morning meeting: "Zitzy, I need you to interview the priest and see if you can develop anything further. And I assume you haven't had a chance to speak with Leasean, May, or Bowditch?"

"No, I haven't; those are on my list of things to do."

"Please let me know when you do. What about the autopsy report?"

"When I called late yesterday, it wasn't ready."

"Well, thinking about it, you already have too many toys on your desk. I'll interview Father Duncan. And Pumpkin, would you handle the autopsy report?" What can I say? Priorities change, and one has to be flexible. The investigative deck of cards is continually shuffled and reshuffled.

"Done." I'll personally go the Coroner's Office this morning."

"Keep me abreast, Pumpkin."

Zitzy and Breeze, ogling her ample boobs with lascivious grins, began to chuckle.

"She can bring me a breast...or two," affirmed Breeze.

"You can gawk all you want, Breeze, but that's the closest you'll ever get to these puppies," said Pumpkin.

"Breeze," said I, "the boss giveth, and the boss taketh away. You'll have to make do without this lovely creature for a while."

"I think I'm going to throw myself in front of a streetcar."

Pumpkin responded with a puckish smile, "Don't do that, you'll just throw the streetcar transits off-schedule and make people late for work."

Assignments allotted, I began to catch up on paperwork. But I couldn't focus. I only had a few pieces to the puzzle and no picture to go with it. And although they were adminicle, I couldn't put them together. I was baffled about the case, but I was now sure about one thing—detecting wasn't my *métier*, and I wasn't the investigator I was cracked up to be.

To hell with the Dome paperwork; it could wait. I felt as if I were an obligate ram ventilator like the great white, mako, and whale sharks. I believed my probe would indeed die if I stopped moving. I had to keep at it. Often in an investigation,

movement in any direction or along any line of inquiry can bring results. Stagnation renders nothing.

So I called Saint Demetria's Church, and I was told Father Duncan was out but should return at about 1:30.

I'd surprise him with a visit.

CHAPTER XXVI
Gayle's Revelations

Because the church was in Bywater, I was reminded of Gayle. Perhaps she had time to look for a journal or a diary. And, who knows? I might be able to get her to recall something I failed to ask or something she didn't mention on the day of the funeral.

When I called, she answered. I identified myself, but she said it was unnecessary; she recognized my voice. "Gayle, may I pass by sometime today and chat with you?"

"Sure; what time?"

"Would 12:30 be okay?"

"I'll see you then."

Trying to be strong, Gayle greeted me with a half-smile. But I suspected my appearance there breached a fissure in the dam of grief she valiantly kept bottled up for the sake of her children. And within a few moments, a cleft ruptured, and she threw herself upon me and began to sob. Words were pointless, so I held her, and I, too, began to tear.

In due course, her wrenching blubbering subsided to small gasps. She let go of me and said, "I'm sorry; it's just that..."

"There's nothing to be sorry about; I understand."

Regaining her composure and drying her tears, she told me she had made a fresh pot of coffee and chicory and invited me back to the kitchen. After pouring us each a cup, she asked, "Have you made any progress?"

"A little, but not enough."

"What can I do to help?"

"Were you able to find a journal or a diary?"

"Not yet; going through his things...," and she again began to shed tears.

When she calmed down, I said, "I know it must be extremely difficult, and neither of us knows whether he kept one or not." She nodded her head, and I continued, "Has anything else—any little thing—come to you that, in the upheaval of losing your husband and the funeral, you might have neglected to say?"

"No; you know how disinclined to talk Langdon was."

"Did he ever speak with you about missing children in Bywater?"

"Well, he did once or twice open up a little bit about one of them, Lashanna Brown."

"Can you remember what he said?"

"Not exactly. But he appeared to be gloomy about it. We both know Lashanna and her family…wait a minute…it's coming back to me. She was lost on a field trip organized by Saint Demetra's Church and conducted by Father Duncan. Langdon criticized Father Duncan for not having taken head counts of the kids.

"And he grumbled about Father Duncan's loss of interest in the case, saying although Father Duncan was upset about it, he airily wrote it off as a runaway. He didn't understand the priest's lack of genuine interest, and he was distressed by that. You have to understand that, while we are Baptist, we still give credence to the Catholic clergy, and because he is a priest, Father Duncan's casual dismissal distressed Langdon even more."

"Langdon didn't think she was a runaway?"

"I don't believe he did. And I think he was unsettled by the matter."

"Do you know if her parents signed permission slips for the tour?"

"No, I don't, and Langdon didn't mention it." I would have to check that out with Father Duncan.

"Is there anything similar you can think of now?"

"No; but if I do, 'I'll let you know."

"Thanks."

"But I have a question," she said.

"Go ahead."

"I don't want to seem to be money-grubbing, but have you had any success with getting his benefits for the kids and me?"

"That's not money-grubbing; you have a family you need to support and protect. But other than a not-well-formulated plan, no. However, I promised you after the funeral, and I promise you now, I'll do everything I can to get it for you. Did you receive the Honor Fund check yet?"

"Yes."

"Good. That should tide you over for six or seven weeks, and it will give me time to organize a plan of action."

I had to first find out what Langdon was doing at the Dome when he was killed. And I had to convince the AG to advocate for her. That would require the help of my supervisor, Jim Chatelain, and a face-to-face meeting with the General who would have to appeal to the Retirement Board.

She thanked me, walked me onto the front porch, and said that her husband told her that I was one of the most honorable men he had ever known. With a rude awakening, I saw myself as a frail Atlas with the weight of the world on my shoulders.

Again becoming lachrymose, she began to sob in my arms. My shirt where she cried was wet as I left.

CHAPTER XXVII
Were Irish Eyes Smiling?

I found Father Duncan in the rectory. He was short and portly, so much so his cassock strained over his round belly, and his substantial jowls drooped over his soiled Roman collar. Grey-haired and bushy, white-eyebrowed; with a swollen, red, gnarled nose liberally diffused across his florid face; and with milky-blue bloodshot eyes, he could have been the stereotypical poster image of an Irish inebriate. *Too many Murphy's Irish Stouts, eh, Father Duncan?*

As with almost all interviews I conducted, while in the church's parking lot, I had turned on my thin Sony tape recorder and slipped it into my blazer vest pocket.

Father Duncan greeted me with a broad grin, and said, "You're lucky to catch me, Lad. I was supposed to be at Saint Cecelia's in Houma today, but my appointment was cancelled."

Was I supposed to be impressed? "Why is that?"

With an exaggerative sigh, he said, "I have an exhausting schedule—I'm what some might call an ad hoc pastor. I'm often requested by the respective dioceses to fill in for other priests in South Louisiana from Lafayette to New Orleans when local curates are temporarily indisposed or when a church has scheduled a big event that requires additional help. Besides that, I work helping inner-city kids. I'm happy to have at least a partial day off." I *was* supposed to be impressed.

So I stroked him, "It sounds like a demanding job to me."

"Yes, it is. My Son, but where the faithful are in want or need, I will go! Anyway, what can I do for you?"

I showed him my credentials and told him I was following up on Agent Dickerson's investigation of the Lashanna Brown missing persons' case. And as ephemeral as a green flash at sunset on a West Florida Beach, I thought I perceived a nebulous scowl fleet across his otherwise smiling visage.

"Ah yes, I heard of you, M'boy. And I know about Agent Dickerson's untimely death; God rest his soul. But I gave all the information I had to the New Orleans police and Agent Dickerson."

The curate then launched a short fusillade of not-unreasonable questions: "Are there any new developments in the case? And why is the Attorney General's office involved in it? How is your group participating in this? Isn't NOPD Missing Persons handling it?"

They were all legitimate queries, but I had the vague feeling that he was a tad more than just simply curious. I learned a long time ago to trust my gut instincts...but only to a point.

"An Attorney General's agent has died as you say, an 'untimely' death,' and that death occurred in the Louisiana Superdome. At present, we are charged by the Governor to assess security there. This was a lapse of security; therefore, that strikes to the core of our responsibilities."

"But why come to me?"

"Because we've received unsubstantiated word Agent Dickerson was working on the Lashanna Brown case off-duty. And although his off-duty pursuits probably have nothing to do with his death, we're only trying to tie up loose ends."

Although he was still smiling, did I detect his smile became a little broader when I said, "probably nothing at all to do with his death"? But I pulled myself up short. I realized I was trying to read something that perhaps wasn't there into it. *Whatever you do, don't fool yourself.*

"I only have a few questions, Father."

"Go ahead, Son."

"Would you recount the events that occurred on the day of Lashanna's disappearance?"

He narrated to me the same story he had apparently given to Dickerson (and I presume to the NOPD—I had not seen the report). And with a disguised air of apathy, he summed up with his opinion Lashanna probably used the opportunity to run away from home.

"What makes you think she was a runaway?"

"That is commonplace in the Black community. It happens every day. You see, My Son, they are always searching for a better life, even if they don't know where they might find it."

"Did you speak with her parents?"

"Of course, I did. But like almost all parents of runaways, they said *their* daughter would never do anything like that. I believe they believed that to be

true."

"Did you take head counts?"

"No, Lad, and I rue I did not. It's no excuse, but I was tired and harried after a long day with forty rambunctious, screeching kids. But if she hadn't run away from home that time, she would have done so at a future date."

"How can you be so sure?"

"I didn't say I was sure. But what I *am* sure of is in today's world in the Black juvenile populace, running away from home is de facto. What you don't understand, M'boy, is that those poor wee ones live in such terrible circumstances that they believe it must be better anywhere else. They don't know where that place is, but they believe it must exist."

"Did you provide an itinerary for the parents?"

"Oh, yes. It went out with the permission forms the parents have to sign if they wanted their children to take the tour."

"Okay Father, thank you for your time.

"Oh, one last question Father. Was the Superdome tour listed as one of the destinations on the tour?"

"I suppose so. Our parish secretary prepared the forms."

"Is she available?"

"No M'boy; she only works until 1:00."

Although said pleasantly enough, did I detect an air of control in Father Duncan's use of "Son," "Lad," and "M'boy"? *You're being hypersensitive and paranoid. Don't let your fragile ego get in the way of the investigation. Get over it!*

As is the case with many investigations, I found myself on a cloudy day in a Southeast Louisiana marshy plain having no landmarks within 360 degrees to guide me.

And other than the impression Father Duncan's runaway theory was prompted by guilt about his failing to be more thorough and more alert, I left gathering no substantial information, whatsoever.

Where to next?

CHAPTER XXVIII
Zitzy Gathers Good Data

At the office, Breeze was attending to his Dome duties. Zitzy, working on his audio equipment, was waiting for me. I played the tape of my conversation with Father Duncan for the two of them and asked Zitzy to share it with Doughboy and Pumpkin then file it for safekeeping. After that, I asked Zitzy, "Do you have anything new?"

"Oh, do I! First, I tried to interview May. Bowditch was working the security desk and refused to call him. I again called Rieglé, and this time, I was met with less resistance; he only asked me why I wanted to speak with May. I told him we were doing an internal audit—that's the rationale for our presence here—of the security force relative to the death of Dickerson.

"I also appealed to his reason. saying, 'Jim, you know the press is in tumult over this death. The faster we can resolve this issue, the better it will look for The Dome's security effort.' I also mentioned that, afterward, I'd like to speak with Bowditch and with him too. He agreed and directed Bowditch to call May and to allow me an interview with him."

"How did the interview with May go?"

"Fairly well. I didn't get a hell of a lot of new Information, except he remembered hearing that Ghost came in sometime before midnight, but he can't recall who the source was. And it was shortly afterward when Bowditch directed him to man the desk.

"He told me Bowditch called him about a dead body at 1:16 a.m. And as we've seen, he duly noted it the log. He followed protocol and called the NOPD, Corbin, and you."

"Yeah, now I remember it was May I spoke with. Did he give you anything else?"

"Well, yes and no. He told me it was highly probable Bowditch knew Dickerson was in the building, because in the past, Dickerson had always entered at the security checkpoint. And May found it odd Bowditch didn't notify him or the other guards of Dickerson's presence as he had done on previous occasions. This seems to be strange, but as of yet, I don't know what it might mean.

"At twelve-thirty, Bowditch called a guard meeting at the command post. And at some time before one, directing May to continue the training, he said he felt woozy, and told the assembled crew he would be back shortly.

"Like Leasean had, he also said, except for extraordinary circumstances, it was unusual for a supervisor to leave the desk during his watch, especially in the middle of a personnel meeting."

"Hmm. We have some anomalies, but they don't lead us to a firm conclusion. What about your interview with Bowditch?"

"Bowditch was different; he was tight-lipped to say the least. But I was still able to squeeze some factoids out of him.

"He told me, on the night of the occurrence, he had symptoms of the flu, and he found the small security kiosk stuffy. So he directed May to continue the training and decided he'd take a walk around the Dome.

"He went out onto the field for fresh air. And as he was admiring the majesty of the enclosure, he happened to see a peculiarity on the Plaza Level near the east entrance. He said it was as if someone had left an overcoat draped over the seats, and that's where he found Ghost."

"Did you ask him if he had seen Langdon enter?"

"I did. But here's the rub—he says he didn't. Anything's possible; however, it's unlikely he didn't see him.

"As I told you, he sat at the command desk, and anyone entering or exiting the Dome without keys would have had to have passed by him. And May said as far as he knew, Ghost always entered at that point. Nevertheless, I didn't want to confront him."

"By the way, did you ask him if, when recovering from the flu, did he lose any work because of it?" "It's probably incidental, but I'm curious."

"No, I didn't." I thought I'd wait until I spoke with Leasean—who is also a supervisor—before I did so. And more importantly, I didn't want to tip our hands by letting him know he might be a suspect."

"Good thinking, Zitzy." *Would have had that foresight?* "

"And, Zitzy, vet him—where he's from, where he lived, where he lives now, where he went to school, work history, criminal records...the full monty."

"Don't worry. I'll get on it."

CHAPTER XXIX

The Autopsy Report, Thanks to Pumpkin

With the exuberance of a *jeune fille*, Pumpkin bounded in. "I have the autopsy report—it's officially classified as a homicide!

"When I went to the coroner's office, the frowzy receptionist with hollow brown eyes dismissed me saying it wasn't ready yet. Her desk nameplate identified her as Katrina de Bella. She had a look as disdainful as the maidservant pouring tea in *Harlot's Progress*, and her cache of amiability was as bare as Old Mother Hubbard's cupboard." (Pumpkin's undergraduate degree was a B.A. in Liberal Arts with an emphasis on art and literature.)

"I asked if she knew when it would be ready, and in a huff, she told me she didn't know. I asked her if I could speak with the coroner, and she snarled 'No!'" Was it de riguer all New Orleans politicians and their petty bureaucratic underlings be uncivil?

"I realized I wasn't going to get anywhere with her, so I opened the doors to the autopsy theater to peek inside, and when I did, she shrieked, 'You can't go in there!' It didn't matter; other than the equipment, the room was empty.

"But her outburst had a positive effect—the coroner came out of his office from behind her and barked, 'What the hell's going on?'

"She squealed, 'She tried to enter the autopsy room!'

"Unfazed by her tantrum, he smiled and asked me, 'What do you want, Ma'am?'

"I identified myself and effecting a demure persona, told him I was there at your request to get a copy of Dickerson's autopsy report. I noticed he glimpsed my unoccupied ring finger, and with a lighthearted grin, he said, 'It's almost finished; come back in about an hour.' And then scowling at the receptionist, he said, 'It will be ready. And when she returns, Katrina, call me.' "

As I had done a week or so ago, she went across the street to the Crescent Bar and ate lunch. But unlike me having eaten a roast beef po-boy, she ordered an oyster loaf, and she had to ward off the drooling advances of the cops eating and drinking there. *With prurient musings, I wondered if oysters were as aphrodisiacal*

for women as they're supposed to be for men.

"When I returned to the coroner's office, I was greeted with only a glower from Katrina, who thrust the report at me. With a wide smile, I said, 'You *do* remember Dr. Odom told you to call him when I returned, don't you?'

"She yanked the phone from the receiver, dialed him, and said, 'That *woman* is here!'

"When he came out, still aglow with his glinting -blue eyes, he said, 'Miss Burchett, here is my card with my home number. Feel free to call me at *any* time.' Katrina rolled her gloomy eyes in disgust, and I thanked him and left."

"Love is in the air," I sang. "Are you going to follow up?"

"I don't know. But he is charming, and I'm considering it."

"Let me read the report."

Shucking the oyster to cull the mussel, I only scanned the procedural aspects of the straightforward document. The meat of it lay in the coroner's conclusion and the facts upon which he based his opinion. His finding was, indeed, "Homicide." And it appeared to me he had more than adequate justification to support it.

Dr. Odom noted Langdon's body had numerous bruises, and some of those were atypical of normal defensive contusions. But others and the accompanying broken bones were in accord with trauma caused by having been manhandled and falling onto the seats.

But the cornerstone of his finding was the lab report coupled with his thorough examination of the body—Langdon had been injected in the neck with etorphine before he fell.

Etorphine is a powerful, fast-acting, semi-synthetic opioid possessing an analgesic potency approximately of 1,000–3,000 times that of morphine. It is legally available only for veterinary use and is strictly governed by law—it is often used to immobilize elephants and other large mammals.

Dr. Odom further concluded Langdon's cause of death was the fall, and if it weren't for the plummet to the lower level, Langdon might have recovered from the injection.

We had more pieces to the puzzle, but as in any breakthrough, they brought up an entirely new set of questions. This was starting to look like a premeditated murder; people don't just carry a syringe and etorphine as a matter of everyday

business.

I would have preferred to have had a chalkboard, a dry erase board, or another vehicle to do this other than my handwritten notes, but the crew and I were faced with a security issue; entrance into our office was unrestricted. So I jotted these down on paper:

- *Who would have had access to such a drug?*
- *Was there more than one perpetrator?*
- *Was the murder spontaneous or rehearsed beforehand?*
- *Was the murder planned to look like an accident or a suicide?*

I shared this with Zitzy and Pumpkin, and I solicited their opinions.

Zitzy said, "A veterinarian or the burglary of a vet's office has to figure into this. And if It's a veterinarian, he's dirty."

And Pumpkin asserted, "I can't see it happening with only one perp; therefore, it was probably well-planned with two or more attackers."

"Of course, they wanted it to look like an accident or a suicide. Isn't that what Macklin indicated at the autopsy?" added Zitzy.

"Zitzy, when you have time, check on burglaries of veterinarian clinics in the New Orleans area."

And I finished with, "And whoever did it must have assumed Dr. Odom was incompetent or could be manipulated. We have some theories, but they're not immutable. Let's flesh them out and, at the same time, try to disprove them."

Zitzy and Pumpkin nodded in agreement.

Pumpkin said, "Do you guys know an asshole named Bowditch on the security staff?"

"Yeah, why?" said Zitzy.

"He's full of himself. He thinks he's suave, but with his beady eyes and hair slicked back with Vaseline, he looks like the quarry in a greased pig contest. He's hit on me three times before, and today, he tried to cop a feel. I called him a disgusting creep and told him to stay away from me.

"His face flushed red. It looked as if he was going to punch me, but when I assumed the position, he backed off and stormed away. I'm not going to put up with that bullshit!"

"There's no need for you to kick his ass—and I know you could," I said to her.

"If he gets out of line again, Pumpkin, let me know, and I'll deal with it."

I ended our meeting with, "Well, other than that, it's been a productive day; let's hit the showers."

Zitzy leered at Pumpkin, "What a fantastic idea! You and I can shower together and support the ecology movement by saving water." *I was thinking the same damned thing!*

"Dream on; that ain't happening, Zitzy," quipped Pumpkin.

CHAPTER XXX
Doughboy Is "Hard at It"

Having dined on Natalie's signature dish—roast beef stuffed with garlic and onions, rice, and a dark-roux gravy—I was relaxing with her while sipping a Port and smoking a cigar. The red wall phone in the den rang.; it was Doughboy. His report and my comments were:

"Yesterday, I told you Jackie and I would be hard at it today. And we were." Thinking about Doughboy's current estate, my unbridled, prurient mind wondered if "hard at it" was a double entendre or a Freudian slip. He didn't say, and I didn't ask.

"I have some news!"

"Tell me."

"It's about Adeline Tournoi, the reason I'm here. Well, Jackie and I spoke with her mother, Céline, Jackie's older sister, today. By the way, you were right; the Saint Martinville tittle-tattle telegraph has been burning up the wires, and it's all favorable chatter.

"Although not as handsome as Jackie, her sister, too, is attractive and well-bred. She echoed Jackie's perception of Adeline as a sweet, timid, and loving little girl. And I verified that, almost identically to Lashanna's disappearance, she went missing while on a Saint Riquier Catholic Church-sponsored tour of the Superdome.

"We asked if she remembered where the rumor about the Superdome being the site of youth abductions came from. She said she had heard it during the first few days of turmoil after her daughter went missing, but because she was so upset, she couldn't recall who told her. And other than remembering the priest who conducted the tour as 'a fat white guy,' she didn't know his name or where he was from, and she could recall nothing else about him."

"The 'fat white guy' might be cog in our case. Have you made inquiries at the church?"

"The church is a one-man show, and the pastor is Father Tobias Hebert. We went there to interview him, but we were only able to speak with his secretary, Camille LeBlanc, a modest, delicate Creole lady just entering the vale of years. She

111

had intellect and sad sepia eyes that shimmered with compassion.

"Jackie knows her, and she knows Jackie. When Jackie introduced me, Camille said she and Father Hebert were expecting us. She further said Father Hebert was anxious to confer with us, but he had been called away and asked us to return when he was available.

"When we began to inquire about the Adeline Tournoi incident, she became distressed and began to weep, sobbing, 'That poor little girl.'

"Responding to our questions, she told us she didn't know who organized the trip or why they did so. It was scheduled for a Saturday—I have the exact date in my notes—and included about forty-five children, ages eight to twelve. And as in Lashanna's case, too, Adeline was not noted as missing until the bus returned to the church.

"We asked if the Dome tour was included in the package, and she told us she couldn't remember, and we'd have to ask Father Hebert. We'll have to wait until tomorrow to interview him.

"We then went to the Saint Martinville Police Department, a small, three-office suite on the rear side of the quaint, antebellum, two-courtroom Saint Martin Parish Courthouse. There, Jackie is well-known, and except for the younger Blacks she had spurned, she was liked and now respected. She asked the petit, aged, but attractive, grey-haired dispatcher/secretary, Calandre, for a copy of Adeline's Missing Persons report, and we waited less than five minutes before we had it in our hands.

"Jackie noted the initial report was taken by Patrolman Pierre Bourgeois. The narrative was, at the very best, flimsy and recorded less than we had already learned. And other than contacting Superdome Security and forwarding the report to the NOPD, there was no indication of any follow-up action taken.

"Jackie asked the dispatcher if Bourgeois was working and if we could speak with him. The dispatcher didn't hesitate, calling Bourgeois on the radio and directing him to return to the police station.

"Bourgeois, was white, unkempt, beard-stubbled, and arrogant. Following his pot belly, he swaggered in and said, 'Yeah?

"Jackie led with the questioning, asking him if he had done any follow-up work not listed in the report. Indignant about being questioned by a Black female civilian, he became surly. Flushing, he said, 'Don't you have my report?'

"I figured I'd better step in. I identified myself, and in a complaisant tone, said, 'Officer Bourgeois, thank you for taking the time to speak with us. And please forgive Jackie; she's distraught over her missing niece. I'm with an AG's detachment working at the Superdome where it's believed Adeline had gone missing. I won't keep you long, but I have a few quick questions.'

"His face softened, and he said, 'Okay.'

"The interview went something like this:

" 'I've read your report, and I noticed there was no other investigation on this end. Why is that so?'

"He responded, 'I wanted to follow up, but the Chief tol' me it wasn't our case—whatever happened, happened in New Orleans. He tol' me to forward the report to the NOPD Missing Person's Bureau, and if 'dey needed any more information from us, I should help them. But as of now, I ain't heard nothin' from them.'

" 'I also see on your report you interviewed the priest, and other than him telling you the last stop was the Dome, you didn't include much else. Can you remember anything else he said?'

" 'Yeah, I do. He tol' me he was on loan to Saint Riquier's church to show the kids religious sites in New Orleans.'

" 'Did he offer a reason or excuse why Adeline went missing?'

" 'Yeah. He told me he was tired and distracted, so he didn't take no head counts, and Adeline prob'ly ran away at one of the stops, most likely McDonald's.'

" 'Why did he think she ran away?'

" 'Oh, you know how Black children are; dey almost always glad to get away from home. And especially 'dose from rural communities like this one. They see the bright lights of the city, and they wanna' be where the action's at.'

"I could see that angered Jackie, but in her wisdom, she said nothing.

" 'Did he say anything more about the Dome?'

" 'No, not in partic'lar. He only tol' me the Superdome was the las' stop, and he didn't know if she was on the bus or not when dey got dere.'

" 'You don't have his name on the report; is there a reason for that? And you have only a very few facts about him in your brief narrative; can you tell me why?'

"That seemed to rile him again. His face crimsoned, and he crossly said, 'Cause he's a priest, dat's why!'

"Sensing we were losing him, Jackie interjected, saying to me, 'The folks in Saint Martinsville are almost all Catholic, and they take their religion seriously.' It seems Jackie and I make a good tag team.

"Bourgeois generously smiled at her—she had made a friend.

"And Bourgeois followed the lead saying, 'Besides bein' a devout priest, he was a helluva nice guy. So when he axed me to minimize his involvement, I was okay wit' 'dat. Besides, like the Chief said, it ain't our case.'

" 'Do you remember the priest's name?' I asked.

" 'No me, not exactly. I think it was Daniels, Dawson, Dalton, or somethin' like that.'

" 'Can you describe him?'

"He was again becoming defensive. 'Why all these questions bout the priest? He's not da bad guy in this; he even blest' me before he left. And the little girl just run away from home.'

"So I responded, 'You're probably right. But like you, I have a boss—a pain-in-the-ass boss who's obsessed with details. If I don't dot the I's and cross the T's, I'm putting my nuts in a vise, and he's going to squeeze hard.'

"Frowning, he said, 'I can understand dat; it happens to me too. Anyway, he was in his fifties, grey-haired, green-eyed, and a bit overweight. Sure 'nuff looked like the perfect pitcher of an Irishman to me.'

" 'Do you know if the Dome was on the list of locations to tour?'

" 'No, I figered Father Hebert handled all dat.'

" 'One last question, Officer Bourgeois: Did he call you Lad or 'M'boy?'

" 'Well, yeah he did; howd'ja know?'

" 'You said you thought he was Irish. And since those are common Irish expressions, I was curious if he did so.'

"You finished?"

"I think so."

"Well, you I pack my ass and get outta' here."

"I might need to question him again, and I didn't want to stir up a hornet's nest, so I said, 'Thank you Officer Bourgeois; you've been a tremendous help, and I'll downplay the priest in my report.'

"Outside, I remarked to Jackie, 'Wow! Can you believe that?'

"She responded, 'You never asked me why I didn't seek employment with the

Saint Martinville Police Department, but that's the reason. And it's even worse than what you've seen—the Chief allegedly only has a GED, and even that is in doubt.'

"I said, 'At this point, I don't think it is necessary to interview him any more right now; and it might be counterproductive to speak with the chief, So I think we should put it off until a later date, if it becomes needed. I don't have much faith in coincidence, and I think we have something here.'"

" 'Neither do I accept coincidence as is.'

"'Okay, let's keep at it.'

"That about wound up our day. Tomorrow, we'll try to interview Father Hebert."

Overall, their interview didn't render much. But it did answer a nagging question I had been puzzling about: Why weren't lawsuits filed in those cases? The simple answer: The laity were afraid to criticize the Church.

I was curious about the honeymoonette, but I was discreet and didn't ask—Doughboy would tell me when he was ready to.

It wasn't a "*Voila!*" moment, but the case was at least moving. Once at home and abed, I slipped into an iron sleep along with Wynken, Blynken, and Nod and didn't awaken until right before dawn the next morning.

CHAPTER XXXI
The Vale of Soul-Making

So profound is Keats. He wrote a letter to his sister and brother in which he offered a view on the significance of life, saying, "The world is the 'vale of soul-making.'" The letter, as are most of his works, is about good, evil, suffering, and self-realization. And with my surplus of insecurities, I tend to read it when I feel swamped and beyond my abilities. I pulled Keats off the bookshelf that morning.

Oscar Wilde wrote: "Most people are other people. Their thoughts are someone else's opinions, their lives a mimicry, their passions a quotation." He was correct, of course; most us strive to blend in with society losing our personal identity as we do so.

But Keats believed we begin as identical bits of God and acquire individuality only by life-defining emotional experiences; i.e., "soul-making." Having my morning cup of coffee, I read it again, and I focused on my two favorite passages: *Call the world, if you please, "the Vale of Soul-Making." Then you will find out the use of the world.... There may be intelligences or sparks of the divinity in millions— but they are not Souls till they acquire identities, till each one is personally itself.*

I wasn't there yet—I wasn't a "Soul." I had not acquired my identity; nor was I personally myself. But I was working on it.

Feeling mentally refreshed, I showered, dressed, and went to work placid and a bit lighter in my step.

At the office, I briefed Zitzy, Pumpkin, and Breeze on Doughboy's report.

"With Duncan, we have a good suspect for an accomplice-assisted kidnapping and maybe the same for a pedophilic perp. But there are still as many loose ends to this case as there are fringe tassels on a cowboy's suede leather jacket."

The ringing of the phone interrupted me.

"Agent Régis?"

"I am he."

"This is Ed Sanderson from the *Times-Picayune*. May I see you this morning?"

"You pick the time."

"Is ten-thirty, okay?"

"Sure; see you then."

I told the crew we were going to have a visitor, Ed Sanderson from the *Times-Picayune*, and asked them to opine what the nature of his call might be. Like me, they had no ideas either. But Zitzy admonished me, "Don't forget he's a reporter—watch your back."

"Thanks. Have you had the opportunity to review the Missing Persons reports Jackson gave you?"

"No, I'm getting around to that. But I will."

"That's okay; I know I've loaded you down with assignments. And we have to prioritize. I think getting information from Leasean, the other security supervisor with whom you've made contact, should come first. If I can find the time, I'll help you with those reports.

"And I'm sure you've already considered this, but don't forget to ask Leasean if he's ever seen Duncan—you have his description—and if so, under what circumstances has he seen him."

"Pumpkin, I have a particularly onerous chore for you."

"I'm up for it," she said.

"Contact Dr. Odom..."

"I'm *really* up for it!" she squealed.

"Okay, but this will require a deft touch. With twenty-five years as coroner, he's bound to have contacts in the overall medical community; he might even have had to perform animal necropsies from time to time. See if he can help us find a dirty veterinarian.

"But in the meantime, touch base with the dioceses in Southwest Louisiana and find out if they have records of the churches to which Father Duncan has been dispatched on an ad hoc basis. Perhaps it would be best if you did it in person. And I think you should start with, the Diocese of Lafayette and following that the Diocese of Houma/Thibodaux. We can save the Diocese of New Orleans for last."

"Why is that?"

"Because Duncan's already struck here. And although the Diocese of New Orleans encompasses more than Orleans Parish, I think it's more likely than not he wouldn't have abducted another one in the immediate area, especially in New Orleans, itself." *Why would you assume that? Don't you know you should gather and consider all the pieces to the puzzle and only discard them later if they don't*

fit?

"What should I tell them is the reason I want the information?"

"Be cautious; you know how defensive of their clergy the Catholics are. Tell them the Governor, along with the AG, are in the process of developing a 'Good Citizen Award.' And someone brought Father Duncan's unceasing labors to their attention.

"And, inasmuch as Louisiana ranks ninth in the nation for a Catholic populace, and twenty-six percent of the State's residents are Catholic, it would be a good idea to start the yearly award with something that would please the Catholic community.

"You can also remind them the Governor and the AG are both Catholic. They are concerned about the Church's besmirched image with the press coverage of pedophilic priests, and they want to help the Church recover the standing it once had. Tell them this is on the QT, and if word leaks out, the program will lose some of its brio.

"But however you handle it, don't speak with anyone in the upper echelons of the dioceses—try to make contact with low-level, secular functionaries."

"I'll get on it right away. And if I don't need to be here when Sanderson comes, I'd like to go to the Coroner's Office as soon as possible."

"Why am I not surprised? Sure, go ahead.

"And Breeze, I have some grunt work for you. We need to put a tail on Duncan. The first two days will be extra-difficult, since you'll have to adjust to his schedule such as his waking and sleeping rhythms. After that, you'll be in the swing of things, and it should slack off a bit. In any event, log your hours; you're going to make a lot of overtime.

"Head up to State Police Headquarters and get a 'cool' car—one that was seized in narcotics bust and has an out-of-state, falsely registered license plate. See Captain Melancon; I'll work out the logistics. And Breeze, change the car out every two days or so."

After he left, I called my friend and contact, T-Claude Melancon, and made the necessary arrangements. *You're still trying to catch all the chickens at once, aren't you?*

CHAPTER XXXII
An Elfin Sprite in a Black Forest Valley

Sanderson arrived promptly. The press had already reported Dickerson's death as a homicide. What more could he want from me?

"Mr. Sanderson, welcome. I didn't think I'd see you so soon."

"Neither did I. Call me Ed."

"Okay Ed, I'm Johnny. What brings you here?"

"For having written an unwarranted inflammatory article about you, I feel I owe you one.

"At about eight-thirty this morning, the paper received a press release from the mayor's office accusing you of interfering with an ongoing police investigation and harassing a Catholic priest.

"The release also goes on to say you were encroaching on a missing persons case the NOPD is actively pursuing, and you badgered Father Baugh Duncan of St. Demetria's Catholic Church.

"The statement, laded with the mayor's office and Father Duncan's what I believe to be hyperbole also gives the date and time of the occurrence. Having met you, I wondered how much truth there is to it. And, I thought I'd give you a heads up."

"Hyperbole is an understatement, Ed. From what you tell me, the only truth might be the date and time I spoke with Father Duncan. I believe if you check the police records concerning missing Lashanna Brown, you'll find the police investigation came to a halt almost when it began. And it wouldn't surprise me if you found out that, shortly after the incident, the case was 'solved' as a runaway.

"I believe that you might also find that it was reported she may have gone missing while visiting the Dome. It is not our job to look for missing persons, but because we continue to audit the security at the Dome, we have to at least consider such reports. I leave it to you to do the fact-checking. Have you done that?"

"Yes, what you say is true. The NOPD informed me the case, although still classified as open, is for the most part, closed—Lashanna was a runaway."

At this point, I was reluctant to divulge I had taped the conversation between

Duncan and me. Although it would have exonerated me, I believed it might inhibit further investigations if it were let out that, with potential or suspected adversaries, it was known I covertly record interviews.

Nevertheless, I told him even though Father Duncan rudely patronized me, I had treated the priest with the utmost respect.

"Well Johnny, you must know it will boil down to a he-said/he-said issue. And as a priest, he is viewed as a pillar of righteousness; you'll receive little support from the community."

"I know; I'm going to have to fade that heat. But as Socrates said to Crito, 'What we ought to consider is not so much what people in general will say about us but how we stand…in right and wrong, the one authority who represents the actual truth.' "

"I'm familiar with the quote."

"Are you going to write the news article addressing this?"

"No, Alvin Katzman with the *States-Item* probably will."

"Is he as good an investigative journalist as I hope you are?"

"You'll have to judge for yourself."

"Ed, have you ever wondered why the New Orleans political machine is so opposed to our presence here?"

"Yes, it is curious."

"These are fig-leaf accusations; someone, somewhere is covering something up. I'm certainly not about to tell you how to conduct your business, but I believe if you look into it, you might have the scoop of the decade. Just saying."

"Can you give me anything else to go on?"

"I wish I could, but I can't now because I don't have anything to give you. However, as soon as I do, I'll let you know. With our limited resources, we're working on it."

"Can you bring me up to date?"

"There's not much on which to update you. We've developed a few leads, but they waned like morning glories do at night. However, we're still plugging away at it." *Print that in the paper, and let our adversaries think we're the Keystone Kops. Maybe we'll get a little slack, especially from Macklin, who would probably see us as clodhoppers and not worry about us anymore.*

"If I write an article, may I quote you on that?"

"Sure...I said it. Should I expect a visit from Katzman?" I had tried to change the subject, but it didn't work.

"I would think so. But I must ask you, 'With the murder and all the other security problems at the Dome, why were you investigating a single missing persons incident?'"

It was what I would expect from a competent journalist, and I sensed he was a perceptive and noble man. He must have felt we were on to something. It was a cheap ruse, and I envisioned myself an elfin sprite deep in Germany's Black Forest valley dancing around my taped interview to keep it secret.

"We weren't investigating a missing persons case, per se. And we're not limiting our perusals of the security function to this incident. But as I said, it seems that a juvenile went missing when on a tour of New Orleans churches and Dome. So, it did merit our attention, because we wanted to follow up on all possible leads. Like so many other ones, that one fizzled too. It had nothing to do with our case."

Sanderson smiled at me. But the smile conveyed to me he knew I was fudging. Which I was.

"Do you think after this assignment is over, you'd take a full-time position here at the Dome or a high-level security post somewhere else?"

Considering that policing was an essential part of my inner being, I responded, "Ed, I just want to go back to being a cop."

CHAPTER XXXIII
A Lost Ball in High Weeds

The Sanderson interview went as well as it could given the exigent circumstances. But I had to call the AG about the forthcoming news reports, and I wasn't looking forward to it.

"Yes Régis," said the AG with undisguised annoyance."

"Reporting in General."

"Okay, tell me."

And he allowed me to speak without interruption for the next fifteen minutes while I mapped out the events and the intelligence gathered over the last few days.

After I finished, he said, "I think you have a handle on it, but be careful. Don't ease up; that's when the hyenas will eat you."

"Will do; thank you Sir."

Maybe he realized what a tough spot he put me in. *Don't be a pansy and feel sorry for yourself, Johnny; suck 'em up and get to work.* And so I did get to work, albeit with a gnawing in my gut.

Katzman called and made an appointment for twelve-thirty.

After a minimum of pleasantries, Katzman dove in. "I know you spoke with Sanderson about the Mayor's Office press release, but I'd like to hear your comments on the matter,"

"It's outright calumny." And I iterated what I had told Sanderson, and he, like Sanderson, focused on the he said/he said issue.

"Did Father Duncan say I pressured him?"

"Yes, he said you were rude and criticized him."

I asked Katzman if he were going to investigate the outrageous claim about the NOPD still working on the case. He told me he already had, and the commander of the Missing Persons Bureau had advised him it was still an active case and one of his detectives *was* currently working it.

"They're putting lipstick on a pig. Did he provide you with any reports?"

"I asked, but he told me he couldn't release them because they were ongoing investigation." Ah-ha! Their chicanery was boundless—one story for Sanderson

and another one for Katzman!

I asked Katzman, "Do you have any evidence to the contrary?"

"No, I don't," he responded. Score one for the bad guys. And the game wasn't over yet; I was going to be placed in an even more delicate position.

He asked the same question as had Sanderson, "Why are you focusing on a single missing persons incident?"

We weren't at all concentrating on that. We're looking at a wide range of potential factors related to potential security risks at the Dome. This happened to be one of them. And as with any homicide investigation or any security audit, we were simply following up on that lead, and it proved to be a dead-end."

"Well, where are you now with your investigative effort?"

"On the same dead-end street. My team and I are the blind men with the elephant. Just as it was with Father Duncan, we come up with leads, we conceptualize theories, but no one has the right answer. Thankfully, we don't go to blows like the sightless pachyderm examiners, but when the smoke clears, we're as lost and flummoxed as we were when we began."

And as I had with Sanderson, I detected what I believed to be skepticism in his eyes...just what my explanation was intended to produce. I *wanted* them to have doubts; perhaps in their perusals, they could ferret out something we missed. I had planted the acorns, and I fantasized they would germinate and grow into mighty oaks.

Later, alone in the office, I contemplated the intelligence we had gathered. It was as if I had a clear picture of the lower one-tenth of da Vinci's *Last Supper*. I could see the cloth-draped table with what appeared to be the remnants of a meal thereon and also what appeared to be one of the table's sawhorse legs.

I could also discern the dress, lower torsos, legs, and feet of two men. Thus, I was able to reasonably surmise the painting depicted a group of persons having eaten at a dinner table in a bygone era.

But that was it. I couldn't envision who the diners were; what they had eaten; what was the reason for their attendance; what were the levels of their participation; when did the coalition develop; when and how often did they carry out the group's mission; where was the base of their activities; why did they band together (money, pleasure, needs?); and what was their business template?

I was a lost ball in high weeds. Would I ever make it to the eighteenth hole?

CAPTER XXXIV
The Vise Tightening on My Nether Parts.

Hurdling through the door and grinning, the impish Pumpkin intruded on my free association. "Charles and I have a date tonight! And he's taking me to Pascal's Manale for barbequed shrimp." *Are her nipples singularly perky? And am I feeling shooting pangs of desire and jealously? Yes, a definitive yes to both!*

"So, is it 'Charles' now?"

"Well actually, no. He asked me to call him 'Chaz.' And he has a BMW K 1600 too!"

"I'm happy for you. But did he give you any information about a possible source of illegal etorphine?"

"No. He was busy; he said we'd chat tonight."

"Good show; do it. And take the rest of the day off; I want you at your best tonight."

Zitzy also entered the office beaming with gusto. *Guys, you have no idea how much your spirit inspires me.*

"Although not hard facts, Leasean provided me with some promising particulars.

"Leasean doesn't like and is suspicious of Bowditch. Even though they work separate shifts, he has heard ominous rumors about him. They center around unusual activity that sometimes occurs when Bowditch is working night shifts."

"Like what?"

"It seems that every so often the evening before a big event, Bowditch orders his entire crew to the security office for a half-hour to one-hour 'briefing and training' by him. As a matter of fact, regardless of what shift he's on, he is assigned to work a special overlapping shift on those nights, outranking the normally assigned supervisors.

He usually starts the briefings by going over Dome security procedural orders which they've heard over and over again. Then he switches to discussing recent Dome security incidences. But the meeting, fueled by coffee and doughnuts, is little more than a bullshit session.

"At some point, he invariably receives a phone call, and the meeting is

abruptly adjourned. And sometimes during a meeting, a few of the guards have thought they heard the 'deliveries-only' back gate open and close."

"What happens with the missed key punches?"

"I asked him that, and he said he doesn't know, but they cannot be made because the Detex watchclocks are still in the possession of the security guards they were assigned to." *Damnit! Another screwup. You should have already had your crew checking those. You would have known about the absences of security coverage, and would have already learned about the training sessions.*

"Who checks the cardboard disks inside the watchclocks?"

"I asked him that too, and he said he didn't know. But I don't think we should pursue that now."

"Why?"

"I think it would it would alert the conspirators we're onto something.

"But it gets stranger. Typically, at about midnight after an event, the same type briefing/training meeting is ordered. And again, some of the guards have heard the back gate opening and closing."

"Does he know if the same type training occurs on other shifts?"

"Leasean said unless he is instructed to do it, he doesn't conduct those sessions, and he doesn't know if the other two supervisors do."

"Have you gotten the schematic?"

"Yeah."

"How close is the back gate to the luxury suites?"

"It's on a different level, but it's easy to reach the suites from there."

"How were Leasean and Ghost?"

"They got along well. In fact, he had discussed what I told you with Ghost." That was a potential security lapse. Why didn't Ghost tell *me* about it?

"Anything else?"

"On a few occasions, Leasean has spoken with Olson's food runners who have asked him why they never have a call to deliver to the mayor's 40-seats box suite on Level 6 during a big event. He told them he didn't know because, unless called, the security guards are prohibited on that level. In fact, there are only twelve of those suites, and there are no watchclock stations in that area."

"Does Leasean know why?"

"No, but he thinks there is so much security on the lower levels that the upper

suites are adequately protected. And although they tolerate an NOPD officer there on event nights, the fat cats object to having security uniforms there. In fact, he's heard a rumor that C&H was planning to hire more guards so that they could station plainclothes operatives there for major events—on their cost-plus contract, of course."

"Who leases those suites?"

"He told me he didn't know, except that one of them is the governor's suite and one is the mayor's suite, which is as large as the governor's suite."

"Did Leasean give you any more information?"

"No, but I plan to speak with him again. I'll also try to follow up with Bowditch about his 'flu.' If you have any other questions you want answered, let me know."

"Did you check on burglaries of vets' offices?

"Yeah, there have been a few. But none of them had missing etorphine.

"You have really done well, Zitzy.".

That afternoon on the front page—this time in the late edition of the *States-Item*—with the byline of Alvin Katzman, the headline read: *AG Security Detachment Interferes with Police Investigation—Harass Priest.*

Withholding that which I had, I left him no other option. And the rest of the article was essentially a summarization of the press release and Katzman's interview with me. It was good and bad press for the AG's Office. The good—we looked like doddering idiots, and the bad—clergy harassers.

The inexorable vise was tightening on my nether parts.

CHAPTER XXXV
L'Amour in Cajun Land

At 10:30 that evening, Doughboy again called me at home from his motel room. He opened with, "I have a blockbuster! We spoke with Father Hebert today. As we suspected, it was Father Duncan who led the tour."

"Good."

"It gets better. Father Hebert had heard about the tours of the churches, and he called the diocese to see if he could set one up for his juvenile parishioners. The diocese apparently contacted Father Duncan, and arranged the time, date, and locations to be toured.

"But here's the rub—the Superdome wasn't on the list.

"After the bus returned without Adeline, Father Hebert asked Father Duncan about that, and Father Duncan said there was a mix-up in the scheduling times, and when they went to the Ursuline Convent, the sisters were in Matins."

"What's Matins?"

"Matins is a canonical hour of Christian liturgy, which was extended in time and number because it was the month of October. October is one of two months that the Catholics have especially dedicated to the Holy Mother.

"But according to Father Hebert, Matins is a morning and evening—not a midday—event. However, when he questioned Duncan about it, Duncan said the Ursulines have expanded it to include the noon hours.

"Duncan told him he didn't want to make the trip a one-pony show, so he took the kids to the Dome. And Duncan further told him Adeline must have bailed somewhere along the way, probably when they went to McDonald's."

"Did he have tour reservations at the Dome?"

"I don't know." *I'll have Zitzy check that out.*

"Did Father Hebert know Duncan beforehand?"

"He knew *of* Father Duncan, but they had never met. Interestingly, I found Father Hebert to be astute. And he volunteered he wasn't quite comfortable with Duncan even before the excursion, but he couldn't pinpoint why.

"Anyway, Father Hebert was distraught—after all, the tour was his idea. And he was angry. So he called the diocese to share his frustrations and concerns. He

told us he spoke with the Executive Secretary of the Office of Diocesan Development in Lafayette. He said, although he was well-received, he felt his anxieties were disregarded because no one called him with results of their purported investigation of the matter.

"I didn't tell him, but I didn't think it was surprising. As you know, the Catholic Church is overrun with reports of pedophilic priests, and their version of Internal Affairs is as unprofessional as a monkey playing a piano at a symphony. And they could ill-afford another firestorm scandal that their clergy was irresponsible with youngsters in their charge. Of course, he was cautious with his criticism, but he was very pleased we were looking into the situation.

"We decided that we didn't have enough time to interview the children, themselves. But we did speak with some of the other parents whose children were on the tour. Almost all said their kids thought Adeline to be a bit odd; she had no good friends, and she was always a straggler when engaged in group activities. But stranger yet, Adeline, like Lashanna, was socially adept with adults—outgoing, chatty, and in sync with them.

"I asked them if their children had noted anything unusual about Duncan's actions while on the field trip. Most of them said no, but two parents said their children told them they had a wonderful time at a McDonald's, where they ate all they wanted for about an hour and a half.

"However, Father Duncan didn't spend much time with them—he mostly left the "babysitting" to the bus driver—because he seemed to make a lot of calls on the pay telephone outside. I don't know if that means anything."

"Did Jackie know what information Langdon had?"

"Only that he was about to wind it up, and he was going to give you a present of it."

"Well, it seems you and Jackie accomplished quite a bit; in fact, much more than I had anticipated. Have you done everything there you think you need to?"

"Yeah. Depending on the traffic in Baton Rouge, I should be in the office at about ten."

I couldn't restrain my curiosity, "Are you going to leave Jackie in tears?"

"Well, inasmuch as you masterminded this jaunt, and because I have no one else with whom I can share, I'll tell you.

"You know about my insecurities with the fair sex, don't you? If I see an

attractive woman, I salivate, stumble, mumble, and walk into a utility pole or a door jamb."

"Yes, I do, but for the life of me, I can't understand it. You're a Renaissance man and a chick magnet, Doughboy. I see them throwing themselves at you, and you're oblivious to it."

"Yeah, yeah, yeah. Anyway, I still feel vulnerable and unsure of myself.

"But something magical has happened. After putting in a long day, we came back to the motel to unwind and have cocktails. But we were only halfway finished the first ones when she said, 'To hell with this; let's fuck.' And so we did.

"It was another voyage to the rapture. Exhausted afterward, we lay entwined in each other's arms. Lying there, I said, 'Jackie, what do you see in me?'

"She said, 'I see your soul. You're decent, kind, compassionate, charming, and from my perspective, lovable.'

"With that, I said, 'You should know I come with tattered baggage.'

"And she responded saying, 'We all do. And I can assure you my baggage is more worn and heavier than yours. I've been abused almost all my life—my paternal uncle repeatedly raped me from the time I was six until he died in a freak accident when I was twelve. The molestations were suspected in our small, backwoods community; and almost as if I were a deflowered single Muslim, I was treated as damaged merchandise and an easy piece of ass.'

"I asked her if Miss Marie knew of the abuse, and she told me she didn't think her mother did, except perhaps toward the end. And of course, I wanted to know why she didn't report the abuse to her mother. She said the uncle threatened to kill the both of them if she did, so she suffered to keep them alive.

"Jackie continued, saying, 'During my adolescence and into my early adulthood, I tried to have relationships with boys and later with men. But they were disasters—the males as well as the relationships. I was objectified and it was dehumanizing. They did so by either putting me on a pedestal like a toy or on a leash like a dog. And it hardened me until I met you.

"'So, I must tell you, even though I recognize what a beautiful human being you are, I'm still guarded. All the men in my life have been pigs, and I'm terrified you might be one too. And right now, my persecution anxieties are telling me you're too good to be true.'

"And with a bewitching kiss, she told me she loved me, and she would never

take advantage of my tenderheartedness."

"Did you respond in kind?"

"Johnny, I might be inept with women, but I'm not a fool. *Of course*, I did!"

"Well, I feel I should be flying around like Cupid...diapered and with a bow and arrow. I'm really happy for you Doughboy."

"I'm glad you are," he said, "but please don't share this with the crew."

"Don't worry. I might not be good at a lot of things, but I *can* keep a secret. By the way, whatever happened to her uncle?"

"I'm not surprised you asked because I did too. That's an interesting story. It seems her uncle moved in with them after her father was killed in an offshore oilfield accident—they never did find his body.

"And one day following a hurricane, the uncle was working on their roof. According to the police report, Miss Marie was assisting him. And when he was at the top of the ladder—a tall ladder, the house is raised—he said he forgot the roofing nails, and he barked at Miss Marie to fetch them, and do it quickly.

"After finding the nails, she rushed back to the ladder, and from the ground, she tried to hand them up to him, but he couldn't reach them. He snarled at her to ascend the ladder to deliver them, and when she was stepping from the first to the second rung, he tried to snatch the bag from her, and the ladder tilted over.

"They both fell to the ground, and she received some bruises. But because he was leaning over, he fell headfirst, broke his neck, and died."

"Does Jackie believe it was an accident?"

"I'm not sure about Jackie, but I don't think it was. I believe Miss Marie learned of the abuse, found an opportunity, and intentionally tipped the ladder. Regardless, the evil cocksucker's dead."

"We've had a lot of new developments here. I'll bring you up to speed tomorrow."

CHAPTER XXXVI
A Danse Macabre

As expected, even before our staff meeting the following morning, I received a call from the AG. He was angry. "What the hell's going on, Régis? Did you see the article in the *States-Item*?"

"Yes, I did, General. And what's 'going on' was what I told you would happen. It was a tough call—I could have played our high trump early on and settled for a split pot, but I chose to hold it and make a split and a rip."

"I don't play bourrée; tell me what you mean by that."

"We could have avoided the bad press by showing our hand, but we would lose our opportunity to 'find the motherfucker, and find him fast'—your words, General. The way I played it—and remember, General, I spoke with you about it before I did it—I'm betting on our antagonists thinking we're hayseeds and perhaps, just perhaps, letting their guards down.

"Moreover, I didn't want to provide them with the intelligence we've gathered; it would tend to drive the bastards underwater like *poule d'eaus* when they sense danger."

"But why haven't you and your staff come up with anything yet?"

"First of all—and I know you're aware of this—there are no simple solutions to complex problems. And secondly, General, the agents you assigned to me are dedicated to start with. And this is one of their own, an honorable man who was a friend. I can't push them any more than they, themselves, are—check their time sheets and see how many hours they're putting in."

"I suppose you're right, Régis, but keep me up to date."

"Will do General," and I hung up.

I didn't have to explain the call to Zitzy and Pumpkin; they understood. "I need updates, and I haven't heard from Breeze."

"*I* did, Johnny," said Zitzy. "He called me about midnight—he didn't want to disturb you—and he said he positioned near the rectory from about 4:00 to 11:30 and he saw no movement. He says the church is on a busy thoroughfare, so he can change positions and try to avoid being detected. He also told me that today his disguise was a beard and a Saints' cap.

131

"He checked the license plates of the two cars parked outside of the manse. One was registered to Duncan and the other to a Regan Gallagher, whom he assumes to be the church rector. He's going to check on it tomorrow, and he'll be on post at about 2:00 this afternoon."

"Okay. When you speak him with again, remind him we need daily updates. What do you plan to do today, Zitzy?"

I glanced at Pumpkin and noticed she appeared to be anxious to give her report.

Zitzy responded, "I'm going to go over all the paperwork that's been piling up. I think I'll start with Jackson's reports."

"Okay Pumpkin, fill us in on your 'activity' last night."

"I caught that 'activity' bullshit, but it didn't happen. Nevertheless, Chaz is brilliant, fascinating, humorous, and very interesting." Did I not detect sparkles in her eyes? *And did I not also perceive a burning in my loins visualizing my having sex with her?*

"That aside, he might have given us a lead. Pauli Courtney, a vet who has a clinic in New Orleans East, which is heavily Asian, has a dubious reputation. The Medical Board has twice reproved him for using his clinic to treat people. Apparently, the folks in the Asiatic community seek out his services for themselves and their children because he charges less than established physicians. And...his services include veterinary care for large animals such as cattle and horses.

"But here's where it gets freaky. Within the past two to three months, two children's naked corpses were found in the marsh in New Orleans East Bayou Sauvage—they had been dead less than six hours. One was a ten-year-old Latino boy and the other was an Asian twelve-year-old girl—both had been raped. And Bayou Sauvage is near Courtney's clinic!

"They each tested positive for etorphine administered in their necks, and they were shot in the right temple with the same .38 caliber Smith & Wesson. The forensic analysis suggests that it was probably an older S&W Model 10 M&P, given the lands and groove markings on the bullets.

"And they were eviscerated! Chaz says the etorphine killed them before the head shots and before they were disemboweled. Chaz also said that the deaths had some of the earmarks of a ritualistic killing, except for the fact that the

children were already dead and the eviscerations were postmortem. Or it could simply be that the killers wanted the bodies to discompose or attract the alligators faster."

I told her we had to think about that congruity, and I instructed her to help Zitzy with the accumulated paperwork. "While you're at it Zitzy, brief her on what she's missed before coming here. And see if you can find an NOPD Missing Persons report on Adeline"

I was confronted with a bird's nest in a tangled fishing reel. The complexities of the case were interwound and knotted, and I was trying to untie the knots and extract order from disorder. Not having any luck, I decided to add to my somewhat trimmed down—but still dismal and formidable—former list, so I deleted some points and made additional notes:

1. *Although we had no physical evidence, we had scads of circumstantial evidence to implicate Father Duncan.*
2. *If he were the perp, Duncan probably wasn't flying solo.*
3. *The assumed abductions probably occurred at the Dome.*
4. *Was it only a coincidence Langdon and the two children had died after having etorphine administered to their necks?*
5. *Who were Duncan's co-conspirators?*
6. *What was their MO?*
7. *Were there more than Adeline and Lashanna abducted at the Dome?*
8. *If so, did the NOPD pick up on that trend?*
9. *What was the motive of the perps; i.e., their end game?*
10. *Did the mayor have a vested interest?*
11. *If not, why was she so antagonistic to our presence in the Dome?*
12. *Was the NOPD and/or Macklin involved in the coverup?*
13. *Did the NOPD receive the Missing Persons report from the SMPD?*
14. *If so, what progress had they made?*
15. *Were there Duncan abduction venues other than the Dome?*
16. *How can I get Sanderson to help us?*
17. *Why is box-level 6 off-limits?*
18. *Follow up on the veterinarian, Pauli Courtney.*
19. *....*

And my phone rang.

CHAPTER XXXVII
Macklin Groveling for Help

It was Macklin. "I need to see you, Régis!"

"Oh, are you going to make an appointment this time?"

Sounding desperate, he ignored the sarcasm. "This is important Régis; I need to see you. And soon!"

"Okay; when do you want to come to the office?"

"Not your office. I need you to meet me in Jefferson—how about Poppa's Poor Boy's on Claiborne Drive right off the Jefferson Highway. And hurry!"

Because I ate there often, I knew where it was.

He was almost pleading, and in the last few seconds, his desperation seemed to have clicked up about five notches.

"Do you mean now?"

"I'm already here; I'll be waiting for you."

"Give me about twenty-five minutes, and I'll be there."

I letter-folded my unfinished handwritten notes and slipped them into my inside jacket pocket, told Zitzy and Pumpkin to continue what they were doing, and said, "When Doughboy arrives, tell him to deliver the same briefing to you as he did to me last night."

They asked me where I was going, and I told them. Concerned about a setup, they began to issue cautions and requests to accompany me, but I was already out of the door.

In my car outside of Poppa's, I clicked on my Sony tape recorder and slipped it into my blazer's vest pocket.

A bit on the seedy side, Poppa's Poor Boy's was a tatty, duskily lit, hole-in-the-wall luncheonette with an uneven, multi-colored painted concrete floor, a miscellaneous assortment of timeworn tables and chairs, and one unisex bathroom. A tiny room with sagging louvered saloon doors was situated outside of the bathroom and housed two video poker machines. And adding to its bag lady ambience, a neglected 40-gallon fish tank with two snapping turtles was *in situ* against a portion of the back wall.

The limited menu featured underground, home-styled New Orleans fare

("good groceries") prepared from scratch by a buoyant, early seventies Black lady named Joyce who served mouth-watering *plats du jour* and, of course, po-boys made with Leidenheimer French bread. Poppa's is an esoteric gem.

Macklin, seated at a corner table near the fish tank, was ashen and as unkempt as the eatery in which I found him. I sat across from him, and the waitress, with a pot of coffee and a coffee mug, came to the table. "Coffee?" she asked.

I told her yes, and after she poured a cup for me, she asked me if I knew what I wanted to eat or did I want to look at the menu first. I acknowledged I did want to check the menu, and finally—at least for Macklin, for he was agitated—she left.

Having lost or shelved his querulous demeanor, he was timorous and fearful, whispering, "I need help."

"Why come to me?"

"Because you're a straight shooter."

"Tell me what's on your mind."

"It's about Dickerson, but there's so much more. I need you to save me from going to Angola." Angola is the sobriquet for the Louisiana State Penitentiary.

I saw panic in his weathered-copper eyes, and I sensed in him a deafening desperation. If Macklin were acting, he should have received an Emmy for outstanding lead actor in a dark drama series.

"What? Slow down and start at the beginning."

"I was told to soft-pedal the Dickerson case because it was bad publicity for the city. In fact, I was instructed to do so even before I reached the scene. And I was told to do what I had to do to keep you away from of the investigation or at least find out what you knew. I was also ordered to write the preliminary report as an accident."

"'Soft-pedal' is a euphemism., Macklin. You must have known it was no accident."

"Of course, I did. But I have a heavy burden, and I was being leveraged."

"How is that?"

"Regis, this is embarrassing as hell, but you need the full story. Because of her illness, my wife of thirty years and I haven't had sex for over a year. So a short while back, I had my first and only extramarital adventure. I know that you probably don't believe me, but that is one indelible fact of my life.

"My lieutenant set it up for me. He said that he felt sorry for me and that I needed to take some of the edge off of my life. Have a little fun, you know! In fact, he arranged a suite for me at the Dome.

"The girl was nubile and so damn desirable. But I suspected she was too young, so I asked her how old she was. She told me she had recently turned seventeen. I was suspect, but in a moronic moment, I let my small head do the thinking.

"About a week later, my lieutenant told me the girl was only fifteen, and "someone" at the Dome had photographs of us in the act. He also told me, 'I now own you Macklin.'"

"Was this the same supervisor who told you to downplay Dickerson's death?"

"Yes."

"What's his name?"

"Oh, don't make me disclose that Regis. If he hears about it, I'm doomed."

"Don't worry; I'll keep it secret."

"No, please, please. I can't, I can't."

I saw what I believed to be terror in his eyes. "Okay, not now. But eventually, I expect you to tell me." Of course, I could find that out on my own.

"Thanks, Regis.

"With my wife's terminal illness, not all her medical bills are covered by insurance, and they're exorbitant. I could retire, but seventy-five percent of my salary won't cut it. Besides, I need a job that provides me a little leeway to check on her during working hours, and I can do that while working homicide." I could have sworn he farted during his narrative; if so, perhaps it was due to angst.

"So, what's the cause for this last-minute panic? You surely tried to get me to withdraw."

"I know. But I was off yesterday. When I got in this morning, Dickerson's autopsy report was in my inbox, and I almost passed out when I read about the etorphine found in him.

"That's the same drug that killed two horribly mutilated, naked children found ten weeks ago near Bayou Sauvage in New Orleans East; both were classified by Missing Persons as runaways. Perhaps the sickos were depending on the alligators to dispose of the bodies, but somehow or another, they didn't.

"You don't have to be a homicide detective to make the connections. Something's up with underage children, Régis; it's big, and it centers around the

Dome. And even with my bullshit preliminary report, I'm being pressured to let the case fall into through the cracks.

"I'm in the middle of it all. If and when it breaks—and it has to—I'll certainly be indicted as a co-conspirator. Even if I were to escape prison, which I doubt, I'll be out on the street with no job and no pension. Please help me."

"Why should I, Macklin? You treated me like a piece of dogshit on your freshly shined shoes." Which weren't at all freshly shined.

The waitress returned, refilled our coffees, and asked us if we were ready to order. Macklin squirmed. I told her no, and she sashayed away.

Macklin said, "I know and I'm sorry. I suppose desperate men do desperate deeds. I can only hope you'll forgive me and help me."

"I suppose you expect me to trust you?"

"Hell no! I wouldn't if I were you. But I'm telling you the truth, and I'm shittin'-the-pants scared." Maybe the fart had been a shart.

"Why did you attend the funeral? How did it help your investigation?"

"Régis, the guy was a cop. I'm a cop. And he died on my watch. Moreover, I felt as guilty as sin for going along with trying to deep-six the case—I told him I was sorry as they slid his casket into the vault."

"I'm curious about this: Why did you have the Mayor's Office submit the press release about our confrontation when you knew I had the tape?"

"I didn't *get* them to submit the release. I told my lieutenant what happened, but I intentionally neglected to tell him about the tape. I wanted my lieutenant, the Department, the Mayor's Office, or all of them to have egg on their face."

"You weren't concerned that doing so would come back and bite you in the ass?"

"Of course, I was. But my story was—and is—that you taped me surreptitiously.

"And I have no proof, only rumors and innuendos, the unknown actors are on to you, and they're afraid of you. And you know fear makes one act with little or no conscience. Watch your back Régis."

"Thanks for the tip. And part of watching my back is mistrusting you.

"However, if you want my help, it's going to be a one-way street—*my* one-way street—until I feel I can trust you. If you put even a toenail over the line, I'll disembowel you like those kids were."

"Régis, you probably won't believe this—and I can't blame you—but I've been a good cop, an honest cop. And I never allowed myself to be sucked into the vortex of graft and corruption as many on the job have. I have kids, good kids. I don't want to die in ignominy. And I want to regain my dignity. I'll follow your lead.

"And besides saving my ass, I have one other small favor to ask you."

"What's that?"

"I know you're going to bust them, and I'd like to be in on it when you do."

"I'm not sure about that; there's still this 'small' matter of trust. I'll let you know.

"Now, here's my plan. First, you'll provide everything—and I mean everything—you have. And make a copy of your entire case file for me."

"That could get me in a lot of trouble, but I'll get everything that I can lay my hands on. I do need you to know up front that the higher ups are keeping a tight rein on the reports—I don't even have my own notes to share with you."

"Macklin, you're already in a lot of trouble. Suck 'em up and do it. Next, wait a few days and then apply for two weeks of annual leave, emergency leave, whatever. Better yet, tell them you have to take care of your wife. You want to be distanced as far away from this thing as you can when the powder keg explodes, and from what you've told me, I'm certain it will.

"I'll need any phone numbers you have so I can contact you without delay. And I'm going to give you my home phone for you to call me, but only *in an emergency.*

"And again, Macklin, if you deviate in any way, I'll be on you like white on rice."

"Okay, I understand." And he hit me with what I was waiting for: "Perhaps if you give me some of what you have, we can work together to solve this case more quickly."

"You think I'm a chump, don't you, Macklin?"

"Oh no, no. As I told you, I'm a cop, and I want to be part of the bust."

"I'll decide what role you'll play and when you'll play it. As of now, I don't trust you."

Cowering, he said, "You're right, I can't blame you. I'll bust my ass to show you that I am a stand-up guy."

"Get the file Macklin. And do it fast. If you dally, I'll assume you're being

uncooperative, and all bets will be off."

He said, "Okay Régis," and I arose, threw two dollars on the table for the coffee and a tip, told Miss Joyce goodbye, and left.

Once in my car, I switched off the recorder and took a deep breath. With a pang of apprehension, it dawned on me that I was going to be fighting off frenzied hyenas on the savanna of UBU synthetic turf in the Louisiana Superdome.

CHAPTER XXXVIII
Brainstorming

When I returned to the office, Zitzy, Doughboy, and Pumpkin were ready for lunch. I suggested we order takeout at Zimmer's Seafood and lunch al fresco at a shelter in the arboreal charm of City Park.

Once seated beneath the shelter near the Sydney and Walda Besthoff Sculpture Garden, we engaged in small talk until after we had polished off our meals.

I led off by asking Doughboy if he informed the crew about his investigative results in Saint Martinville, and he said he had.

I said, "Listen to this," and I played the Macklin tape. After it ran through, I said, "Like the extraordinary moment that occurs at the end of the third movement in Beethoven's Fifth Symphony, this case is building up to a crescendo. The skirmish has become a war.

"Zitzy, make several copies of this and keep them in safe places.

"Also, until Zitzy sweeps the office this afternoon and every morning thereafter, we won't discuss the case while there; that's why we're here now."

The three of them started talking at once, but I interrupted, "Wait a minute, before we begin, I want you to read some notes I have handwritten at different times; some of the tasks have been accomplished, and some of the questions answered; I plan to trim them down and consolidate them soon. Disregard those we know the responses to and those tasks we've already completed.

"We can't fulfill all of them at one time, so focus on the critical ones—there might be some duplicates. When I have a chance, I'll redraft and condense the issues, and we can look at them again. You'll see they're in chronological order, page one being the first set I wrote. Pass them around."

Page 1:

1. Who killed Langdon, and why was he killed?

2. How was Langdon killed? (The autopsy report should reveal that.)

4. Was the murder a conspiracy?

5. If so, who were the conspirators?

6. Who were the Saint Martinville fonts of the rumors about the sex slave trade at

the Dome?

7. How and why was Langdon involved?

8. Why did Langdon persist after he told me he was shutting the "inspections" down?

9. What did Langdon know?

10. With whom did Langdon share his intelligence?

    Gayle,

    Jackie,

    Jackson?

11. Why didn't Langdon share his information with me?

12. Macklin—background, Zitzy.

13. Jackson—possible source, Zitzy.

14. Leasean—possible source, Zitzy.

15. Rieglé—background, Zitzy; interview, me

16. Zitzy—schematic.

17. May and Bowditch—log anomaly, Zitzy.

18. Jackie—press for more info, Doughboy.

19. Autopsy report, Doughboy.

20. Follow-up—Gayle, me.

21. Langdon's benefits—Gayle, me.

Page 2:

1. We know where—the left rear side of Langdon's neck—but how was the etorphine administered?

2. Who would have had access to such a drug?

3. Was there more than one perpetrator?

4. Was the murder spontaneous or rehearsed beforehand?

5. Was the murder planned to look like an accident or a suicide?

Page 3:

1. Although we have no physical evidence, we have scads of circumstantial evidence to implicate Father Duncan.

2. If he were the perp, Duncan probably wasn't flying solo.

3. The assumed abductions probably occurred at the Dome.

4. Was it only a coincidence that Langdon and the two children had died of etorphine administered to the neck?

5. *Was it a coincidence the two missing girls were timid?*

6. *Who were Duncan's co-conspirators?*

7. *What was their MO?*

8. *Were there more than Adeline and Lashanna abducted at the Dome?*

9. *What was the motive of the perps; i.e., their end game?*

10. *Did the mayor have a vested interest?*

11. *If not, why was she so antagonistic to our presence in the Dome?*

12. *Was the NOPD and/or Macklin involved in the coverup?*

13. *Did the NOPD receive the Missing Persons report from the SMPD?*

14. *If so, what progress had they made?*

15. *Were there Duncan abduction venues other than St. Demetria's Catholic Church. and St. Riquier's church?*

16. *How can I get Sanderson to help us?*

17. *What information can we get from the housekeeping crew?*

18. *Follow up with the veterinarian, Pauli Courtney.*

19. *Are the children confined until they are sold, and if so, where?"*

"And I've buttoned on another one: Does Duncan make reservations for his Dome tours?"

After they had each read the notes in silence, they all wanted to contribute their ideas. But I said, "Let's get up to date, and we'll be in sync. Zitzy, what do you have for us?"

"I spoke with Breeze again last night, and it seems Duncan had a visitor—Donatien Huberty. Huberty stayed at the rectory for about an hour and left. Breeze wanted to tail him but decided it was better to sit on Duncan. He now thinks it would have been best to follow Huberty, because Duncan didn't move for the rest of the afternoon or evening."

"When you speak with him again, tell him there's no need for Monday-morning quarterbacking. Duncan is our prime suspect, and at this time, we have a bird in the hand and we don't want to lose it in attempt to get two in the bush."

"I've already told him that."

"Good. What is his time schedule? And is he changing disguises?"

"He put himself on a variable twelve-hour schedule. It's hit-or-miss, and he's limited, since he is the only one on point. He doesn't like having to get off-station

either. But when he slips away to stretch, eat, or use the facilities, it does afford him an opportunity to reposition.

"He says he doesn't think it's worth the effort to lose time by going to Baton Rouge to change cars, so somehow, he has managed to get other non-registered license plates, and he changes them daily. He also dirties the car one day and cleans it the next. One day he even hung fuzzy dice from the rearview mirror.

"Enlisting the aid of his wife, who, after taking his measurements, bought him two dresses. a bra, and a pair of woman's shoes to disguise him as a female—she also garishly applies his makeup."

"Tell him to make sure he records *all* of his time; he's going to have a helluva paycheck next month. Also remind him to put the dresses, the bra, the beard, and any other accessories he has to buy on his expense account. That should drive Larry Messina in Finance crazy.

"I don't suppose you and Pumpkin have had time to go through Jackson's reports?"

"We've begun. But except for the fact there are many more missing children than we first thought, we haven't found any that are directly related to our case, including the one on Adeline."

"If you can't find that one, see if Jackson can get it for you. And don't forget to sweep the office this afternoon. Also, contact Leasean, and find out if Duncan makes reservations. When you're finished with those tasks, continue to pore over the Jackson reports and pull any ones that might even be remotely related to missing children in the Dome.

"And by the way, Zitzy, can you determine if the telephones in our office are tapped?"

"I'm not sure; I'll try."

It was a sucker punch out of nowhere. I realized I had not been allocating resources to our best advantage. We were fishing with worms when we should have been baiting our hooks with live shrimp. We had multiple gossamer leads, but the most substantial one at the moment was Duncan. Even though he might be a bit player, he was the one we were most certain of. *How did you miss that? Were you really cut out for this work?*

"Pumpkin, this afternoon, contact Breeze on the radio. Meet him somewhere near the stakeout, and work out a schedule with him so the two of you in separate

vehicles can provide more coverage. Perhaps Duncan's moving during hours when Breeze is not on stakeout.

"But before that, early tomorrow morning, head to State Police Headquarters in Baton Rouge, and pick up a cool car. Ask for Captain Melancon; I'll work out the details. After you and Breeze agree on a schedule, call and inform Zitzy what it is. And stay in touch. After our meeting, go home and rest; you have a long day ahead of you tomorrow."

Pumpkin replied, "You know I've not had time to contact the dioceses regarding any other tours conducted by Duncan, don't you?"

That was important enough for her to delay her surveillance, so I told her to continue west through Baton Rouge tomorrow morning and go to the Lafayette Diocese and pick up the cool car on her way back.

"Got it," she said.

"Doughboy, you can help Zitzy with those reports."

"Done."

"This didn't happen in a vacuum; the clues are out there; we just have to dig— and maybe dig some more—until we find them. Okay, now we need some bleeding edge ideas."

Doughboy started, "Regardless whether or not Duncan has to make reservations, I think we've established a firm link between him and the Superdome. The two "missing persons" cases—Lashanna and Adeline— probably occurred at the Dome.

"Breeze saw Huberty going into the rectory. Why would he visit the priest? The Dome was not on the Saint Martinville itinerary. And I'd bet Duncan doesn't have to make formal reservations; he just has to make sure there are no other tours or events going on at the time when he conducts *his* tours.

"Therefore, I would say Duncan's co-conspirator or co-conspirators are in supervisory and/or administrative levels in the Dome, and Huberty is one. Perhaps because of your visit, Duncan is shaky, and he needed a pep talk."

"We should keep that on the table" I replied.

Pumpkin said, "I think, based on everything we have *and* the unverified rumors of sex slave trade, our working theory should be the children have been abducted for that reason."

Doughboy interjected, "This might be in left field and perhaps a logistical

unfeasibility, but if we consider that the Dome is a focal point, and if we accept Pumpkin's theory, could those 'off-limits' Level 6 suites be where the sex slave enterprise takes place?"

"It's a long shot," said Zitzy, "but we have to consider all possibilities."

Pumpkin offered, "Would the kids be rented or sold?"

Doughboy hesitated and then responded, "Perhaps both, but if they are sold, the buyer would have to pick up his purchase at another location."

Pumpkin posited, "Langdon must have discovered something critical, so the perps had to eliminate him. I say 'perps' because this couldn't have been a solo hit."

"Why?" I asked.

"Because the space between the seats and the wall rail in Section 347 is narrow. I think they hemmed him in between them. I also theorize that he was struck from behind with the etorphine hypodermic, and if so, the killer was left-handed."

"You've checked out Section 347?" I asked.

"Of course, I did; it was the scene of the crime!"

With admiration, I said, "Very well done, Pumpkin. And I believe your theory has merit; I, too, think we might be looking for a lefthanded assassin who injected him from behind."

"Perhaps Langdon was still looking for—or had found—the finishing touch, and that is why he didn't give up his investigative efforts after he told you he would," said Doughboy.

And we all agreed.

I asked, "Is there a connection between the two juvenile murders and the presumed abductions at the Dome?"

Zitzy said, "Other than the endorphin, we don't have a direct link, but I think we seriously should consider there is one." Doughboy, Pumpkin, and I agreed.

"Is it simply a coincidence the two missing girls were timid?" I queried.

Doughboy said, "I think not. First, it would be easier to isolate them. Secondly, because they were respectful and trusting in elders, they would more easily respond to an adult, especially an adult who would take an interest in them. And lastly, from what we've learned, Adeline and Lashanna are reclusive, and they would be the ones less likely to be missed."

"Good points!" exclaimed Zitzy.

"Was the murder planned to look like a suicide or an accident?" I questioned.

There was no consensus on this. The three of them tossed around suggestions from, "Yes, it was," to "The murderers didn't care, and it was lagniappe the mayor, via Macklin's lieutenant, pushed him to write it up as an accident."

"But in any event, it had to have been planned well beforehand." said Zitzy.

"I agree," I said. "Why do you think Langdon was killed?"

Doughboy fielded that one. "Jackie confirmed Langdon indicated he was winding up his investigation, and he was preparing to give you a report. He must have unearthed a critical aspect but was discovered in the process. And like Pumpkin said, the conspirators had to prevent that, so they killed him."

"I think you're right. Is the Mayor a suspect," I asked the group?

Again, there was no agreement; the responses ranged from her just not wanting us there to yes, she is part of the enterprise. Zitzy's answer was, "She's a nasty bitch, but that doesn't make her a co-conspirator. Nevertheless, a lot goes on in the sleazy backwater politics of New Orleans, so I don't think we should eliminate her."

But Doughboy was adamant, "The Mayor *has* to be a suspect. Why else would she be obstructing our investigation?"

"Well," said I, "inferring that might be a big leap. She could simply be concerned about the PR aspect for the city. Poor Dome security tarnishes her public image. And under her leadership, 'her' police are viewed as incapable to do the job at the Dome we're doing, and she's not happy with that."

Doughboy's rejoinder was, "Quite frankly, I think she's running the entire operation, and she's sexually abusing the children, herself. I just believe she is that kind of person."

"That sounds like a stretch, but we can consider it," I dubiously responded, since I believed Doughboy's take on the mayor's involvement was nothing more than an illusion fueled by his animus toward her.

Nevertheless, this group was brilliant, far more perceptive than I. Besides, I would shoot myself in the foot if I were to discourage them for blue-sky thinking. So even with Doughboy's questionable hypothesis, I said, "Exceptional ideas! Let's give them serious consideration. Any other comments?" And at that moment, there were none.

Changing the subject, I asked, "Okay, what would it tell us if we were to learn Duncan needs no formal reservations to tour the Dome?"

Pumpkin said, "I don't think it points to any one person in particular—except maybe Huberty—but it would be highly suggestive Duncan has connections at the Dome. Whether those connections are part of a conspiracy is speculative."

"I would give it more weight than speculative," countered Doughboy. "Look, we're almost certain Duncan plays a significant role in the abductions. He doesn't do it alone, and there is some relationship between him, the Dome, and Huberty. Although not independently conclusive, when taken together, those factors are more consequential than 'speculative.'"

"Any other impressions?" I asked.

"My impression is that we get back to work," said Zitzy. "And I'm going to chat with Leasean if he's available and burn some midnight oil going over those reports. Are you in, Doughboy?"

"Sure," he responded. But I wondered if he would have been so enthusiastic if Jackie were not still in Saint Martinville?

"I'd like to help you guys, but I have a working date tonight," said Pumpkin smiling.

With a salacious grin, Zitzy said, "Yeah, we know what you'll be working on. *Did I not feel stabs of lechery and envy of my own?*

I cautioned them, "This probably goes without saying, but don't leave any of your notes in the office; we're vulnerable there. And do not discuss this business aloud in the office until after Zitzy sweeps it."

Nodding their heads in unison, we headed back to the Dome.

CHAPTER XXXIX
More Questions and Skeleton Theories

I called the AG's Office and spoke with the General. "We have a delicate situation here, General; can you call me at home tonight?"

"What the hell's going on, Régis?"

"I don't want to discuss it now; will you please call me tonight?" Although piqued, he agreed, and we signed off.

And I revised and consolidated my handwritten notes. The results were:

Outstanding questions.

1. Who killed Langdon, and why was he killed?

2. A coverup—why?

3. Was the murder a larger-than-two conspiracy?

4. If so, who were the murderous conspirators?

5. How was Langdon involved?

6. What did Langdon know?

7. Langdon's benefits, Gayle?

8. How was the drug administered?

9. Who would have had access to such a drug?

10. Who were Duncan's co-conspirators?

11. What was their MO?

12. Were there more than Adeline and Lashanna missing (or abducted) at the Dome?

13. Did the mayor have a vested interest?

14. If not, why was she so antagonistic to our presence in the Dome?

15. Was the NOPD and/or Macklin involved in the coverup, and can Macklin be trusted?

16. Did the NOPD receive the Missing Persons report from the SMPD?

17. If so, what progress had they made?

18. Were there Duncan abduction venues other than those related to the Dome?

19. How can I get Sanderson to help us?

20. Why is box level 6 off-limits?

21. Who leases suites on Level 6?

22. *Are the Level 6 suites, more particularly, the mayor's suite, off-limits for the housekeeping crew?*

23. *Why were the two Bayou Sauvage children killed and afterward eviscerated?*

24. *What is the connection, if any, between them and the two abductees?*

25. *Did the veterinarian, Pauli Courtney, play a role?*

26. *Does Duncan make reservations for his Dome tours?"*

27. *Who is Duncan's mystery assistant?*

28. *How were the abductions carried out?*

29. *What is Rieglé's background, and how does he fit into the picture?*

Working theories (subject to change):

1. *Langdon had discovered something important about pedophile sex trading in the Dome, and he was murdered because of it.*

2. *The two missing girls, Lashanna and Adeline were most probably abducted at the Dome.*

3. *Although we have no physical evidence, we have enough to implicate Father Duncan in child abductions.*

4. *It is likely Duncan isn't flying solo.*

5. *Most likely, the motive of the perps is sex slavery and reaping the profits therefrom.*

6. *There are connections among the abductions of Lashanna and Adeline.*

7. *There is a connection between Langdon's murder, and the killing of the two juveniles.*

8. *Huberty is a new—and viable—suspect.*

9. *The mayor might or might not be involved in the scheme.*

After completing the notes, I went home and awaited the AG's call.

"What do you want to talk about, Régis?"

"We've had some major developments here, General. And I am not sure at the moment that the phones in our offices are secure." After I related to him that which we had carried out and uncovered, I said, "We need more manpower."

"I can't help you there; it was a stretch to send Pumpkin. You're going to have to make do. Watch your ass, Régis."

Natalie had overheard my conversation, and she brought me a glass of Cabernet Sauvignon. She rubbed my shoulder, while plying me with all of the right

questions to animate my mental process, but it was unavailing. At length, she asked me if I weren't placing myself in danger, and I replied, "I don't think so." But my response fell way short of placating her, and I suspected it would be a two-rosary night.

I dreamt I was alone on a butte in Monument Valley with no way to climb down. And I could see a dust storm kicked up by the horses of my nemeses who planned to hurl me off. *What ever happened to those most pleasant erotic sex dreams I used to have?*

Tormented the Dome situation was way beyond my ken, I slept the sleep of the damned.

CHAPTER XL
The Uprise of Piquant Facts

Zitzy had swept the office and found it clean. And although he couldn't be sure, he believed the phones were not tapped. He next chronicled his progress.

"I was able to speak with Leasean. He told me that Duncan never made formal reservations when he brought his tours to the Dome. The security supervisors were notified of the group's impending arrival and directed to allow them access. And it was always when there were no other tours going on."

I asked, "Who notifies them of the field trips?"

"Most often, it's Rieglé, and sometimes it's Huberty. But there's a strange twist. The security officers are called from their posts and provided with training throughout the duration of the tour.

"It seems to me that the security force receives an inordinate amount of instruction. And one should expect at least some security to be around during a tour. It doesn't make sense.

"Nevertheless, the supervisors are told that the kids are inner-city residents, and they are averse to authority figures in uniform. He also noted that Duncan is assisted by a tall, thin, unknown Hispanic female who meets him at the entrance when he arrives."

Zitzy continued, "Leasean thinks that the kids are allowed to run helter-skelter around the Dome, and when it's time to leave, Duncan summons them with three blasts on a whistle. Immediately afterward, Duncan scurries them out of the building onto the waiting bus. But it is peculiar no one ever sees the Hispanic lady leaving the Dome.

"He also said that some of the rank-and-file security officers have remarked about hearing the freight entrance opened and closed when the children are in the Dome, because they are concerned one or more of the kids might leave the Dome, and they'll have to spend the day looking for them in the surrounding area. Moreover, it seems the kids are using the Dome's electric golf carts, as the officers find them repositioned when they return to patrol duty."

"Unfortunately," I said, "I didn't have that information when I questioned Duncan. Among other things, I'm curious about the carts and the Mystery Lady.

But we sure as hell can't question him now without raising another shitstorm and revealing our strategy.

"What about Jackson's Missing Persons reports?"

Doughboy said, "Nothing jumped out at us that could directly help our case. But we were both amazed there are so many missing children reported in New Orleans. And we noted a trend; most of them were Black, Hispanic, and Asian.

"And, even more interesting, they are almost all are classified by the NOPD as runaways, yet the narratives of the reports indicated the parent or parents didn't believe it was so. Something's wrong with that picture."

"It's another piece to the puzzle, and I'm not sure if or where it fits. But we need to remember that anything that does not make sense, or seems out of place could be a clue."

Pumpkin called collect. "I just left the Lafayette Diocese. I spoke with a transitional deacon; it's the last step before receiving Holy Orders and being ordained a priest. Johnny, I have to tell you; I think the gay pedophile image is overblown. This guy was as straight—and as randy—as they come. He was not at all bashful about hitting on me; he even asked me for my phone number.

"But anyway, at first he didn't want to give me any information; you know what with the pedophile scandals how tight-lipped those Catholics are. But when he—Michael—started to flirt, I decided to reciprocate. And before I did, I went to the restroom, where I unbuttoned the top button of my blouse and fluffed my hair. When I returned, I leaned over the desk and gave him a full view of my décolleté, and he started to not-too-subtly rub his crotch.

"To make a long story short, I gave him my phone number, and he gave me the information. Father Duncan is no longer performing ad hoc duties, nor is he conducting tours, at least not in the Lafayette Diocese. I suppose it was a wasted trip."

"No not at all. Pick up the cool car, and when you arrive back in Metairie, call Zitzy or me. Station yourself outside our parking lot exit, but don't bring the recon car into the Dome. Tell Captain Melancon I again said thanks."

"Okay, I should be there in about three or four hours."

CHAPTER XLI
Is Macklin Bridling Me?

I called Macklin and reached him at home. "Do you have those reports for me?"

"Yeah, but it wasn't easy…"

I cut him short. I didn't need to hear how he sacrificed himself for the cause. "Meet me in an hour at Gennaro's on Metairie Road in the shadow of the Causeway overpass."

"But…"

"No buts, Macklin; be there!"

"Okay." He seemed to be vexed.

"Zitzy, we're changing the game plan." This was becoming a common occurrence, but not out of the ordinary for a complex investigation. "Get in touch with Breeze and have him meet us in about three or four hours at the same location in City Park. Pumpkin is going to call; have her meet us there when she gets back from Lafayette and Baton Rouge.

"Doughboy, I want you there too. In the meantime, Zitzy, do some research on Rieglé. And Doughboy, you do the same with the veterinarian, Courtney. Also, Zitzy, find out from Breeze what car Huberty drives.

"Doughboy, contact Jackie and ask her if she knows anyone on the security staff who has horses or contacts at the Fairgrounds [the New Orleans hippodrome]."

"What's going on," asked Zitzy?

"The short story is I believe Duncan is running scared, and we have to change priorities. I'll give you the rest of it at City Park."

I reviewed my lists and reflected on my meeting with Macklin.

I grew up five blocks away from Gennaro's. It is one of the oldest bars—if not the oldest—in Metairie. It was established in 1937 and has not missed a beat yet. Their menu includes some of the New Orleans area's best comfort food around.

It's a combination bar and restaurant, and the sprawling bar is a work of art, especially the back bar which is hand-carved and sports a large, sculpted, bevel-edged mirror. Metairie residents were eating and drinking there before I was

born.

Parking under the four-level Causeway Boulevard overpass, I turned on my recorder.

Seated at a four-chaired table, Macklin was eating the specialty of the house, a roast beef po-boy. He didn't get up nor offer to shake hands which was just as well, since they were—as they should have been—covered in mayonnaise and gravy.

As I was sitting down, the waitress appeared, "Coffee, iced tea, beer?" she asked.

"Coffee. What do you have Macklin?"

With a mouthful of food some mayonnaise and gravy on his chin, he pointed to two new, thin file folders on the table. I picked them up and said, "Is this all there is?"

"That's what I was trying to tell you. That's only the preliminary report; the rest of the investigation is shuttered and put on ice. Moreover, I was ordered to give all of my field notes to the lieutenant. I'm in homicide, and it's supposedly my case, but I couldn't even get close to it. I have no access to what any of the other investigators have found, and I can't get the forensic reports, just the coroner's report"

"You're bullshitting me Macklin. It *is* your case. You're holding out on me."

He winced and said, "No, Régis, no. I tried! Right now, I'm not the most liked guy in the group. I even got a veiled threat that if I persisted, I was going to be retired. Why would I lie to you? You're my only hope; you're my lifeline.

"I don't even understand why some of my good friends on the Homicide Unit are avoiding me like the plague. These are guys that I have known and trusted for years. I told you that you're my only hope. I don't want to go down on the wrong side of this.

"I don't blame you. You have no reason to trust me after the way that I treated you, and the way that I gave in to the politicos. But I'm telling you the truth"

I scrutinized his face and studied his body language for a sign or signs of prevarication, but the only thing I could see was fear; thus, I had to accept it *faute de mieux*. "I'm not sure I believe you, and if I find out you lied to me, I'll cut your balls off.

"Why do you think the case is so under wraps? Is it a coverup to avoid bad

press for the city or to hide criminal activity?"

"I suspect criminal activity. I overhear rumors—just rumors—that the Chief is nothing more than a marionette, and the mayor is pulling his strings. He's hanging on to his job like I am with mine."

"Well, you must still have some friends there. See what else you can dig up."

"I will, I still have a friend or two there...I hope!"

CHAPTER XLII
New and Intriguing Developments

Outside, I called Zitzy on the radio. He told me he had arranged the meeting in City Park for 2:00.

I headed to my rumination spot to mull over the situation. As before, the lake and the lakefront were serene and conducive to reflection. I knew we had something, but I didn't know what that "something" was. For the moment, I had to accept how inadequate I was at this, because no new revelations knocked on my conscious cognitive portal.

The crew was awaiting me, and we sat en banc.

I gave Zitzy the recorded Macklin tape and the skimpy reports I had received from him, and I directed Zitzy to review them and provide me with a synopsis. I thereafter apprised the crew with the results of my meeting with Macklin. Their general consensus was espoused by Zitzy who said, "That motherfucker!"

"Maybe so, Zitzy. But somehow, I don't believe he was lying. I get the feeling that he is on the level, which adds another area of complexity to all of this." Even as I said that, I hoped I was not getting soft on Macklin.

We again addressed the possibility of the mayor's involvement, and Doughboy said, "Even though it's only a distant firefly blip in late evening, I don't think we should ignore the possibility of the mayor's part in the abductions. For something like this to work, it has to be handled at a very high level."

Breeze, checking out Pumpkin's boobs, was somewhat distracted. "Glad to have you with us, Breeze. Do you have anything new to report?"

"No. Except for Huberty's visit, Duncan is sitting tight," and he returned his gaze to those delightful gourds.

I asked Pumpkin to fill the crew in on her visit to the diocese, and she did. Following up, I asked Zitzy and Doughboy if they had made any progress on the assignments I had given them.

Doughboy reported he had asked Jackie about anyone on the security staff who had horses. "She told me she didn't, but she had once overheard Bowditch telling someone he had, at one time, been a trainer at the Fairgrounds. And she also told me that, although she has no compelling reason for it, she's wary of

him."

Zitzy said "So far, Rieglé is clean. I called Kim Felder, the General's administrative assistant. As you know she's our unofficial liaison with the FBI. She said she'd get on it as soon as possible and call me back with whatever else she can find out. And I took it upon myself to call Jackson to ask him if he could locate a report on Adeline. He told me he would try, and he would let me know."

"Good," I said, "tell Jackson we need as many juvenile Missing Persons reports from throughout the city as he can get us."

"I had a little more success with Courtney," reported Doughboy. "As Chaz told Pumpkin, he has been disciplined by the Medical Board on three occasions for medical treatment of Asians, and he presumably does have a large-animal veterinary practice, mostly cattle and horses.

"But the interesting part is he lives in a 6,000 square-foot house in Eden Isles and has three vehicles registered to him. All later and expensive models, they are a Mercedes 600, a Mercedes 450 SLC, and a Ford 350 Econoline panel van. The obvious question is: Where does a veterinarian with a practice in New Orleans East get the money to live that lifestyle?"

"It convinces me we have to again reallocate our resources," I said. "Breeze, spend this evening and tomorrow morning and afternoon at the rectory. Starting day-after-tomorrow, I need you to stake out Courtney. I would suggest you find out what his office hours are and arrive there about three hours before closing. I don't think you'll have to continue past one or two a.m., but if he's on the move, follow him until he returns home. As before report in to Zitzy."

Breeze asked me, "Why not stay on Duncan; isn't he the firmest suspect we have?"

"Yes, he is. But I believe he's gone white feather, and at least for the time being, he's out of the abduction business.

"Along with that, Doughboy, check with the New Orleans Diocese to see if Duncan's notified them of his 'tour' retirement, too. Try to do it this afternoon and let me know as soon as possible."

"Will do," said Doughboy. And soon afterward, he notified me Duncan had withdrawn from the excursions.

"And Pumpkin, I want you to start tailing Huberty and essentially keep the same schedule as I told Breeze to do with Courtney. What kind of a car does he

drive, Zitzy?"

"A new maroon Buick Skylark 4-Door Sedan, and he parks on the same level we park."

"Zitzy, there has to be a lead in those Missing Persons reports, so you might want to go over them again. Or perhaps you might discover something in the new ones you'll hopefully receive from Jackson—press him for those. Also focus on the number of missing juveniles from the New Orleans East area."

Asking the group if they had any questions for me or their colleagues, I was answered with mumblings of noes and uh-uhs. So I said, "I'm working on a plan I can't now disclose to all of you, so in the future, if the need arises, you won't have to perjure yourselves under oath.

"This case is more complicated than the *New York Times* Sunday crossword puzzle. We're given clues, but they're nebulous. Nevertheless, if we work on it as a team, we should be able to solve this conundrum." But I wasn't as confident as I had projected.

Frenetic about the children, that night I faced another nocturnal monster. I dreamt I was a medic on a battlefield surrounded by death, dying, and anguish. I couldn't do anything for the dead ones. And worse, the only relief I could give the dying was a bullet to the head and, to the others in excruciating pain, only aspirins. *I had to save those kids!*

CHAPTER XLIII
Father Confessor Goes to Confession

When he slid open the confessional window, I said, "Bless you Father for you have sinned," doing so as deftly as I could with the best alto I could muster.

<><><>

After I left the crew at City Park, I went home. Taking a cue from Breeze—and Sherlock Holmes—I said, "Natalie, I need your help."

"What's that?"

"I'd like you to come with me to a thrift store and select a wig, a woman's dress, and a handbag for me."

"Why?"

"Because I need a disguise for tomorrow morning."

"Again, why?"

"I'll tell you about it later; let's go."

When in the car I explained the situation to her, she said, "This I have to see. Can your male ego handle it?"

"I hope I can, but I'll need lessons from you on how to be a doddering old lady."

"Hey! What makes you think that I would know how to be a doddering old lady?" she responded with a plucky half-smile. Considering I had already pushed the envelope, and out of a strong sense of survival, I elected not to answer.

We first went to Fifi Mahoney's Wig Shop in the French Quarter, where she picked out a shoulder-length, dirty-blond wig with bangs to cover my forehead. At a Goodwill store, we bought a long-sleeved, button-up, brown and beige checkered dress; a long-sleeved button-up sweater; a beige and white, daisy print headscarf; a DD-cup bra; white knee socks; somewhat soiled tennis shoes; and a large, well-worn, paisley, steampunk carpet bag.

When we returned home, I had a dress rehearsal. After donning the bra stuffed with socks, I admired myself in the mirror. Swirling, and squeezing my "tits," I said, "Oh, look at this luscious rack I have." *Did I have latent desires to be a crossdresser?*

Her rejoinder was "Yeah, you do have the doddering old lady thing right, but

you're one ugly woman."

Everything fit, but I was uncomfortable as hell—thank goodness I didn't have to wear panties. *Would I have liked to have done that too?*

Natalie would painstakingly put makeup on me in the morning. And it perplexed that me women had to brook so much inconvenience.

<><><>

Both surprised and irate, Father Duncan said, "What the…. I beg your pardon, Ma'am!"

<><><>

The night before, I had called Breeze and asked him to change plans and pick me up from my home at 7:30 the next morning. Seeing me in drag, Breeze chaffed me, saying, "Your tits are bigger than mine were, but I was still sexier than you."

Directing him to drive me to the church, I told him to wait outside. I realized I was perilously pushing the boundaries of my abilities. *Am I up for this?*

I seated myself in one of the last pews and ostensibly participated in 9:00 Mass. Shortly after the service, I saw Duncan enter the confessional. There were a few hangers-on—those who felt a spiritual need to regenerate their souls and needed more grace than Mass and Communion could give them, as well as a handful of self-perceived sinners waiting to seek dispensation for their misdeeds.

As the confessions progressed, the faithful who had needed lagniappe grace filtered out. The penultimate, conscience-stricken flagellant was a diminutive granny. And after she entered the right side of the confessional, I hesitated, and I went in on the other side. Except for Duncan, the little old lady penitent, and me, the church was deserted.

I could hear the oldster sob as she told Duncan she had been lusting after and then masturbating because of her young bodybuilder neighbor. And after five or six minutes of confessing her other nonexistent sins, Duncan gave her absolution with a penance of saying a rosary, which she was probably going to do anyway.

I had arranged the tape recorder in my bra, and I had stuffed my purse with newspapers. And considering the possibility Duncan was armed, on top of the papers, I had placed a .32 caliber automatic with a silencer.

<><><>

Sotto voce, I said, "If you have a gun, don't go for it. I have a thirty-two with a

160

silencer pointed at your heart. I have no intention, whatsoever, to shoot you unless you try to shoot me."

"I'm a priest, and priests don't carry guns."

"But you're a dirty priest, and I don't trust you."

Fidgeting, he said, "What do you want?"

"I want to save you from going to the electric chair,"

Still irate, but a little more shaky, he said, "What do you mean?" Duncan conveyed an aura of intelligence, but having led a somewhat cloistered life, he fell well short on street smarts.

"You're a pathetic fallacy. We know what you've been doing, and we have enough evidence to have a grand jury indict you. Resigning from your 'tours' and hiding behind the mayor's skirt isn't going to save you.

"Even if she could rescue you—or even want to, which I doubt—from State prosecution, the FBI will pursue you with Federal charges. And you know how relentless they are in their persecution of child abduction cases."

A little shakier, he tried to muster bravado, "Who the hell are you?"

"I'm Matilda, and you're going to waltz with me or be executed in the State Penitentiary."

"What evidence do you have I performed those preposterous deeds?"

"We have you cold for two abductions, and we believe there are more—we'll be certain in a couple of days. But I think we can also prove you were involved as an accessory in the gruesome murders of the two children found near Bayou Sauvage."

He responded quickly, maybe too quickly, "It wasn't me! I didn't have anything to do with that." That was a tell; I knew I was on the right track.

"Perhaps not, but you knew about it and you concealed it. How is it going to look when a pedophile priest—one to whom they've trusted and confess their sins— is tried before a jury of his peers, and besides being a pedophile and responsible for the abduction of innocent children, covers up the brutal murder of two other children?"

"I swear to God, I didn't know anything about it."

"God doesn't like liars, Father, especially when they invoke his name to do so. Isn't that called blasphemy?

"Oh yes, you knew about it. And even if you didn't—but you did—who's going

to believe you; you, the worst of all hypocrites, who has hidden his abominable deeds behind his white collar and has betrayed his flock? I'll tell you who—no one! Unless you come forward, you're going to fry on Earth in the electric chair, and after that, you're going to roast in Hell."

"You might be a hypocrite too. Why do you want to help me?"

"I might be an unflagging optimist, but I believe at one time you were a good priest. Yet you're Irish, and like all Irishmen, you are highly sexual. But you were restrained by the asinine and oppressive vow of celibacy. You couldn't risk being ensnared by a woman who might tell all, so you chose a safer route—altar boys. And I believe you were found out and subsequently blackmailed into doing the 'tours.'"

He started to cry without restraint, and between wails, he repetitively pleaded, "God, please forgive me." Yet another tell.

"You more than anyone should know confession is good for the soul. And in this case, it might be good for your well-being. Let's sit in the back of the church and talk." With that, I slipped my gun back into my purse, and we both arose.

But as we exited the confessional, I sensed dubiety in him. And he began to reach through his cassock pocket opening. I spun him around, tripped him, and he fell to the floor. Kneeling on his neck, I frisked him, and unsurprisingly, I found a .32 caliber revolver in his pocket. This was a third tell—he was afraid of something or somebody.

"Were you going to shoot me and add to your already long list of crimes and sins against your God?"

"No, you didn't give me a chance. I was going to surrender my gun to you. You're not a woman; you're a man!"

I ignored the obvious question.

Perhaps he was telling the truth…or he could have had plans to kill me and claim it was self-defense. But no matter what he might have done in the moment, he was in fear of his life.

"Now, do you want to help yourself, or are you going to keep playing games. I have our confessional—and confrontational—conversation on tape. If I leave now, you'll be vulnerable to Federal investigation. Or worse, much worse, I can provide the tape to those who are your associates. "They don't like weak links, and they have already determined you are one. Didn't Huberty recently give you

a pep talk?"

Astonished, he said, "How do you know about that?" This was the fourth tell in less than that many minutes—I was on a roll.

I again ignored the question, saying, "Think about what they'll do to you if they believe you are going to go canary on them; you'll probably meet the same fate as did those innocents. And you'll have the opportunity to see your guts spill out of you before you die an agonizing death."

He continued bawling.

"It's over for you, Duncan. And you can take my word; if I walk out of here now—with your gun—I won't hesitate to provide the tape, of which there shall be multiple copies, to the FBI *and* your associates. And I'd bet my balls your accomplices will get to you faster than the federal authorities will.

"On the other hand, I can't promise you a reduced sentence if you cooperate. But historically, the courts have looked with favor on participants who have provided evidence in big cases. Who knows? In the best of all worlds, you could be farmed out to the pedophile-priest treatment facility in Jemez Springs, New Mexico."

"Who *are* you?"

I dropped the feminized voice and showing him my ID said, "I thought you would have guessed by now; I'm Agent Johnny Régis, the same guy who interviewed you a week or so ago. You didn't think we were going to stop investigating simply because of the bogus press report couched in tumid political prose put out by the Mayor's Office, did you?"

"I was hoping it would." And another tell.

"As you know, hope is one of the three theological virtues. But there was no virtue in that hope, nor was there virtue in the faith you placed in the mayor and perhaps others. And what charity have you dispensed to those innocent children—the charity of suffering and death?"

"No, no, no," and he began to bawl again.

We sat in the back of the church, and I decided to give him a litmus test. If he failed, it would hamper our investigation, but if he passed, he'd be an invaluable font of information. "You're not under arrest; you're free to go anytime you wish. But if you leave, this recording will be in the hands of the FBI and your criminal confederates today.

"I'm stepping out for a few moments. You can choose to run back to the rectory; I won't pursue you. But you should wait for me. If you cooperate, I'll not forward the tape to either of those groups at this time—I may, however, have to eventually turn it over to the FBI. Before you make your decision, think about what your blackmailers would do to you.

"But more importantly, I believe religious dogma still lives loudly within you. I think you still believe in the New Testament passages, more particularly, 1 John 1:9 which says, 'If we confess our sins, He is faithful, and just, and will forgive us our sins and purify us from all unrighteousness,' as well as the many other ones that speak of God's forgiving nature. Let your conscience be your guide and decide what you want you to do."

Outside, Breeze was awaiting me, and his sapphire eyes, deep-set in his thin face, alit when he saw me. With a heartfelt grin, he told me he was beginning to worry. I narrated what had transpired, and I asked him to turn on his recorder and accompany me into the church.

Entering there, I was relieved to find Duncan where I had left him, kneeling on the kneeler with tears running down his flushed wet cheeks, and his hands clasped apparently in prayer.

Seating ourselves on either side of him, I said, "Father, this is Agent Dan Brisolaro, and we both have questions for you." Breeze and I withdrew our tape recorders and announced we were interviewing Father Baugh Duncan who has volunteered to be an informant without any promise of eliminated or reduced sanctions against him. After giving him his Miranda rights and with the usual prefaces (date, time, location), the highlights of that which we learned were:

- He had indeed been blackmailed for pedophilia with two Black boys, and the blackmailer was Huberty.
- The Mayor and Huberty were an item. (I almost felt sorry for Huberty.)
- But he didn't believe they were associates in the child abduction scheme. In fact, from his perspective, the mayor, having done so much for the Black community, was an altruist. *But if she weren't involved, why had her office so desperately tried to protect him?*
- He surmised the children were farmed out for sale to millionaires during major Superdome events.
- He didn't know where the children were kept or how many there were.

164

- He had taken part in the abduction of three other children, one from Santa Maria Church in Houma, Terrebonne Parish; one from Saint Bartholomew Church in Raceland, Lafourche Parish; and one from Mary Queen of Asia Church in New Orleans East.
- He also informed us Saint Bartholomew was a predominately African-American church, Santa Maria was mostly Hispanic, and as the name implied, Mary Queen of Asia was chiefly Asian. (I planned to later have Zitzy or Doughboy check them out.)
- He said he believed all the children he abducted were sold to millionaires who could give them a better life. (I, on the other hand, believed it was a self-deception he fostered in an attempt to assuage his guilty conscience.)
- He had heard a rumor one of the abducted boys about seven years old had two functional penises, and he was going to be sold for close to $250,000. He couldn't recall who told him, but he thought it was Huberty.
- Informing us of the MO he employed at the Dome, he said as they entered the building, he met an Asian female. (But hadn't Leasean told Zitzy the woman was Hispanic? Nevertheless, because I didn't want to break his oration, I decided not to press him on that issue.)
- He didn't know her name or who her employer was, but someone had told him she was the wife of a doctor.
- Having been with the children throughout the day, he would select a child who would be most vulnerable, and he would subtly point her or him out to his anonymous accomplice.
- He said the abducted children were offered a ride in one of the electric carts, and they were then whisked outside through the freight door to the doctor's van. But he didn't know where they were taken after that.
- Except for vaguely recalling someone indicating the two slaughtered children were Asian runaways who might have been sex slave children, he had no further knowledge of them, except one of them could have been a girl he abducted from Mary Queen of Asia.

Throughout the interview, Duncan cried, shuddered, and shook his large head from side to side. As heinous as his deeds were, I felt a twinge of pity for him.

This could be the touchstone of our case. So I decided not to arrest him; doing

so would drive his confederates underground. Instead of that, I told him that we could offer him witness protection, but I would have to arrange it through the AG's Office, and it would take a day or two. "In the meantime, stay low."

He agreed, but I again stressed to him how foolish it would be to notify his associates of our meeting. "If you do that, it will be your death warrant, Father, and I'm certain they won't tarry." We left him sobbing in the back of his church.

Perhaps this was our big break, but we still had a lot more weft and warp to spin before we had a tapestry. *You might have carried the day with this one. But don't be too cocksure; recognize your world of shortcomings and allow for them.*

We were at an inflexion point. Duncan's confession became a menopause in our probe, and it beseemed a "menostart." Now unencumbered with interruptive investigative menses, we had a fresh impetus, and our investigation took on a new life.

CHAPTER XLIV
Following Up on Duncan's Leads

While Breeze was driving me back home to change, I directed him to pair up with Pumpkin, inform her of the new developments, and for the two of them to each work overlapping shifts, Pumpkin to surveille Huberty from 11:00 a.m. to 11:00 p.m. and Breeze to surveille Courtney from 1:00 p.m. to 1:00 a.m. I felt the most productive movements would be between 4:00 and 9:00 in the afternoon and evening hours, and it might require a double team to avoid losing them.

Relieved to be out of drag and free from the makeup Natalie had virtually plastered on with a mortar trowel, I returned to the office in the afternoon. Once there, I briefed Zitzy and Doughboy about the morning's events with Duncan and the surveillance arrangements for Breeze and Pumpkin.

I gave the Duncan tapes to Zitzy for duplication and safekeeping. He told me he had contacted Jackson, and Jackson was going to work on obtaining other youth Missing Persons reports. Zitzy also said he again went through the files we had but could not find an NOPD Missing Person's report for Adeline.

I asked him if he had yet vetted Rieglé and Bowditch, and he said he had not. I responded, "Get on it as soon as possible and continue working with Jackson to get the other Missing Persons reports." I was clearly weighing Zitzy down.

Doughboy confirmed Duncan had terminated his tours with the New Orleans Diocese. So I directed him to research the missing juveniles from the three other churches where Duncan said he had abducted children. And I asked him, "Has Jackie returned to New Orleans?"

"No, she's supposed to come back in three days."

"I think it would be advantageous if the two of you went to Saint Bartholomew's, Santa Maria's, and Mary Queen of Asia's together. They're all minority churches, and I believe you'll have better responses with having a minority alongside you. I also suggest you head to Houma this afternoon and spend the night there, so you can get an early start tomorrow. Maybe Jackie can meet you tonight."

"I'll get on it."

"I bet you will 'get on it.' Good luck, Lover Boy. In any event keep me posted."

I called Macklin and told him to meet me tomorrow at 8:00 a.m. for breakfast at Denny's on Veteran's Boulevard in Metairie. I didn't have much to discuss with him, but I wanted to keep him on tenterhooks.

Conrardy entered the office. "Johnny, some people are beginning to question why you and your staff members are so noticeably absent from the office, and they are complaining you've forgotten about your mission here. What's going on?"

"They're right, Willy. We're investigating Dickerson's murder, and we have limited resources. And as of now, we're far flung, and the murder is taking precedence; however, we haven't forgotten the other security concerns here at the Dome.

Moreover, the murder, per se, is an indication of the lax security here. But we'll get back to only in-house security as soon as we can. Do you think you could divert some of the heat for us?"

"I'll do my best, Johnny. Where does your investigation stand now?"

"For all our efforts, we have yet to uncover any significant clues, and the NOPD is uncooperative. But we're working on it." I so desperately wanted to tell him about our progress, but secrecy was our crucial asset.

I knew I was pretermitting my Dome obligations. But my head was swimming with the ongoing investigation. We were sorely shorthanded, and the Dome security function would have to wait. And I was thankful to have Willy ease things up for me.

After arriving home, Doughboy again called me. He had acquired a motel in Houma, but Jackie would be unable to meet him until tomorrow morning. "That's good; you need to be on your toes tomorrow and thinking with your big head and not your little one."

I settled in for a light dinner of catfish fillets and pan-fried plantains. I was just thinking about dessert when Natalie came behind me, put her hands on my shoulders, and kissed my bald pate. I knew in a moment what my dessert was going to be.

Natalie was ravenous, and she again conveyed me to the welkin. When we were done, she said, "I love you," and all my worries drifted away like silent fairy leaves floating on a languid bayou toward the yawn of the Gulf of Mexico.

CHAPTER XLV
Macklin Extols Huberty

"How's your wife, Macklin?" I asked over coffee the following morning.

"She's fading; I can see it every day."

"I'm sorry, but I'm glad you're there to take care of her. Were you able to get those reports?"

"I'm telling you I can't get any more than I've already given you, Régis."

"You're stalling, Macklin."

"Why would I stall? I want to solve this as much as you do."

"Maybe so, but I still don't trust you. What do you know about Huberty?"

"Great guy. He once saved a cop's life."

"How's that?"

"About two years ago, a white patrolman was called in to the Desire Street Project—which is all Black—on a domestic dispute. A woman with five kids was being beaten by her boyfriend, and it was still happening on her stoop when the cop arrived. He tried to arrest the offending male; the male resisted; and they got into a scuffle.

"The event drew a crowd of onlookers, and they were cheering for the arrestee. Among them was Huberty who, as you probably know, doesn't live there. But because he was a philanthropist and economically ministered in the housing projects, he was well-known and respected there and in the other projects.

"And as so often happens in these cases, the victim turned on the policeman, and she joined in on the fray. Somehow, she seized the cop's service revolver, and she was about to shoot him when Huberty drew his permitted firearm and capped her. She fell to the sidewalk and dropped the gun. Huberty retrieved it, and he stood off the angry neighbors.

"By then, a dozen or so police units responded to the scene, the almost mini-riot was quelled, and the abuser was arrested. Huberty was hailed as a hero by the police, and I believe that helped him and Corbin land the security contract at the Dome."

"What happened to the woman?"

"They transported her to Charity Hospital where she lingered for about eight hours and died."

"Was Huberty charged?"

"No, he was cleared. The District Attorney made a presentment to the Grand Jury, and the jurors issued a 'No True Bill' declaring there was no probable cause to decide a crime had been committed."

"I'm going to cut you slack with the homicide reports. But I do need juvenile Missing Persons reports dating back for two years."

"I think I can do that; I have a friend in Missing Persons. But I can tell you now, most non-Caucasian children are written off as runaways, just like Homicide pays little heed to the murders of prostitutes."

Redolent of a leopard in a tree, Zitzy was waiting to pounce on me at the office. "We have a huge development!" he exclaimed. Breeze and Pumpkin reported in last night and informed me Huberty was on the move yesterday. At about six, they followed him to—of all places—Pauli Courtney's veterinary clinic."

"And...?"

"They don't know what transpired. The meeting was brief, and other than Huberty's, there were no other cars in the parking lot. Breeze reconnoitered the building, and they learned that rather than being a small office, the physical plant was prodigious, and there is a large garage door at the rear.

"When Huberty left, he went to Don Villaso's cocktail lounge, where he stayed for the next three hours. And afterward, he went to his home in Eden Isles. About a half-hour after Huberty departed, Courtney left from the garage, and he too went to his home in Eden Isles."

"That does it! We have to include Courtney as a suspect. Have them each continue to work twelve-hour shifts, 1:00 p.m. to 1:00 a.m., Pumpkin on Huberty, and Breeze on Courtney. Also, find out when the "Aint's" will next be playing—or should I say "losing?"

"Next Sunday at three p.m."

"Good. It gives us four more days to intensely surveille them. In the meantime, check to see which shift supervisor will be working that day."

"Okay. Jackson managed to get us additional Missing Persons reports; I'll go over them."

"What about Rieglé?"

"Kim's done some preliminary research. So far, he's clean, but she's going to do more."

CHAPTER XLVI
A Bowling Alley in the Chapel

The phone rang; it was Macklin. "Régis! Have you heard about Father Duncan?"

"No. What?"

"You might want to know he hanged himself from the choir loft in his church. And Régis, it was grisly, even for the homicide detectives. Due to his weight and because he had to fall about six feet to do so, the noose decapitated him.

"His body fell straight to the floor, but when the stretched rope recoiled like a spring after a weight has been lifted, his head champagne-corked off and rolled like a bowling ball up the aisle toward the altar."

"Do you have any more information?"

"Yeah. He left no suicide note. And a passerby reported that, earlier in the day, two churchgoers, a dowdy old woman and a youngish, handsome male, both Caucasians, left the church together in late morning, well after the usual time for confessionals to be over.

"The passerby, a longtime member of the parish, said the two strangers were unknown to her. The male was driving a black Pontiac Firebird with a Texas plate. But although she couldn't get the number, she had seen a similar car in the area several days before.

"And Duncan's rector, Father Gallagher, said because of Duncan's heavy workload of outside assignments combined with his regular duties and his grief about the missing girls, he had for quite a while been fatigued, depressed, and sullen. Father Gallagher also said, after confessionals this morning, he could hear Duncan rotary dial two phone calls, but he didn't hear Duncan actually speak with anyone.

"Father Gallagher added that Duncan was particularly morose after hearing confessions; however, Duncan didn't indicate why. Gallagher suggested perhaps Duncan had heard a grievous confession, he was agonizing over it, and burdened by the regular duties, that's what pushed him over the edge."

Albeit still with trepidation, I was beginning to trust Macklin. Or was he trying to pump me for information?

That seemed to get Breeze and me off the hook, but I was certain the homicide detectives would be curious to know why he had killed himself, who the unidentified visitors were, if they played an active role in the suicide, and what part, if any, did they have in the ensuing event.

As a citizen, I was under no legal obligation to report a criminal act, whether I knew about it in advance, witnessed its commission, or found out about it after the fact. And besides, suicide, per se, is not a crime.

However, I was not "just a citizen"; I was a law enforcement officer. As a matter of policy, which is subject to justifiable deviation, law enforcement agencies should cooperate, but it is not requisite they do so.

Moreover, in Massachusetts, prosecutors had charged several juveniles with causing the suicide of a female schoolmate. The case is on the periphery of manslaughter, and the prosecutors have an uphill battle against legal challenges. In my precarious position with the city administration and the NOPD, a spurious charge could be lodged against me, and it would significantly hamper our investigation.

Besides that, I was between Scylla and Charybdis. If we disclosed our findings, we would lose our momentum, and all the intelligence we had obtained would have been for naught.

Furthermore, I didn't trust the NOPD. Even if the NOPD didn't feed the information to the perpetrators—which they might have done—they would leak it to the press. The sex slave traders would go off the grid, and any element of surprise we might have would be forfeited. Therefore, it was a gray area, and I chose not to divulge the results of Duncan's confession.

The front-page article in the late edition of the afternoon *States-Item* parroted what Macklin had told me, but the writer focused on the reason for the suicide and the presence of the two strangers. The piece noted they were persons of interest and the police were soliciting information about the mysterious duo.

I realized Breeze had had no disguise, so I decided to keep him veiled from public view for a while. *Another screw-up. I should have curtained him as well. When was I ever going to learn?*

Nevertheless, it was serendipity the NOPD did not conduct a thorough investigation and did not connect my earlier publicized visit with the priest's death. It wasn't until later that I was to learn why.

It was time to update the AG, but I decided to ask him to call me at home in the evening; I still did not trust the phones in the office. I later spoke with him from home, and told him what had happened. He confirmed my decision to stay mum about Duncan's confession and told me not to worry about it.

But, of course, I did

CHAPTER XLVII
Rieglé's Observations

I chose to interview Rieglé without the benefit of in-depth vetting. Wanting to put him at ease, rather than our offices, we met on the Plaza Level in the empty stadium. After the niceties, I said, "Jim, why'd you leave the FBI?"

"I'm a born and bred Yat [the demonym for a native New Orleanian], and the FBI kept transferring me around the country to every place that wasn't New Orleans. I wanted to be back home."

"How'd you end up in the private sector instead of law enforcement in the public milieu?"

"Régis, you should know better than anybody—Louisiana law enforcement doesn't pay well. But why the questions?"

"I'm curious about Corbin and Huberty's indifference to the murder of a law enforcement officer in the arena where they are responsible for security."

"I honestly don't know, Régis. I've asked them about it on a few occasions, but their responses have been it was out of their hands and in those of the NOPD."

"Well, do you have any theories?"

"Yes, but that is what they are—theories, only theories."

"Would you share those with me?"

"Because I have no proof, I'm reluctant to."

"Well, how about it if we reduce it from theoretical to hypothetical?"

"I don't know whether to trust you or not."

"Jim, you have no reason to mistrust me. Like you, I'm a cop. I and—I believe you, too—want to find the son of a bitch who killed an AG agent and my friend. Other than that, I have no ulterior motive."

"Okay. I'm taking a chance, and I am going to confide in you, but keep this between us.

"You know what the drill is. This is New Orleans; politics reigns supreme. The politicians are endlessly concerned about their political image, so they pander to the public, while they clandestinely cut their deals over cocktails at Le Pavilion.

"At first, I assumed it was Louisiana politics as usual—nothing more than

smoke and mirrors to avoid bad press for the Dome. But when I began to dissect it, I realized there are some deeper issues here. I don't know what they are or even what they might be, but I'm uneasy with the entire situation.

"Of course, I realize that's nothing more than a gut reaction. And I can't offer you anything than what I've given you."

"As Chief of Security, why weren't you at the scene of the crime?"

"I'm curious about that, too. No one notified me, and I didn't find out about it until `I arrived for work at 9:00 the next morning. I've spoken with the shift supervisor about it. He told me he thought Corbin or Huberty would do so."

I considered asking him what he knew about Duncan's Dome tours, but I realized it would be exposing our hand. "You have my word; your insights are safe with me. We've been working on a few flimsy leads that have not yet gone anywhere. Therefore, I have nothing to share with you now, but if and when they develop, I'll keep you posted. In any event, we should keep in touch."

I left the interview with a positive impression. Perhaps if there were a conspiracy, Rieglé was not part of it. *But don't flag now; there's danger behind every tree and bush in this quagmire of lies, deceit, and depravity.*

CHAPTER XLVIII
A Bleak Portent

I thanked Rieglé and returned to the office. Once there, Zitzy said, "I checked out Bowditch with the NOPD Records Bureau—he's clean. And I found Adeline's Missing Persons report. Like so many others, the investigating officers' assessment was that she was a runaway. In my opinion, the missing persons detectives are engaged in a massive coverup, or they're just fuckin' lazy—they can't be that dumb."

Could the deception be that prevalent? If it were, it was on a grand scale, and the foes were redoubtable. I was up to my ass in a South Louisiana swamp with territorial, voracious alligators surrounding me, and all I had was a culm of bamboo to beat them off. *Just because you're paranoid, doesn't mean they're not really after you.*

I told Zitzy to inform me posthaste when he received the reports from Breeze and Pumpkin. And with nothing more of consequence I could do for the day, I went home to wait for the call from the AG.

"We're in murky waters, General," I said. And I outlined to him the data we had accrued. "Of course, except for Duncan's confession, it's all circumstantial at this point."

"Well, Régis, I think that you are on to something, but we have another investigation going on up north, so you're on your own when it comes to staffing. I'll have my secretary send you a quick memo authorizing you to use as much overtime as you need." And the sole solace he rendered was an echo of what he earlier said to me, "Don't let the hyenas eat you."

I wanted to employ the scientific method in the investigation—a) observation, b) the formation of hypotheses, c) experimentation, and d) the development of a theory. But there was a Catch-22—without exposing our hand, we had scant opportunity for experimentation. We had a few suspects, but we couldn't question them without exposing our strategy.

One of the variables in my theory—one that I could not account for at the moment—was that I did not know why Ghost was murdered or just how many people might be involved in this. And absent that, all we could postulate were

watery hypotheses. It *was* a fast-moving case, but where in hell was I going? I felt like the Lewis Carroll misquote, "The hurrier I go, the behinder I get."

The outlook was grim. It was a parlous trek, but other than slogging through the mare's nest of possibilities, I had no other options. *Suck it up; life is not always an evening stroll on the beach. Remember JFK: "We choose to go to the moon in this decade and do the other things, not because they are easy, but because they are hard."* And I was shooting for the moon.

Spooning with my mainstay, Natalie, I went to sleep expecting a phone call from Zitzy about Pumpkin and Doughboy, but when I awakened at 6:00 the next morning, I had received none.

CHAPTER XLIX
Willy Pulls Johnny's Ass from the Fire

Arriving at the office earlier than usual, I was unsurprised to see Zitzy there. Like the rest of the crew, he was dedicated, and he was immersed in the investigation. "I didn't want to awaken you last night, but we've had some developments," he said.

"Tell me."

"There was another Huberty/Courtney meeting at the veterinary clinic yesterday afternoon. After the meeting, Pumpkin followed Huberty east on US 90, Old Spanish Trail, to a farm north of 90 on Mississippi Highway 604 in Pearlington.

"She was wary of entering the gate behind Huberty, but there was enough light left for her to see pastureland with horses and cows grazing there. She gave me the address listed on the mailbox, and I'm going to check for ownership of it today. Huberty stayed there for a little over an hour and returned home to Eden Isles afterward.

"Nothing notable took place with Courtney. After the meeting, he too went home to Eden Isles.

"But interestingly, Breeze reports that, at least in the afternoon, Courtney has very few patients. In fact, there was only one visitor later in the day—a tall, thin, Hispanic lady, without an animal, who stayed there about an hour and then left."

"Did he say Hispanic or Asian?" *Hispanic or Asian? Was this our Mystery Lady?*

"Hispanic."

"What type car did she have?"

"Breeze didn't say. He supposed it was just someone seeking medical treatment."

"If she returns, ask Breeze to get a detailed personal description as well as the make, model, license plate, and registration of the car." It was pure speculation, but could she be Duncan's mystery woman who was married to a doctor? Yet Breeze and Leasean had said she was Hispanic and not Asian as Duncan had said.

Zitzy followed up with, "I also received a call from Doughboy who told me he hit paydirt at both the church in Houma and the one in Raceland—each had a

missing girl on a field trip with Duncan. I told him to book a room in Houma and follow up with the respective police departments today. And, oh, he has Jackie with him."

"Another honeymoonette of the company's nickel! When he gets back, he's going to be as desiccated as a three-day roadkill frog on a hot asphalt roadway."

I received a call from Sanderson who said he wanted to meet with me. We scheduled a time, and he came to the office.

Wearing his journalist hat, Sanderson got right down to business, "Agent Regis, we received a tip you and your agents are somehow involved in the recent suicide of the priest, Father Duncan. Moreover, the tipster said you are sitting on evidence about child abduction cases. Is that true?"

A nauseous riffle coursed through me; the war zone was now defined. But if Sanderson's article were to be published, I hoped it would convince our nemeses we were inept, and we weren't pursuing the abduction case of Adeline, Lashanna, or any other abductees.

"Your source is a fabulist. It's not just misleading; it's absurd and deceitful. Much of our resources are now dedicated to solving the murder of our agent, Langdon Dickerson. You should also remember that we are also doing a security audit of the Dome. There had been some rumors that a child went missing while on a tour of the Dome. But that investigation, if there is one, would clearly fall to NOPD.

"Between the murder and our evaluation of the Dome's security system, I hardly have time to turn around in the shower much less investigate missing children's cases. Maybe the tipster, himself or herself, has some information we don't have that could help us solve this case. Do you know who provided it?"

"We do, but the party has told us off the record and wishes to remain anonymous."

"We're being gaslighted. You and I both know that in the real world, nothing is 'off the record.' Did they provide any factual data?"

"Only that you had harassed Father Duncan."

"You should know better. Do you believe it's newsworthy?"

"Not in and of itself; that's why I'm speaking with you."

"I hope you do run the article." And with the anticipation of spicing the sauce to lull the malefactors into a false sense of security, I added, "We *do* have an

ongoing investigation into the murder of our agent, but so far, we haven't developed even one significant lead, and the few we had have all petered out. Of course, that doesn't mean we are going to let it get lost in this political imbroglio and allow it be forgotten."

"Then, why did you question Father Duncan about a missing child?"

"We received information Dickerson had spoken with Father Duncan about a missing daughter of one of his neighbors. We were just doing what any other investigator does; that is, retrace the activities of the victim to see if there might be a correlation between his previous activity and the murder."

"And was there a connection between Dickerson's inquiry and his murder?"

"There was no connection at all. It turned out to be a mere happenstance that had nothing to do with the murder."

"Isn't the murder investigation the responsibility of the NOPD?"

"Undoubtedly it is. But I do have five significant points to make. First, we are a statewide law enforcement agency; we have authority to investigate criminal activity throughout the State, and this investigation is, of course, within the scope of our authority. Secondly, any citizen has the right to investigate a crime, provided he doesn't disrupt the police investigation—and we certainly haven't done that.

"Thirdly, we've tried to check on the progress of the NOPD investigation, but all we have been told is the lead investigator, Sergeant Macklin, is on leave. Fourthly, what kind of clowns do you think that we would look like if we did not conduct an investigation into the murder of one of our own? And lastly, the murder was a breach of Superdome security, and problems with Dome security is why we're here."

His expression of intensity and his hasty scribbling of notes indicated to me he was listening with rapt attention to everything I was saying. And he continued, "The anonymous source also said you *are* interfering in the police investigation."

"That's a straw-man attack. Did he or she offer any facts to substantiate that accusation? How can one interfere with a phantasma? We have no idea what they're working on to avoid interfering with them.

"Moreover, the NOPD has never—not even once—informed us we've been an active hinderance to their efforts. As I told you, we've tried to establish communication with them, but we've been stonewalled. If we've crossed paths,

I'd like to know where."

"What progress have you made in the murder investigation?"

"As I indicated, none, absolutely none. Every lead we've had has led us into a cul-de-sac in which we keep going round and round with no sustainable results."

"What are your plans?"

"I don't want to throw in the towel, but we're shorthanded, and with the complete absence of data, finding a solution looks bleak. At some point in the near future, we might have to cold-case the investigation and hope the NOPD can solve the murder. They have many more resources than we do, plus they have the homicide experience we're sorely lacking."

"Our source also said you're neglecting your responsibilities to oversee the security functions at the Dome; is that true?"

"Ed, Socrates said, 'When the debate is lost, slander becomes the tool of the losers.' And that's what's happening here. And to some degree, yes, we are. We haven't forgotten our Dome obligations, and we're still working on those.

"But we have to prioritize. One of our agents was murdered in the Dome, and it takes precedence. We haven't shelved the work we were doing on the Dome's security operations, however, at this point, that function is on a slower track than the murder investigation.

"And to complicate our situation, nefarious instigators are lighting infodemic brush fires like this in an apparent attempt to derail our already tenuous and circumscribed inquiry. And we have not received one iota of help from the city— help that could be advantageous in solving the case. Rather, we have to expend much-needed man-hours with distractions like this.

"This is not about glory. We don't care who provides the dénouement to the murder. We simply want to close this case, so we can return to addressing the function to which we were initially assigned; that is, improving Dome security.

"And if you run the article, you can quote me on this: It seems there is a concerted effort to oust the AG's Office from the Superdome."

Through the open door, Willy had entered the office as I was answering the last four questions. He must have known Sanderson, for interrupting he said, "Ed, cut Régis some slack. One of his agents was murdered, and he's trying to find the killer. He is overwhelmed at the moment, and we have his assurance he'll be on top of the security function as soon as he can."

Willy had thrown me a much-needed life preserver; he really did have my back!

Inclining rearward, Sanderson seemed to nod in quizzical agreement. He smiled and thanked me, and told me he appreciated my candor. But he did not indicate whether he was going to publish the article. Nor did I ask him if he would.

After Sanderson left, I thanked Willy for his support. He told me that he was glad to be of ancillary assistance to our investigation, and he then queried me, "Have you developed anything new?"

Willy wanted to help and be a part of our probe. Thus, I felt guilty lying to him, but I said, "No, Willy, this has been a Sisyphean endeavor—we push the rock up the hill, but before we reach the top, it comes rolling down and flattens us again."

"Well, if I can check out a few things for you, let me know; I have a substantial bank of resources."

"I might take you up on it; thanks."

My father used to say, "You can't get christened without a godfather." I felt I had a godfather in Willy, and I knew in him I had a trump card. But I wouldn't play that ace until I was in dire need of it.

CHAPTER L

Virtual Dumpster Diving

After the interview and Willy's departure, Zitzy informed me the Mississippi farm was owned by a Gerald M. Bowditch. It was too coincidental not to be *our* Gerald Bowditch. But the answer to the ownership question opened a rabbit hole of other answerless questions and possibilities.

There appeared to be a linkage among Huberty, Courtney, and Bowditch. Courtney would have access to etorphine, and with livestock, Bowditch would probably be familiar with it. Bowditch discovered Langdon's body.

Langdon was injected with etorphine which might have been used to kill or subdue him, and the Bayou Sauvage supposed "runaways" were killed by that drug. Moreover, Bowditch was working on the night of the murder. Evidentiary? Yes. But it was all circumstantial, and it was no smoking gun.

But how could a Dome security officer afford to have a farm with livestock? With his security job keeping him away from the farm, he would have to hire others to care for the animals. And if he were wealthy enough to have such a spread, why would he be working as a mediocre security officer? Moreover, Bowditch would need veterinary care for the farm menagerie which would also require a sizeable income to afford.

Perhaps—probably—Courtney was his veterinarian. It was plausible Bowditch would be knowledgeable of the dosing requirements of etorphine, and via Courtney, he could have access to the drug. Moreover, he was the one who found Langdon's body. Bowditch had, indeed, become a person of interest.

"Zitzy, did you find out where the mayor's suite was located and if the mayor's suite has food delivered there?"

"Leasean told me the mayor's suite was the last one at the dead-end from the east ramp on Level 6. And the concierge food service does deliver frozen food from their expensive menu to that suite but only thirty hours or so before an event and none, whatsoever, during the event.

"All sixth-level suites have standard refrigerator/freezers and microwaves. And like the Mayor's suite, meals and hors d'oeuvres are also delivered to those

other ones in advance of major Dome expositions. Oftentimes, the other suites call for replenishments during, and even after, the event, yet that never happens at the mayor's suite."

"Who receives the food at the mayor's suite?"

"Most often, it's Huberty; sometimes it's Bowditch.

"And during that time, the stadium viewing windows are almost always shaded, but from the stadium, one can still see that the lights are left on.

"He further told me members of the janitorial service have remarked they are amazed by the amount and nature of the refuse in the mayor's suite following major events."

"Why is that?"

"The janitors say the trash in there is two to three times more than any other suites, so much so they had to provide the suite with three extra trash cans."

"Do they know why?"

"Wait, there's more, much more! The clean-up crews say that more than half the waste is discarded fast-food-to-go receptacles from Popeye's, Burger King, or McDonalds. It's difficult for me to believe big-time operators would be dining on drive-through fare. But children would." This was to be a bijou in our case.

"I agree."

"And even more interestingly, Leasean told me when there is a big event and Bowditch is working, he assigns a subordinate to the security command desk, and then he disappears." This, too, was a jewel in our investigative diadem.

"Did you ask Leasean if Huberty was in the Dome on the night of the murder?"

"No, but I will."

"Did the NOPD run Bowditch through the National Crime Information Center or only through their records?" NCIC had just recently been formed.

"I don't know for sure. I assumed they did a national search."

"Just in case, ask the State Police to process him through NCIC. And also, arrange a full staff meeting tomorrow morning for 11:00 at our provisional office in City Park.

"And have you had the time to further vet him?"

"No. As you know, I've had other priorities, but I'll get to it when I can."

"I agree, and I understand."

\

CHAPTER LI
Finally, Some Good News...and a Big Break in the Case

Walking into the office the next morning, I found Zitzy and Doughboy grinning like Cheshire cats.

"What's going on, guys?" I asked.

Zitzy thrust the morning copy of the *Times-Picayune* into my hands, saying, "It worked!"

"What worked?"

"Read the article!"

Although there was a similar, but more objective, news article on page 2 of the *States-Item* by Katzman, burnishing the AG's Office and me on the op-ed page opposite the editorial page in the *Times-Picayune*, Sanderson had written:

Attorney General Investigator Beleaguered by New Orleans Politics

Special Attorney General Agent Johnny Régis, assigned to review security at the Superdome, says he and his team being thwarted in the murder investigation of AG Agent Langdon Dickerson at the Dome.

Besieged with accusations and rumors, Régis claims his investigation has been derailed by a political machine. He has been accused of expanding his efforts of Dome security and the murder of an AG agent into an investigation of missing persons.

Régis says that is absurd. He is shorthanded, and with his two probes, he doesn't "have time to turn around in the shower much less investigate missing persons cases."

Régis has also been accused of neglecting his Dome security investigation, but Wilhelm Conrardy, the Dome's Operation Officer is satisfied with Régis' performance.

The murder investigation is at a standstill. He says he has pursued every possible lead, but all of them have dead-ended. He indicated he is almost ready to cold-case the murder and hope for the best with the NOPD.

Régis also noted because he has received so much criticism and no help from the city, there seems to be an effort to remove the AG's detachment from the Superdome.

If that were to happen, the citizens of New Orleans would lose a striver who is working in their best interests.

We wish Régis wind at his back and hope he and his team remain on-site until the murder is solved and security at the Dome has been improved.

I had been having an ominous feeling the investigation was spinning near light-speed around a black hole, and it was teetering close to the singularity that would spiral it in where it would be forever lost. But this turn of events might have been a fortuitous aberration to belch it from that perilous orbit and allow the inquiry to traverse the Superdome cosmos in a surreptitious search for answers.

It was much more than I had expected, and I became aware I had two extramural allies—Sanderson and Conrardy. But unfortunately, I could not disclose the status of our case to either of them.

The article had to draw the attention of the regnant mayor and her disciples. Perhaps it was too much to hope for, but I was sanguine about the possibility the hyenas would lose the scent, and we'd have free range and undetected mobility in our investigative pursuits.

Shortly after I arrived at the office, and I had read the article, Willy notified me I was summoned to provide a state of security report at an extempore Superdome Advisory Board meeting scheduled for 3:30 that afternoon.

Later, Doughboy informed me the Raceland and Houma Police Departments treated the missing children much as had the NOPD and the Saint Martinville Police—the missing youths were classified as runaways. Why was there such a dearth of communication between police agencies?

Zitzy, with a face-crinkling grin, told me that, via Leasean, he confirmed Huberty *was* in the Dome the night of Langdon's murder and he left at about 6:00 in the morning. And still grinning, he said, "The NOPD was sloppy, lazy, or deceitful in their records search of Bowditch. Although not in New Orleans, he does have a record in neighboring Mississippi."

"What for?"

"In adjacent-to-Louisiana Hancock County where his farm is, he was twice arrested for carnal knowledge of a juvenile."

"What were the dispositions of those cases?"

"Both charges were dismissed. Perhaps he has heavy political clout. Or perhaps in both cases, the complainants declined to provide any additional information or testify after making the complaint because they were bought off or received threats.

"And Johnny, it is said extra security personnel are needed depending on the size of the event like a Saints' game. Bowditch is scheduled to work a special shift

from 6:30 a.m. until 12:00 a.m. on the day of a game or concert, even though Leasean and another supervisor are scheduled to work 6:30 a.m. to 6:30 p.m. and the 6:30 p.m. to 6:30 a.m. shifts.

"Plus, he'll be the 'Chief Supervisor,' out-ranking Leasean and the other supervisor on the same shifts during that time." I so wanted to ask Rieglé about those arrangements, but doing so would divulge our tactics.

"Doesn't the NOPD usually back up the security contingent on game and concert nights?"

"Yes, they do. There's enough security; that's why this situation is so odd."

"Zitzy, I have a wild hunch. Find out which automobile Bowditch drives and check to see if his car is here Saturday night and Sunday morning."

"Why?"

"I have this crazy idea; I'll let you know if it pans out.

"And gather the crew together for an 11:00 meeting in City Park."

CHAPTER LII
Sous les Chênes

An ambitious autumn day with a crystalline azure sky. The wind's breath in the City Park environs was replete with the balsam of blossoming clerodendrum, forsythia, and French lavender, as well as the live oaks with their vacillant Spanish moss.

The bonhomie ambiance of the surrounding milieu was as contrasting to our case as torpid Bayou Lafourche is to an enraged, innudative, springtime Mississippi River racing to the Gulf of Mexico. But I conceded it was appropriate—New Orleanians had for many years dueled "under the oaks," where many lives were lost and scores settled.

With expense funds, I had sent Zitzy to Maspero's Restaurant in the French Quarter for our lunches and soft drinks. He was a familiar face there, always received good service, and never had to stand in line to enter. We ate first and after that began to discuss our case.

In the late 18th century, Maspero's Slave exchange was where slaves were sold and Andrew Jackson met with the Lafitte Brothers and planned the defense for the historic and epic Battle of New Orleans.

Opening—and later closing—the discussion with an admonition for secrecy, I laid out what we had accomplished to that point except for Pumpkin's and Breeze's reports from the preceding day and early morning. Nevertheless, they had little to report; unlike the night before, Huberty and Courtney had engaged in no unusual activity.

"We don't have a catechism to guide us, and this might sound bizarre, but stay with me." I then posited my quite dubious working theory. I proposed that the abductors' business strategy was pedophiliac sex and football. I suggested there was a definitive link between the abductions and the Superdome.

Going beyond my window of skill and way beyond my investigative pay grade, I offered an exotic hypothesis: The abductees are either rented, or sold, or both to high rollers during major Dome events. I also noted Bowditch would be the shift supervisor on Sunday, the day of the game. If he were involved, and if there were to be activity with the children, that would be the time for it.

I was counting on the principals to be greedy; they had only a limited number of big events to sell their products. That, coupled with the incapable image I had projected, I contended that the deviants might be likely to consider the rewards high and the risks low and continue forward with the venture.

Reaching even higher, I postured that on game-day, there were probably pedophiliac sexual activities in the mayor's suite. And for an exorbitant fee, one-time patrons and prospective buyers could sample the wares and decide to buy one or more of the juveniles or pay on a short-term rental basis. I further speculated that perhaps the kids saw a way out of the captive situation they were in, and they performed at their very best.

"I know my ideas might sound outlandish, but at this point, we have nothing else. Moreover, I know you'll have long working hours ahead of you, and you'll be away from family—in your cases, Pumpkin and Doughboy, your heartthrobs. However, unless you guys can come up with a better theory or strategy —to which I'm wide open—this is the best we have. Any comments?"

Doughboy and Pumpkin both facetiously moaned, but they were in for the duration, and along with them, Breeze agreed it seemed plausible.

Breeze said, "Well, if the illegal activity is happening at the mayor's suite, wouldn't it follow that she is part of the scheme?"

"Not necessarily," countered Zitzy. "Because of her elected position, she has a free lease on the suite. So she could be sub-leasing it to someone else—Huberty for example. And do you really think the mayor would be that foolish?"

I started to say, "I don't know, but...," when I was interrupted by Doughboy.

"Zitzy, I think the power's gone to and infected her head. Hasn't that been the case for almost all despots throughout history?"

Zitzy responded, "Maybe you're right. But maybe you just have an axe to grind with Langlois."

"Okay guys; the crux of the matter is we don't know, and unless you have other ideas, at this time, this is our only theory. Unless...unless...one of you has another one. Again, I'm wide open"

The crew nodded, and no one offered a second opinion. So, I continued, "In any event, this is top secret. Tell no one, including your wives, lovers, sisters, or brothers, what we're up to. Secrecy is our major asset, and ineptness is our theatrical poster. If we blow those, we expose our hand and possibly place our

190

lives in danger."

Of course, I wasn't so naïve to discard the dictum of the New Orleans' Mafia's *capo di tutti capi*, Carlos Marcello, who reportedly said, "Two people can keep a secret if one of them is dead."

So, what makes you think you can keep this on the sly until you nail the son of a bitch or sons of bitches?

Pumpkin and Breeze went to their surveillances, and Zitzy, Doughboy, and I returned to the office to outline a plan of action. As crenulated as it might have been and knowing full well my theory was subject to change, or worse, not materialize, I said, "This is what we're going to do..."

CHAPTER LIII
Cat on a Hot Hypalon Plastic Roof

At 3:30, the Superdome Advisory Board, sans Langlois, was seated with barely a quorum due to the assembly having been so hastily called. But the press, puzzling over the abruptness of the special session, was there in full brunt.

Everyone marked time until twenty minutes after the scheduled hour of the meeting, when Langlois, insouciant and unapologetic arrived. And with a gleeful abuse of power, she pavonine-strutted in, leaving behind her what I perceived as an illusory smog of smegma. She took center stage, and then—and only then— *Ludi incipiant.* (Let the games begin.)

Langlois and her parvenu henchmen who luxuriated in well-upholstered sinecure and copied their antediluvian governing genre from the Romans' *panem et circenses* (bread and circuses). Their cant was to provide subsistence programs (bread) and, more particularly, sports—the circuses of football, basketball, and other entertainment at the Dome—to conciliate the New Orleans hoi polloi.

Moreover, in a long-standing tradition, the mayor and her minions resorted to the dog whistle exploitation of New Orleanians' parochialism. Indeed, most of the New Orleans populace were insularities. Discounting Copernicus' heliocentric model, they believed, "Doesn't *everyone* know the world, nay, the universe revolves around New Orleans?" Living in their Bacchanalian holographs, Yats are disinclined to take the red pill.

Her gynocentrism had secured a bloc vote of New Orleans females. And with that, Langlois had also channeled New Orleans' provincial persuasion into her election stratagem—it's us (New Orleans) against them (the State of Louisiana) she pandered to the sectarian New Orleanians. Thus, the State Attorney General's Office, mostly populated by men, was cast as a hostile alien entity.

Johnny Régis was fast becoming a buzzing maringouin with the blare of a train horn in the mayor's ear. Besides Sanderson's galvanizing article, our investigation into the murder was an oblique threat. If I validated the claims of deficient security, or if I found the murderer was tied in with the Dome, I would bollix her political agenda.

I suspected this encounter was designed to render the *coup de grâce* to our

murder investigation. After that, it would be lagniappe for her to politicize the issue and pressure the Governor to remove us from there. To achieve her goal, she and the Board were going to spin the AG's Dome undertaking into a nativist issue.

This was not going to be a vanilla inquiry. No mere contretemps either, it was to be an inquisition, a kangaroo assize headed by a contemptuous judge and designed to smear my name and vilify the AG presence at the Dome. I was to be stigmatized and flagellated in the court of public opinion. Thus, I was being forced to adhere to the atavistic code, "Eat or be eaten."

Prima facie, I was expected to demonstrate accountability concerning our group's activities at the Dome. But as if I were barefooted walking alone on the Dome's Hypalon plastic roof in the excruciating August sun, I was the only attestor, and I was going to have to hop lively to prevent my feet from being roasted.

I was afraid. But I wasn't afraid of the mayor or her chickenshit advisory board. I was afraid of me.

A secret I kept buried even deeper than my licentious desires for Pumpkin was a dark side for demonic vengeance toward those who harmed me, or my loved ones, or committed vile social injustices. I rarely met a grudge I could not keep, and I didn't easily "forgive and forget."

Machine politicians like those on the Board were running roughshod over the public they were supposed to serve and, at the same time, stealing the soul of the once blithesome Crescent City in which I had wassailed as a youth, adolescent, and young adult. I was troubled that, if pushed too hard, the beast within me might be freed from the captivity in which I kept it.

Seated there facing the Board members, I was pilloried. But I had a ruthless urgency to "...find the motherfucker and find him fast." Adamantine, I wasn't going to let hack politicians stand in my way. I forced myself to remember the Latin maxim, *"Levi fil, quod bene fertur onus,"* (A burden becomes lightest when it is well borne.) Therefore, I pledged myself to endure the onus before me to my advantage.

Surveying Langlois' coterie of Board members, I visualized a diorama of Botticelli's *Calumny of Apelles*, for they sat enshrined by bovarism and arrogance. Each one of the prima donnas could have been archetypes of one or more of the

painting's implied vices—Perfidy, Conspiracy, Calumny, Slander, Rancor, Envy, King Midas (or in this case, Queen Midas), Ignorance, and Suspicion.

As much as I might have implied it, although unattractive, Langlois was not a superficially ugly woman. However, installed as the chairperson at the head table, she gave the impression of a bumptious gargoyle protecting her edifice of oily, parasitic ass-kissers who probably couldn't masturbate without a manual. Her weapon of choice was going to be invective; mine was going to be insidious mockery intended to mislead and infuriate.

Taking her sweet time with clipping, toasting, lighting, and then taking a couple of puffs of her *Robusto,* she finally called the meeting to order. And pulling a constipated face as if she had just taken a hefty dose of cod liver oil, Langlois bowed up and pointed her stubby finger at me.

I didn't think my Cheshire Cat grin sat well with her...I *hoped* it didn't.

With palpable animosity, she said, "Why are you smiling, Agent Régis—do you see something funny in these proceedings? This is business, serious business. We have no need for frivolous smiling here Agent Regis." Was she aware my smile was in truth a smirk?

In American English, "Madam" is démodé and most often used in a disrespectful way, a term usually used to address a woman running a brothel. And repeating it conveys the same sarcastic slur as Mark Antony's repeated aspersions of Brutus at Caesar's funeral, "And Brutus is an honorable man."

Thus, I responded, "No, Madam," with an inflection on *Madam*, "not at all; I was just trying to be pleasant. And yes, Madam, I have been duly cautioned about being amiable."

"What is the declared mission of the AG's Office here at the Superdome?"

"To improve security. Our objectives are to review and evaluate the security function and make recommendations for enhancement."

"Do you think you're accomplishing that?"

"We're making headway, but it's slow, Madam Mayor."

"And why is that?"

"Because we're also trying to find a murderer, Madam."

"Is that why you were assigned here?"

"Of course not. No one expected an AG agent would be murdered in the Dome."

"But isn't the homicide investigation within the purview of the NOPD?"

"Yes, it is, Madam. But as a crime and a breach of Dome security, it is not without the orbit of the AG's office either."

"What progress have you made with your investigation?"

In an effort to affirm my investigative naïveté, I answered, "I'm sad to report we have made very little progress—for all intents and purposes, none at all."

"And didn't you just tell the press you're overwhelmed and ready to cold-case the investigation?"

"Yes, I did, Madam. It looks like we might have to do that."

"Then, why haven't you already done so?"

"Madam Mayor, it doesn't look like were ever going to solve this case. But Dickerson was one of our agents, and I could never forgive myself if I believed we didn't exhaust all possible leads."

"Have you gotten to that point yet?"

"Not quite, Madam. But it doesn't look promising, and it seems we're within just a few days to packing our bags and calling it quits."

"Obviously your rustic approach isn't working, so why don't you leave the investigation to the more professional NOPD? After all, they have many more resources than you do."

"Rustic" and "more professional" were rude *défis*. Rudeness is indicative of a lack of manners, and a lack of manners betokens an absence of morals. I felt my choler rising, and although I vowed retaliation, I choked back an angry reply, saying, "I agree they are, and they do, Madam. But it does no harm to have an additional investigation. Although remote, it is possible we might stumble across something they've missed, which at this point, seems to be a lot."

"Why haven't you shared the fruits of your investigation with them?"

"I thought I made that clear. As of now, Madam, our fruit baskets are empty; we've made no headway, whatsoever. Moreover, the NOPD has shared nothing, absolutely nothing, with us. We can't even get a copy of their preliminary report. Of course, that wasn't true, but I was not to give up our collaborator, Macklin. "Do you think you could help us with that?"

"I don't interfere with the operations of the police department; that's why I have given the chief full autonomy." *Er, Madam Mayor, shouldn't that "onomy" be heteronomy?* "Perhaps the NOPD doesn't want you interfering in their

business."

"Pardon me, Madam, but I don't understand."

"I said it in plain English; what is it you don't understand, Agent Régis?"

"What puzzles me is how can I know if I'm interfering in the NOPD's business if I have no inkling as to what their business is? We could be on the same track as they are; we might be on a separate, but parallel, track; we could be on the same track but going in opposite directions; or for all we know, they might not be on any investigative track at all. Again, Madam, we can't even get a copy of their preliminary report."

She said, "*I* say you're interfering! And it is the consensus of this Board you should be attending to your Dome duties and leave the homicide investigation to my much more competent police department."

"I'd consider doing that, Madam, but as you know, the murder did occur in the Superdome, and that's a breach of Dome security. So, if for no other reason, it falls within the scope of our responsibilities here."

Perhaps it was just wishful thinking, but she seemed to cringe every time I said "Madam."

She shrieked in antipathy, "You're in the city of New Orleans, Agent Regis. And *we'll* determine what's within or without the scope of your responsibilities!"

In my self-determined role of provocateur and intending to egg her on, I responded, "I respectfully disagree, Madam."

"Agent Regis, you're aware, aren't you, that you are here at the pleasure of the City of New Orleans and the Superdome Advisory Board?"

"I was *not* aware of that, Madam. Rather, it is my understanding I was assigned here by the Governor, via the Office of the Attorney General. And although I'd prefer working with the NOPD and the Board, neither entity has given us any assistance in solving the vicious murder of an AG Agent."

Wow, did that ring a bell! And it prompted an enraged response.

"Well, you're aware of it now, Agent Regis!" she shrilled. The imperious czarina was habituated to being accommodated. And I had no intention of being accommodating.

With the energy she invested in that delivery, she must have assumed I would deliquesce. But with muted antagonism, I said, "I understand what you're saying, but again, I respectfully disagree, Madam. Perhaps you should speak with the

Governor about your viewpoint. Good luck with that."

The obloquy of my comment wasn't lost on her; it was incendiary and impudent, as I had designed it to be. Committing the unpardonable crime of *lèse-majesté*, I had become her Mephistopheles, her *bandillero*, incensing her to abandon her composure. And it worked!

My taunts had been akin to sticking pins in a voodoo doll. One of them must have punctured her liver, because she had become bilious. With her squinty eyes even more shadowed than normal and in a shrieking timbre suggesting I was seditious, it appeared she, like the Queen of Hearts, was going to bellow, "Off with [his head]!"

But instead, with only a slight diminution of her wrath, through clenched teeth and with veins throbbing on her squat, reddened neck, she waved her cigar scepter and hissed, "You're dismissed, Agent Régis!"

With a not-too-stifled smirk, I violated her "no amiability" admonishment, and I replied, "Thank you, Madam; have a nice day." Pomposity can withstand almost everything except being laughed at. For all her efforts to hear the band play *Hail to the Chief*, all she took in was a charivari. I wondered if she could detect my amusement.

I felt I had achieved two goals. The first was painting a *trompe l'oeil,* lulling our adversaries into a forged sense of security. And secondly, I had led the mayor to the watering trough laced with anger, and she had drunk of it with vigor. I wanted to believe I had provoked the virago to the point of rashness.

If she were part of the conspiracy, due to rage, she might be bold enough to make a foolish mistake. And even if she weren't, the news that we were stymied and ready to shut down the investigation would be publicized for all to know.

It is said that the media crave conflict. And this was conflict! Print, radio, and TV seized the opportunity to publicize the turmoil. Although a few obscure tabloids with a parochial bent endorsed the mayor's position, while most of the high-profile media advocated for the AG.

Ed Sanderson had attended the meeting. The next day, an op-ed article with his byline read: ***Mayor Hectors AG Agent Johnny Régis***. He reported the clash between the mayor and me almost verbatim, well-illustrating her vituperations yet minimizing my taunts.

Continuing, he said, "Régis is frustrated his probe has gone nowhere. And it is

indeed interesting the Mayor and her Board want the AG's Office out of the homicide investigation."

Saying the mayor's jingoism was flagrant, he went on to quote her condemnation of our "rustic approach" as the mayor's reason to oust us from the probe. "But it is ironic," he wrote, "the NOPD—or as the mayor has said, 'her' police force—has not solved the murder case either." Sanderson had stultified the mayor's challenge for me.

He closed the piece with, "As Régis has said, perhaps the mayor doesn't want the AG's Office at all in the Superdome. And the obvious question is why?"

But although her vitriolic comments limned her as a contumelious bully who was trying to impede our search for the killer, it was still a hung jury as to whether she was a player in the suspected pedophilic slave trade.

Langlois' histrionics and fiery gasconade had immolated her argumentum ad baculum. With her ad hominem rants and her aborted struggle to marginalize our presence in the Dome, the Mayor had sabotaged herself. Her tyrannical recriminations boomeranged and left a nasty gash on her eminence in the New Orleans community. Even laissez-faire New Orleanians have limits to their indulgences.

You won this battle, but do you have the wherewithal to win the war?

CHAPTER LIV
Sophie's Choice

With four days to go before game day, Pumpkin and Breeze reported riveting and critical developments in their surveillances. And those particulars changed everything.

At 5:30 on Wednesday evening, Pumpkin trailed Huberty to Courtney's clinic, where Breeze had been sitting on him. Breeze reported the only "client" during his surveillance was the same Hispanic woman, who had no animal with her and who was still there. Breeze had run the license plate of her car and learned the vehicle was registered to Courtney. So, was this the Mystery Lady—Courtney's wife or partner—who abetted Duncan with the Dome abductions?

At about 6:00, Huberty and the Mystery Lady went to their respective automobiles and waited. A few moments later, a blind van (no side panel or rear windows) driven by Courtney, decamped via the clinic's garage door and began to head toward the inner city in tandem with Huberty in the lead.

Pumpkin and Breeze trailed them to an old, weathered, two-story, almost-windowless, brick warehouse on Tchoupitoulas Street quite near the Dome. Once there, a large garage door opened, the three of them drove in, and the door closed behind them. About an hour thereafter, all three left the warehouse and went to Eden Isles, Huberty to his house and Courtney and the Mystery Lady to Courtney's house.

I had an afflatus. An embryo of a theory, it seemed to me the warehouse might be makeshift prison housing the abductees ready for rent or sale. And that premise led to the fragile speculation the rental or sale of the sex-slave children played out in the mayor's Dome suite before, during, and after major events.

If we wanted a large roundup, that might be our time and place to strike. We'd still miss a few who would evaporate like the angels' share, but the distillate of criminal activity would comprise most of the barrel.

So I said, "We have yet another change in plans. I suspect Courtney has been holding and/or delivering abducted children to the warehouse, and from the warehouse, they are transported into the Dome via the back gate on the night before a game.

"Doughboy, get the address and the description of the building from Pumpkin

or Breeze and stake it out from twelve noon to midnight until you hear differently from Zitzy or me."

I was faced with a Sophie's Choice. We could rescue the children now, but other evildoers would escape. Our ambuscade, if it were to come to fruition, would corral most of the predators I suspected to be in that horrific exploitation. On the other hand, waiting could result in another Bayou Sauvage incident. Or worse!

Nevertheless, our North Star was saving as many children as we could, now and in the future. I resolved that this heinousness had to stop, and I decided on the surprise attack...but we had to work fast! *Johnny, you're on a tightrope; you're clumsy to begin with, and you're all-in, drawing to an inside straight flush.*

CHAPTER LV

Requesting Assistance...from Macklin

The next morning, I called Macklin. "I need to meet with you this afternoon."

Without hesitation, he said, "Where?"

"CC's near the riverbend at the foot of South Carrolton Avenue close to Saint Charles Avenue."

"When?"

"At about two."

I next called Mike Christodoulou, the most erudite—and colorful—attorney on the AG's staff. Mike was a large man and could easily be intimidating. He's one of those rare individuals who is not pugnacious by nature but pugnacious by circumstance. Unless riled or advocating in the courtroom, he was a marshmallow—sympathetic, empathic, understanding, and caring. His jocund demeanor was a spirit-lifter for everyone around him.

And Mike was erudite, a breathing, walking, talking encyclopedia of law...and life too! I knew I would receive top-drawer advice from him.

While in the Army as a lieutenant, Mike had pissed on a general's leg. As the story goes, the general was "fighting" a battle while hiding in a bunker. He almost screwed the operation up, but for the steadfastness of Mike and other field officers who ignored him, the battle was won.

When the general finally made it to the battlefield, well after the firefight, he is recorded as having made the statement that he was pissed off at the rebellious actions of his subordinate officers.

Mike walked up to him, pulled out his penis and let loose a stream of urine on the General's leg, while saying in a load voice, "Now you have been pissed *on* as well!"

He was told his days of defending the United States were short. But the war was heating up, which resulted in a huge demand for seasoned warriors, especially accomplished field commanders like Mike.

Cooler heads prevailed, and Mike's punishment was mild—five days in the stockade. The general, given a desk position in logistics, was encouraged to retire.

And within two years, Mike was promoted to lieutenant colonel...and awarded the Silver Star.! I liked Mike.

After explaining I needed two warrants and why, he said, "It sounds like you have something there. Go for it." But he also enjoined me to do so only with the most ethical jurist in the city.

With the two of us enjoying café au lait, Macklin provided me with a stack of Missing Persons reports. I asked him, "I need two warrants; who is the straightest judge in the New Orleans judiciary?"

Again, he didn't hesitate, "Roberta Giaccone." She's the most noble, intelligent, and fairest jurist in New Orleans or anywhere else for that matter. She's had a lot of heartache in her personal life, and she's ultra-compassionate."

But he was a cop and curious. "What do you need warrants for?"

"I can't tell you now. Can you get me in there to see her?"

"Yes, I can. But why won't you tell me why you need two warrants?"

"Because I can't trust you yet. Moreover, it has nothing to do with Dickerson's murder. But I'll tell you what, Macklin—give me some time to think about it, and I might include you if you want to participate."

"I'm a cop, Régis. If I can help you, I'm ready and very willing to do so."

"Thanks. Can you arrange for me to see Judge Giaccone tomorrow?"

"I have a good relationship with her; I'm sure I can. You'll have to prepare affidavits to get the warrants. But a word of caution: Don't try anything fancy with her; she'll see through it in a heartbeat!"

"Duly noted. But I have no intention of misleading her; we have a good case. I'll have them ready in the morning. Call and let me know what time she'll see me."

Calling Zitzy, I said, "Zitzy, it's going to be a late night for you. Tomorrow morning, we'll need affidavits to get no-knock search warrants for the mayor's suite and the warehouse on Sunday.

"I know you've prepared many of those, but carefully bullet in detail all the facts we've gathered for Judge Giaccone and stress the risk to the children if we have to tarry to save them. If you need to come in late tomorrow, that's fine, but hide the affidavits in the office, and let me know where they're hidden—wake me up if necessary."

"Better than that, I'll put them in your home mailbox tonight."

"Terrific! Also pull Doughboy off his stakeout, and have him head to State Police headquarters tomorrow morning to pick up a State Police sport utility vehicle with a heavy-duty grille guard, seven flack vests, fifteen extra sets of handcuffs, and two police door-breaching rams. I'll make the arrangements with Captain Melancon. And tell Doughboy to keep the vehicle away from the Dome and the warehouse until our sorties."

I had to track down Captain Melancon at his home, but he assured me he would have the equipment ready for Doughboy in the morning. A cop, he wanted to know for what reason we wanted the equipment. But I said to him. "I'm sorry, but I can't tell you, T-Claude. Just please trust me on this." And because we had worked well together in the past, he did.

Later during supper with Natalie, she told me she sensed my anger and apprehension. "I know you Johnny, and something's going on." I tried to squirm my way out of it, but concerned and ever-perceptive, she persisted.

I finally had to tell her it was a secret I couldn't share, and the best thing she could do to help me was to accept the situation as it was. She was disconcerted with it, but she seemed to understand. And again that night as I was falling asleep, I heard the familiar tinkle of rosary beads.

CHAPTER LVI
Macklin's Connection Yields Fruit

Awakening at dawn the next morning, I made haste to our mailbox, collected the affidavits, and placed them in my briefcase. After a breakfast of coffee and toasted French bread slathered with butter and a thin film of fig preserves, I showered, dressed, kissed Natalie, and told her not to worry. Of course, saying that to her was futile—she was going to worry anyway. I suspected it was going to be a two-or-three rosary day.

Alone in the office, I pored over the Zitzy's paperwork. From my limited perspective, except for a few typos, they were perfect—they included everything we had unearthed. But I had little experience preparing affidavits. I anxiously began to pace the enclosure biding my time awaiting Macklin's call. Did he sell me out? Did I expose my gut-shot hand?

Shortly before ten, Zitzy came in, and after giving him the reports I had received from Macklin, I complimented him on his work. Together, we reviewed the requests. Except for the typos he corrected with dispatch, the affidavits appeared to be pristine.

Filling in the time, we discussed our strategy: I would notify Zitzy via radio when we were going to force-search the mayor's suite, and simultaneously, with the State Police vehicle, he would batter open the garage door of the warehouse.

Zitzy, along with Breeze and possibly Jackie (to care for the kids), would make any needed arrests and set free and patiently begin to interview the children. He would also notify social services and request their assistance at both locations. And if all went well, we would also have the aftermath assistance of the NOPD and the FBI.

When the phone rang, I lurched for it. It was Macklin. "Régis, Judge Giaccone will see you in her chambers at 11:45. Do you have your affidavits prepared?"

"Yes, I do. Thanks."

"I know you're going to make a bust. You know I'm a cop, and if it has something to do with Dickerson's murder, I'd like to be in on it."

"But I can't trust you yet. As I told you, it has nothing to do with Dickerson's

murder. But I'll tell you what, Macklin—give me some time to think about it, and I might include you if you want to participate. You're growing on me, but I can't tell whether you're a wart, a freckle, or a beauty mark. Remain on standby, and you might hear from me."

"Please, Régis."

"I have to go. Stay on standby." And I disconnected.

"Has our surveillance team come up with anything new, Zitzy?"

"No, except for the comings and goings of unidentified men at the warehouse who appeared to be going out to procure food and drinks, it was quiet last night."

"Schedule a meeting for tomorrow morning at 10:00 in City Park. And work on an action syllabus; I'll be back later."

CHAPTER LVII
No Buts, Agent Régis

Judge Roberta Giaccone! She was a petit, russet brown-haired, and handsome lady. In contrast to most dull-eyed New Orleans politicos, she was discerning and refined. Her jade-green eyes glittered with perception and intellect. *Woe to the poor bastard who gets on her wrong side in the courtroom*, I mused.

All business, she said, "I have an active docket today, and I'm doing this for Macklin. Do you have your affidavits?"

"Yes, Your Honor." and I presented them to her.

She read them through and remarked, "Even though they're largely circumstantial, and most of it is hearsay, I'm inclined to issue the warrants. Do you have any physical evidence?"

No, Your Honor. But may I remind you that 'absence of evidence is not evidence of absence'?"

"There's no need to lecture me, Agent Régis! Why do you want no-knock warrants?"

"Because innocent children are involved, and I'm concerned that if we're delayed, they may be taken hostage in an attempt by the perpetrators to escape."

"Are you going to enlist the aid of the NOPD?"

"No, Your Honor. I'm afraid some members of the Department are part of the conspiracy. As it is, we've struggled to keep this under wraps, and we don't want to tip our hands. I shall, however, put the FBI on notice that we might need their assistance. But until we make the busts, I'm not going to advise them of our mission."

"I'm aware of the politics that's been going on at the Dome, Agent Régis, and I'm sensitive to the aspects of your situation. I can read between the lines of the newspaper articles and TV newscasts about your efforts."

Apparently, Zitzy had done a spectacular job, because she said, "These are the most thorough search warrant affidavits ever presented to me. You even included the fast-food refuse in the mayor's suite. And it's interesting that Level 6 is off-limits to even the security personnel.

"Therefore, there's more than enough reason for probable cause.

"But this is ultra-high-profile. You know you're going way out on a limb, don't you? I have full immunity, but if that limb breaks, I'm going to fall but not as hard as you. You'll be savaged and devoured by the New Orleans cannibalistic political machine, and your bones will be strewn across the cityscape to parch in the relentless New Orleans sun."

"I know that, Your Honor, but what choice do I have? Let me correct that. If you believe—as you should—that written in the affidavits is true and that I'm willing to risk my career on it, what choice do *we* have?"

"Technically, I do have a choice, Agent Régis. But as a mother, a human being, and an attentive observer, I have little wiggle room. And again, I have a good idea of what's been going on. I'm going to issue the two no-knock warrants...but with one stipulation."

"What is that, Your Honor?"

And she taser-zapped me, "That you include Rosh on the bust."

"But..."

"No buts, Agent Régis. Sergeant Macklin is the reason you're here. Without him asking, there would be no warrants issued to you from my bench.

"He's a broken man. I know all about the blackmail he's had to endure and the distressing situation with his wife. But I also know what a noble human being he is, both professionally and personally. He made a mistake—we all do—but he's paid a heavy price for it.

"This would be his opportunity to regain some of his integrity, and I want him to have that opportunity, especially before his wife dies. If you don't like my caveat, peddle your affidavits elsewhere." *Wow—she means business!*

There would be no productivity arguing with her. Besides that, I had toyed with the idea of including him, and we could use the extra help. Thus, it was moot; Macklin would be in on the raids. Prithee, let him be a demon-cum-angel.

So, I called him.

CHAPTER LVIII
Matriculating an Outlier into the Team

Returning to the Dome with the warrants, I directed Zitzy to have the team meet at the shelter near the flying horses tomorrow at 10:30 in the morning.

I dialed Macklin. I hoped I didn't disturb his wife, but if he were to be part of the team, he would have to participate like a team member. "Macklin, Régis; I hope this call didn't unsettle your wife."

"She's sedated; she could sleep through a hurricane."

"Thanks to Judge Giaccone, you're in. Can you leave your wife alone for a while?"

"Really? I can get her sister to sit with her. Am I really in?"

"Yes, you are. We're going to muster at the City Park shelter near the flying horses at 10:00 tomorrow morning. I'll fill you in sometime after that."

"I'll be there, and thank you!"

CHAPTER LIX
Living with a Guilty Conscience

I told Zitzy about Macklin, and he provided me with the strategy of assault he had written for me in my voice. As expected, it was almost flawless. He also informed me that Doughboy had procured the State Police sport utility vehicle and was on his way back to New Orleans from Baton Rouge.

I said, "Get his ETA, meet him at his apartment, notify him of Macklin's inclusion, and bring him back here."

"He should be nearing Jefferson Parish now." Zitzy contacted Doughboy via the handheld radios and said, "I'm going to head to his apartment. We'll be back shortly."

Reading Zitzy's outline, Willy interrupted me. "How's everything going, Johnny?" It bolstered me that he was so supportive. And I was certain that, in my hour of need, I could depend on his help.

"Well enough," I said, shrugging my shoulders to indicate otherwise.

"No new developments?"

"We keep getting stalemated, and we've run out of leads. I don't think we're ever going to solve this case. We've had a few developments, but they just didn't pan out. You know how it is; you think that you're onto something, and in the blink of a cat's eye, it's little more than thin air."

I hated to be lying to an ally, but other than providing moral support, there was nothing he could do. Moreover, if I disclosed my intentions, he might consider it to be bad press for the Dome and, therefore, try to dissuade us; he might try to impose an alternate strategy on us; or he could want to participate. But I had to make an eagle, and I was already teeing off with variable crosswinds of unknowns, so I was not inclined to add another potential complication.

I also harkened back to an apothegm my Daddy had bequeathed me, "Never let the left hand know what the right hand is doing." And this situation demanded I follow his advice.

"By the way, thank you for helping me with the interview."

"You're welcome. Is there anything else I can do?"

The game was going to be played on Sunday, and I needed a cover for us being

at the Dome on our day off. "Well, yes, there is. My crew and I are exhausted; we're going to take a much-needed break this weekend and temporarily put work aside. Do you think you could get us tickets to the game on Sunday?"

"You don't need tickets. Unfortunately, it's not a sell-out. Choose any vacant seats you like."

"Thanks, again, Willy."

"And my offer is good. If you need any help with the investigation, let me know."

"I might do that. However, as of now, we have nothing for you to assist us with." *But if we misfire, I'll need you to help with damage control.*

CHAPTER LX
Jackie Is Invited to Come Aboard

When Zitzy and Doughboy came into the office, I instructed them to pair up tomorrow and both of them to continue Doughboy's surveillance routine in Zitzy's assigned unmarked unit. Zitzy had already updated Doughboy on Macklin's involvement and our and plans for the assault.

Doughboy's eyes were twinkling, he was jaunty, and his face detonated with an exhilarated smiling-face meme. Nevertheless, I asked the superfluous question, "Has Jackie returned to New Orleans?" And with a contented warble, he confirmed she had.

I segued, asking, "What do you think about including Jackie in our foray; hasn't she had police-type training?"

"Yes, she has."

"Do you think she would be amenable to do so?"

"I can't speak for her, but you do remember why she's working here, don't you?"

"Well, if she's interested, have her come to our meeting tomorrow."

And tomorrow, I would have to call the AG. I wasn't looking forward to that.

I was awash with doubt. *You're the poster boy for the Peter Principle—you've promoted yourself to your level of incompetence. What in the hell makes you think you can make the grade with this grandiose gambit?*

But I found it odd I was composed. Oh, I was still burdened with doubts and unanswered questions. But I had a blueprint, and all I had to do was follow it. Contingencies were acceptable, but worrying about pratfalls was counterproductive. And I needed a good night's rest.

That evening, sweet Natalie had prepared Crawfish Monica, and to a slight degree, it assuaged my anxiety. Trying to give me solace, she said, "This too shall pass," but that did little to allay my apprehensions. Nyx, with her gloom of night and Eris disconcerting me, I slept the sleep of a tormented man. (Nyx was a Greek goddess of sleep. And Eris was the Greek goddess of discord and strife.)

CHAPTER LXI
Assemblage of a Motley Crew

Ah, autumn in New Orleans—clement and delightful, especially in City Park. But alas, it did not presage benevolent developments within the next thirty or so hours.

When I arrived at the shelter, the re-formed team, including Jackie, was there, and Macklin was beaming a silver dollar smile. But frowning, Pumpkin and Breeze inundated me with quizzical miens. They appeared to be astonished an outsider—especially an outsider such as Macklin—was present.

Directing my comments toward Pumpkin and Breeze, I said, "Here's the situation; we're going to serve two warrants tomorrow, and we couldn't have obtained *safe* warrants without the help of Sergeant Macklin. Besides that, we're shorthanded."

Pumpkin, sui generis, part cultured lady, and part no-holds-barred gamine, railed, "But Macklin? Hasn't he been an obstructionist adversary since the beginning?" She didn't question Jackie's involvement. (Jackie had taken more k-time to work with us.)

"Yes, he has. But he's changed his attitude, and again, we couldn't have obtained the warrants without him."

Macklin interjected, saying, "I don't blame you, Miss Burchett. All I can tell you is I've been a cop—a good cop—since I was twenty-one years old. And I want to catch these slimeballs as much as you do."

Pumpkin replied with a "Humph," and said, "But…."

I interrupted, "Pumpkin, he's on the team and we have to deal with it."

"Okay," she responded, "but I don't like it!"

Changing the subject, I said, "Here's the plan." And I went on to narrate the following that Zitzy had mostly prepared:

1. "Before we go operational, continue the surveillances. If there are no further movements, we'll postpone the raids.
2. "We will split up into two teams; Zitzy, Breeze, Jackie in one, and Pumpkin, Doughboy, Macklin, and I on the other.
3. "We'll synchronize the raids for 3:00.

4. "Zitzy and his team will batter down the garage door with the State Police sport utility vehicle and serve the warehouse warrant.

5. "Pumpkin, Doughboy, Macklin, and I will serve the other warrant on the mayor's box office suite. We, too, will batter down the door to the suite before entering.

6. "Doughboy, we'll smuggle the ram into the Dome with a guitar case. Buy one if you have to, and the AG's Office will reimburse you for it. (This was pre-9/11, and we were law enforcement officers; entry with the case would not be a problem.)

7. "At all costs, take care to ensure the safety of the children.

8. "There's a female on each team, and there's a reason for that. These children are going to be traumatized, and they might be suffering from Stockholm syndrome.

9. After the perps are arrested and handcuffed, you ladies will need to calm the kids down as only your gender can.

10. "These will be crime scenes; make every effort to preserve them.

11. "Today, Zitzy will call Kim and have her put the FBI on notice we might need two response teams for major busts at two different locations at about three on Sunday afternoon involving the violation of state and federal laws in Jefferson Parish. But also tell her not to divulge our plans to them.

12. "Additionally, tell her I know it's tricky, but use her charm to finesse it. Naturally, we'll inform them immediately if it's a no-go.

13. "Zitzy will call Kim as soon as possible after the scenes are secured, and have her get the FBI there posthaste; their office is only a few blocks away.

14. "Stay in constant radio contact; each member will carry a portable.

15. "Zitzy, you and I must make sure we have our search warrants, as the NOPD will probably descend upon both scenes in seconds.

16. "Doughboy, at 2:30, I'll need you to check out who is manning the security command desk.

17. "Everyone will be armed.

18. "Everyone must wear a bulletproof vest.

19. "And this is a team effort; one weak link breaks the chain."

"Are there any questions? Have we overlooked anything? Comments?"

Breeze asked, "Why do you want to lie and tell the Feebs that we will need them in Jefferson Parish?"

"Because it's a secret, and secrets spawn paranoia. What guarantee do we have that some of their agents are not in on this too? I'm not ready to risk that, especially when we don't have to."

"It looks like you put together all in all a motley crew—church member, atheist, gentile, and Jew, to quote a poem," said Pumpkin. "How about including Chaz?"

"A good idea," I said. "Contact him ASAP, and see if he's receptive. He's the coroner, so I won't have to deputize him as I am going to deputize Jackie. He can be on Zitzy's team, and I think a doctor would be an asset there. We don't know how much medical attention the children—if there are any—might need.

"Moreover, if our assumptions are correct, we ought to be met with less resistance at the warehouse because all the heavyweights should be in the mayor's suite. If Chaz comes along, make sure he has a sidearm and a vest.

"Any other comments?"

"I'd like to be on the same team as Chaz," Pumpkin said with a facetious twinkle.

"I know Pumpkin, but the two non-law enforcement persons should be on what appears to be the least dangerous assignment. And I think those children might need medical attention."

Pumpkin smiled and nodded her head in agreement.

"Besides your paranoia, are there any other reasons why you don't want to get the FBI involved beforehand?" asked Breeze.

"I've deliberated that. It's a close call, and I struggled with the decision. We could certainly use the resources, backup, and oblique political support, but I'm afraid they'd take over the investigation and sit on it."

"You mean you don't want them to take the credit?"

"That's not at all what I mean! We've set the hook, we're reeling in, and it's a big one. It's amazing we've been able to keep this invisible as long as we have. And we don't know how far the cancer's spread. Again, one or more of the Feebies might be involved too.

"Moreover, the FBI isn't going to take our intelligence and run with it; they're

going to have to develop their own database and make their own analyses before they take action. And that will take time, a commodity we and those children don't have."

"But we could certainly use more help and time to confirm our presumptions," said Breeze.

"You're right; we *are* a small crew, and we're working on a short run. But we're between the hammer and the anvil, and 'more help and more time' are luxuries we don't have. For us, this is like show business, 'The smaller the theater, the faster the music.'

"These are children—think about Bayou Sauvage. It's another Sophie's choice, and I'm not willing to risk it." Rage coupled with fear of failure incited the beast within me to jolt its cage, but I forced myself to stay calm.

"I'd rather, 'Do good by stealth, and blush to find it fame.' As far as the credit is concerned, it could be given to the NOPD, the FBI, Vinson's Security Services, or Joe Shit, the Ragman; I don't give a damn. But what I do care about is the welfare of those kids!"

Zitzy asked, "When and where are we going to muster tomorrow?"

"It depends on the surveillance results tonight; Zitzy will let you know. Give your reports to Zitzy, and keep your radios charged and on. Zitzy, call me immediately when you get their reports."

Breeze, Doughboy, and Pumpkin dispersed to their assignments, and I brought Macklin au courant. I couldn't help but notice the resolute gleam in his eyes, the same one the crew had and other cops before us have had before a bust.

But glancing at the flying horses, I thought, *Maybe all we're doing is going around in circles. And if we were, would we be able to snag the brass ring?*

Zitzy and I went to the office, and Jackie and Macklin supposedly to their homes. Once there, I decided to call Ed Sanderson. "Ed, Johnny Régis here. If I can contact you tomorrow in the afternoon, I might have a scoop for you."

"Can you tell me what it's about?"

"No, you'll have to trust me. The call is yours to make."

"I'll be expecting to hear from you tomorrow."

Later, Pumpkin called and said Chaz was in. And I then said to Zitzy, "There's not much more we can do for today. Let's chuck it in; we'll need to be rested for tomorrow. Zitzy left for home, and I went to my meditative stupa, the Lakefront,

sat on the seawall, and reflected, *Tomorrow the fat lady sings. Will she be celebrated, or will she be panned?*

CHAPTER LXII
The Ducks Are in the Decoys

I still had to call the AG, but it was better to do so from home. When I did, I gave him all the intelligence we had, and I outlined our plan as I had earlier done with my crew.

He didn't try to dissuade me, but he said, "If you're successful, my office will bask in the limelight, but if you fail, I'll probably have to fire you."

I was disquieted but found myself with a Panglossian perspective; therefore, I said, "I've already considered that General, but I'm going forward with it."

"Then you're on your own Régis."

I tried to eat dinner—Natalie's spectacular lasagna—but I had no appetite. I showered and readied myself for bed. And after Natalie went to sleep, I sat brooding and awaited Zitzy's call.

At 10:05, the phone rang. I snatched it from the cradle and said, "Tell me."

It was Zitzy. "Everything's falling into place. Doughboy and I observed Huberty leaving the Dome at 4:35 p.m. He proceeded to Popeye's on Saint Charles Avenue where he went through the drive-thru. He had a large order, and he pulled to the side and waited about fifteen minutes for it to be delivered. And from there, he went to the warehouse, arriving at 5:20.

"Breeze reported that, at 5:10, Courtney and the Mystery Lady left his office in the panel van, and they entered the warehouse at 5:42. Along with Huberty, the three of them remained there until 7:05 when Huberty, and Courtney with the Mystery Lady, drove in tandem to the Dome, and we followed them.

"At 7:18, Huberty parked his car in its regular spot. At 7:30, the Dome's rear service door opened, and Courtney drove the van inside. A half-hour thereafter, Courtney and his partner left the Dome and went back to his office, changed vehicles, and proceeded to his home.

"Huberty stayed at the Dome. We terminated the surveillances, and I don't know what time he left."

"The ducks are sitting in the decoys. Tell the team I said good work, Zitzy. Notify them we'll muster at 10:00 tomorrow, again in City Park. I'll call Macklin and have Doughboy call Jackie. Also, have two vehicles available for your team— the State Police SUV and your assigned unit. You can pick up Doctor Odom, and

Doughboy can pick up Jackie.

"And sometime after our raid, contact Popeye's for a copy of the receipt. I suspect we'll find Popeye's boxes and chicken bones in the mayor's suite tomorrow. Thinking about that, have Breeze sit on Huberty starting at 6:00 tomorrow morning. I believe Huberty is a part-time 'cafeteria man' for the children when they're in the Dome."

If the kids were in the Dome, Johnny, who was babysitting them? And although you've accounted for those you believe are the key actors, there are other multiple unknowns you haven't answered for. Will there really be abducted children in the Superdome? And even if there are, will we find them in the mayor's suite?

I was riddled with uncertainty. But because of the crew, I had to posture an image of confidence and fortitude to avoid casting the shroud of my apprehensions over our planned operation.

So I focused on Shakespeare, "Defer no time; delays have dangerous ends." And one way or another, it would all be over tomorrow.

CHAPTER LXIII
Suiting Up to Slay the Dragon

Awakening refreshed and virile in the morning, I knew I had been neglecting Natalie, but that was not the reason for my sexual puissance. I was a warrior going into what I envisioned would be a metaphorical life-or-death battle, and my subliminal primal instinct to procreate was preeminent.

When we kissed, it were as if a high-voltage electrical charge had fused two sundry metals. Natalie worked her magic, and Johnny Régis was ready to do combat.

Following the afterglow as I lay there exhausted, Natalie said, "Whew, Don Juan! You were great! Whatever prompted it, keep it going."

"You want to tiptoe through the tulips again?"

"Come on! Who are you kidding? After those gymnastics, you won't be ready to do *anything* in the tulips until the middle of next week. But I do expect an encore, so take care of yourself."

Perhaps because I realized how much I loved Natalie, or for some other unknown reason, I was thunderstruck by the realization that my theretofore lust for Pumpkin had vaporized. I still saw her as the beautiful human being she was, but at least for the moment, my innate sexual urges toward her had vanished.

Without being aware of it at the time, I had followed Carl Sagan's "Baloney Detection Kit" And I had appointed that our plan was the poetry of logical ideas. But I also considered the reality that poems like *The Bells, The Raven,* and *Ode to Silence* could sometimes be dreadful.

With squabbling birds in the trees overhead and a refreshing breeze tousling our coifs, it was a sensuous Indian-summer day belying the challenge and the quandary that lay before us. Yet the crew, including Macklin and the civilians, Jackie and Chaz were as wired as I was.

Using the authority given to the Attorney General and delegated to his senior agents, I deputized Jackie. I cautioned her and Chaz about the inherent dangers they might face. "Desperate men do desperate deeds, so be alert and follow Zitzy's orders." And with pronounced nods of their heads and sets of their mouths, they let me know they understood and agreed to do so.

Sitting close to one another with oeillades passing between them, Pumpkin and Chaz both glowed like three-wicked Yankee candles, as did Doughboy and Jackie. It didn't take much imagination to divine what they had done last night.

"I suppose Pumpkin apprised you of our situation, Doc?" I asked.

"She did," he replied. "And it seems to me you have a good case. Thank you for inviting me; I'd like to get the bastards too."

"And thank you for your help."

Macklin's enthusiasm was palpable. He, too, was as charged as a lightning bolt as was the rest of the team. And the crew's collective body language shouted, "Let's nail their asses!"

"Did Huberty move this morning, Breeze?"

"Your hunch was right. He left home at 7:05 and headed straight to McDonald's on South Claiborne Avenue. Like what happened at Popeye's, he went to the drive-thru and waited about fifteen minutes to receive a large order. He drove to the Dome and entered the parking areas.

"I didn't follow him; rather, I came to the park early to enjoy this pretty morning. And much to my surprise, Macklin was already waiting here smoking and drinking a cup of coffee when I arrived."

I still had doubts about Macklin, but they were now somewhat allayed.

Zitzy informed me he had checked on Bowditch's car yesterday evening and again this morning. Indeed, it appeared Bowditch spent the night in the Dome. Another hunch had borne results.

Bowditch was probably the babysitter. But they would need more than one. Who was the other? It was a loud noise in our investigative data.

"Did you contact Kim, Zitzy?"

"I did, but I haven't heard back from her."

"That's okay. When you do, tell her to call the FBI at 3:15 and request agents at the warehouse and the Dome after that. Ask them to also go to the Tchoupitoulas warehouse and, when at the Dome, to proceed straightaway to Level 6 on the LaSalle Street side.

"I've changed the time because at least some of the group in the mayor's suite might be distracted by the first plays following the kickoff. Also, ask Kim to assure the FBI that if we're successful, they can take all the credit for the bust. Call me via radio with updates as soon as you hear from her. And because of our high

220

profile, tell her to avoid letting them know we are involved.

"Doughboy, did you find a guitar case?"

"Yeah, I borrowed an old one from my nephew. It's in the SUV with the ram inside; it's one heavy motherfucker. I also have the second ram if we need it."

"Well, load it down a little more with the rest of the handcuffs you don't issue to Zitzy, Breeze, Jackie, and Chaz."

"Pumpkin, have you had time to apprise Chaz of our enumerated operational plans?"

"I caught your 'had time' innuendo," she said with a foxy smile. "And yes, we had time to work it in."

Eureka! As if shocked by a stun gun of clarity, an epiphany galvanized me. I had evolved...I felt no pangs of jealously! Perhaps my longing for Natalie at this critical juncture was the catalyst, but my bygone coveting of Pumpkin was now only an ephemeral memory. And with relief, I was certain I was past the point of no return.

"I bet you have had time to work 'it' in. Sorry, Doc; we're cops, and we tease hard."

Laughing, he said, "If a coroner wouldn't have a sense of humor, he'd go battier than he already is."

I iterated our bulleted plans but added the few tweaks I earlier mentioned. "Are there any questions or comments?" Does anyone think we should cancel or postpone?

Hearing no responses, I said, "Pumpkin, I know you and Chaz would like a little 'alone' time, so would the two of you go to Central Grocery and get muffulettas and soft drinks for us?"

She said, "Of course, if you're buying. But I expect a tip."

That prompted Breeze to say, "Oh, I bet you want more than just a tip!"

"Why? Because all you have to offer is a tip, Shorty?" And she took our orders.

I gave her eighty-five dollars and instructed her to bring me the receipt; this was to be courtesy of the AG's Office.

In less than an hour, they returned, and Pumpkin said, "Here's the receipt and the cash you gave me. Chaz picked it up."

"That's the least I could do," said Chaz. "After all, it was because of you guys I met Pumpkin. By the way, why do they call you Pumpkin?"

"It's a cute story contrived by these little dicks; I'll tell you later," replied Pumpkin with a wide grin. Apparently, Chaz was not underendowed.

"Did you get your tip, Pumpkin?" asked Breeze with an insinuating leer.

"I'll get it tonight, Danny Boy. Your pipes won't be calling, but mine will."

Unknown to us at that time, our luncheon would have some parallels to the Maundy Thursday feast.

Laughing and thanking Chaz, we blitzed our sandwiches and made small talk as we ate. Finishing our meal, I said, "Doughboy, are the vests in the van?"

"Yes, they are. But with the addition of Chaz, we're one short."

"That's okay," I said, "I'll go without one."

Amidst a cacophony of grumblings and suggestions, I was adamant, "This is my show; I'm responsible for all of you. My mind is made up. Get into your gear."

Doughboy gathered and distributed the vests among the crew, and in groups of twos and threes, they went to the nearby restrooms to don them beneath their shirts and blouses.

After that was finished and the extra handcuffs were issued, I said, "Zitzy, you and your team can hang out, but I want you in position at least fifteen minutes before our assaults."

My team and I headed to the Dome. Once there, I still had to listen to grousing about me not having a vest. Pumpkin, full of verve and always decisive, said, "When did 'everyone,' 'team effort,' and 'weak link' stop including you? You're trying to be macho, you motherfucker [delivered in her mezzo soprano enunciation], and I for one am not impressed."

But with an air of bravado I didn't have, I lit a cigar, leaned back in my swivel chair, and was able to calm them down.

"Our entry tactics are: Doughboy will batter the door in and back off. I'll lead, and the three of you will follow, entering with guns drawn. To whatever extent possible, we need to keep a 360, but when we make entry, remember, we'll only have a 180."

We're each going to have three extra sets of handcuffs—I'm assuming you have your issued ones. When we make the arrests, Macklin and Pumpkin will cuff the arrestees, and Doughboy and I will cover them.

At 2:00, Zitzy called Kim and then called me. "Kim has made the preliminary arrangements with the FBI, but she hasn't yet given them the nature of the case,

the times, or our locations. She said they aren't happy with the situation, but they were enticed by the carrot of getting full credit for the bust—whatever it was—if it were to be successful."

At 2:35, Doughboy informed me another supervisor, Arthur Terrebone, whom we hadn't interviewed, was manning the security command desk—Bowditch wasn't. I directed Doughboy to go into the arena and check whether or not the draperies in the mayor's suite were open or closed; five minutes later, he informed me they were shuttered.

At 2:50, I called Sanderson, "Come right now to Level 6 on the LaSalle Street side at the Superdome and by the end of the day you might have a lock on a Pulitzer."

Without hesitation, he said, "Okay," and we hung up.

CHAPTER LXIV
Strumming "Let Me In"

Antsy, I was in a *pater semper incertus est* quandary. No mere nostrum, this was like Coca-Cola—the real thing! I knew the perils that lay ahead were made even more mercurial by so many tasks left undone and a host of unanswered questions left on the table. At best, the outlook was for success 70/30 or, probably closer to the mark, 50/50.

But we might not have a more suitable time, and without going forward, we would have to brook at least another three weeks of trepidation knowing innocent children were suffering or then save the kids and let the perpetrators slip away.

Hoping for the best, we headed up to Level 6. *You better hope, Johnny; one way or another, they'll be looking up your ass.*

And still not one hundred percent convinced Macklin was not batting for the other team, I had resolved to kill him if he turned on us, even if it might cost me my life.

At 3:10, on the west side of the Level 6 ramp, we were stopped by a New Orleans police officer. "You can't go in there," he said. *If this were a setup, would he have tried to stop us?*

"Oh, yes we can officer," and Doughboy, Pumpkin, and I showed him our blazer pocket badges. "We're with the Attorney General's Office, and as you might have heard, we're doing a security review here. You probably know Sergeant Macklin with Homicide." And Macklin flashed his ID.

"Yes, I've heard of you; what's in the guitar case?"

"A guitar of course. The mayor has asked us to entertain her guests. Didn't she inform you? Oh, I guess not because we're adjunct to Dome security. We sing, and Agent Dosstein plays a mean guitar."

Leering at Pumpkin who was flashing her "come hither" smile, he said, "Do you dance?"

Effecting a kittenish air, she said, "Yes, but never fully clothed."

"I'd like to see that! Have a good time," and he waved us through.

Walking down the corridor toward what I presumed would be the site of

despoilment, I thought, *There are a lot of bad people all over the world. But why in the hell do we have such an abundance of them here?*

CHAPTER LXV
The Precarious Crapshoot

In front of the mayor's suite door waiting for my card to be dealt, I noted that eleven suites from us in the otherwise empty corridor, the police officer had turned away and was chatting up an attractive middle-aged lady.

This was going to be the big divulgence! I was going to fill in the inside straight, or I was going to go tits up. But in any event, *alea iacta est.*

I made a quick radio call to Zitzy to proceed, and releasing the falcon, I said, "Now, Doughboy; do your stuff."

The door was a flimsy one, and it only required one ramming to open it. Tax, license, and insurance, it was all there in a watershed moment, an eyeblink of eternity.

Bolting into the Mayor's lair, I had effectuated the hand I sought, and it was an inside straight flush, no less, with the Ace of spades leading the way! We were jarred by a plangent, bittersweet panoply. The sweet: I had surmised unerringly— the children *were* there; we had saved them; and I wasn't going to shatter my career.

But the bitter was stupefying: What we encountered was surreal, and we were sickened and aghast; we were in a mosh pit of mostly naked bodies. The gods of depravity ruled with might and main; the New Orleans *haut monde* were frolicking in an abhorrent pedophiliac orgy. It was sensory overload.

The kids...the kids...those woeful children! The room was crowded with about thirty-five or more adults and juveniles, most of whom were naked. Contrary to what I had presumed, no one was interested in the football game below; in fact, the draperies were still drawn.

The mayor—grunting, groaning, and having a ball—was on her back on a sofa being screwed by a young Hispanic boy no older than twelve. At the same time, she was performing cunnilingus on a diminutive white girl of about nine squatting over her face, the two children almost lost in her oleaginous rolls of fat. In an instant, I realized how prescient Doughboy had been, and I had disagreed with him, when he opined about her involvement.

Another pre-adolescent white girl was performing fellatio on a naked

injured or killed us and innocent children as well.

And in a moment after that, the NOPD officer with whom I had spoken must have heard the battering of the door or Pumpkin's shot, and he burst into the room shouting, "What the hell's going on in here!"

By then, we were overwhelmed with neural inundation. So at a reckless turning point, my team and I were easily distracted; our heads swiveled, and we looked behind us.

Bowditch had to have known it was finis. With what I assumed was extracting revenge for the indignity Pumpkin had foisted on him, he drew his gun and shot her in the dorsal left side of her head.

She dropped her sidearm, and she, along with her zest, sagged to the floor—a worn-out rag doll with red fingernail polish in its cornsilk blonde hair. In my later fantasized recollection, I saw three seraphs swoop in and whisk her soul away to the vault of heaven.

Amidst panicked screaming, with what I believe to be was Bowditch's choler with Macklin for being a Judas Iscariot, he fired again, hitting Macklin in his arm. And Macklin, too, let fall his service revolver onto the black and gold fleur-de-lis-impressed Mohawk "SmartStrand Forever Clean" carpet.

It was apparent Bowditch, armed with a revolver, had little police firearms training, for he paused before firing again. Then, when he was about to get off another shot at the wounded Macklin, I leaned forward, lunged between them, thrice rapid-fired my Browning Hi-Power semi-automatic 9mm-caliber pistol, and hit him with all three in his chest. He fell to the floor with his penis still projecting from his open fly.

But Bowditch consummated the omega! As he was being ferried by Charon the ferryman across the River Styx, he fired once more. And amid the screaming, the last thing I remembered was bearing witness to a supernova stellar explosion.

PART TWO

CHAPTER LXVI
Lucky to be Alive

As if in a pea-soup, fog-enshrouded Honey Island swamp, I awakened in a hospital bed. My vision was out of focus, but I could discern three doctors and a nurse surrounding me. One of the doctors, with what seemed to be the voice of a frog croaking in a drainage pipe, was saying, "Mister Régis, can you hear me?"

My head was hurting like hell; I was cantankerous; and all I wanted to do was sleep. But with a dry mouth and a brittle voice, I answered, "Yes."

"Can you move your fingers?" I could, and with my arms still on the bed, I shot him the bird with my right hand to prove it.

He chuckled and asked me, "Where do you live?"

"Old Metairie."

"Are you married?"

"I sure as hell hope so; where's my wife?"

"What's her name?"

"Natalie. Now stop asking me all these stupid questions and get my wife!"

"Only two more. What is twelve squared?"

"Is this a fucking math quiz? One hundred forty-four. Pi is 3.1248 into infinity. The hypotenuse of a right triangle is equal to the square root of the sum of the squares of the other two sides. And the Hippocratic Oath includes, 'First do no harm.' Now get me my wife!"

"He seems okay to me," said another doctor. "I think it best we not distress him; we can do further testing later."

The doctors left, but the nurse stayed with me. And within a few moments, Natalie, with tears cascading from her viridian eyes, was at my side. "Oh, Baby, oh Baby," she bawled, as she buried her wet face in my chest. I tried to hug her, but my arms were leaden.

"Please Ma'am," said the nurse, "he isn't to be moved. Perhaps you can hold his hand."

She did and, with an efflux of compassion, entreated, "How do you feel?"

"I feel like I've been beaten with buzzard guts and drug through hell backwards. But it's all okay with you at my side."

Fatigued and with her face drawn, she appeared to be feeling my pain. She said, "Where do you hurt?"

"My head hurts...bad."

Out of the corner of my eye, I saw the nurse nudge her. The nurse instructed Natalie, "Continue to hold his hand." Natalie did, and I could hear the rustle of the nurse's scrubs as she moved about.

"What happened to me?" I asked. And once again, I could see the nurse nudge Natalie.

Natalie said, "We'll talk about it tomorrow."

"But I want to...," and I lofted to an undefinable, nebulous place, where, I slipped into an artificially induced hibernation.

I next awakened to hear someone calling my name, "Johnny, Johnny Régis." Opening my eyes, my vision was again blurry, but it seemed I could see the same three doctors and the same nurse as before.

"How do you feel, Mr. Regis?" one of them asked.

"I just told you. Why are you back here again? Where's my wife? She was with me a few moments ago!"

"That was yesterday," he said. "Mr. Régis, you suffered a serious head injury due to a gunshot wound. We had to perform brain surgery on you and keep you in a medically induced coma for six days. You're lucky to be alive."

And with the flash of a strobe light recalling the events preceding my hospital confinement, a tsunami of anger roiled within me. That motherfucker Bowditch shot me!

"You're in the Intensive Care Unit at Charity Hospital, and we would like to place you in a room, but we have to run some more tests on you first. Please try to cooperate with us, and we'll get you out of here as quickly as we can so you can be with your wife and visit with the droves of people who want to wish you well and are now filling our lobby and corridors."

Even in my groggy state, it made sense. "Let's get it on!"

"How do you feel?"

"A little woozy, like I had too much to drink."

"Does your head hurt?"

"Yes, but not as bad as it did earlier...er, yesterday."

"Can you move your fingers?"

I said, "Yes," and I moved them on both hands.

One of the doctors said, "Well, he didn't flip us off today," and they all three chortled.

"Can you lift your arms?"

Thinking back to how leaden they were yesterday, I could raise them this time, although it required an unusual effort.

"Can you wiggle your toes?" And I did so with relative ease.

"Can you lift your legs?" I did, but only barely so.

"You're doing well, Mr. Régis. But you suffered a traumatic injury and underwent a delicate surgery. You can't let yourself get excited; if you do, it will delay your recovery. Or worse, we might have to put you in a medical coma again, and those are always dicey.

"We're going to keep you in ICU a few more days, and we're going to restrict visitors except your wife."

"What...no math problems today?"

"No, but I'll give you a little physics quiz. If a car going 20 m/h skids with locked brakes on a certain roadway for x feet, would it skid $2x$ feet on the same road at 40 m/h?"

"You gotta' be shittin' me."

"Caught you on that one, didn't I?"

"You didn't even catch a cold. It's all about kinetic energy; the car would skid $4x$ feet."

"You might be out of here sooner than you think, Mr. Régis."

"Wonderful! Now would you send in my wife?"

Five minutes later, Natalie, as alit as City Park at Christmastime, came rushing toward me, and the nurse again cautioned her against moving me. Natalie did, however, adorn me with soft gentle kisses. "The doctors said you're going to be fine!" she said with glee. "But you have quite a road to recovery—we can do it together."

She told me about my injury. The bullet cracked my skull and caused a buildup of fluid on my brain. I was rushed to Charity Hospital where a neurosurgeon—

Tommaso Canale, the best in the city and probably the doctor who questioned me—performed emergency surgery to relieve the pressure and excised a tiny portion of my left cerebrum that was damaged.

"Well, the unsubstantiated trope is we only use ten percent of our gray matter anyway," I joshed.

"And I've always said you have a hard head," she teased. "Johnny, you've always been my hero, but now, you're everyone's hero."

"Why? Because I was shot?"

"You saved Macklin's life. You took a bullet for him. You eradicated a horrendous and widespread pedophiliac sex slave ring. You outright rescued forty-four innocent children and probably saved hundreds more.

"You demolished the Vatican of the New Orleans crime syndicate and annihilated its Pope, Mayor Luna Langlois, its Cardinals in the New Orleans City Council, and the lords of pedophilia who have tithed the Devil Incarnates' sanctum."

"But I couldn't have achieved anything without you. You have been my Eirene and my life's compass."

Again hearing the whoosh of scrubs, I saw Natalie nod at the nurse. And I said, "Nothing I did was important, all I ever wanted was to be your he…"

Descending into the abyss. I recalled the words of Kurt Vonnegut, "We are here for no reason unless we can invent one." And I wondered…had I yet invented mine?

CHAPTER LXVII
The Dearly—and Not-So-Dearly—Departed

Fallout funerals in New Orleans had made front-page newspaper and afternoon TV lead stories.

Pumpkin was buried with honors, pomp, and gravitas. The Governor, the Attorney General, one of Louisiana's two U.S. senators, J. Benjamin Johnson, and the Superintendent of State Police, Colonel Dondre Theriot—all exceptional orators—eulogized her. Her Pastor, Monsignor Algernon Marchand of Saint Louis King of France Catholic Church, administered the last rites.

Pumpkin's service was held in Metairie, and she was placed in a grave downtown in Saint Vitus Cemetery, the same cemetery in which Langdon was interred. Her 25m/h cortege tied up traffic on I-10, I-610, and many of the surrounding streets.

Chaz, on his BMW, pulled a small, new, flatbed aluminum trailer onto which Pumpkin's casket was secured. Alongside the multitude of colorful sprays surrounding it, the casket was strapped to the trailer and topped with a large pumpkin. After all, that's what she was called, and it was fall—pumpkins were in harvest.

In addition to a multitude of civilians—including almost all the populace of Bucktown—at least a hundred somber police officers from throughout Louisiana, thirty-one other States, and even an RCMP from Canada attended the funeral. With their piebald potpourri of dress uniforms, they rendered a semblance of a Picasso abstract.

The cortege was escorted by a phalanx of forty-two multicolored, multidistrict motorcycles with a cacophony of sirens clamoring. The NOPD motorcycle squad led the procession. And six Louisiana State Police motorcycles trailed the three-quarter-mile procession to prevent frustrated motorists from interposing themselves in the motorcade.

At the burial, the tocsin of a bell rung seven times with seven-second pauses between each chime tolling across the necropolis and the surrounding neighborhood. On its heels, a lone bugler mournfully played *Taps*, and that was followed by a 21-gun salute. Benicia Burchett, we miss you.

I later learned Gayle again hosted an intimate funeral party. She presented the same buffet as she had after Langdon's funeral, and amid the tears, the mourners devoured the fare. Maybe they did so to assuage their grief.

With an overflow of contributions, a white, six-foot, Italian Carrara marble cenotaph dedicated to Benicia (Pumpkin) Burchett was sculpted. And the owners of One American Place in Baton Rouge, the private office building where the State rented workspace for the AG's headquarters, generously donated twenty square feet of their plush lobby for it to be sited there. Besides her name, DOB, and DOD, its epitaph was, *She Died Protecting Our Children.*

I was sickened at the thought that my former debauched desires for Pumpkin had exposed me, if only in secret to myself, as the lowlife I had affirmed myself to be. And that weighed on my soul.

The next big funeral was for Shallier Corbin. He had been cleared of any involvement. But because he was ultimately responsible for Superdome security, he was fully accountable for not having been cognizant of the detestable affairs occurring on his watch and the criminality of his partner, Huberty.

And Corbin, Richard Cory's counterpart, "one calm [autumn] night, [...] went home and put a bullet through his head."

Perhaps he had been successful with other ventures, but the opportunity that could have propelled him to legitimate status and prosperity was snatched from him. Sad to hear of his death, I believed that under different circumstances, we might have been able to have been friends.

But Corbin's Pontius Pilate attitude of non-involvement had come back to crucify him. One of his last reported utterances before he killed himself was, "That nigger motherfucker, Huberty, ruined me."

Nadeau had been a leading light in New Orleans politics, loved and respected by both Blacks and whites. He was an almost shoo-in to be the next mayor when Langlois' eight-year term limit expired. And later perhaps, the State's first Black governor.

However, he died in infamy. His closed-casket, private funeral was attended by only a few family members, and his burial was so disregarded he could have been a homeless wino interred in potter's field.

Bowditch was buried on his farm; there were less than ten people—not all mourners—present for his last rites.

Our bust was a parabolic regicide. And the biggest funeral was for the death of the New Orleans parasitic juvenile sex crime fiefdom and, buried with it in the sepulcher of parish prison, the toxic sludge of humanity's most heinous lowlifes.

The solipsistic psychopath, Mayor, Luna Langlois, was held without bail on both State and Federal juvenile charges for kidnapping, aggravated rape, accessory to murder (three counts), the Mann Act, and pedophilia.

Based on their financial resources and the possibility of flight risk, those who were eligible for conditional release had high bonds assessed upon them, and their passports were revoked.

One judge and four of the seven New Orleans Council members—three men and one woman—were held on charges of aggravated rape and abetting child trafficking. Their bonds ranged between $150,000 to $250,000. The council members not charged were one male and two females...the angels' share?

Due to the unwritten "Code of Honor" among imprisoned hardened criminals who abominate child rapists, many of the arrestees would eventually die violent deaths while incarcerated. The best the male sex-slaving pedophiles could hope for were hemorrhoids.

The mayor's toady, Irvando, was charged with the Mann Act, aggravated rape, abetting child trafficking, and kidnapping; his bond was set at $225,000. There was no doubt he, too, would not survive imprisonment.

The duplicitous fifth columnist, Willy, was indeed the "Operations Manager" for not only the Superdome but also the pedophiliac sex trade and child abduction syndicate. He kept the operation's books which were seized to be used as evidence and to expand the inquiry in order to net other sickos.

But his most critical job was extensive and intensive vetting of potential buyers to prevent moles or undercover agents from joining the society, a task he did with surgical precision and dynamism. The entrance fee alone was $25,000, part of which was spent on the vetting process.

Even if the NOPD had not been so corrupt and dismissive of the missing "runaways," its detectives would have first had to have an inkling of the operation, which was well-hidden. And besides that, the police department would have been unable to front that much money to place an undercover agent in that high-ticket sphere.

Willy, too, was charged with the Mann Act, aggravated rape, kidnapping, child

trafficking, and accessory to murder. (It was he who orchestrated Dickerson's killing.) His bond was the highest, set at $350.000.

Because of the perceived flight risk, bail bondsmen would have chosen to put their balls in a meat grinder before doing business with any of them.

Interviewing the children, the FBI learned Courtney had injected the two Bayou Sauvage children who had tried to escape with etorphine. Then to put even more fear in the other children to shun flight, Huberty had shot and eviscerated the two would-be runaways in front of their cellmates. Courtney and Huberty were charged with aggravated rape, child trafficking, and three murders. Like Langlois, both were held without bail.

The team led by Zitzy at the warehouse had encountered no resistance. Two Hispanic Dome security guards and jailers, Jaime Suite and Jacques San Romano, were arrested there and charged with aggravated rape—with the cookie jar so close at hand, they, too, had availed themselves to pedophilic sexual treats—abetting child trafficking, and accessories to murder. Their bonds were set at one hundred fifty thousand dollars.

Suite copped out on the other eight warehouse guards, all convicted felons. They were subsequently arrested and had high bonds set against them too.

Considering how it was used, the State Police vehicle suffered little damage; it was nothing that couldn't be repaired at the State Police Motor Pool.

Having received a report of an SUV crashing into a warehouse door, the NOPD converged onto the warehouse scene. But by then, Zitzy's team had matters under control.

There, they found twenty-eight children in two gender-separated cells hastily built within three weeks or so around two pre-existing male and female bathrooms. Each enclosure had steel bunkbeds, footlockers with Goodwill clothing, a toilet, and a shower. Other than the odiferous toilets and the floors, the only places for the children to sit were the sides of the bunks and the small clothing trunks at the ends of the beds.

The youngsters were confined like cattle in pens waiting to be slaughtered. One of the cells held eight boys, and the other immured twenty girls. Those children who weren't crying displayed vacant stares.

Physical examinations and blood tests of the children in the warehouse revealed many of them were malnourished, some had gonorrhea, and almost all

tested positive for high levels of lorazepam, a benzodiazepine that works in the brain to relieve symptoms of anxiety, administered to prevent a *Lord of the Flies* scenario from occurring. Most of the children were zombie-like.

The floors were strewn with fast food containers, plastic cups, and straws—the wild animal cages at the Audubon Zoo were more orderly and sanitary than those occupied by the confined and exploited children.

Would those poor innocents ever recover?

Would *we* ever recover?

CHAPTER LXVIII
Aftermath and Media Praise for the AG's Office

Ed Sanderson had followed hot on the heels of the police officer who had entered the mayor's suite, and both witnessed the shootout when Pumpkin, Macklin, Bowditch, and I were shot. And somehow or another, Sanderson wasn't later barred from the scene.

On the front page of the *Times-Picayune*, a full banner-headlined article with his byline shouted:

Titanic Pedophilic Sex Slave Ring Sunk by AG Sortie
Three Dead; Mayor, Judge, Council Members, Others Arrested.

The news story continued, "In simultaneous raids, a limited team of five Attorney General agents, one off-duty NOPD officer, Coroner Charles Odom and a deputized Dome security guard made the biggest pedophiliac sex-slave roundup in Louisiana history.

"A miscellany 'doodlebug squad' razed what had been an ineradicable pedophilic slave-trade temple of iniquity and depravation.

"One AG agent, Benicia Burchett, and two suspects—City Councilman Roy Nadeau and Dome Security Officer Gerald Bowditch—were killed in a firefight. And AG Agent Johnny Régis and off-duty NOPD Sergeant Rosh Macklin were wounded in the operation."

Without being unduly graphic, but not overly painting over it, Sanderson also described the scene in near-Gothic phraseology as he had witnessed it at the time of the raid.

The piece further detailed the names of the arrestees, praised the AG's office as the most competent law enforcement agency in the State, and extolled me for orchestrating the raids and as a hero for saving Macklin's life.

Sanderson said our operation was a tourbillion of ingenuity and persistence, and he contrasted our diminutive team to the huge NOPD complement. Analogizing it to the Battle of Thermopylae, he wrote, "Against incredible odds, Attorney General Agent Johnny Régis rendered a stellar performance, and he and

his diverse crew of seven accomplished what 1,700 NOPD officers were unable to do."

Mostly quoting Zitzy, who gave justified credit to the FBI and the NOPD for their assistance in making the arrests, the article continued. And omitting pertinent details saved for trial presentation, outlined the maze we wended through to make the apprehensions.

Part of Sanderson's article was written in the first person, wherein he reported witnessing the killings of Pumpkin, and Bowditch as well as the wounding of Macklin and me.

And the article provided additional details, some of which were:

The lone uniformed NOPD officer had seized my gun that lay on the floor at my side. He, and to some degree Macklin—who, until the ambulance arrived, had retrieved his sidearm with his good arm—a flood of additional NOPD officers summoned from their Dome security posts, and the FBI made the physical arrests.

Because Nadeau had produced a gun "out of nowhere," all the adults were arrested and cuffed as they were found—clad and partially clad, but almost all nude. It wasn't until a thorough search of their clothing could be made that they were one-by-one unhandcuffed, allowed to dress, and re-handcuffed before being taken away. Their culpability was not going to be a hard sell to a jury or juries if they were tried separately or en masse.

Thinking ahead, Sanderson had brought his mini-camera, and he took photographs of the naked arrestees in the progress of their uncontestable evil. The photo editor of the Times-Picayune artfully blurred out the arrestees' genitalia, the females' breasts, the faces and genitalia of the children, and the dead bodies.

The newspaper ran one of the retouched photos along with Sanderson's article, but even with the retouching, it was unmistakable that almost all of the participants were in the buff.

Without delay, the children had been segregated from the crime scene clad in assorted clothing provided by other box suite attendees—mostly men giving their shirts—and whisked to a private area. New Orleans and State social workers as well as the medical community swoped in and pooled their resources to calm and attend to the young victims.

Doughboy had been too preoccupied to make any arrests. Giving me aid, he

had torn off his shirt to stanch blood loss from my head wound. And he went in the ambulance to nearby Charity Hospital with Macklin and me.

Sanderson ended the piece saying, "Macklin is recovering from an arm wound, and Régis is in ICU in critical condition with a bullet wound to his head. Hopefully, he will recover. Régis will fare well without the Superdome. But will the Dome fare well without that cop?"

The Emergency Room had been notified of the imminent arrival of two injured police officers, one with a head wound and one with a gunshot to the arm. And in Charity Hospital practice for police officers injured on duty, the decks had been cleared expecting us.

One ER doctor, one neurosurgeon, and two nurses were waiting on the emergency ramp when the ambulance, escorted by two NOPD squad cars, sped up and onto the elevated emergency vehicle ramp.

The AG's office did not solicit limelight for the apprehensions. But the New Orleans Chief of Police seized upon the NOPD officers' and Macklin's presence at the scene and effected an ostentatious effort to claim credit for the captures. The Chief's assertation was so ludicrous he became the laughingstock of the New Orleans media.

Editorials on local television and in the two major New Orleans newspapers portrayed the Chief as a pompous buffoon. And a *Times-Picayune* editorial cartoon pictured him as a rotund, bulbous-nosed police officer in uniform wearing a king's crown emblazoned "Chief." With a nightstick held over held at a forty-five-degree angle, amid battered children lying at his feet receiving care from an AG agent, he was saying, "I, alone, am the guardian of my subjects."

Although the FBI New Orleans Special Agent in Charge also tried to gain credit for the bust, the lengthy *Times-Picayune* front-page article by Sanderson and a similar one published in the *States-Item* by Katzman precluded him from doing so.

Two days later, the *Times-Picayune* again lampooned the NOPD, but this time along with the FBI, too, for their vapid attempts at self-aggrandization. Another *Times-Picayune* editorial cartoon pictured the uniformed police chief, this time with a police hat saying, "NOPD," and a portly, bow-tied, pork-pied-hat bureaucrat with "FBI" on the hat's crown. The two in the parody-captioned "Superdome" sketch were fighting over an oversized football lettered "Child Sex

Trafficking Bust." Each was saying, "It's mine!" And a caricature of an AG Agent holding an entitled "Game Ball" was standing at goalposts in the background laughing at them.

One of the attendant articles also criticized the NOPD for having refused to work with us, a just commentary for such a derelict agency.

Already short of staff before the raids, the deaths of Langdon and Pumpkin as well as my injury ended the AG's participation in the review of Superdome security. But the Governor dispatched a detail from the State Police to take over where we had left off.

With new security contractors, the LSP tenure in the Dome was uneventful. Absent the nemeses we withstood, they were able to facilitate many much-needed changes in the Dome's security system and thereby revitalize the Dome from its theretofore haunting and dystopian image.

CHAPTER LXIX
Queen City on the Mend

Zitzy, Doughboy, and Breeze collaborated in the preparation of a fifty-eight-page report documenting our activities and findings leading up to and including our raids, and they provided a copy to the FBI. Afterward, Zitzy was temporarily assigned to assist the Bureau with the continuing investigation, and Doughboy and Breeze resumed their regular duties.

The FBI did eventually receive much-deserved credit because their agents commandeered the follow-up investigation and did a laudable job with it. Besides ferreting out a great many pedophiles burrowed like termites in the woodwork, they made multitudinous arrests, and they reunited most of the abused children with their grateful parents.

Utilizing their prodigious resources, the FBI disgorged the garbage of humanity from their once-secured dumpsters of iniquity into a refuse collector. Most of them would be disposed as slag heap in prison, and others would be incinerated in the electric chair.

Using Willy's books, Langlois' labyrinth was deciphered, and throughout the New Orleans metropolitan area, a manifold of other affluent pedophiles and sex slavers took the fall. Even an FBI agent was one of those arrested.

And what a monolithic enterprise their pedophilic slave trade had been! Quite the entrepreneur, Luna Langlois had extended her network of perversion and atrocities up the East Coast as far north as New York and even into Canada. The FBI estimated all the key players had become millionaires in the process.

The degenerates had established a Maginot Line. Because all the participants were complicit, none would have bailed on the group, for they would then would have had to acknowledge their collusion and involvement.

Almost all transactions had been made in cash; indeed, no one—seller nor buyer—wanted to leave a paper trail. Thus, in the process, most of their proceeds had been deposited into multiple domestic banks and from there into offshore accounts. With the cooperation of other countries, those assets were methodically seized by the IRS.

But as cunning at business as the traffickers were, they wallowed in stupidity.

Hoisted by their own petards, they mistook feigned form for substance. And as if wooed by sirens' songs, their ship grounded on a reef of retribution and sunk in their sea of insatiable prurience.

An accomplished drug dealer doesn't make use of his wares. But Langlois and her group did avail themselves of their commodities. With unbridled arrogance, they felt they were invincible; after all, Langlois "owned" the city. She had the City Council, the NOPD, and much of the New Orleans judiciary in her crawly grasp—surely, someone, somewhere, somehow would tip them off about a forthcoming raid.

But Goliath met David, and the perverts trivialized their "bumpkin" adversaries. Obsessed and blinded with power, they were witless to their chimeric air castles. Most dictators self-destruct, even Mikhail Gorbachev, the last Soviet president, admitted as much. "Absolute power corrupts absolutely" ...and makes one foolish too.

Courtney had fled. But with the combined efforts of Zitzy, Doughboy, and the FBI, he was learned to have a fishing camp in Happy Jack, located in Port Sulphur. Zitzy and Doughboy staked it out, and when they found him to be there, they, along with the FBI and the Plaquemines Parish Sherriff's Office took him into custody without incident.

A search of Courtney's office premises evinced two cells similar to, but smaller than, the ones at the warehouse. They were, however, empty. Later-collected evidence would establish the cells were way stations used to detain some abductees—most often from New Orleans East—before they were ferried to the Tchoupitoulas Street warehouse and then to the Superdome.

Breaking the *omertà*, Courtney became a high-profile snitch. Terrified of going to the electric chair, he made a deal and sang like Pavarotti belting out *Pour Mon Âme*. He blamed Dickerson's murder on Huberty as well as Conrardy, who allegedly orchestrated the execution. Doing so, he fitted together most of the remaining puzzle pieces.

With his admissions, the history and machinations of the child human trafficking unfurled, exposing their craven stripes and razing the inner sanctum of the transgressors. According to Courtney, the enterprise, founded by Conrardy and Langlois, had been in existence for a few years before the Dome opened. The Dome simply provided an almost tailor-made venue for the pedophilic sex slavers

to ply their wares in upscale ambience.

I was wrong...again. Father Duncan *did* have street smarts. Salting his confession with some truth, he had held out on and lied to his confessors, Breeze and me. Indeed, Duncan and Courtney's live-in, the Mystery Lady, were a team and the principal procurers of the children.

Besides the Dome abductions, they posed as volunteer social workers, luring children with candy, pastries, McDonald's burgers, and oftentimes marijuana. The duo had ready access to those who depended on the benignity of others, and they were responsible for up to seventy percent of the abductions!

They were nihilistic farmers, planting seeds of cash and feigned compassion in the abundant fields of poverty and then reaping the harvests of indigent and innocent children. But they became overweening, extending their operations into the Superdome "tour" business. Had they not done that, they might have remained will-o'-wisps for a limitless time.

It seemed Duncan wanted to protect the mayor too. Duncan had told Breeze and me she was an altruist, and to his knowledge, she was not involved in the child trafficking ring.

Was Duncan in it for the money? Or was his payoff simply pedophiliac sex? If it were the latter, the scenario could have been a takeaway from the monastery scenes in de Sade's *Justine*.

Perhaps just before his suicide, Duncan realized the operation was coming to an end, and he and his partner would be exposed. And by then, the priests' pedophile rest home in Jemez Springs would be way beyond his reach.

I also considered that maybe Duncan had developed a fondness for Quintero. With his Asian/Hispanic attempt at deception, he had tried to cover for her. He might have even been hiding the salami with her. And hoping to give her time to flee to Colombia was why he left no suicide note.

Huberty, the "patron saint" of the fertile grounds of the housing projects, was another procuring entity. He was a wholesaler. Beyond his complicity in the Dome snatchings, his MO was to buy children from derelict drug addicts and poverty-stricken parents who could no longer feed, care for, control, nor in some cases, even want their children.

Both Huberty and Duncan projected *trompe l'oeil* altruism. Perhaps they fell victim to Oscar Wilde's quote, "Charity creates a multitude of sins." Or they were

truly sociopathic and used the humanitarian facades solely to satisfy their pedophilic perversions and aggrandize their lucrative juvenile sexual enslavement enterprise.

Courtney declared Huberty and Conrardy had told him they had information Dickerson might have unearthed their criminal activities. Conrardy said Dickerson had to be handled, and Courtney, Conrardy, Huberty, and Bowditch devised a plan to intimidate and interrogate Langdon by confronting him at the Dome during one of his meddlesome midnight specials.

The veterinarian further said he and Huberty boxed Dickerson in on the Loge level next to the balcony (as Pumpkin had said). And when Huberty buttonholed him, Langdon lashed out. Huberty, weighing almost twice that of Langdon, seized him and told Courtney to inject him.

But according to Courtney, a southpaw, he did so only to subdue him. And he maintained that, in the fray, he accidentally administered more etorphine than he had intended; whereupon, Dickerson immediately went limp and died. Of course, the autopsy report contradicted him.

Trying to make it look like an accident or a suicide, Huberty threw Dickerson over the balcony. We never did learn why Ghost was where he was when he met his demise.

Courtney also said Bowditch, sharing in the profits of the operation, had been a key player. He was present on the stadium field when Langdon was killed, and he served as the lookout, coordinating the restriction of the guards' movements when the murder occurred.

Further incriminating Huberty, Courtney also claimed that, inasmuch as Huberty, along with Corbin, were the security contractors, they had keys to all the Dome's portals. Therefore, covertly getting his partner, the Mystery Lady, and the children in or out of the building was effortless.

Courtney's was a doomed man's confession, and it was unlikely a jury would exculpate him for that. But for providing that information and testifying for the government, he would probably escape the death penalty. While in Angola—aka, "The Farm"—maybe, he would be pressed into service to treat prisoners or at least the large herds cattle and the horses used in agriculture and the yearly convict rodeo.

Vehement in his denial, Huberty repudiated Courtney's account and declared

246

the veterinarian was lying, insisting he was asleep in his office at the time of Dickerson's murder, and he didn't find out about it until he left the Dome at 6:00 that morning.

He also denied his involvement in the Bayou Sauvage children's murders. But a search of his house unearthed the S&W Model 10 that matched the bullets recovered from the two Bayou Sauvage victims. It is amazing that so few killers fail to dispose of the weapon used in their homicides—the literal smoking gun.

An exorcism of the vile demons within Huberty would be futile. The only cure for thar execrable disease was euthanasia. And to meet that end, doomed to perdition, he was a prime candidate to be a *cochon de lait* in Old Sparky.

Upon further questioning, Courtney disclosed it was he who supplied the lorazepam the warehouse guards slipped into the children's beverages. But the group made sure the kids who were to be on the auction block two days hence were not given the drug beforehand—business acuity ordained that sexual zombies wouldn't sell well.

Besides the two Bayou Sauvage children who were disemboweled, Courtney said a few others had died in captivity. Due to fast-food-only malnutrition, they had fallen ill and although he tried, he was unable to heal them.

Their corpses were immediately taken away, and they, too, were disposed of as offal in the Bayou Sauvage marsh. It appeared the degenerates had then had more luck with the alligators than they had with the disemboweled latest two, for their bodies were never found.

Courtney's partner, the "Mystery Lady," who was later learned to be an ex-con narcotics runner from Colombia named Ileana Quintero, was charged with kidnapping and child trafficking. Because of the egregiousness of her crimes, her flight risk, and her criminal history, she, too, was held without bail. Quintero was not present at the bust, but trying to abscond to Colombia two days later, she was arrested at the Louis Armstrong International airport.

Confirming what Duncan had told Breeze and me, Courtney also revealed how the children were abducted at the Dome. After the young ones entered, Duncan and Quintero would take the kids on rides in the electric carts. And Quintero would offer the designated targets, who were usually wandering on their own, a ride. She would then drive them to the freight entrance; Huberty would open the door; and she would deliver them outside to Courtney.

247

From there, Courtney would place them in his van and whisk them away to the veterinary clinic, where, they would be held until transported to the warehouse. Saying he was just in it for the money, he denied having pedophilic sex with any of the children.

Chaz refused to perform the autopsy on Pumpkin. He solicited another pathologist to do the postmortem.

Riegelé was investigated, but he wasn't charged with anything. Even though he was innocent, he would forever be stigmatized with the scarlet letter "S" as in "Superdome."

He had enough of his beloved New Orleans. It was rumored he left New Orleans in search of greener pastures and less corrupt politics. That wasn't difficult; he had a multitude of better options available to him.

Additional arrests seemed to multiply like Burmese pythons in the Florida Everglades, and a host of pedophile sex traders and sexual deviants were arrested both in and out of State.

Quite a few handcuff carriers in the NOPD surrendered and gave evidence of corruption. Conspiracy charges were filed against several high-ranking officers there, including Macklin's former lieutenant. The Missing Persons Unit was gutted. A few of the officers were criminally charged, others were fired, a few demoted, and some were transferred to desk duty, their career advancement opportunities forever lost.

There was no way possible the conspiratorial whoresons could ever propitiate the goddess Themis.

Macklin was promoted to lieutenant in charge of Missing Persons and given as much time off with pay and allowances as needed to recover from his gunshot wound. And Jackson, was promoted to Detective Sergeant and assigned to Missing Persons to work with Macklin. Jackson would later go on to become an assistant chief of police.

The city was in shambles—an ant on a floating stick thinking it was in control. So much so that in the interregnum, the Governor stepped in and appointed an ad hoc mayor and ad hoc council persons to replace the jailed ones to administer municipal operations until a special election could be called.

It appeared another of my theories was correct—most of the children were suffering with Stockholm syndrome. Having been trapped into drug addiction

along with the associated emotional trauma, most of them were resistant to returning home. As such, it would take years of counseling to reintegrate them into orthodox society.

Thus, the State Legislature overwhelmingly passed a bill to provide funding for extended medical care and long-term psychological rehabilitation for the abused innocents.

Although ravaged with the detritus of ruined lives, the Queen City was on the mend. Perhaps after a convalescence, she would recapture some of her lost innocence, and her inhabitants could again gambol and rest easy in the Big Easy.

CHAPTER LXX
Hospital Visitations

My recovery was arduous—MRIs, CT scans, physical rehabilitation, and other ministrations. But I was persistent; I wasn't going to let Bowditch cripple me. I had no intention of going "gentle into that dark night."

And I had Natalie, *The Wind Beneath My Wings*, to nurse me. Sleeping in the lobby and later on a cot in my private room, Natalie had left the hospital only twice during my recovery and that was just for her tooth brush, quick showers, clean clothes, and to check on our home. Surely, Paris made a mistake when he awarded the Golden Apple to Aphrodite instead of her.

When the doctors transferred me from ICU with a bandaged head and a plum-tinged face, I was the cynosure of the hospital. My private room became overfilled with bright rainbow sprays of almost every flower one could obtain in New Orleans, and they were also lining the corridor outside. Many of them were from total strangers. Natalie had removed the attached cards, and I would later call or write the well-wishers to thank them.

Lifting the veil, Natalie filled me in on those events that occurred when, due to the wonders of propofol, or pentobarbital, or thiopental, I was out somewhere in the rings of Saturn.

More than anything, she described Pumpkin's televised funeral, and I wept profusely—not just because of the injustice of it all, but unknown to Natalie, also because my guilty conscience about my theretofore lechery burdened my soul.

Exacerbating that, even though I recognized it wasn't my fault Pumpkin died, I drowned myself in self-recriminations—if only this; if only that….

Natalie told me the AG had contacted one of his in-pocket legislators who was going to submit a bill in the Louisiana Legislature to extol me for being a state hero.

She also notified me what a coup the bust had been. She said, "It not only made national news, it was picked up by the AP and it made international news too—the BBC had aired it, and *The Australian*, *El Pais* in Spain, *la Republica* in Italy, and even *Haaretz* in Israel had run front or second-page stories about it. What particularly fascinated them was Sanderson's retouched photograph.

With so many well-wishers, the doctors, via the nurses and Natalie, had to limit the time of each visitation. *Fame and glory are leaves on a deciduous tree— pretty to look at but easily blown away to wither on the ground. Don't forget that!*

The first visitors I had, except for Natalie, who wasn't a visitor anyway, were Doughboy and Jackie, both of whom kissed me. With an impish grin, I asked, "You two aren't married yet?"

"No, we can't," said Doughboy.

"Why in the hell not?"

"Because we need a best man, and you're in the hospital, damnit!"

"Well, what's going on with the two of you?"

"We're pre-honeymooning," said Jackie. And they were both beaming, their pearly whites glistening like high-wattage fluorescent bulbs.

Zitzy, loyal Zitzy, visited often; he was working at the FBI office, only a few blocks away from Charity Hospital. "Zitzy, with my injury, I stole all the limelight, and your indispensable contributions have gone unnoticed; I'm sorry," I said.

"I wasn't in it for fame, and I know you weren't either. We wanted to get the slimeball motherfuckers, and I'm glad we did."

"I don't care. I'm going to put you in for a commendation. And by the way, as I told you, I didn't need a bulletproof vest." And I bantered, "Of course, I could have used a bulletproof helmet."

Macklin came to visit. And even though his arm was in a sling, it was refreshing to see him tidy and well-groomed.

Irvando, Macklin's niddering shadow "handler" and the source of the specious press releases from the Mayor's Office, in a moronic effort to obfuscate his involvement and save himself, had tried to deflect his guilt by pointing out Macklin's encounter with an underage teenager. But by then, the blackmail threat was irrelevant.

Neither Irvando nor Macklin's lieutenant could provide the juvenile's name; no young teen had come forward to accuse him; and in their multitude of searches, the FBI found no photographs of Macklin in the illicit act. Perhaps it had all been a ruse, and the girl wasn't underage after all.

Macklin didn't come alone; he came with his wife, Miss Etta, who was in a wheelchair. Both wept as they entered my room, and they thanked me with effusive ardor. It seemed the FBI ballistics experts had determined my skull had

deflected the bullet that whizzed nearby Macklin's ear would have otherwise struck him square in his face.

Miss Etta took my hand in her wrinkled one and said, "Mr. Régis, we've been praying for you."

"And I shall pray for you, Miss Etta."

"Thank you, but I'm a goner. However, you gave me my husband in my last days, and for that I'm profoundly grateful."

"Natalie and I will pray for you anyway, and I hope you and Rosh enjoy your time together."

"God bless you, Mr. Johnny."

Breeze, too, came to see me often. I already knew he was jocular, but I had never fully realized what a splendid sense of wit and droll humor he had until then.

On his first visit shortly after I was released from ICU, even though I was recovering, Natalie had called a priest to administer the last rites in the event I died. When the priest arrived, Breeze intuited he should leave. But before doing so, he arose, kissed me on my cheek, and said to the cleric, "Padre, don't give him Extreme Unction until he assures you that I'm in the will." Natalie and I found it hilarious, and I laughed so hard my head hurt.

On another visit, as he entered the room, in a feigned gruff voice, he said, "All right, quit the malingering; get your lazy ass out of bed and go to work!"

"Can't you see I *am* working"; I responded, "I'm working at making sure you do your job—and not in your preferential drag this time." And the same type of repartee was repeated on his other visits. As I had told Chaz, cops tease hard.

Without success, the AG had unsuccessfully tried to politicize his way into the ICU to see me. Now that I was in a room, he paid me a visit. "How're you feeling, Régis?"

"Fairly well, thank you General."

"By now, you must know what a tremendous success you were?"

"Not me, General, it was my team. And I'm not so sure we can claim success with the loss of Burchett." In my charged emotional state, I began to weep.

Surprisingly, the old curmudgeon teared up too, and his face became even more florid than it already was. And through his weeping, he said, "She was an outstanding agent and a wonderful person."

Recovering his composure, he continued, "But I'm not here to make you sad. If you haven't already heard, Red Prudhomme, the state representative from Evangeline Parish, is going to introduce a bill to designate you a state hero."

"I've heard, General, but I'll refuse it unless they posthumously confer the same honor on Benicia." I felt I had done a decent job, but I refused to rationalize away my lapses and errors, and I gave myself a B-minus. If I had truly been on top of things, perhaps Pumpkin and even Langdon wouldn't have been killed.

"You're making it difficult, but I can see your point. I think we can get it done.

"But I'm also here to give you options. If you decide to stay with my office, I'm going to reorganize, and I'll promote you to Agent IV. Chatelain will be the only Agent V on my investigative staff. Or if you'd prefer to retire, you can do so with seventy-five percent pay and full allowances. It's your decision."

"I'll have to talk it over with Natalie, if you don't mind."

"Of course."

"But enough about me, General. I'd like to ask you for three favors for others." *Call in the IOUs now—if there are any. They're perishable, and you might not have another opportunity to do so.*

"Go right ahead. Indeed, you've guaranteed my reelection."

"Could you write a letter of recommendation for Jackie and pull any political strings you have to get her a job with the U.S. Postal Inspection Service?"

"Have her contact me. I'll give it my best effort."

"And General, this wouldn't have panned out without Leman. He was brilliant and worked his ass off for this bust. Can you do something for him?"

"I'm ahead of you on that one. If you take the promotion I offered you, I'm going to elevate him to your spot."

"Would you give him a commendation?"

"Of course."

"And would you please petition the Retirement Board to provide Mrs. Dickerson with Langdon's full pay and allowances? After all, if it weren't for Dickerson, the streets of New Orleans and elsewhere would still be overrun with the menace of pedophiliac sex slavers and murderers."

"You're absolutely right, Régis. I think I can swing that."

Economically, it would have behooved me to take the early retirement. But I first discussed it with Natalie, my awesome consigliera and Fidus Achates. I told

253

her I could work another job, and we would have two incomes.

With an effusion of energy, she told me we could use the extra money, but we didn't *need* it. I should do what I enjoyed doing; and she would support me in whatever I chose. I suppose Macklin and I were cut from the same cloth—cops *au fond*. Plus, Zitzy deserved a promotion.

Perhaps one can take the cop out of policing, but policing cannot be excised from the cop.

CHAPTER LXXI
A Blush of Anemones

With our newfound celebrity, the media vetted the crew and me under the glare of harsh spotlights, and we all were endorsed with Triple-A ratings. Subsequent to that, some of the news outlets ran glowing, albeit short, bios on each one of us, including Ghost and Pumpkin.

Zitzy and I received our promotions. And at a formal gathering of AG members, state and local police officers, the governor, and State Police Colonel Dondre Theriot, Zitzy received his commendation from the Attorney General. And at the same fanfare, Doughboy and Breeze received commendations too.

Via a bill conjointly passed by both houses of the State Legislature, Pumpkin (posthumously) and I were fêted with encomiums, replete with a lot of wherefores and whereases. The Governor made the presentations on the floor of the House. I personally accepted mine, and Sam received Pumpkin's.

And with the attendance of state representatives and senators; Louisiana sheriffs and police chiefs; Louisiana political office holders; state, parish, and municipal police officers; family; and friends, it was an SRO. *Glory is fleeting, Johnny, and vainglory is lethal.*

Gayle frequently visited Natalie and me. Although Langdon had worked for the AG's office for only nine years, Gayle was awarded what would have been Langdon's twenty-five-year retirement (75% of his salary) with full benefits and allowances. She several times, thanked, hugged, and kissed me. She had gone through all of Langdon's personal effects, and she had not found a diary or a journal.

Until I was in the hospital, Natalie and Gayle had never met. But when they did, it was instant synergy; they bonded as if they were sisters. After my release from the hospital, they shopped together, went to movies together, shared tea together, exchanged recipes, and lent one another clothing and jewelry. Gayle's children became enamored with Natalie, so much so that "Miss Natalie" became "Aunt Natty."

Melding their culinary talents, Gayle and Natalie collaborated on scrumptious soul food, southern, and Creole cookery for us, and I began to gain weight. Gayle

and her children were frequent overnight guests at our home; it felt empty when they weren't there. And every time they visited, I would greet them singing, *Ain't No Sunshine When [You're] Gone.*

Jackie went back to work at the Saint Martinville Post office. Apparently, the AG had exerted some influence, for in a short time, she was accepted as a U.S. Postal Inspector. After training, because she was French/English bilingual, she would be stationed in Lafayette, the heart of Cajun country, not far from Saint Martinville.

Following the bust and co-authoring the report, Doughboy asked for and received a transfer to the AG's Lafayette office. He and Jackie bought a modest Southwest Louisiana honeymoon cottage in Cecelia similar to Miss Marie's house, midway between Lafayette and Saint Martinville. Many of their free days and evenings were spent caring for and enjoying the company of Miss Marie.

Breeze continued to work out of the New Orleans office. And in his inimitable style, he emotionally nourished a troupe of pulchritudinous damsels who venerated him.

Rosh recovered and bounced back with unprecedented élan, but he didn't immediately return to work. Rather he used the opportunity to spend time with, and nurse, Miss Etta.

We still experienced mournful remembrances of Langdon's and Pumpkin's sad demises. But blessed by Demeter, our team's lives' meadows brandished a kaleidoscopic blush of perfumed, dewy anemones which were delicately nudged to undulate and sway by tender breezes of contentment dancing around them.

EPILOGUE

Eros was quite sprightly that day, for the redolence of budding magnolias, fantasy, placidity, and romance filled the air. Approaching the winter solstice, cool, spirited zephyrs invigorated the enthralled wedding party and the hundred or so guests.

We were in Saint Martinsville's Evangeline Oak Park in the middle of the Atchafalaya Basin where feral flora and fauna abounded. And where the biota flourished was of their own choosing.

The ceremony was held on the west bank of Bayou Teche, both sides of which were threaded with weeping willows, tupelo gums, elephant ears, and the ubiquitous cypress trees, their knees like phalluses pointed at the sky.

Sprinkled between them in the arborescent leafage were a few wizened and hoary Black men seated on plastic five-gallon paint buckets fishing with bamboo poles for *sac-a-lait*, alligator gar, bream, and the occasional bass.

Persuaded by a delayed and lengthy Louisiana fall, the leaves of the myriad of heterogeneous terrestrial trees were emblazoned with hues vying to eclipse their cousins. And the fulvous foliation, having fallen in acquiescence to autumnal inducement and gentle airs, murmured and pirouetted around the feet of the wedding party and the guests, most of whom were denizens of that Creole township.

With a permit from the city, an area had been cordoned off for the nuptials and the reception. And except for a slight pall owing to Pumpkin's and Langdon's deaths, the Jackie and Doughboy mid-afternoon nuptials abounded with jubilation.

By city ordinance, Jackie and Doughboy had to hire an off-duty police officer for a security detail. And who else but Officer Bourgeois had been first up on the detail roster!

Doughboy was taken aback by how much he had changed. Clean shaven, somewhat thinner, neat, scrubbed, and pleasant, Bourgeois presented as a man who took pride in himself. Surprised after having heard Doughboy's former description of him, I wondered what had occasioned the transformation.

Jackie's sister, Céline, was the Matron of Honor; Gayle was one of the

257

bridesmaids as were two of Jackie's high school friends, Lizette and MaeMae. Recently rescued Adeline and Lashanna, aglow in matching sherbet-orange dresses, dutifully served as flower girls.

Zitzy, Breeze, and Macklin were groomsmen, and as decided by Jackie and Doughboy, I was the best man, an honor I cherished, but didn't think I necessarily deserved.

Lissome Jackie was ineffable—a study of comeliness. Stunning to begin with, her cinnamon complexion offered a charming contrast to her champagne, tea-length, A-line bridal gown.

Her brother, Célestine, a prepossessing lad of nineteen known with affection as Tin-Tin, had taken time off from his oil-rig roustabout job and gave his elder sister away.

Doughboy, who had begun to absorb the Cajun culture with zeal, welcomed the guests with, *"Comment ça va?"* Of course, most of the New Orleanians greeted him with "Where ya at?" He was aglow with a buoyant gladness and attired in a creamy-beige linen-cotton suit. It was difficult to determine where the raiment retired and Doughboy began.

Miss Marie, Céline, and Tin-Tin had welcomed Doughboy into the family as a son and a brother. And Miss Marie, determined to keep him "rosy-cheeked and healthy," fed him so much Cajun fare he had to rent his formal wear a size larger than his previous measurements. Moreover, she maintained a ready supply of candied orange slices—his favorite dessert—in her undersized kitchen refrigerator-freezer.

Miss Marie declared Doughboy—although she didn't call him Doughboy; rather, she called him Dave—was a gentle man within a gentleman.

And with an unceasing grin, Miss Marie was resplendent. She wore a knotted-waist, Bohemian maxi-dress in brilliant fall colors of oranges, yellows, and golds. Her wide-brimmed bonnet, too, reflected the autumnal landscape with the bright shades of fall leaves and flowers.

As graceful as a lotus flower, Natalie, was ravishing...no surprise there, since she is a paragon of muliebrity. Attired in a navy-pink-and-teal, off-the-shoulder ruffled neckline, bandana print jersey maxi-dress with an empire-waist and a wide pink sash, she was a highlight of the bubbly gathering. But forasmuch as her warmheartedness and Southern propriety prevailed, she considerately avoided

upstaging the bride.

I, on the other hand, was accoutered in a navy-blue blazer, khaki pants, a white dress shirt, and a red and black striped tie which I promptly shed after the ceremony. The only remarkable feature of my attire was one of two boutonnieres Celine had pinned on the lapel of my coat and the other one on Doughboy's tuxedo jacket.

The AG was unable to attend. Because of our bust, he was hastily designated the second keynote speaker at the National Conference of Attorneys General in Atlanta, Georgia. However, Jim Chatelain, along with other agents from the AG's Baton Rouge and Lafayette offices were present with their wives or significant others.

Zitzy's wife, Tressa, a vivacious, personable, and quite pretty lady, enlivened the gathering, as did Zitzy, himself. Zitzy was indeed a lucky man.

Miss Etta couldn't make the trip, but she was still alive and sent her best wishes. And Breeze's wife was not in attendance either, ostensibly due to a "headache"—she sent no wishes.

Jackie, Miss Marie, Céline, and Gayle had planned the wedding and the reception. The costs for food and beverages were minimal, as those were supplied potluck by the guests who had already been fond of Jackie and now revered her as a local hero. Friends and family also pitched in and decorated the wedding area of the park.

The couple exchanged vows in the gazebo near the *Evangeline* Oak. (It is a common practice in Louisiana to assign names to old, stately oak trees.) The legendary giant oak tree memorialized in Longfellow's poem *Evangeline* graces that attractive park in Saint Martinville.

Leasean, having been confirmed as a minister, gave the invocation and the benediction afterward.

With her customary aplomb, Judge Giaccone, in her judicial attire, officiated the marriage. Having suffered her own tragedies, she began the ceremony with an elegiac lamentation entreating the rest of Ghost's and Pumpkin's souls. And before reciting the Declaration of Intent, she lauded the couple for their bravery, dedication, and industry in the eradication of the New Orleans pedophilic crime syndicate.

After being pronounced "man and wife," the then-married couple kissed, and

their wassail ritual was quite longer than most other matrimonial couples' toasts. Finishing that, in Jewish tradition, Doughboy broke his wine glass by crushing it with his right foot. And the guests, mostly Catholic and with Cajun accents, shouted "*Mazal Tov!*"

Following the benediction, an almost two-minute eruption of whistles, cries, and applause erupted. The musicians' who had played at Ghost's funeral, entertained us. Their prothalamion was *If Ever I Cease to Love,* the official theme song of the New Orleans Mardi Gras Rex krewe.

The ladies ruffled their lace handkerchiefs and tissues to dry tears of joy from their eyes and cheeks. And the men queued up to buss the bride. Paraphrasing Dante, I saw them gathered together bound by love into a single volume.

And the roistering *fais do-do* began. *Laissez le bon temps rouler!*

Befitting a mixed marriage, the reception sphere was themed-bedecked in black and white trappings—crepe paper hanging from the colossal live oaks, tablecloths, balloons, and napkins. The popping of champagne corks, the snapping of beer can pull tabs, the tinkle of cocktail glasses and ice, and the raucous laughter of the attendees infused the ever-so-slightly crisp air with jubilance.

For our audible and terpsichorean pleasure, the duet played jazz, blues, hip-hop, and oldies but goodies. I learned the bass player's nickname was "Acapella," for he sang many of the songs without instrumental accompaniment.

The occasion presented a blissful and romantic panorama. Yet somehow, the joy and the ambiance awakened in me a semblance of synesthesia of Pumpkin, and I could have sworn I had seen her blithesome specter mingling with the invitees.

I sadly thought how happy she would have been to be a live part of it. But as New Orleanians ask, "Aren't there more ways of showing one's respect than to beat one's head against a wall?"

The provided hors d'oeuvres were reminiscent of a *réveillon.* Except for the addition of raw oysters; cracklings; chaurice, fried alligator; boudin balls; chicken and sausage jambalaya; hot and spicy seafood gumbo occasioned, noted for by a piddling cold front, and sweet potato pie instead of cake; the fare was almost a mirror image of that which we were served at Langdon's funeral party. It was bounteous, and the guests gormandized it.

The AG, with his unflagging support for the oyster industry, had capitalized on the felicitous occasion to politic. A prime benefactor of his endeavors, Pitor Drago, had dispatched a truckload of oysters and two shuckers to delight the participants. We'll never know how many votes that garnered, but owing to my prurient imagination, I thought of how the testosterone levels would peak sexual activity that night.

Funeral, weddings, and crises—all are venues for romance. Breeze was about my age, picaresque, and strikingly handsome. Was it my imagination, or had he become intrigued by one of Jackie's alluring, doe-eyed bridesmaids, Lizette? And gazing into his shimmering blue eyes, did she not become enthralled by him? They certainly seemed to spend an inordinate amount of time chatting together.

Indeed, when they strolled away from the reception milieu to a quieter section of the park, I thought perhaps in the future, Breeze might be spending more time in Saint Martinville when his wife experienced her frequent and curiously convenient headaches. I suppose it was his perk to himself for having so diligently participated in our successful operation.

A modern-day Casanova with a Romanesque countenance and a cleft chin, I then knew why he was called Cool Breeze. It was not only a play on his surname, but with Dionysian flair, he was "cool," as in urbane and suave. And he was almost always surrounded by besotted and adoring *tee-nah-nahs*.

Although a philanderer, Breeze was not bad; he was just naughty—I fancy that was my way of reconciling the irreconcilable. With Pumpkin, I had almost let myself slip in to that entanglement myself...and I didn't have a headachy wife! So, inwardly snickering, I said to myself, *Go for it, Big Boy!*

Ed Sanderson was in attendance too. He told me because of us, he had the biggest scoop the *Times-Picayune* had picked up in the past two decades. It was so notable it had occasioned a rare special edition of the daily to be issued.

And Ed, having authored the lead story with his byline, had acquired a large eagle feather in his reporter's hat. Moreover, with his article and photograph, he had been nominated for a Pulitzer Prize in "Breaking News Reporting."

By then, my first interview of Duncan and his in-church confession had gone public. Thus, I had the opportunity to tell Ed why I couldn't disclose that to him during our discussions. He told me he understood. As I had suspected, he had read the subtext, and he surmised I didn't harass Duncan and that we had more

than we could make known.

And the apogee was what he told me next—it was staggering. The same Willy who had "defended" me at Sanderson's second interview was the one who had provided the tip that prompted our last encounter in the first place!

"So, was that the reason for your wry smile at the end of our last session?"

"Yes, it was. The newspaper had received the screed in writing; it was from Conrardy with the stipulation he remain anonymous. It seemed that, in physically writing the tip, he was giving us an outline of questions to ask you.

"I couldn't figure out what his end game was, but I suspected he was trying to use the newspaper to extract information, or harass you, or both, especially after he entered your office to ostensibly defend you.

"I began to think perhaps he was your unknown nefarious instigator. So I went back and reviewed and compared his written tip with previous press releases negative about you.

"My career has been devoted to writing, and I can usually pick up on others' techniques. The patterns in those were almost identical. Although the other releases came over the signature of Luis Irvando in the mayor's office, I concluded Conrardy had been their ghost writer. And that was why I wrote the article the way I did." Obviously, Sanderson had heeded my Cassandrish harbingers.

"Did Conrardy ever tell you why he interrupted you during our interview?"

"Yes, he did. He called and told me that in overhearing the last part of our chat, he realized perhaps his information was in error."

"What a phenomenal achievement that was! In every sense of the word, you are a true investigative reporter" I said to him.

"Thanks for the compliment. But I didn't make the connection between Conrardy and the Dickerson murder."

"Nor did I, Ed. In fact, I believed he was a staunch ally. And it also appears Willy must have tagged us for involvement in the Duncan suicide." What dumb luck I had when Willy was unable to help me with extra manpower!

"Apparently so," said Ed. "Of course, I didn't make that connection either."

"As I told my crew, the investigation was analogous to quantum theory—it was fuzzy and uncertain. We suspected individual characters, and we conjectured particular crimes. There was some dark, unexplainable symmetry there, but it was smeared.

Except for estimating probabilities, we couldn't definitively put the two together at the same time and in the same place until the bust. And had any one variable been ever so subtly different, we might have been met with disaster."

"But you did put them together."

"Yeah, but sometimes I felt I was being used as a trendy experiment in survival.

"You must be aware of the Stupefied Syndrome, wherein organizations hire smart people but then positively encourage them not to use their intelligence. Asking difficult questions or thinking in greater depth is seen as a dangerous waste. In hindsight, I realize the AG is not cut from that cloth.

"I didn't recognize it, but the old man was smarter than I gave him credit for. He pressed us to utilize our cerebral abilities. Except for Dosstein, we aren't polymaths, but the circumstances required us to be resourceful. And it worked!"

Always in journalistic mode, Ed asked, "How does it feel to be the victim of a shooting?"

Without a breath of hesitation, I said, "That's the way the press labeled me. But Ed, I don't feel victimized; I was just a guy doing his job. If I had to sit down and write what I was a victim of, I'd end up with a blank page."

"As I see it, your *tour de force* was persistence. Even with all the adversities, you were like a bulldog with a bone—you wouldn't let go. Johnny, everybody's looking for it, but you got it." Ed and I subsequently became fast friends.

At one point, Macklin, who was once again well-groomed—even his shoes were shined! —pulled me aside. Glassy-eyed, he hugged me and said, "Thank you, thank you." And in typical cop gallows-humor, he gruffly said, "And thank you for getting me shot too!"

"You deserved it for fucking with me," I said with a grin.

"Seriously, Johnny, you saved my life. And there's no residual damage. Indeed, because I was shot, I was declared a hero and promoted, too. But more importantly, I have regained my self-respect, and being injured has given me more time to spend with Etta. I'm certain that's why she's still alive today."

"You really owe Judge Giaccone."

"I suppose you know about Irvando hanging himself in jail?"

Yeah, I saw that in the newspaper. Good riddance.

"Have you heard about Dr. Odom?"

"No. With my convalescing, I've been behind the curve."

"Do you know that, four years ago, he lost his wife to a thug in a carjacking?"

"No."

"Well, the rumor mill has it, with that and Pumpkin's death, he started drinking heavily. And if he doesn't retire beforehand, he's not going to run for coroner again when his term expires in January."

"So that's why he's not here today. Jackie sent him an invitation, and he didn't RSVP. Those motherfuckers fucked up a lot of lives.

"But I need to ask you a question, Rosh. Why didn't the NOPD connect Duncan's suicide with me?"

"*I* did; that's the reason I called you! But unfortunately, we only have a few from the old days who can think outside the box; the lead investigator didn't play Connect the Dots when he was a kid. And I wasn't about to share my theory with them."

"With little effort, they could have gotten pictures of me and my staff and shown them to the tabby who had seen us at the church and could have identified Breeze."

"Of course, you're right. But the lead investigator proffered a theory, and the rest of the detectives were lemmings. He plagiarized his conjecture from Father Gallagher and built his case around it." With still-lingering shame, I recalled a case when I was in JPSO homicide, and as the lead investigator, I did almost the same thing.

"What were his conclusions?"

"He's a lazy ass, so he glommed onto Father Gallagher's premise. Almost quoting Father Gallagher, he 'deduced' that, with Duncan's extracurricular duties, a history of long-running depression, and probably hearing a shocking confession to which he was required to give absolution, the priest was overwrought and decided to end it all."

"Well, that 'could' explain why Duncan committed suicide. But why did they not follow up on the old lady and the young man?"

"Again, they were lazy. They simply assumed the two were mother and son, and the son had driven her to church. Because they had already locked in to a provocation for the suicide, why bother with such small trivialities?"

"It wasn't reported that way in the media."

"That was just pansies in a window box to give the public, via the press, the

impression they were hotshot investigators exploring every avenue of a complicated case.

"And as I told you," Rosh continued, "I immediately figured you were somehow involved in the suicide. But I must admit, because of your disguise, I didn't make you or your group for the Duncan visitors. However, in accord with good investigative protocol, I would have followed up on the 'unrecognized visitors' aspect. And I think doing so would have eventually led me to you."

"Probably so."

"Hell, Johnny, I sized you up at our first meeting in your office, and I knew you were on top of your game. But you played the role of an Inspector Clouseau for your adversaries so well, you could have gotten an Oscar. That's why they so underestimated you. You and those with your artistry should be on the endangered species list.

"And you knew the Devil is in the details. Isn't paying attention to the minutiae exactly what you did to solve the case?"

"I suppose so, Rosh, but we had to poke a lot of dead frogs." I conceded how extensive and how overwhelming for me those nuances were, and that we were only successful because of our collective acumen.

Macklin segued, "I hope you realize how lucky you were?"

"It seemed to me you just implied we made our luck."

"No, not that. You *did* make your luck in busting the case. But do you remember that I told you to watch your back?"

"Yeah?"

"What I mean when I say you're lucky is I believe you narrowly missed having a hit put out on you—and they had the means and the impetus to do it. I'm almost certain that, if you hadn't projected an incapable bumpkin image, or if you would have delayed a little longer, or if you would have otherwise tipped your hand, you'd be having coffee with Dickerson and Pumpkin right now."

I realized how right he was and how naïve I had been for not having considered that imperilment. And with having it laid out to me as Macklin did, I shuddered at the thought of Natalie being hurt as collateral damage. Perhaps her rosaries worked after all.

Macklin added, "And I was all wrong about Huberty. I fell victim to the halo effect. I let his one good deed cloud my judgment, and I should have known

better."

"It doesn't matter, Rosh. You're my horse if you never win a race."

Macklin and I eventually became good friends. And a few months later, I was at his side to give him solace when Miss Etta died.

All those revelations made me realize how much I had underestimated Doughboy's prescience. He was able to dissect, examine, scrutinize, tear, probe, and polish muddled data until he had a clear picture of the issue. But the misguided would still view it as rubbish. In a thousand years, I would never be the analyst or be as intuitive as he was.

Nearing the end of the festivities, Officer Bourgeois motioned me aside. "You're Agent Dosstein's supervisor, aren't you?" he asked.

"Well, I was; he's been transferred to the Lafayette office."

"I thought you might like to know that he and his wife are class acts. And I was rude to them. Even so, they gave me a new look on policin' and even life for that matter. I shoulda done more work on that missin' girl's case. But because they impressed the hell outta me, I'm gonna lose weight, get in shape, improve my English, apply for the State Police, and get outta this rinky-dink department."

"Thank you for telling me; that's good to hear. And I wish you the best."

Natalie and I danced to many of the songs, especially the oldies but goodies. Holding her in my arms, a frisson of exhilaration ran through me. Her fluidity and sense of rhythm fused us into gracefulness, so much so my tone-deaf ears and two left feet didn't realize I couldn't dance.

When we swayed to our song, *I Left My Heart in San Francisco*, we had the air of eluding the constraints of gravity. And when she whispered those cinnamon words, "I love you," in my ear, everything beyond us was non-existent.

I had become pleasantly tipsy on mint juleps. So, at the first sign of an early scarlet and mauve- and salamander-tinged twilight—"Red sky at night, sailors' delight"—Natalie and I decided to leave.

With bald eagles winging to their aeries, ducks roosting on grassy hummocks, alligators lumbering back to their self-excavated swamp holes, hairy bats sallying forth from their arboreous roosts, and the furred nocturnal wildlife commencing their hunting forays, we said our goodbyes, and Natalie drove us home.

On the two-and-a-half-hour trip, perhaps inspired by mint juleps, I reflected on my circumscribed world. Of me, I had slight standing to be haughty, for I was

just an ordinary chap. With the exception of the Dome experience, I was living, and satisfied with, a pedestrian life.

Traversing the Atchafalaya Basin, I mused, *Johnny, you learned a lot, but the two most important lessons of all were the awareness of the preciousness and fragility of life and knowing what you don't know.* Those were truisms that would remain with me for the duration of my time on the planet.

LA DERNIÈRE BOUCHÉE

The wedding and the reception had kindled in me the realization that, although capricious and sometimes unfair, living was good—very good!

Life is a succession of endless possibilities; happenstance is the rule. The megillah and chaos of the preceding two months had broken the hymen of my political innocence and throttled me into a posture of personal reconnaissance.

And it had borne fruit. The recognition of my naïveté and the sequence and outcome of the events unnerved yet irradiated me, and it sated my inner beast. I had been out of my league. I was lucky...except Macklin had said I made my luck.

I suppose the best one can wish for is to change things for the better. I felt I had, but I realized that my contribution was infinitesimal in the greater scheme of things. In a meager few succeeding months, it would go as unnoticed as a single drop of precipitation in a crawfish pond during a rain shower.

Yet except for a lingering sadness about Ghost, Pumpkin, and the children, I was content with that; I had Natalie and my tinsel memories of triumph to sustain me.

I felt I had cast a long shadow at the Dome, and I had breached the bulwarks of New Orleans political knavery. The rabid hyenas we corralled would no longer be free to feast on vulnerable prey, and our efforts might deter a few others from doing the same.

It is said that the most gratifying things in life are merely on loan from the universe and granted us for the time being. Nevertheless, my mojo was at its pinnacle. Like Hercules, I felt I had diverted a river to pass through the mucked-up stables of the Superdome and along with it expelled the putrid dung of society.

Moreover, I had high-wrought expectations that Ghost and Pumpkin could now *requiescat in pace*. I woolgathered they were in heaven swinging censers and chanting, "*Ut benedicat tibi Dominus.*"

Except for Natalie, my raison d'être had been policing. However, the raw, pristine environs of the park along with the affinity of the wedding party and the assembled guests sheathed me in a rare sense of rapture and peace, a phenomenon unlike any I had ever before experienced. It was as if body and spirit

had coalesced in a resplendent synthesis. Being a cop was still a significant part of my life, but it had lost the preeminence it once had.

The next day, Natalie and I would leave on a two-to-three week, as-promised, loosely-mapped-out vacation—perhaps a road trip to North Carolina, where we'd amble the rich hills of the Blue Ridge Parkway, and from there on to Virginia. We considered returning via blue-grass Kentucky and then home following the flow of the Father of the Waters down the Blues Highway, US 61.

That evening, it was nippy outside. But once in our cradle of love, Natalie, my sage and loving wife warmed and cocooned me inside her inviolable chrysalis. Entering through the vale of soul-making, I slumbered in the Arcadia, a utopia somewhere beyond space and time. And there, I experienced a metamorphosis that was destined to perdure.

Keats would be pleased; I had my life-defining emotional experience. Acquiring my identity and becoming a "Soul," I knew and accepted who Johnny Régis was and wasn't…I had become my own personal self. And I was ready for a sea change.

With the evening red-sky promise of lucent days ahead, I scuttled the barque *Johnny Régis*, awakened the wind, hoisted sail, and set asea on the *Johnny Régis II*.

AFTERWORD

As noted in the *Disclaimer*, this is purely a work of fiction. For example, the Office of the Louisiana Attorney General's Sexual Predator Unit simply oversees the statewide implementation and enforcement of Louisiana's sex offender and child predator registration and notification laws.

That is, the AG's Office renders a reactive, rather than a proactive, law enforcement effort, and it deals mostly with litigation. In essence, it is primarily a prosecutorial agency. And the Office does not have a large staff of law enforcement investigators.

Moreover, in writing this novel, as I would with crawfish, crabs, boudin, or red beans and rice, I have helped myself to generous servings of poetic freedom. For example, there is no sixth tier of enclosed box suites; there was no canteen at the Superdome; the Dome's seating and suite arrangements in the novel do not reflect its actual layout; etc. Moreover, to my knowledge, no law enforcement officer has ever been murdered there.

New Orleanians will readily notice I've also taken creative license with some of the New Orleans geography. For instance, there is no City Park shelter near the Sydney and Walda Besthoff Sculpture Garden, there is no address of 581 Piety Street, and there are quite a few other fictional physiographic anomalies in the book. I hope you die-hard Yats and Coonasses (bantering slang for "Cajuns") will forgive me.

For four months, as a Louisiana state trooper I was once assigned to the Superdome as Chief of Staff Security. I supervised a team of five or six troopers—it varied. The thrust of our work was to oversee and review the security function and to make recommendations for improvement. As such, we were not line officers there; i.e., we did not perform functional security or law enforcement activities within the Dome

Shortly after taking the assignment, I joked about security—or lack thereof—at the Superdome. When friends would ask me if the security was as inadequate as reported, I usually narrated this fictional tale:
During the opening of an early event, newly arriving patrons found a man who appeared to be drunk sprawled across their ticketed seats. Unable to rouse the somewhat inert individual, all they could elicit were groans from him.

270

After they summoned a security officer, he too could evoke only moans. Relatively new in his position, he was unsure what his course of action should be, so he called for New Orleans Police backup.

In typical New Orleans police fashion, an NOPD officer swaggered into the milieu. And after being advised of the exigent circumstances, he, too, tried to roust the alleged inebriate. But other than evoking more groans, he had no success. He then slapped the bottom of the recumbent's shoes with his nightstick, gruffly saying, "Who are you? Where did you come from?

The hapless man shakily extended his arm upward and falteringly said, "The bal...con...nny."

Perhaps there was a problem with security at the Superdome.

I found the Superdome to be a political cauldron, and I was plunged headfirst into it. And as it was for the naïve Johnny Régis, the landscape was alien, enigmatic, and perilous for me.

Nevertheless, our State Police presence brought a small ray of sunshine to the veiled machinations that were previously ongoing with the stadium management. Some of the newspaper quotes in the book are closely plagiarized from news and editorial articles written about me during and after my tenure there.

Again, this is a work of fiction. Except for possible criminal incidences with the Dome's engineering firm, neither I nor my team ever uncovered any illegal activity within the Catholic Church, the Dome's administrative staff, the Louisiana Superdome Commission, the Dome's sub- and sub-sub-contractors, the NOPD, nor with any New Orleans politicians.

(This book is self-published and, with the exception of *Word Grammar and Spellcheck*, mostly self-edited for composition. Thus, please pardon any errors in grammar, syntax, spelling, etc. you might have encountered while reading it. You may direct any comments you might have to the Facebook page entitled John Rigol.)

ABOUT THE AUTHOR

John (Johnny} Rigol enjoying a daiquiri and a Cuban cigar
at the Havana Yacht Club, La Habana, Cuba.

Hyenas, John's first novel, is the outgrowth of Rigol's nearly four-month 1976 tenancy as Chief of Staff Security at the Louisiana Superdome shortly after it opened in late 1975.

Due to adverse publicity about derelict security at the Superdome, he was temporarily assigned to the post from the Louisiana State Police at the direction of the Governor, via State Police Colonel Donald Thibodeaux, to oversee the security function and make recommendations for improvement.

Only a State Police lieutenant, Rigol was catapulted into ground zero of Louisiana and New Orleans politics. And he found himself in an intricate weave of intrigue alien to him.

Now retired at eighty, when John is not writing (which is rarely), he reads, and he enjoys traveling—anywhere, any time. Besides many monographs, he has also written his autobiography as well as an exegesis about God, religion, and the Bible.

www.ingramcontent.com/pod-product-compliance
Lightning Source LLC
Chambersburg PA
CBHW070217030726

47505CB00006B/1710